THE
Attractiveness
OF WISDOM

JUDY
KELLY

Black Rose Writing | Texas

ISBN: 978-1-68433-850-4
PUBLISHED BY BLACK ROSE WRITING
www.blackrosewriting.com

Printed in the United States of America
Suggested Retail Price (SRP) $21.95

The Attractiveness of Wisdom is printed in Sabon

*As a planet-friendly publisher, Black Rose Writing does its best to eliminate unnecessary waste to reduce paper usage and energy costs, while never compromising the reading experience. As a result, the final word count vs. page count may not meet common expectations.

For Stephon, whose words of encouragement keep me writing.

The Attractiveness of Wisdom

THE ATTRACTIVENESS OF WISDOM

Wisdom is radiant and unfading, and she is easily discerned by those who love her, and is found by those who seek her.

–The Wisdom of Solomon 6:12

For wisdom is more mobile than any motion; because of her pureness she pervades and penetrates all things. For she is a breath of the power of God, and a pure emanation of the glory of the Almighty; therefore nothing defiled gains entrance into her.

–The Wisdom of Solomon 7:25

CHAPTER 1

Hamilton Maddox, a man of strong conviction, believed in two things his father taught him. First, make yourself an honorable person by being trustworthy and honest so you can find a good woman. Make her your wife, trust her, honor her, make her happy, be faithful to the marriage vows, and do everything for the family. The second was vengeance belongs to the Lord. Never stand in the Lord's way by doing His work. Never fill your heart with hatred and anger. You can't be trustworthy, or a good person, or honor your wife with a heart filled with hatred and anger.

He had heard his father's advice from the time he was born, it seemed to him, until he went off to college. It was the only thing he thought his father had given him, and his father's words were etched in his brain just as the stars were permanently etched on the Hollywood Walk of Fame.

So, it was not only heart breaking and devastating but also unbearable for him to sit in this courtroom now, staring down at the irregular patterns in the wooden table, as the gavel firmly wrapped in the judge's hand, slammed down, and echoed throughout the courtroom, echoed throughout his body, echoed throughout his heart stunning him and causing a minor shake like an electrical shock of a stun gun. Divorced. The judge had just pronounced him divorced. He was now a divorced man, despite everything he wanted. The deafening silence left him shaken. The heat from the hot and humid 100-degree early July afternoon swirled around him, and choked him, annihilating him, as if the divorce wasn't enough.

He sat on the opposite side of the aisle from his now ex-wife, HolliAnne, and her live-in boyfriend, Todd, and watched her smirk throughout the proceedings. He noticed her quiet, covert elbowing she gave to Todd, her gesture that said, "I told you so," the same sneaky, easy-like nudge she used with Hamilton. An intimate communication he always thought was theirs.

Perspiration ran down the sides of his head into his shirt collar, irritating him, and he wanted so badly to loosen his tie. HolliAnne's uncomplimentary comments about him squeezed the life out of him, leaving him hollow. Perspiration ran down his back and caused his shirt to stick to his back, and he stopped himself from loosening his tie. From the off and on rattling noise, the air conditioner struggled to put out cold air, and Hamilton strained to feel even the tiniest bit of a cool wave settle on him. He tried to avoid looking in HolliAnne's direction as much as possible. He couldn't let her see how devastated he really was over this divorce.

Just a few minutes ago, HolliAnne, on the stand, peered over at him with her big brown eyes that made her look as if someone had just surprised her, had asked him outright in the courtroom how in the world he didn't see this divorce coming. A sharp pain pierced his heart at the sound of her question, much like the time he played the "Hit the Bell" game at a carnival—one hard hit, the bell sounded, and the game ended. Worse was that he and those in the courtroom, including his three children, had to hear how selfish, inconsiderate, controlling, and inattentive she said he'd been to her for the past twenty-seven years.

He slouched down in his seat, as much as his six-foot body would allow, his shoulders rounded. Perhaps he should have seen this coming, but he tried hard to trust her, believe in her just the way his father had taught him. Hamilton liked HolliAnne enough to want the two of them to grow old together. He couldn't believe his ears when he heard her say to the judge that she wouldn't stay in the marriage and grow old with him because she didn't want to take care of a contrary old man who would just make her life even more miserable.

"All rise," the bailiff said, interrupting Hamilton's thoughts. Hamilton rose and looked over at HolliAnne. She had added a few extra pounds over the past year, but she was still beautiful. When she saw him watching her, she grabbed Todd's hand and then gave a sideways glance back at Hamilton, who hastily turned away. Maybe her comment about not wanting to take care of him was a valid one. It made the judge a little more sympathetic toward him, it seemed, and he really needed that now.

"Well, you're a free man, now," his attorney said as he hurriedly jammed a handful of papers into his leather briefcase. Hamilton stood there eyeing the attorney, thinking about how he was now a free man. He had been with the same woman in what he had thought was a tolerably good relationship for longer than he could remember; how was he free?

"You know, Hamilton, I wouldn't worry about those things she said, especially the part about her not wanting to take care of you. I'm sure she was just angry, that's all. It's been my experience that people say ugly things out of anger. Things they don't mean, things that really didn't happen. You understand," the attorney said. "At least you got what you wanted. Your children will continue living with you in the house."

"Well, what do I do now?" Hamilton said, half to himself. Deep down inside, he had hoped HolliAnne would come back to him. They would tell each other how sorry they were, promise to change, and agree to start again. He had held out hope until the last possible moment. What would he do, now?

"It's all over. Go home. Start a new life."

"Start a new life," Hamilton repeated. "Start a new life."

"That's right," the attorney began, "do what you've always wanted. Get what you've always wanted."

Hamilton tried to smile, but at this moment he felt like he did when he had visited his cousin, Morton. When he was ten, Hamilton watched his seven-year-old cousin, Morton, run down the road after his father. Late one afternoon, during another screaming match between his cousin's mother and father, Morton's father drove away in his beat up old green Ford, to where he said was a better life for him. He left Morton, who was wearing one of his father's old navy-blue plaid shirts, in the middle of the road crying and yelling out to him. Hamilton had a hard time watching Morton, especially when Morton dropped to his knees, begging, and pleading for his father to come back, even after the car was long gone. That just broke Hamilton's heart.

The fact that HolliAnne brought her boyfriend and told her lawyer in a voice loud enough for Hamilton to hear, so Hamilton thought, that they'd been living together for a year, did little to bode well for her. Hamilton was sure she did it to show him a thing or two. Besides, there was no way he could drop to his knees and ask her to come back in front of her new man. The reward from the proceedings so far was the graciousness of the judge in giving him the house so his kids could continue living with him.

Hamilton stood in the courtroom, a place where strangers cast judgement; the place where Hamilton had to turn over everything personal and private to absolute strangers. He watched HolliAnne, in her newly dyed and coiffed brunette bob and stylish gray silk suit, leave holding hands with her boyfriend. The two attorneys — his and hers— who also knew each other, walked out together. Hamilton turned back to the empty judge's bench where the man in a black robe made decisions about his future sat. He and HolliAnne were married longer than the time it took for the judge to pronounce him divorced.

When he turned around again, everyone had left, except his daughter, Anna. She stood in the back, waiting at the double doors. He prided himself on showing his children how to be strong, and he had never cried in their presence. His head down, he approached her, ready to take her accusations, admonishments, and insults, but only saw her tear-filled eyes. He tried to open his mouth to speak, apologize or something, but words refused to come.

"Dad, can I take you home?" Anna asked, her voice cracking.

He watched for that one-sided smile that she always gave off when everything was all right with her. "Yes," Hamilton answered. He tried not to show his surprise at her emotion.

She put her arm through his and looked up at him the way she did when she wanted something. "Let's go home."

Hamilton gave her a slight smile. He wanted to wipe away her tears and comfort her, but he couldn't get out of his mind the fact that Anna had heard her mother call him selfish, controlling, thoughtless and other things he didn't think of himself. He had always wanted to do whatever he could for his family. He was certain that he honored his children and loved them, no matter what. He always thought he showed them he was a better father than what his daughter and sons heard in that courtroom earlier. If HolliAnne was angry like his attorney thought, then maybe his children also saw that.

HolliAnne had asked him why the divorce was a surprise to him. He never thought it would happen. Sure, they were having problems, but no worse than other married couples. He was willing to accept what they had. One night, after a time of coital bliss, HolliAnne confessed the truth about how she grew up; the hate, despair, and disappointment she felt.

Her parents were avid churchgoers. They went to church for Bible class, to help feed the homeless, to do something almost every weekday evening, and almost all day on Saturday. At first, she and her sister had to go with them. It was not a choice, but a demand.

When she was older, she told her parents she had homework, and they excused her. According to HolliAnne, her parents quoted the Bible to them when they made mistakes or didn't do what they were told. Her parents dragged her and her sister to church every Sunday, no excuses. She hated it. Her parents never held her, comforted her when she was upset, or told her they loved her. They never showed her what she most needed – affection.

HolliAnne told Hamilton she would try to love him, but over time, Hamilton discovered she didn't know how. Even though he accepted what she offered, Hamilton needed more. So, over the years, he had consumed himself with making himself an honorable person, caring for his wife, and doing everything for his family. Even though he knew they were both unhappy, he made himself believe his marriage was improving. He thought of himself as a good husband and father, so how could his marriage fail.

But time sped by so quickly and before he knew it, he was caught up in a divorce process. He didn't have time to think, to stop the divorce, to fix what HolliAnne said was wrong in their marriage, and what they both knew was wrong.

Hamilton and Anna walked out of the courtroom into the wide and busy hallway. Small groups of people talking; a man waving his hands, obviously making a point; people shaking their heads, maybe not agreeing with their lawyer; the clicking of shoes as women walked by him, all filled the hallway. HolliAnne stood with her boyfriend, Todd Wilson, talking to her attorney. Eric and Jeremy, Hamilton's sons, sat on a bench opposite them. HolliAnne insisted their three children be present, something Hamilton hated. He never wanted them to see the other side of their marriage.

Hamilton and Anna turned and walked outside into the heat to the parking lot to find his car. He took his keys out of his jacket pocket and she opened her hand for the keys. This was not the time to struggle over who would drive. Hamilton gave her the keys and went around to the passenger's side.

After they got in and settled, Anna turned to him. "Dad, I'm so sorry. I know you didn't want this."

"I'll be okay. Don't worry about me, sweetheart, okay?" He wanted someone to worry about him, but he didn't want to burden his daughter. Finally, he loosened his tie and unbuttoned the first two buttons on his shirt. Anna pulled the car out of the lot, made a right turn onto Montgomery Avenue, and drove down the street toward home.

The temperature in Rockville had risen and the heat from the afternoon sun rose from the asphalt in shimmering waves, giving the impression that the street was too hot even for the sun. He turned up the air and sat back in his seat. Hamilton looked over at his daughter, the one who was always the peacekeeper. Anna was a teenager, and they fought from time to time. But when he needed her to be forgiving, she always made him feel appreciated.

He didn't want to think about what he would do next. He stretched out his legs and sat back in his seat as he tightened his seatbelt.

Maybe he should have done what his now ex-wife did. Maybe he should have bailed on the marriage. But he had his three children to think about. He couldn't have asked them to fit in to that world. It would not have been fair to them. They weren't responsible for the change in their status.

Reaching home, Anna pulled the car into the driveway. "Dad, are you going to be all right? I would stay, but I have to go to work."

Hamilton reached over and kissed his daughter on the cheek. "I'm fine, sweetheart. Go on to work. You only have a couple more weeks before we have to take you to New York, anyway."

"Dad, I can call in. I can stay if you want." She paused. "If you're not feeling well."

She had just turned eighteen, and she was already a responsible adult. "I do want, but you go to work. I have some thinking to do."

"I'll call you later, okay?"

"That'll be nice."

Hamilton waited until Anna left before he entered his house. He opened the door, stepped into the foyer, and walked to the steps to the upstairs, as he always did when he came home. He stopped himself from calling out, "HEAJ," a word he made up for HolliAnne, Eric, Anna, and Jeremy, and used every time he came home. Hamilton made up his own pronunciation for this word he created. He said it was He-A-ja, but his kids told him he was wrong, and each had their own pronunciation. Hamilton smiled when he thought about how they wanted to take his word and make it their own.

On the table just before the stairs, he laid his keys on the key dish, the blue and green fancy one that Eric made for him in art class during his senior year in high school. It was hard for Hamilton to believe that Eric will begin his second year of college in a few weeks, and Anna will leave for her first year in college in a few days. He touched the key dish again, with a smile, thought about his oldest son, Eric, and how he had named it "key dish" and wouldn't let anyone use the key dish if they didn't call it that.

Hamilton turned from the steps and walked down the hallway to the kitchen, the place where they had to eat. He and HolliAnne were very stern about that. They all had to eat dinner together. Hamilton looked at the wooden floor and the recess lights in the ceiling.

Early on, he had read an article in Parents' Magazine about how parents should do things to keep their children close to them as they got older. The article focused on teenagers. Parents should engage in conversation with their teens and, as they grow, understand the changes in them and get to know their friends.

Keeping them close could help them stay away from drugs and that corrupted lifestyle. At that time, Eric was almost thirteen, and the article gave Hamilton the idea to add on to their house. He wanted a spacious family room where they could all spread out. He had convinced HolliAnne they needed to add on by promising her he would only design the room and she would oversee the color scheme. She agreed. They added on from the kitchen to create a family room, with a big stone fireplace almost taking up one wall, and stylish French doors that opened onto a large deck. HolliAnne filled the new room with cozy furniture, and they added new computers for study and games.

After the room was completed and furnished, it seemed to fill with teenagers. First, Eric's friends from his science club, then Anna's debate club friends, and about two years ago, Jeremy's friends. It was nice to have the house filled with young people laughing and joking and studying together. Now Hamilton stepped into his family room that only filled him with loneliness.

Even though HolliAnne told him, it was hard for Hamilton to accept that his wife couldn't love him. No matter what he did or could have done, she just didn't love him; she didn't know how. Now, what he wanted more than anything else was for someone to love him. He wanted a marriage where he and his wife supported each other, inspired each other, and loved one another beyond his imagination. This was all he wanted. Could this be so impossible?

The phone on the side table blinked. Just as he reached out to lift it, it rang. Hamilton picked up the phone. "Oh, hello, Dr. Mitchell. Yes, I can come in tomorrow." His doctor wanted him to come in and talk about how he was doing after his near fatal accident the day of his original court hearing.

Driving to court, Hamilton had what he thought was a heart attack and ran off the road into a ditch. He must have blacked out for a while and when he came to, a man had opened his car door and was shaking him, yelling for him to wake up. The man told Hamilton he saw Hamilton veer off into the ditch and figured he needed help. The man called for an ambulance and stayed with Hamilton until the ambulance arrived. Hamilton was in the hospital when he should have been in court. He asked a nurse to call the judge's office and let the judge know. The assistant said they would reschedule the hearing. Later, the ER doctor gave him a prescription for beta-blockers and told him to follow up with his regular doctor for a complete diagnosis. But what was the point?

As he put the phone down, he turned all around, taking in the still beautiful family room. The emptiness of the room overwhelmed him, and he realized how small he was, how almost insignificant he was now.

CHAPTER 2

Hamilton sat up in his bed listening to the weatherman, Goodness Dave, on the morning news announce another sweltering day with high humidity. Typical weather for Maryland, he said. He cautioned people again, for the eighth day in a row, about exercising in the heat.

It was yesterday when the judge slammed that gavel down, making him a divorced man. Free. A man unchained, his lawyer said. The problem with this freedom was he wanted a marriage. This divorce decree left him hollow, lonely, betrayed, and cheated.

He reached for his cell phone on the table next to his bed. It would be a good idea to call in sick on this day. Since he had been at the university beginning as a professor, then department chair and now dean, he rarely called in sick. He took off when each of his children was born, when any of them were sick, or on special occasions. Other than that, Hamilton was at the University of Maryland.

The thing about calling in sick this time was everyone would know he wasn't sick, or not physically ill. Calling in sick would call attention to himself, and if he didn't go in, he would avoid the stares, the conversation starts and stops, the pitiful looks his office staff would give him, or the brave ones just coming right up to him and asking how he was doing. On the other hand, the president and senior vice president told him to take all the time he needed.

Hamilton believed in being responsible. He performed his duties and responsibilities, no matter how he felt. He was not one to show weakness, and if he took a sick day, his coworkers and office staff would have to think he needed it. He didn't want anyone to know that inside he felt like pieces of a puzzle all strewn out on a table, needing to be put together to make a complete picture, to make a complete Hamilton. He got up and went to the closet to select a suit to wear.

Even though he loved to bike to work, he would drive to the university this morning. He began biking ten years ago when he was a department chair. Since he had been dean of the college of education, and because of the many hours he worked, he found it difficult to take a bike ride after work. He remedied his situation by riding his bike to work; and riding the university's bike path around the lake, whenever he could take a lunch break.

Every time he rode the bike path that surrounded the lake, he always thought of his father's vineyard. Hamilton loved the lake and the things that grew in the lake, the same way his father loved growing grapes. His father's grapes made the best wine in Maryland. He knew his father didn't realize it, but he taught Hamilton so much about the soil and how to make anything grow.

When he rode, he loved to stop near the lake and take in the lotus bowl lilies, always appearing on the water in perfect form, as if the lake had always been their home. He enjoyed the pickerel wood plants with their heart-shaped leaves and violet-blue spikes extending about the water. He enjoyed watching the ducks try to get to the tuber of the duck potato plants. Unfortunately, the ducks always came up empty. The arrowhead duck potato plants with broad leaves shaped like arrows with small white flowers that seemed to dart out like an actor dashing out on stage at the right time, demanding to be seen, daring anything else to take their spot. The water lilies with large round leaves and banqueting themselves as they exhibited their vibrant shades of green.

Each day he tried to pick out the plant that had grown; which one grew taller, which one spread a little more. He loved the smell of clean air that seemed to hover over lakes and the pure smell of water. There was something cleansing and rejuvenating about inhaling clean air, and when he inhaled, he allowed it to flow through his body, bringing life to his lungs, his heart, his brain. It gave him a sense of renewal and sometimes he stopped and watched whenever a family of Canada Geese swam and played in the lake.

The lake was a wooded area before it became a lake. Hamilton couldn't wait for the construction crew to break ground. He had spent the year before pushing through requests and proposals to have the dead and decaying trees taken down and a lake put in the area. When he finally got the Grounds and Beautification committee to agree, he became "The Man Who Made the Lake." After that if anyone needed anything done, particularly of that magnitude, they asked Hamilton.

Early one morning, Hamilton heard the rumbling of big trucks outside. From his office window, he watched a construction crew of four dump trucks stop in front of the trees. Several men got out, walked through the trees, and, as men do, consulted one another on the project. They shook their heads, went through the trees one more time, and one man climbed into a truck, pulled it away from the trees, turned around, and drove away. Then the others drove off.

The following week, the men returned and took down the trees. With a backhoe, they tore down into the earth, leaving a gigantic hole about a half-mile round. One evening, after the men had left for the day, Hamilton went down to the enormous hole, moved the barrier just enough for him to get through, and stood near the edge. He reached down and picked up a handful of dirt, feeling its smoothness, its coarseness, searching for its power. He realized its power was in the mass, the bulk, the quantity. He picked up another handful and rolled it in his hands, feeling it go from moist to dry in a few seconds.

Like all of nature's changes, it went too quickly for him. He picked up another handful and tried to see the exact time, find the exact moment when the dirt changed from moist to dry. But the elusiveness escaped him. It was like when he was growing up and he wanted to know the exact day and time he grew an inch. When he was in high school, he stayed up all night measuring and watching as hard as he could, but one day he was 5'11" and the next day he was almost 6 feet. Or the time he wanted to know exactly when his face changed from smooth to wrinkly. One day it was smooth, and the next day he had lines. Change was like that. It couldn't be seen; it just happened. One day he believed in something, and the next day, just as quickly as that, he believed in something different.

As was his usual way, he was the first person to arrive in his office wing. He went about turning on the lights and the copy machine and started the coffee for everyone. Then, after a trip to the gym across campus, he made his way to his coveted office overlooking the lake where the low water level and surrounding wilted trees, flowers and weeds were now the scene. The sun was already preparing itself to scorch the earth, and there were only a few brave and strong people dedicated to a good work-out on the path. This morning, he didn't bring his bike; he drove. He wasn't one of the strong ones today.

Before he had gotten much done, the outer office came to life. The aroma of coffee permeated the air; the secretaries or administrative assistants, as they liked to be called, were busy at their desks; student workers answered the phones or on computers; and the sound of copy machines thumped in rhythm. He looked at his calendar he always kept on top of his uncluttered desk and felt good that he was ready for the department chairs meeting.

He had open communication with his department chairs, and since his first semester as dean, he made it a point to meet with them before each semester. They were under his area, and he wanted to be sure they solved all problems, and each chair had all the resources they needed for their departments. He gathered his notebook titled "Department Chairs Meetings," and walked down to the end of the corridor to the conference room.

After the meeting began, his mind was elsewhere. He worried that someone would ask him how he was holding up, or ask if they could do anything for him, or pity him. He didn't want to be pitied. Then, the fact his doctor needed to see him made Hamilton a little nervous. The tests he had taken at the hospital were okay, so the ER doctor told him. Hamilton didn't understand the need to see his doctor. Besides, Dr. Mitchell knew he was a man who avoided doctors as much as possible.

However, it worried him that Dr. Mitchell wanted him to come in, instead of a phone conversation, their usual way.

All the department chairs were present, even Doug. He forgot about Doug, the consoler. Doug would say something to him about the divorce. It would be a disaster for him if someone asked him how he was doing. What would he say? Why didn't he think of Doug earlier? He was the leader; he had to show strength to his group.

He eyed the department chairs who sat at the long conference table, all watching him. He had to arrange this meeting so that he stayed in control, giving no one a chance to say anything to him. He should have thought of all this earlier. He opened his department chair notebook for his notes, but they weren't on top where he put them. Looking up from his folder, he smiled at the chairs and flipped through the notebook for his notes. While he continued to search, he gazed at Doug again, seated next to Pat.

Doug looked up at Hamilton, and Hamilton quickly turned away. "I know they're in here," he said as he continued his search. The room was quiet. No one uttered a sound; not even a cough escaped from any of the chairs, which made him more nervous.

Hamilton peered at Doug again and this time noticed a white envelope sitting on top of Doug's folder. The envelope was the kind that held a birthday card, a Christmas card, or a sympathy card. It would be like Doug to give him a sympathy card. How could he accept it?

When he left, he could just leave it on the table unopened. But he couldn't do that. Did they all sign the card for him? Would they also say something to him? What would he say back? For now, he had to calm down.

However, his nervousness grew, and a slight haze of perspiration broke out on his forehead. He was sorry he had to return so soon. Why didn't he take the time off his vice president and the president encouraged him to do? A shuffling noise came from Doug's direction and Hamilton saw Doug had changed positions in his seat. Doug picked up the envelope and fanned himself with it for a few moments. Hamilton finally found his notes.

"Good morning everyone. I trust everything is going well. No problems this semester?"

"I would like to say something," Doug began. He picked up the envelope.

Hamilton's heartbeat sped up. He tried to relax. The words, "Please don't pity me," ran through his mind, but he said, "Doug, is this about your department?"

"Not really." He quickly opened the envelope and took out a card. "I just wanted to thank everyone for remembering my birthday and this really beautiful handmade card."

After Hamilton arrived at his medical center, a nurse directed him to Dr. Mitchell's office. Dr. Mitchell, in his white coat, was already in his comfortable-looking office and seated at his desk, typing on his computer. When he saw Hamilton, he waved him in. Hamilton took one look at the white coat and sensed a seriousness of the visit. After they shook hands, Hamilton sat in the chair opposite the doctor's desk.

"I don't have a lot of time. I have to get back to the office."

"I understand. Everybody is busy, but we have some things to talk about." The phone rang, and Dr. Mitchell picked it up. "Sorry, Ham. I've been waiting for this."

Hamilton got up and stood out in the hall. He paced back and forth and stopped himself from loosening his tie. The tests he took at the hospital were all positive. They must have missed something. He felt all right, no pain, no broken bones, no trying to get his breath. The doctor broke into his thoughts when he called Hamilton back. Hamilton stood in front of Dr. Mitchell's desk.

"Maybe we can do this another time."

"Sit down, Ham."

"Tell you what, I'll call for another appointment."

The doctor stood up behind his desk and motioned for Hamilton to take a seat.

Hamilton sat.

"Ham. I asked you in this morning to find out how you're doing. Are you taking the beta blockers that the ER doctor prescribed for you?"

"I'm doing fine. No, I didn't get the beta blockers." Hamilton cast his eyes down at his hands as if he discovered a mole or something that he hadn't noticed before.

Dr. Mitchell didn't respond. Hamilton could feel his stare, but he couldn't look the doctor in the eye. After a moment, Hamilton turned his head up to Dr. Mitchell. "I think I need to start again. I had an accident in my car on the day I was to go to court. Someone called an ambulance; the paramedics took me to the hospital where I took some tests. What else can you tell me?"

"Sure." Dr. Mitchell gave a slight smile, one that said, "I knew you didn't understand everything that happened to you." He sat up close to his desk and leaned over. "First, Ham, the reason I've been trying to get you back here is because you need to know the results of your tests. You've been avoiding me." He picked up some papers and began reading from them.

"I know the ER doctor went over this with you. I just want to go over it again in case you have new questions." He paused, looked at Hamilton as if waiting for him to respond. Then, "At first, the EMTs and ER doctors thought you were having a heart attack. They began treating you for that since you reported you were having chest pain, shortness of breath, a sharp pain in your arm and you were sweating profusely, an EMT described. At the hospital, you received an angiogram, an echocardiogram and a TTE. An angiogram gives images of the major blood vessels that supply your heart."

He pulled out a picture from his papers and showed Hamilton a picture of his heart. "During a heart attack, one or more arteries," he pointed them out with his pen, "are blocked, but in your case, the blood vessels were okay. See here? You also took an echocardiogram that shows pictures of your heart," Dr. Mitchell showed Hamilton another picture of his heart, "and may reveal a heart to be shaped like a fishing pot. See, here it is."

"So, this is what my heart looks like?"

"Yes. In your case, it is. See this image here? It shows that the left ventricle of your heart is shaped like a fishing pot."

"What does that mean? Do I need a new heart?"

"No. It shows what we call stress-induced cardiomyopathy, or takotsubo cardiomyopathy, the medical terms. Most people may know it as broken heart syndrome."

"Then I didn't have a heart attack?"

"No."

"I've never heard of broken heart syndrome."

"Yes, you have. Almost everyone has. You know when you see it, but rarely do people recognize it as a medical condition."

"Do you mean like Sandra and Bob Durant from church? They were married for 65 years."

"That's a lifetime of being with one person. What would it be like if one lost the other?"

"Sandra was left alone after a lifetime with Bob. I remember hearing her say she wanted to be with him. She wouldn't eat, sleep, or leave her house."

"That was how she responded. With you, what happened, your accident, was the way your body reacted to extreme stress. This condition usually comes after a trauma, like the death of a loved one, such as in Sandra's case. It can be a mugging, an accident, or any traumatic event. With you, it's the loss of your marriage and family structure that, no doubt, caused the accident."

"I feel like some kind of psychotic person."

"Absolutely not. Ham, you don't have any way to let out the stress?"

"My biking."

"When you ride, do you ever think about whatever may cause stress with you?"

"No. I just ride."

"When you came in, I asked you how you were doing, and you said everything was fine. Don't you face things?"

"When there's a need."

"I see. Ham, a divorce is a very tragic event. You can't take that lightly. When you're under severe stress, you need to deal with it. You can't just let it accumulate and continue to say that nothing is wrong. This could happen again. When you have an episode, the heart muscle can be affected to the point where it can't pump blood out to your body in a strong enough manner. This could be fatal, life threatening for you."

"What do you suggest?"

"First, take those beta blockers. I have the address and phone number of a therapist, someone you could talk to, just when you feel stressed." He didn't look up, just wrote the information.

Hamilton accepted the paper when Dr. Mitchell handed it to him.

"And get those beta blockers today."

"Okay." Hamilton didn't tell Dr. Mitchell about the guilt he carried. He found out before the divorce he had caused HolliAnne to lose her job. She was let go because he pushed her into something she couldn't handle. All she wanted was to be a pre-school teacher. But he wanted her to have higher aspirations. Could beta blockers stop him from feeling guilty?

"Make an appointment. I want to see you back here in six weeks."

Hamilton stood, they shook hands and just as he turned to leave, "Ham, this divorce thing has been hard on you. Maybe you should try to get away for a few days. Relax, enjoy doing nothing."

"You think so?"

"In fact, I recommend it. Take a week or two off and just relax. Think of nothing but doing nothing," He chuckled.

Walking down the hall, he thought long and hard about getting away. Maybe that's what he needed.

CHAPTER 3

"Dad, wake up. Dad, Dad, wake up." Hamilton heard from very far away, as if in a dream.

"Dad, Dad? Dad? Wake up." Another voice, one more urgent and louder. Something shook him and he moved from side to side. Hamilton opened his eyes. His three children stood over him, calling out to him to wake up.

"Dad, are you okay?" Eric asked.

Hamilton sat up on the couch in the family room. "I was asleep."

"Are you feeling, okay?" Anna asked.

"Yes. I just dozed off." He rubbed his face and stood up. "Are you guys hungry? Let's see if we can find something to eat." He started toward the kitchen. His children followed him.

"Dad, I called you at your office and your assistant said you left to go to a medical appointment," Anna said.

"That, I did." Her question made him a little nervous. He didn't see the need in talking about his fishing pot shaped heart.

"I thought the ER doctor said everything was okay. Is there something else?" Eric asked.

"Dad, you're okay, aren't you?" Jeremy asked. Even though he smiled, Hamilton sensed an uneasiness in his voice.

"What is this? Am I being interrogated?"

"Yes, but no, if it upsets you," Jeremy said, a wide smile on his face.

Hamilton rustled his amber-brown hair. "Buddy Boy, you don't think you should take a serious stand on this one?" He sat a bowl and spoon in the places where his children normally sat at the kitchen counter. Hamilton went back to the cabinet for cereal.

"What about your mother? Did you say goodbye to her before you left?" He pulled out a box of cornflakes and sat it on the counter as he tried to divert their attention.

Anna pulled out a stool from under the counter and sat down. "We told her we were going home." Her comment made him feel valued, but he was sure it hurt HolliAnne.

"She knows we're here," Eric said.

"We just spent the night. It's not like we actually live with her and Todd or anything," Jeremy said.

"Computer class. What time is it?" Hamilton asked. "Jeremy needs to get to computer class, and then to church for his acolyte meeting."

"We have enough time. Tell us about the appointment," Eric said.

Hamilton sat down on a stool. "Dr. Mitchell called, and I went to see him."

"So, what did he say?" Anna asked.

"There's nothing to worry about." Hamilton didn't get the beta blockers he needed, and he didn't want to say much about his broken heart syndrome. He couldn't have his children worrying about him, and he'd never been the kind of father who talked over his problems with his children.

"What does that mean?" Eric asked.

"Isn't it clear enough?"

"You said there's nothing to worry about," Anna repeated.

"That's right. There's nothing to worry about."

"Dad, you're being vague. Why? It's creeping me out," Eric said.

"Me, too. What did the doctor say?" Anna asked.

Fear swept through him and overwhelmed him, and he was weak in the knees. His children needed his strength and needed to feel secure. He couldn't let them see his vulnerability.

"How about you guys take Buddy Boy to his computer class and his acolyte meeting?"

"But dad, you had an accident," Anna said.

"I know that." He gazed at the clock on the stove. "Bud's class starts in a few minutes."

"What did the doctor say was wrong? Why won't you tell us?" Anna asked.

"There is nothing wrong."

"But we want to know what the doctor said," Anna said; her voice filled with distress.

"Dad, we're worried about you. Tell us please," Eric said.

"I just told you. If I seem troubled, it's because I have some things to think about."

"Like what?" Eric asked.

"For one, Buddy Boy and I will miss you and Anna."

"Are you thinking of selling the house?" Eric asked.

"Why would you think that?"

"Mom said you would," Anna said.

"That's my decision to make and I haven't made a new decision about the house."

"I don't have a problem with you selling the house, but if you do, you have to use the money for whatever the doctor said you need to do," Eric said in a loud voice.

"Eric—"

"No, Dad. Anna and I will find a way to pay for our college, and we'll help Jeremy when it's his time."

"Even if it means we have to transfer here to where you are," Anna said.

"You can't change our minds. We already talked about it and decided. This is what we want to do," Eric said.

Hamilton saw how worried and determined both Eric and Anna were. "Okay, I'll tell you what. Take Buddy Boy to class and we'll talk about it later."

"Dad, we have to talk about this," Anna said.

"Eric, Anna, you wanting to pay for your college education is very admirable. It makes me feel proud of you, both. But paying for your college education is my job and I intend to do my job. And I'm not selling this house."

Eric, Anna, and Jeremy left. Hamilton stood on the porch and waited for them to pull out of the driveway and turn down the street before he went inside.

Hamilton remembered that a few days ago, while they were still at church, Jeremy was upset and wanted to pray for his father. Hamilton saw his apprehension, and they went to see his brother, the rector at the church.

Hamilton and Jeremy caught Taylor in his overcoat and coming out of his office.

"Fr. Maddox, Jeremy wants to pray."

Fr. Maddox opened his office door and invited the two of them in. He motioned for them to sit in the leather chairs, and he took off his coat.

"Tell me what you would like, Jeremy," Fr. Maddox asked.

"I want to pray for my father, but I don't know what to say or how."

"Why don't we go to the sacristy?"

They left Fr. Maddox's office and walked into the nave of the church and down to the Altar. On the Altar sat a large gold cross with a light behind it, beckoning people to come toward it. The candles and chalice along with the other things that were on the Altar earlier, were now removed. The light behind the cross was the only light in the sacristy, giving the Altar a mystique aura. Fr. Maddox stood in front of the railing. Hamilton put Jeremy between them, and they knelt on the cushion at the railing in front of the altar.

"Jeremy, we are here in the heart of God's house. Just tell Him what you want Him to know. He already knows what's in your heart, but just say it out loud," Fr. Maddox said.

"Okay."

"Whenever you're ready."

After a few minutes, Jeremy began his prayer. "God, I love my father so much. You know I do. He's the best father in this entire world. We all need him, my sister, Anna, and my brother, Eric. Even my mother needs him." Jeremy tried hard to hold back his tears, but he couldn't. "But God, I really need him. I need him to be well. God, I want you to keep him healthy. Please, God. I just don't know what I'd do without my father. I don't know what will happen to me." He stopped for a moment to wipe his eyes and nose. "He does things for us. He's like you, God. He's always showing us love. My father loves us; he encourages me, my sister and brother, and he supports us in everything we ask of him. He protects us, Father, just like you do, so I want to ask you to protect my father. God, please keep him well. Amen."

"Father, we pray this in the name of Jesus Christ. Amen," Fr. Maddox added.

Hamilton reached over and grabbed hold of his son. They held on to each other as tears flowed from Jeremy and Hamilton. Fr. Maddox stayed with them, his strong arms around his brother and nephew, sheltering them.

They pulled away. "Jeremy, you prayed a very powerful prayer for your father, but you must realize that everything is in the hands of the Lord. Understand?"

In the family room, he walked back and forth thinking about how his divorce left his children confused and him worried about how others would treat him. He didn't want to worry his children, but they were concerned and had questions, particularly Jeremy. Naturally, they would want to know what would happen to them. He'd always told them that the house was their house, too. Why would HolliAnne say such a thing? A warm sensation came over him and he felt his problems crowding him, stressing him, and burying him. Funny how he never felt that way during the marriage, even though he was the one to make almost all the decisions. Knowing HolliAnne was there gave him the security he needed; another reason he didn't want the marriage to end.

Dr. Mitchell recommended he try to get away. It would give him the space he needed. He was no longer a married man. He had to get control of his new life as a single man with two children in college and one at home, soon off to college. He had to realize that no one pitied him. He had to rid himself of those thoughts.

In his home office, he sat down in front of the computer and typed out two letters. When he finished, he folded it, slipped it inside an envelope and addressed it to the president and VP of his university. The second letter he left on the kitchen counter for his kids. His detailed instructions and the detailed schedule, including a calendar and instructions for thawing, were enough for them. He explained he needed space to think.

The kids all had keys to the house and cars, and there was always an extra set on the hall table next to the key dish. He called his brother, Taylor, and his best friend who lived down the street on the corner to look in on his children. He asked Taylor to take Jeremy home after his acolyte training. Then he called the airlines. On the way out, he checked the door and got in the taxi he ordered. It pulled out of the driveway.

The cab driver drove him first, to the university. In his office, he sat for a few minutes behind his mahogany desk and looked out over the lake, his lake he liked to say, and the walking trail. Then, he stood in front of the bookcases that spanned the long wall opposite his desk and ran his hand over the books and manuals he had written, the policies and procedures he collaborated on, and the myriad of awards and plaques he had earned over the twenty-five years he'd been employed at the university.

He knew he would miss his work; he'd never taken a vacation by himself. He'd miss the "hurry to meet deadlines," the "what to do about an unexpected increase in enrollment in his department," and "the trying to figure out how to add new life to his college of education," not to mention the ever-dreaded budget; these things that excited him.

He began his career at this university, first as an instructor, then professor, and after he earned his Ph.D., he asked to be addressed as Dr. Maddox. After all, he had the right, given the work he put into earning his degree. He couldn't imagine his life without the university, but at one time, he couldn't have imagined his life without HolliAnne, either.

Even though he would only be on leave from the university for five months, he packed up his awards along with his pictures of his family, friends, and people he'd met over the years. He wanted those things with him in his home. The VP may want to turn his office into a temporary conference room while he was on leave. He didn't want people handling these things that were so special to him.

At the door, he turned around to look at what he had accomplished so far. He recalled he didn't have to put up much of a fight to get the office larger than the others, with windows letting in the light and overlooked the lake. In fact, he thought there must have been something wrong with it when they gave it to him. But it turned out to be the best office in the building, almost as nice as the president's. He was told he'd earned it.

Before he changed his mind about taking a leave of absence, he turned around and started out of the office, but his eye caught something on his desk. He almost forgot it. In fact, he wished he could forget the letter and what happened. He hesitated a minute. He could just leave it for his return. But it was confidential, and he didn't want to just leave it. He didn't want HolliAnne's jobless situation to become a conversation in his office. He took the letter and put it in his jacket pocket.

"Josie don't stop your typing. I'm just gonna put this letter right here on top of these papers." He took the letters he'd carefully typed and put them on Josie's desk. The wonderful thing about Josie was she was overbearing and liked to take charge over matters not in her domain and without letting Hamilton know what she had done.

He and Josie often fought about who supervised the department. Hamilton was not a man to be stepped on. Sometimes, when two department chairs couldn't agree on something, she would try to settle the matter. Several times Hamilton asked her to stay out of it and let him handle the affairs of his office. But she continued interfering. According to Josie, she often handled situations better than Hamilton did, and she tactfully told him so, so she said. He placed the letters on her desk, knowing she would take matters upon herself.

Josie turned around to him. "Letters? What letters?" She picked up the letters and as she opened one, Hamilton turned to leave.

"Wait a minute Dr. Maddox. Don't go anywhere. I may need you for something. Oh, no, Dr. Maddox," a look of sorrow on her face. She held up his letter and pointed to the bulging box he carried under his arm with his pictures and plagues protruding over the top.

The others in the office looked up at him and, embarrassed by Josie's reaction, Hamilton turned and hurried off toward the elevator. So far, he had been strong. But she was causing him to break down. On the elevator, he tried to compose himself. It stopped the next floor down; a man got on and Hamilton blinked away his tears. He took a deep breath and straightened his shoulders.

As soon as he stepped off the elevator into the garage, the security guard approached.

"Dr. Maddox, your office called down and asked me to have you wait. Your assistant needs to talk to you," he said.

"Sean, I can't." Hamilton handed Sean the box with his plaques and awards, along with an envelope. "Here you go. Just mail them for me, like I asked. Okay? Everything you need is in the box," Hamilton said.

Sean took the box. "Just wait here, sir. She said it'll only take a minute." Sean said.

"Thanks for your help, Sean."

Hamilton escaped him and avoided a car speeding past him. He made it to the cab parked near the entrance of the university garage. As they pulled out and turned down the street, he thought about going back, to explain everything, let everyone know he needed a little time. But everything they needed was in the letter. He explained he was taking the president's and vice president's suggestions and he would be on leave effective immediately. There was no need to torture himself and return. He was sorry he didn't give them all a proper goodbye, his second family, but this way was best. The cab driver made it through the next light before it turned red.

CHAPTER 4

As Hamilton got off the plane in Hawaii, and walked toward the main concourse, his legs were a little unsteady. He had done nothing this daring since he had asked HolliAnne to marry him. The airport, expansive and airy, with skylights that spanned the ceiling, and huge, luscious, dark green plants that traversed the wall on both sides of the walkway, and boldly crept onto the walkway, gave him a sense of peace.

Sun rays pierced the glass ceiling, leaving streaks of light in his pathway as if they were spotlights aimed at him. The people going in different directions, talking to each other, on cell phones, and hurrying by, all seemed a slight intrusion on his scene. Women in their traditional grass skirts greeted the passengers and one woman, who didn't look much like a Hawaiian to Hamilton with blond hair and blue eyes, offered him a lea. He accepted it, then followed the signs to baggage claim.

After he checked in at the Hilton Hotel and found his room, Hamilton weighed the benefits of going down to the bar to have a drink. But he couldn't wait to get started on the reason he, at the last moment, decided on Hawaii.

Ever since he had read about the Rain Forest in a magazine when he was in the fourth grade, he had always wanted to see the Rain Forest in Hawaii. He had read so much about the luscious green plants, the constant rain, and the size of the leaves. He saw pictures of leaves on some plants that were much larger than elephant ears. He wanted to see how the sun came streaking through from some places in the forest, while darkening other parts. Maybe he could take something back and grow it at the lake when he returned to his university. But he knew the danger in that.

He also came to get away, think, come to conclusions about his life, and this was as good a place as any. Maybe the lady on the plane who sat across the aisle and kept smiling at him would be in the bar. In his twenty-seven years of marriage to HolliAnne, he never once strayed. Even if the lady on the plane were there in the bar, at this point in his life, he wouldn't know what to do or say. Instead, he opted to go for a walk on the beach, take his shoes off and let the water surround his feet and ankles.

In the hotel, he decided on something else he always wanted to do first. He arranged to SCUBA dive and the next morning went to Living Ocean SCUBA to plunge into something he had never done. He joined a group of six other divers, both men and women, who were also taking the introductory boat dive. After the morning-long instructions in the meeting room, one diver fitted them with gear and gave them time to change. After everyone changed, the two professional divers took the group of seven out to the cabin cruiser with the words "Living Ocean" painted across the side and steered them to Hanauma Bay for the afternoon's SCUBA adventure.

The lead instructor reminded everyone of the instructions and, one by one, the group members jumped into the water. Hamilton was the last to jump into the warm water. His body had forgotten that he hadn't been in the water for a few years and when he hit the water, he splashed around, breathing hard while slapping his arms and hands hard in the water. Then his brain remembered, and he settled himself, curled over, and dove under.

The teacher, whose obvious job was to make certain everyone was in front of him, caught up to Hamilton in the water, and, using their sign language, asked him if he was okay. Hamilton flashed back the "thumbs up" sign. He wanted to be last so he wouldn't embarrass himself by having everyone watch his clumsy dive with each leg going in the opposite direction and arms flailing like a wild man, but he forgot about the teacher.

Once under, Hamilton looked up, amazed that the sun didn't break the surface. It settled on top of the water as if it were not invited into the underwater world, according to the rules of nature. Hamilton looked up as he felt like someone had closed an immense door to the life above and everything in the green water was serene and beautiful as waves gently flapped against him.

Hamilton and the second teacher found the group where the lead teacher had stopped. A shark headed their way, and Hamilton remembered the lead teacher said earlier when they came across a shark, he would stop. Hamilton relaxed as the shark moved so close to him. He could feel the smooth edges of the shark's skin, understand his need to find food, feel his desire to stay alive, and appreciate his kindness in leaving them alone.

After the shark swam on, Hamilton looked all around him again. The busy anxiety-filled world, his world, the world of humans, seemed so far away at this moment, and replaced by this unique world of easiness and relaxation. It gave him a sense of freedom he had never felt before. The water gave him a weightless feeling and all his burdens seemed lifted off him.

Life for sea creatures seemed easier than the life of man with his wants, needs, and agenda. Sea animals lived in their hidden, carefree world, swimming from place to place and resting whenever they were tired. He turned in all directions, as yellow, orange, and gray sea creatures of all distinct shapes, sizes and types swam passed him. Many he could not name. He could see why man wanted to be in the sea. The sea offered a serenity often missing in an earthly world. Hamilton resolved to enjoy life rather than have life; live life, rather than let life pass him by.

The leader gave them a sign, and the group followed as he took them farther down. Hamilton flinched at first when he saw eels; after all, they looked like snakes. But a kind of peace came over him again and he relaxed. He passed a huge sea turtle bigger and taller than he if they were to stand side by side.

Though he moved his legs in a scissor-like fashion, he moved through the water with an effortless glide, almost feeling like he was a sea creature himself. He glissaded beyond a small shark and a scorpion. He followed the leader as they dove deeper. Hamilton saw the unique colors of the corals — the pale pink, soft corals, and the red corals that looked like cups. He wanted to touch them but remembered the instructor's warnings. Some of them were sharp and meant to catch fish.

Hamilton couldn't remember a time when he was as relaxed as he was now. He, as best he could, looked in the eyes of the sea creatures as he slid by giant-sized turtles and a spray of tropical fish. He coasted by the clear-looking glass anemone and the pale pink swimming anemone that looked sticky the closer he got. He passed by the gray ghost tube, the yellow sunray, and the rubbery zoanthids, all spread out and covering the floor. He went over these names in his head and tried hard to remember the scientific names, even though he didn't think he had them right. But he wanted to remember the time he went SCUBA diving.

He pulled away from the coral and went up a little to get a better look at the magnificent array of the yellow, pink, white and red colors of the sea formation and the sea creatures that all passed by. He watched as a scorpion circled around the rubbery coral. Hamilton thought the scorpion was going after his meal, and he hoped it wouldn't.

When he asked during the information session, the instructor said scientists were not sure how these wonders were formed or how they were used. They knew the coral had been in the sea for thousands of years and they provided so much to the sea. Hamilton wanted everything he did at the university over the years to be used to improve his department and have an impact on the world, just as the coral had a powerful impact on the sea world. Before they left, the leader took them to Shipwreck Reel where they saw remnants of a ship from long ago, and where a giant turtle had made the wreckage its home.

The next day, Hamilton and a small group of five hikers gathered to walk up to Manoa Falls. One man who said he and his wife had hiked it last year when they came, was made the hike leader. He said last year it took them one and a half hours to hike to the falls. After passing through the gate, there were several signs in the Hawaiian or Asian languages, Hamilton guessed, and English, warning of the dangers of the trail. No one wanted to turn back.

The first part of the rugged trail took them through the edge of the Rain Forest and led to another more rugged trail, that wasn't as much a trail as it was a very narrow passageway covered with overgrown weeds, trees, bushes, and limbs that steeply spiraled upward. They hiked until they came to a clearance. Hamilton found it hard to breathe.

"We can stop here, take a rest," the leader said. He sat on the edge of a bolder. The others found places to sit.

"Mighty steep," a male hiker said.

"It's difficult. The trail is not very worn," a female hiker said.

Hamilton had to look at her twice. She looked like the lady on the plane who sat across the aisle.

"I don't think many people want to climb after a certain point," the leader said. "You have to know what you're doing."

"You've done a lot of hiking in tough places, it seems," Hamilton said to the leader.

"My wife and I," he pointed to his wife seated on a large rock and eating a protein bar, "do a lot of hiking. The tougher the terrain, the better we like it."

"The brochure didn't say it would be this hard," a woman hiker said.

"Everyone, we need to get moving if we're going to the top. We want to be back before we lose the light. If you can't go any further, wait for us here. We'll all get down together."

"He's right," a male hiker said.

"You may want to find a sturdy stick or limb to help you climb," the leader said.

After about forty-five minutes, they made it beyond the barren trees and then into the Bamboo Forest. The atmosphere was cool for the time they were in the forest. Hamilton wiped the perspiration off his face and neck and took in the clean forest air. He took a few more steps into the forest to see and feel its beauty. He could hear the rustling of trees and bushes, but he didn't see any animals in the forest. He got back on the trail. They came to another narrow dirt path after about another forty-five minutes of a grueling climb.

"Ahhhhhh," a woman's voice yelled out.

Even though she was in front of Hamilton, the denseness of the trail with overhanging limbs and vines made it difficult for him to see her. As he moved forward, he looked over the side and saw her hanging on to a root protruding from the cliff below. He looked down at her; her face filled with fear. He looked for a way to get down to help her but saw no way. He could see nothing below her. She struggled, legs slicing in a scissor-like motion as she tried to find some place to put her feet.

"Help, Help!" Hamilton yelled as loud as he could.

"Help me, please. Don't let me fall, please." Terror in the woman's voice.

The leader arrived, looked down over the side of the trail and saw her hanging on to something. "Oh, my goodness. We gotta get her up."

"Please, I can't hold on much longer."

The others returned. The leader opened his backpack and pulled out a blue-colored rope that looked like a huge bungee cord. His wife appeared, and she pulled a cord out of her backpack and handed it to him. Hamilton heard a loud crack and a distant thud sound.

"Ahhhhhh," the woman yelled. "Part of the limb just broke off. I don't have much to hold on to. Please don't let me die here."

"If she tries to grab the cord, she could easily lose the grip she has and fall," Hamilton began. "We need to use both cords."

"Let's see if this will stretch from that tree down to where she is." The leader pointed to the tree on the other side of the trail. The leader and one of the other hikers tied the bungee cord around the tree and then dropped it down the cliff. They looked and saw it reached the lady.

Hamilton tied the second cord around his waist. The other hiker began pulling the first cord up.

"No. Leave that one there. I'll help her tie that one around her waist." Then he yelled down to the lady. "Don't try to do anything with that cord just yet. I'm coming down to help you tie it around your waist."

"Can you please hurry? I don't think I can hold on much longer."

"I'm on my way." Standing close to the edge, Hamilton tied the second cord around his waist and held onto it.

"Are you sure this will do it?" asked one hiker.

"Do we have anything else? We could use a cord long enough to go around the waist and legs, but we don't have that."

"I just have the one cord. Does anybody have another suggestion?" The leader turned to everyone. No one answered, just shook their heads.

"I think this is our only and best choice," said a hiker.

"Okay, then," Hamilton said.

"When she is ready, three of you pull her up. But don't drag her all at once. Pull, wait, pull, wait, like that. Pull about three or four times, together. Once she passes the root where she's holding on, she'll have something under her feet and can help you. Pull us up one at a time. Pull me the same way. Pull, wait, pull, wait, about three or four times, three men pulling."

Hamilton started down the ledge and then onto the cliff. He dropped himself below the cliff to get to her, but he was startled at the drop and the fact that he had nothing to stand on, and nothing to hold him there but that bungee cord. He thrashed around like a fish caught on a hook as he tried to find a place for his feet. Then he tightened his grip on the cord and got his breath. He reached for the lady's waist and tied her bungee cord around her waist. "Hold on to this. It'll help with the tightness of the cord around your waist. When you're ready, call out to them to pull you up. Help them pull after you get to where you can use your feet."

She thanked him and called out to the people on the trail above. They began pulling her up. Anxious, she thrashed around, frantic, as she tried to find a place for her feet. She let out a loud, gut-wrenching noise. When she reached to where she could use her feet, she slipped down, and in her fear, she kicked Hamilton in the head. He shook his head to keep himself awake.

He swung back and forth, his legs kicking, arms splaying and slicing through the air. Suddenly, the cord tightened around his waist, and he knew the man who held his cord saw he was in trouble. He looked up and saw the lady swing back and forth, trying to hold on with one arm. Hamilton pulled himself up on his cord and took the woman's arm. "Grab the cord," he said.

"I can't."

He took her hand and put it on the cord, then took hold of his cord. "Pull her up, again," Hamilton tried to yell.

"I'm ready," the lady yelled.

The leader pulled her again. "You're almost over, wait. Okay, now use your feet to help pull yourself up."

After she got up, they pulled him up. Hamilton crawled up on the trail and took off his cord. "These things are very handy," he said to the hiker. He turned to the lady. "Are you okay?"

"Thank you so much. I don't know what happened."

"Take a minute and get yourself together." He looked to the others, "The rest of you should go on."

"We could wait with you both," the leader said.

"Why don't you go on," Hamilton said to the leader. "We'll find you up there."

"Yes, go on," the woman said.

"We'll be right behind you. She just needs a minute," Hamilton said.

The leader and the others left, and in a few minutes, the woman stood. She decided she could make it and they proceeded up to the falls.

They finally reached the top of the falls, where the others were. After he got his breathing under control, and his ears popped, allowing him to hear better, he stood up straight. Hamilton turned around in all directions. He had never seen a more breathtaking sight. No one spoke. Everyone seemed mesmerized by the beauty and massiveness of nature.

He stood as close to the barrier as possible. On the other side of the falls, a flock of birds flew in and out of the forest. They were too far away, and Hamilton couldn't make out the type of birds. He tried to count them, but they flew in and out so quickly, he couldn't. The air, even though warm, was fresh and clean. He stuck out his hand to let the air settle on it. The air seemed to rejuvenate him and instead of discomfort from the height, he was calm, and filled with an indescribable sense of peace and relaxation, a slightly different feel from the ocean.

He stood there, taking in the magnificence of these islands. He was so high up it seemed to him, if he stood on his toes, he could actually touch the sky. He should have been frightened, being so high up, but the trees behind him provided security. From where he stood, he could see a tiny village nestled in the trees on the other side of the falls, and over to his right, Honolulu, according to his guess.

He remembered a time when he was eight years old, and he told his parents and brother he was Superman. He found a long red towel and said it was his Superman cape. He cut it and made it so he could tie it around his neck. His parents, as he recalled, were worried because they thought he thought he was Superman. Hamilton would even sing out the name SUPerMAN as he ran around the house in his red cape and jumped off furniture. After he jumped, even if he stumbled, he would straighten himself and stand with his hands on his hips singing, "SUPerMAN." Several times, his mother asked him not to jump off the coffee table or the end tables or the couch.

One day, he showed her he was Superman and Superman couldn't get hurt. He climbed up on the china closet. His mother came into the dining room and saw him on the top, trying to stand. She cried out to him, "Hamilton, get down from there, now." She reached out her hand. "Give me your hand. Let me help you down." She stood on the same step ladder he used. The china closet was tall, and it was about three feet from the ceiling.

Hamilton couldn't stand up straight. Instead, he could only bend over in a jump position. He was Superman. He jumped off the cabinet and landed on both feet. Even he was stunned for a moment as he looked at his body and saw he hadn't fallen or broken anything. Then he sang out SUPerMAN, several times. "Look mom, I'm Superman." His mother ran to him. He was okay. She couldn't believe he hadn't hurt himself.

As he recalled this event, he recognized he'd been a superman all his life. From the time he jumped off the china closet, to high school, to college, to marriage, and to the work world. He had always been the decision maker in his family, the provider, the cook, the driver for his kids, the man who fixed everything from skinned knees to broken toys.

That invincible man somehow disappeared when his marriage began to fail. He needed that invincible man now. He couldn't remember why Superman disappeared when he needed Superman the most. Standing at the top of the mountain and looking out at the massiveness and power of the falls with the beauty of the multi-green forest behind him, he needed the strength and courage of his Superman, the ability to be free, to let go. At this moment, he didn't know how he could turn things around for himself.

He stood there at the falls, listening to the power of the water. He saw the strength of the whitecaps below and understood he was so busy controlling what he thought was his life, what he thought he wanted, he missed enjoying life. He controlled everything with HolliAnne. She said he controlled her education, how many children they would have, their house buying, the finances, everything. He controlled even his rise at the university.

The leader stepped back. "We need to start back," he said. The others, one by one, followed the leader back down the trail. The woman who he just helped and looked like the woman on the plane, stood beside him. She whispered something, and then threw what Hamilton thought were ashes, over the barrier and into the falls. She gave a quick glance at Hamilton, wiped her face, and followed the leader.

He took a step closer to the barrier and gazed down. The rushing water of the falls was strong, and he knew he had to make a change. At that moment, he wanted that part of him whom he thought of as Superman to return to him. He had always wanted to be a dutiful father to his children to prove to his father he was a good man. He had proven that.

Now, more than anything, he wanted to love again. He wanted what his father told him all his life to get for himself. He took a deep breath before he turned away from the falls. When he got a little farther away from the barrier, he stopped for a minute and turned back to the falls one more time.

The waterfalls, with its rhythmic sound, filled his ears, and in that moment, a thought came to him. He smiled so wide it covered his face, almost as if someone had shined a light on him. He now knew what he had needed for most of his life, why even though he loved his kids, there was still that hollowness, that void he could never fill. Then, he nodded and quickened his pace to catch up to hike back. Superman.

That evening, the lady on the plane who sat across the aisle and who was also on the hike, entered the restaurant where he was having dinner. He had just ordered when he saw her. Hamilton looked around the restaurant and saw all the tables were full. He summoned the waiter.

"She's with me. Would you direct her here?" he said, pointing to the lady.

The waiter brought the lady and seated her.

"We were on the hike together," Hamilton said.

"Yes, and you sat across the aisle from me on the plane."

"Yes. How are you feeling?"

"Much better. It was a scary thing. I thank you so much for risking your life to help me." She looked over at him. "And thank you for doing this. I was about to leave when the waiter came."

"I had an extra chair, so why not.... We didn't introduce ourselves. I'm Hamilton Maddox."

"I'm Anita Brown." She reached her hand out to him.

The server returned and she ordered. Anita was a sociology teacher in a high school. This trip was to be her honeymoon trip.

"Two weeks ago, my fiancé was in a hit and run. When he woke up in the hospital, he said he didn't think he would make it and he made me promise to take this trip to Hawaii. He died the next day, a week before we were to get married." She wiped at the corners of her eyes.

Hamilton took a sip of water. He could see why she was so fearful.

Loud laughter came from a group of people two tables over. Hamilton recognized them. They all sat together on the plane. They raised their glasses in good cheer. He turned back to Anita.

"He had always dreamed of going to Hawaii and told me he had even made a list of all the places to visit and things for us to do."

"Today was on the list?" Hamilton asked.

"Yes." She dabbed her eyes again. "Today helped me see how hard this is going to be. It's not the same without him." She took a sip of wine. "What about you?"

He saw how she struggled to maintain her composure. "I'm divorced."

"Do you miss being married?" She asked while mixing her salad dressing into her salad.

"I do. Until my divorce, I used to think a person would be happy to break free. But it's not that easy. It's almost as if I left one world and entered another."

"That's exactly how I feel. Only I don't fit in with the single people anymore and I don't quite fit in with the married people either."

"Misfits. Are we misfits?" he asked, a smile on his face, as he tried to change the mood.

"I don't want to be. My fiancé loved the fact that I'm a teacher. He always said that teachers inspire so they don't give up." She blinked away her tears. "I don't know what's next."

"Why worry about what's next? Enjoy your trip. Make the effort for you both."

"Eventually, I'll have to allow someone else into my life," she said.

"Eventually."

"I think Ron was the only one for me. We were one, perfect. Is it possible for there to be more than one perfect person?" she asked.

"Perfect is what you want it to be." He forked a few green beans, put them in his mouth.

"Let's make each other a promise, right here and now. What about that?"

"A promise?" Hamilton was reluctant to make a promise with a woman he didn't know. "What sort of promise?"

"A promise to keep ourselves alive." She took more salad.

"I don't make promises." He straightened himself, took a sip of wine this time.

"Yes. We promise that from this day forward, we will reach out, take a risk, and go on with our lives. We will honor what's now behind us, but we will not hide from romantic encounters, including love. We will be brave and find our way."

"As I said, I don't make promises, shaking his head."

"But we have to; we just have to." She rested a forkful of linguini on her plate.

"I couldn't do that, anyway."

"Why not? What's wrong with making a promise?"

"It's not simple. Promises are simple. I don't think I could keep that promise. So, it makes little sense to say I would." He didn't understand her purpose.

"We have to believe we can." Her voice was frantic.

"I don't make promises I'm not sure I can keep."

"How you get there is your choice, but we must not shy away," she said, now sounding a little irritated.

"Why don't you make that promise yourself," he paused for a moment, "Why me? Why not make it with someone you know?"

"It's easier to make a promise with someone you don't know."

He took a sip of wine, then a forkful of his mahimahi. As he put the mahimahi into his mouth, the power of her eyes, filled with tears, penetrated him, and begged him to make the promise. The heaviness of her stare and tears rolling down her face, pulled his body down into the chair, making it difficult for him to move. He turned away from her, wishing now he hadn't offered her the seat.

"Oh, come on. If you don't promise, I won't do it either." She sat back in her seat. "I have to know you'll do this with me."

"But you don't know me."

"I know."

"I don't want to promise anything."

"You're saying that you don't make promises with strangers. Some people whom we've never met are not strangers."

"I'm saying I know what I'm planning for my life." He had to soften things. She was upset. "You have to do the same." He turned away from her to the people at the table across from them. Maybe he could excuse himself and leave.

He finished his meal and put his knife and fork in the center of his plate. He gazed up and she was still watching him. He could just say the words and not mean it. But he was not that kind of man. He motioned to the waiter for the check.

When the server brought the check, Anita reached for her handbag. He held up his hand to her. He signed the check and gave it back to the waiter.

Hamilton looked all around the room, at Anita, again, at the couple across from them, and the group two tables over, all laughing and talking at the same time. Anita eased her chair back and placed her napkin on the table.

When she looked up at him, he thought he saw disappointment on her face and in her eyes. She slid her chair back again. Hamilton leaned in and, looking directly into her eyes, said, "Okay."

"What?' she asked.

"Okay. I promise." Why not give a little?

She smiled.

After dinner, in the cool warmth of the evening, they walked along the beach. Swimmers and sun bathers gathered up their things and left for the evening. Hamilton turned to Anita. "Anita, thanks for having dinner with me."

She raised her eyebrows. "I would have had to wait longer if you hadn't offered me a place at your table."

He extended his hand to her. "Do what your fiancé wanted you to do. Go through that list and experience everything."

Her hand in his, she nodded. "Thank you. Don't associate with strangers and don't forget our promise. Maybe we'll run into each other again during our trip."

He gave her a half-smile. She was lost and hurting, feeling pain the same way, he felt pain. Earlier, when he turned away from the falls, he decided to do something about his pain, so he agreed to Anita's promise. He would go to the rain forest tomorrow, the one they skimmed through on the way up to the falls. This time, he would take his time and stay as long as he could.

Hamilton turned to leave. Anita needed to carry out her husband's wishes. But life is so that people come and go. They each leave a little something behind for the person they just met, and he hoped he had left something behind for her—something she could use to help her mourn and put her fiancé behind her. Hamilton used to say people were like hotels, where we all stop over for a while to enjoy the company or to learn something from each other. When our stay has ended, we pick up everything we've learned, that are now our belongings, and go onward to the next stop. He now saw his marriage was that way.

CHAPTER 5

It was late in the evening by the time Hamilton reached his home. When he saw his car sitting in the driveway as he got out of the cab, he knew his children were home and his thoughts went to Anna. Knowing his daughter, she had worried about him. He unlocked the front door and stepped inside. A faint light cast itself from the hallway to the living room, and a flickering light came from the family room in the back.

He started up the stairs, but when he heard a noise, he turned and went to the family room instead. Jeremy lay balled up on the floor in front of the couch, a blanket over him, and Anna stretched out on the couch, with Hamilton's favorite throw over her. The television was on to the evening news. When Hamilton cut the TV off, Anna changed positions. He stepped around Jeremy, leaned down, and gave Anna a kiss on her forehead. Jeremy sat up and looked around.

"Dad," he yelled out, and attempted to get up.

"I didn't mean to wake you," Hamilton whispered.

Jeremy jumped up, gave his father a hug. Anna awakened, reached over, and held on to her father's arm. He took one arm from around Jeremy and hugged Anna.

"I thought you both would be on the internet or playing games or something." Slightly pulling away from them.

"We were worried about you. Where were you? Your note didn't say where you were," Anna said.

"Sweetheart, I don't want either of you to worry about me. I said that in my letter. I just had to think, that's all."

"We knew you needed the time away. Eric said it would be good for you. You needed it. It's just that we didn't know where you were," Jeremy said, pulling back.

"Dad, you've always had us around. This time you needed time alone. We understand," Anna said.

"You weren't afraid, were you?" Hamilton asked.

"No. We know what to do."

"Eric is right. I just needed some time away. You had everything you needed, right? And your uncle Taylor took excellent care of you, right?"

"I—I — I...," Jeremy tried to speak.

Hamilton rustled Jeremy's hair and Jeremy calmed down. Hamilton looked around the room. "I guess Eric left already?"

"He called to let us know he arrived safely, and said everything was okay, and for us not to worry about you," Jeremy said.

"How'd your acolyte meeting go?" Hamilton asked.

"It was great." A big smile across his face.

"Good. So, you want to serve and help train others, then?"

"Yes. The leader will send out a schedule soon. I want to serve Thanksgiving and at the Christmas Eve service."

"I thought you were going to drive me to New York?" Anna whispered.

"I am, sweetheart. Indeed, I am." Hamilton had to see his daughter off to college, that next stage of life. She had always fought him whenever he tried to control her, and he was glad of that. She is now a strong woman with a mind of her own, and he wasn't afraid for her any longer. He knew she would make good choices for herself.

"Am I going, too?" Jeremy asked, half-smiling.

"Yes. You are going, too." He turned to Anna. "When are we leaving?"

"I have to pick up some things, first. I have a list. Remember, you asked me to put a list together?"

"Yes. I do."

"We have to do the list tomorrow. We can do it tomorrow, can't we?"

Hamilton took Anna's hands in his. "For now, I'll unpack, and make us all something to eat. We'll take you shopping tomorrow, first thing. How's that? When you are packed and ready, we'll drive to New York."

By mid-morning, they were on the road. When they got to Havre-De Grace, Maryland, they pulled into the parking lot to stop first at Tydings Park and Promenade. The coolness of the early fall air and the heat from the late summer made the day pleasant.

"What're we stopping here for?" Anna asked.

"I thought we'd stop here and have lunch." Hamilton cut the motor off and turned to Anna.

"Dad, I have to be there early. I'm meeting friends." Anna crossed her arms, a look of irritation on her face.

"Okay, but we can do this too, can't we?"

Anna peered out of the car window again. "Is this a park? Are those swings?"

"Let's get out and go for a swing," Hamilton said.

"I'm not a child," Anna said as she got out of the car. She found a bench and slammed herself down. Hamilton and Jeremy ran for the swings and began swinging back and forth.

"Come on Anna. Let's see who can swing the highest," Hamilton said.

Anna rolled her eyes. "Dad, come on. I told you I had to be there by this afternoon."

Hamilton stopped swinging, and Jeremy slowed down until his swing stopped and then pumped again to get his swing a little higher. Jeremy was afraid to jump out of the swing until one afternoon Hamilton showed him how to do it. Now that he knew how, Jeremy slowed down and jumped out of the swing.

Hamilton looked over at Anna. He waved her over to swing in the one next to him. "Come on, Anna. Just one swing."

She turned her head away. Hamilton was careful with Anna. She was strong, stood her ground, and refused to be controlled. Hamilton often backed down and gave in to her. He was afraid if he didn't, he'd drive her away.

"We want lunch, but you have to come and swing with us first."

"Dad," Anna sighed loud, long, and hard, "this isn't a game. I have to be in my dorm by—"

"Come on, Anna." Jeremy said. He picked up a handful of sand and let it slip out between his fingers.

"Anna. If you would just take one little swing, we could eat. What's it gonna be?"

She got up from the bench and sat on the swing. Hamilton pumped himself to make his swing go a little higher. Anna smiled and pumped a little harder.

"I remember how you loved to swing," Hamilton said. He turned to Anna as he continued swinging. "You always wanted me to push you. 'Push me higher, Daddy,' you used to say—"

"Push me, Daddy, push me higher," Anna said. She pumped her legs to go higher.

Hamilton got out of his swing and pushed Anna in hers.

After he'd pushed her long enough, Hamilton got the lunch that he had packed. Anna turned to her father as she took out the sliced turkey sandwiches with lettuce and tomatoes, ridged chips with sea salt, sliced melon and apple and the oatmeal raisin cookies, all her favorite foods. With tears forming, she helped him set the lunch out on a picnic table.

She wiped her tears with the back of her hand and picked up the package of oatmeal raisin cookies. No one else in the family liked the cookies as much as she did. Hamilton gave her a kiss on the side of her head, and whispered, "I love you."

As they ate, a sadness came over them, and they were quiet. The three of them just ate and watched the boats, some small, some large, some with cabins, some without, as they moved in and out of the dock on the mouth of the Susquehanna River.

Just before they packed up, Jeremy wanted to play their version of "I think I know," a game that Hamilton made up one Christmas when he wanted his children to guess their presents.

"I think I know the man who owns that yacht. He's me." Jeremy pointed to a cabin cruiser.

"Jeremy, that's not a yacht. It's only a boat," Anna said.

"A cabin cruiser, I know. But now it's my yacht."

"What do you think, Anna?" Hamilton asked.

"I think the boat has a dead body, and the owner is trying to find a spot to dump it in the water."

"It's a murder mystery," Jeremy yelled out.

"Yes. Anna is very creative," Hamilton said.

"I'm going to be a journalist and a novelist."

"An award-winning journalist and novelist," Hamilton added.

"Can we get started now? Dad, I have to be there in a few hours. My new roommate texted me and said she had gotten together a group of freshmen and we were all meeting for dinner. I can't miss that."

"Anna let's clean up and put everything away. We have time. We can take a short walk down the boardwalk to the museums and then to Concord Point to see the light house, if you two want to do that." Hamilton gazed at Anna. She loved museums and history and never seemed to get enough of how things were created long ago. Anna read up on things and could correct anyone about historical facts. When she began putting things away, he relaxed.

They went to the Maritime Museum where a man hammered and banged on a piece of metal on what looked to be a shovel with a long handle. He held the shovel over a pit fire for a while and when he saw the metal was melting or bending, he pulled it away and began shaping it into something for a ship, so the sign next to Hamilton said. "Look," Hamilton said, pointing to the man, "He's making something for a boat." When Hamilton asked, the man said he was building some portion of a ship.

Anna pointed to the boats and ships and told them how they could tell the difference. Jeremy walked over to the other side to ring the big bell that was almost as tall as he. He tried to move the bell. The man said the bell—looking much like the Liberty Bell, Jeremy said — was made in place and couldn't be moved. He challenged Jeremy to try again, to move it, and as hard as Jeremy tried, he couldn't budge it. They went inside a U.S. Coast Guard boat the man said he helped make. Then they were off to the Decoy Museum, where Jeremy liked the shotguns and decoy ducks.

Anna couldn't wait to see the lighthouse at Concord Point. Later, at the gift shop, Hamilton bought Jeremy a lighthouse. Anna wanted a ceramic plaque of the ships and boats on the Susquehanna River. As the day wore on, the sun was in and out leaving a fall chill in the air. No one noticed. They were too busy enjoying the trip and each other.

In New Jersey, they went to the Brandywine Zoo, a small place. After Hamilton paid the entrance fee, Jeremy went first to the tigers, then to the snakes. Hamilton pointed out the pair of Asian bear cubs. Anna couldn't get over their small size. They went for the cotton candy that Jeremy saw at a stand, and each got one.

In Cherry Hill, New Jersey, they stopped at the Garden State Discovery Museum, a hands-on museum where the three of them could hold the dirt, measure the growth of plants, and see what came out of the dirt. Hamilton thought about the lake at the university where he biked and his father's vineyard. He always noted the growth of the land plants and how water changed the growth. He liked the feel of dirt in his hands, and how good it felt to be so close to nature.

It was early evening when they arrived in New York. Hamilton didn't drive them to Anna's apartment. Instead, they stopped to eat. They didn't have to; he just needed the time. Jeremy ordered a burger and fries, and Anna and Hamilton ordered salads. When they finished, Hamilton took Anna to get her key card she needed to enter her apartment. Then he drove her to her apartment, where he and Jeremy carried in her things. Her roommate hadn't arrived yet.

Even though they had visited the university months earlier, Hamilton looked around the room inspecting it for something; what, he didn't know. But at this moment, he was overwhelmed with the reality he would no longer drive his daughter to school every morning; she would no longer call him every day; she would no longer ask him to pick her up from parties and other places; she would no longer ask him to taste her new made-up recipe; and he would no longer ask her to go walking or biking with him. Anna would be away at a university. Every day, he would miss her smile; he would miss her.

Jeremy had to use the bathroom.

"Do you want us to help you arrange your towels and everything?"

Anna laughed. "No, Dad. I'll be fine."

Hamilton took her hands in his. "Anna, this will be the last time we will have the time we had today. I hope you understand. The next time

I see you, you'll be a young lady with your own plans and dreams and a wonderful start on your future. I just wanted my little girl one last time."

"I know, Dad. I know." She hugged her father, and Hamilton felt her arms tighten around him.

"But know that no matter what, I'll always think of you as my little girl," he said as he pulled away, tears forming.

Jeremy came out of the bathroom.

"Ready Buddy Boy?"

"Yeah. Bye, Anna," he said, his voice monotone, but he stood there looking down at the floor.

"Oh, come here, Buddy Boy." Anna stretched out her arms.

Jeremy gave his sister a long hug. He held his head down as he pulled away and left the room. Hamilton followed. Just as she closed the door, he heard her sobbing on the other side of the door and wanted to turn back. But he thought it best not to. He promised himself the same promise he made to Eric last year on his road trip—he would stop trying to control them. They needed to live their own lives.

They drove to New Jersey and when they got to Princeton, Hamilton dialed the emergency number he had to get Eric to meet him. Hamilton and Jeremy saw Eric standing outside his Residential College.

"Eric, you missed it," Jeremy said.

"What's that, Buddy Boy?"

"We took Anna to her university. On a road trip to a museum, a zoo, oh, man, you missed it. We ate something we hadn't had in a long time–cotton candy."

"Wow, you guys have had an enjoyable time." He smiled at Hamilton. "Hey Dad."

"Son, I'm so sorry. I wanted to bring you here."

"No, Dad. That's okay. I wanted to get here early, anyway."

"Are you all settled in and everything, then?"

"I'm fine. I told you not to worry about it two weeks ago. I know you've had a lot on your mind."

"You have your car with you?"

"Yeah. I drove up."

"Is it all right? I thought we would put it in the shop first."

"No. It's fine. I won't be using it much, anyway."

"Eric –

"Dad. Everything is okay. I mean it."

"I guess you have to get back to class, or whatever you were doing. I'm sorry I had to pull you out like this, and I know it's getting late, but I just had to see you."

"You, coming here, checking up on me, that means a lot to me. I love you, Dad."

Eric reached for his father and Jeremy held on to both. Again, Hamilton thought about time and how time had just slipped away from him. His two children were both off to college. When he would see either of them again, he would see other people, not the children he spent the bulk of his life caring for. Everything he had was easing away from him.

Hamilton and Jeremy started toward the car. "Dad," Eric called out. Hamilton turned around. Eric shrugged his shoulders. "You know. Thanks, thanks for coming." Hamilton nodded, smiled at Eric. Jeremy waved goodbye, and the two of them left.

Just before they arrived home, Hamilton pulled to the side of the street, cut the headlights, and stopped the car.

"Buddy Boy, I'm going to drop you off at your mom's."

"Why?"

"I'm leaving in the morning to go to your Grandpop's."

"We're leaving in the morning."

"Sure?"

"Very sure."

"Okay."

He needed Jeremy now to keep him grounded. More than likely, Anna and Eric will be back for Thanksgiving and Christmas, but they will come home to visit. He wanted his children to concentrate on their education, and their lives, not on him. When Eric was born, Hamilton promised himself that he would do what he needed to provide for Eric's future. Even if that meant he would have to make sacrifices.

He was used to making sacrifices. He had made them when he was growing up and he made sacrifices for each of his children. HolliAnne said she wanted kids; a house full, she said before they married. Hamilton wanted four, and she agreed. But that was what she must have thought at the time.

After they married, she said she could only handle one because she wasn't good with children. She reminded him she had come from a family that didn't show affection, and parents who wanted to belong to church clubs and organizations rather than be with her or her sister.

When Hamilton found out HolliAnne only wanted one child after telling him she wanted four, he felt deceived and gave thought to divorcing her. But he was used to making sacrifices, and he remembered his father's advice. Even though he wanted a large family, he also wanted to keep his marriage together and make his marriage work.

Every time he came to her at night, she pushed him away, feigning a headache or something else bothering her. Now and then, she allowed him, and he was like a man who had just won the thousand-dollar sweepstakes. He wanted her to remember those times, to make it easier for him the next time. Soon, she let down her guard, but when she discovered she was pregnant with their second child, whom they later named Anna, HolliAnne kept him away with every excuse she could think of. Hamilton came to realize that she not only kept him away from her physically, but emotionally, as well.

HolliAnne said often enough that she didn't grow up in a house where her parents freely showed her love, and she was always afraid to accept love from anyone, when she didn't know how to return love. Hamilton didn't improve her situation for her. He only expressed love to her when they were intimate. But they were married, something she had wanted more than he did in the beginning. HolliAnne wanted to get away from her parents, who smothered her with church activities and what they said the Lord wanted. Hamilton liked her enough and decided he could grow to love her. And now, they had started a family. He had always wanted his children to have a stable home life with a mother and an attentive father.

Hamilton took over the parenting of both Eric and Anna. HolliAnne suffered from postpartum depression after Anna was born, making it hard for her to tend to Anna or Eric. From the time they were born, Hamilton changed most of their diapers, fed them both, and played with them. If anyone had asked Hamilton why HolliAnne didn't bother to hold her children or play with them, he would have said it was not depression, not that she didn't know how to love, but she just didn't try. She was convinced she wasn't a good mother, not because she wasn't, but because she refused to do much with them.

HolliAnne tried to explain to Hamilton about postpartum disorder, but he refused to believe anyone could turn away from their children. Hamilton wanted her to go to a therapist after her diagnosis, but she rejected the idea. She said he was trying to make her do something she couldn't do. He wanted to turn her into someone else. Hamilton left it alone. He settled for having two children. They both were careful after that, especially HolliAnne.

Five years later, and three months after a lengthy night of celebrating their anniversary, HolliAnne announced she was pregnant again and broke out in tears. Throughout her pregnancy, she had bouts of depression and cried almost daily.

Hamilton knew the effects that her mental state would have on the baby, and he tried to do things to make her laugh and take her mind off her pregnancy. "Like that's possible," HolliAnne told him. But he tried anyway.

After Jeremy was born, Hamilton fed Jeremy, changed him, and played with him. HolliAnne couldn't look at Jeremy and sometimes refused to hold him. She could only think about going back to work and losing weight. Hamilton took Jeremy with him to the university's day care center, the same thing he did with Eric and Anna. That way, he could go see Jeremy whenever he had a free moment. Often, he brought Jeremy to his office while he worked.

His children had always been his life and the focus of his marriage. Eric and Anna were college students and away from home. He would soon have to refocus his life. Hamilton wanted to do whatever he could to keep Jeremy close to him, to watch him grow up; watch for those moments of change. Sooner than he will want, he will take Jeremy on his road trip to the Grand Canyon, the place of his dreams.

CHAPTER 6

"Dad, Mom called. She's on her way over to pick me up. I thought I was going with you to see Grandmother and Grandpop."

Hamilton could only hear the fear and anxiety in Jeremy's voice. He stopped eating his oatmeal and put his spoon down on the granite counter, pushed back on his stool and turned to Jeremy seated next to him. The sun streamed through the window across the room and reflected on the metal pot of oatmeal left on the stove.

"I didn't call her. I thought it best to tell her in person. What's wrong, Buddy Boy?"

Jeremy didn't respond. He sat eyeing his bowl of cornflakes, his hands in his lap.

"Hey, Buddy Boy."

Jeremy picked up the carton of milk in front of his bowl and poured more milk over his cornflakes until all the flakes were hidden under the milk.

"Is there something I should know?"

"He doesn't like me."

"Your mom's boyfriend?"

"He doesn't like me. He hates everything I do, everything I say."

"Something must be wrong with him. How can anyone hate my Buddy Boy?" He reached over and mussed Jeremy's hair. "Why not give him a chance?"

"I do. But he blames me for things, and he won't listen to me when I try to explain."

"Neither do I."

"I know, but you're different. You understand me."

"Bud, I'm going to see your grandfather today—"

"Me too, Dad."

"Okay. Then pack some clothes and bring along a toothbrush. You know, just in case you could need it."

"Ha, ha. Very funny."

Hamilton went to his office to print the schedule again.

A few minutes later, the doorbell rang, and Hamilton went to answer it. HolliAnne stood in front of him, looking surprised. And there was something else, but he couldn't put his finger on it. She looked slightly different.

"Is Jeremy ready?"

"Come on in, HolliAnne." He offered her a seat in the living room.

"He's not ready yet?" She stood in the hallway.

"No, he's going with me, HolliAnne," he paused. "I'm going to see my mom and dad."

"There you go again. We agreed." She turned to face him.

"He doesn't want to visit you and Todd right now."

"No, we agreed. He's going to stay with us until school opens."

Hamilton looked around for Jeremy. He didn't want Jeremy to overhear. "He doesn't want that." He offered her a seat in the living room again, but she didn't move. "HolliAnne, Jeremy has his things he wants to do. You can expect to see him when he doesn't have conflicts with school or church or with the things he and I do together."

"That leaves little time for me," she said.

"When you want to see him, you must pick him up from here, his home, and bring him back to his home. When he visits you, you must be there with him during the entire visit, and the two of you do things together. I don't want him to have any contact at all with Todd."

"I can't ask Todd to leave home when Jeremy visits. That's insane." She leaned toward him, pointed at him.

"We have to think about Jeremy."

"You can't do that. You can't just tell me what to do in my house. Why are you keeping him from me?"

"I don't want Todd to be the one telling Jeremy what to do, accusing him of things he didn't do and whatever else."

"Todd and I love each other. We live together. I want to see Jeremy." she paused, her anger mounting from the look on her face.

Hamilton didn't speak.

"Jeremy's just like you. Todd tries to tell him things, but Jeremy decides for himself. He can't listen. I know he and Todd don't get along. I wish they could do better, but they are constantly at each other's throat. They have to learn to get along with each other."

"You'll have to do something."

"Ham, I want to see my son. You have no right to stop me."

"You're his mother, all right, but look at your situation."

"My situation? What do you mean?"

Hamilton was silent.

"These are modern times, Ham. You should know that by now. I know my place isn't as big as this, or my situation ideal according to your standards, but Jeremy has his own area. You can't control everything. I don't understand why you think you can."

"For now, it'll just be better for him to skip the visit with you. I think that'll be better for him." He picked up a schedule from the table in the living room. "I've completed a calendar with his schedule and the times and days you can see him. You have it, but here it is again."

HolliAnne took a step back and refused to take the schedule. "Ham, I'm so tired of this. You're always trying to control my life. You see how well that worked out."

He handed her the schedule again. She looked down at it, then again took a step back.

"HolliAnne—" Hamilton began. He opened the front door for her. "Goodbye." He handed her the schedule again. She looked down at it again, then put her hands behind her back, shook her head. Hamilton continued to hold the schedule in front of her. She walked around him and stood in the doorway.

"I understand, really I do. You think I'm a terrible influence."

"Are you a terrible influence? What kind of environment have you created?" he asked.

"Everything always has to go your way and at the cost of others."

"I don't want to argue with you."

HolliAnne started out the door. "Jeremy is too smart to let you control him."

Hamilton closed the door and then put the schedule on the hall table.

Hamilton pulled into the driveway of the last house on Stevensville's main street, the two-story house where he grew up, and the house where his parents still lived. Since there was a big lot between his father's house and his neighbor's house, his father's house was located just beyond the town limits and therefore, not subject to the town ordinances about animals. The house sat far back off the street with a large lot behind it, so even his mini farm couldn't be seen from the street.

As he got older, his father, George Maddox, liked to get away with whatever he could, particularly since he retired. He told Hamilton and Taylor he kept two cows, chickens and grew corn, peas, tomatoes, and several other vegetables behind his house. To hear him talk, George had grown or tried to grow just about anything that would come up out of the ground. Hamilton didn't have the heart to tell him none of that was against the ordinances or laws of the town, or the county where he was located.

Mary, his mother, in a flowing bright yellow dress making her look youthful, opened the door, and started out to greet them. Several times she turned toward the house calling out "George, honey. George, they're here," as she continued toward the car. At the car, Mary turned toward the house. "That man. I asked him to stay here and told him you were coming, but he's gone, anyway." Jeremy got out of the car.

She turned around and reached for her son and grandson, and the three of them held on to each other. Hamilton relaxed a little when he heard his father wasn't there. He was afraid his father would make him feel like a failure — he couldn't keep his marriage together because there was something wrong with him.

Even though his father never said things like that out loud to him when he was growing up, Hamilton always thought his father was judging him and, in that judgement, Hamilton didn't meet his expectations.

"Come on in. I know it was a long ride. Come on in. I made some tea and Jeremy's favorite lemonade with my secret ingredient, and some homemade cookies and cupcakes."

Hamilton went back to the car to get the suitcases and brought them inside. He set them near the upstairs steps. Hamilton wasn't upset his father wasn't there to greet them. His father was often absent from the house when he was growing up. It was as if he didn't want to be around Hamilton, since he was such a disappointment to his father. His father made him nervous, so when his father made a grand appearance, Hamilton fumbled with his words, not knowing what to say or how to say it. Hamilton thought it was just as well he wasn't present, now.

"Mom, the house looks great. I thought you said it needed some work." Hamilton took a tour of the first floor as he made his way through the living room, dining room, office, family room, screened-in porch and then back to the spacious kitchen and breakfast room where his mother and Jeremy stood.

"I finally hired someone to do it all. I was afraid someone would try to take advantage of us, but the town's people got together and now we have a new law. Our neighbors and many elderly people were taken for all their savings. I was afraid that would happen to us."

"It's a nice job."

"We can sit out here on the porch," she said as she led the way. Hamilton picked up Jeremy's glass and his glass and they followed her out to the screened porch. Jeremy sat on an ottoman, near his father, but facing his grandmother.

"Jeremy, I guess you're looking forward to your new school, huh?"

"Mom, he'll have one more year in middle school."

Jeremy gave his father a wide smile, love spilling out.

They talked for a while about the vegetable garden in the back.

"Why don't you two go upstairs, unpack, and take a nap? My sister, your Aunt Deborah, and Uncle Silas are having their annual barbeque later. They're looking forward to seeing you two."

Hamilton's father, George Maddox, drove them, as he had for many years, in his dark red 1995 Mercury Tracer, to Deborah and Silas' house, where the barbeque was under way. Hamilton relaxed and smiled as soon as they got out of the car and saw the smoke, knowing from years past what to expect. In one part of the yard, smoke curled upward from a large grill where ribs, burgers, corn on the cob, and chicken breasts roasted.

On the opposite side, a pit with a pig rotated on a rod. Every year, Jeremy asked the same question, "Is that a real pig?" and every year everyone just laughed. No one ever answered the question. Hamilton never answered it either. This year, he only got out, "Is that...." before he knew it was. Hamilton looked down at Jeremy, rustled his hair.

"Buddy Boy, why don't you get yourself some salad and corn or something and go say hello to your cousins." Hamilton pointed to a group of girls and boys sitting and standing under a tall oak tree, laughing, and talking. Jeremy didn't move.

"Go. Have fun."

Jeremy got a plate, filled it, and went to his cousins.

Hamilton got a plate of potato salad, green salad and a chicken leg and sat on a picnic bench with Deborah and Silas' son, Ken, as they watched the older kids play volleyball. Ken was a little older than Hamilton.

"You remember doing that, Ham?" Ken asked.

"Long ago undergrad years," Hamilton responded.

"I heard you were good at volleyball," Ken said.

"That I was."

"Let's try it. Come on. Just for old times' sake," Ken said.

"Yeah?"

"Yeah. Just for a few minutes because I think that's all I can stand."

"You're on."

The two men asked to play, and the kids allowed them in, but on opposite sides. Hamilton served the ball, and, to his surprise, it went over the net, but into the hands of an opponent. When the ball came in Ken's direction, he hit the ball over the net. Hamilton hit the ball over the net and volleyed with Ken a few turns until, in returning, the ball hit the net. The two men played until they could see they were no longer the stars they used to be and then sat down.

"George, I hear you've started growing vegetables now," Silas said, holding a chicken leg in one hand, his plate in the other.

"You heard right."

"You can't just sit back and enjoy life?" He bit into his chicken leg.

"If you do nothing, you have nothing to enjoy. I've been working all my life, Silas. It's hard for me to do nothing." George filled his mouth with green salad.

"I know, George. I know. I had trouble when I first retired," Seth, Silas' twin brother, said.

They paused for a moment and Hamilton thought they were thinking about the time when they worked. He stopped to think about his first job as a professor's assistant at the university.

"Hey, George, do you remember when you and Mary, Deb, and I were out on the beach? The kids were little then. It was late in the evening, and we were trying to decide whether we should go home and get cleaned up for dinner or just fill up on the junk food from the stands at the beach. Deb thought I was going to feed her and our kids popcorn and hot dogs for dinner."

"She and Mary both were all upset, lecturing us about a proper dinner," George said. The four of them laughed as they recalled that time. George put his plate on the table next to him.

"I remember that Memorial Day. Ham went to put something in the trash can and we waited for him to come back so we could go get dinner. But he didn't return. I looked over at the trash can where he went, but I didn't see him. I stood up and looked all around, but I didn't see where Ham went. Mary went to the trash can and came back to tell us she couldn't find him. I climbed up on the Lifeguard's chair, remember that?" George said.

"I remember that. You climbed up and made the lifeguard get down. The lifeguard tried to argue with you about giving up his chair, or something," Silas said.

"He said he was the lifeguard, and he couldn't get down until a certain time. Mary was screaming something. I couldn't figure out whether she was yelling at me or the lifeguard. But I heard her say 'Get down' so I figured she was yelling at the lifeguard. I grabbed his arm and pulled him down out of the chair. He came down on the other side."

"Nobody knew why you were climbing up there," Silas said.

"I was so rattled I didn't think to tell the lifeguard. All I knew was I had to see where Ham went. I grabbed hold of the seat to hold on to as I climbed up and looked around. Then I climbed down a bit, told the boy he could have his chair back, jumped the rest of the way down and ran."

"I saw you running. It's tough to run in the sand, but you were moving," Silas began. "Then, I saw you coming back with Ham, holding on to that boy like a fly caught in a spider's web. I don't think anything could have pried that boy away from you that day."

"You remember all that?" Mary asked.

"Worse day of my life," George whispered.

Hamilton turned to his father. A mixture of astonishment, shame, and pride flooded through him.

"I never saw you do anything like that before," Silas said.

"I remember that time," Ken began, "that man Ham was with was the same man talking to Ham earlier when Ham and all us kids were playing in the water."

"What happened to him? Did the police come?" Deborah asked.

"I called them. I told them what happened, and George described the man. Other people on the beach knew him and knew where he lived. The police picked him up at his house," Mary said.

"I don't remember that," Deborah began, "Did Ham have to identify him or something?"

"I wasn't going to let either of my boys get involved in identifying or anything like that," George said.

"Do you remember that, Ham?" Silas asked.

"I remember talking to a man on the beach. He was there before, and we talked before. I remember he told me about something that he had at his house, but the first time he told me, Taylor said we had to go home. We left. The next time, I think Mom came, so I had to leave. The time Dad came, the man had asked me to walk along the beach with him. I thought I was just walking along the beach with a friend."

"But that wasn't the worse part. Tell em', George, what happened when Ham went to school."

George gave off a loud guffaw before he began. "Ham went to school the next day, and when he took off his jacket, there was a big bruise on his left arm. The principal called us both in and said she had Child Services standing by."

"Are you kidding? Naw," Seth said.

"I was so mad in that meeting. All I could think about was how Mary felt. I was worried that she thought their comments were a reflection on her. So, I let them have a piece of my mind."

"Which didn't help any because now they saw him as an angry man who could have bruised his son," Mary said.

"So, after Mary's elbow nudging, I calmed down and told them what happened. When I saw him, from the lifeguard's chair, that man was holding Ham's hand. I caught up to them. Ham was about six or seven at the time, and he walked slowly. So, I caught up to them and grabbed Ham's arm. I wasn't going to let him go, and I didn't think about how tight I must have been holding on to him. I pulled Ham, but he didn't want to come. I was a little behind them, but when he turned around, and saw it was me, he let go of the man's hand. I grabbed him up, held him in my arms and said, 'It's me, Dad. It's me, Dad.' That little boy wrapped his arms around my neck so tight he almost cut off my air." George wiped at his face, cast his eyes down.

And there was a silence as Mary, too, wiped away tears. "We almost lost our son, that afternoon," Mary said.

"I tried to put Ham down, but he wouldn't let go of my neck. It feels good when your kids hug you."

On that afternoon, for the first time, Hamilton saw his father as the bulwark—the father who protected him, the father who loved him. At the barbeque, Hamilton found out more about his father than he had all his years. Hamilton didn't remember the story that way. Until now, he'd always thought his father was upset with him because he didn't do what his father asked of him — to return quickly after he put his trash in the can. He had thought of the man as a friend and the friend said he would help Hamilton find his father. The friend said he saw Hamilton's parents leave, and he would take him to his parents.

"All I remember was I thought Pop was angry because I didn't come right back. Ken was right. He had talked to us several times before."

A few minutes later, Silas had a hard time catching his breath. He gasped and wheezed loudly, as if he was trying to get air into his lungs before he suffocated. Hamilton had Silas sit down in one of the lounge chairs off the patio. He leaned back so the air could flow through his lungs.

"Give him CPR," yelled Seth. "Silas, you're a doctor. Do you need CPR?"

"I just need to stop and relax a little. I'll be okay."

Hamilton sat beside Silas. Even he breathed better.

Jeremy ran over to his father. "Dad—"

"Hey, Buddy Boy. Thought you were having a good time with your cousins."

"What happened?"

"Nothing. Uncle Silas just got out of breath, that's all."

Later, Hamilton and Jeremy walked down to the Bay Bridge Marina to watch the boats on the bay. He looked down and heard the water slapping the pier where they sat. For a moment he was back in time, a time when he was a young boy, sitting on the pier and watching the boats come in and out.

He had missed the sounds of the bay. The sound of the waves, and the birds, and sea gulls cawing and flying over the water. He missed the water splashing on his feet and ankles when he ran along the shore. He missed the sun that surrounded him and gave him a feeling of safety. He missed the sound of the motorboats roaring and slamming against the water. On this evening, Hamilton noticed how the drivers lined up, one boat after the other, waiting their turn to enter their slip and dock. Several drivers, who had cabin cruisers, had to come out and start again.

Every evening when the boats and cruisers returned, there was an aura of sadness for Hamilton. A time when the town and all the people stopped and just closed down. The party goers would quietly return, spent from their celebrating; families returned, children half asleep; and eased into their slip. It was as if the sun going down with its red, orange, and gold colors set the time for all noise and motion on the water to end, and the fascinations and excitement the day had brought would be saved in memory. Another day down. He also learned to see it as a time to revive and prepare for the wonders of the next day.

A motorboat, last in line, slowly pulled out of the line and, before moving beyond the boats, halted. A woman in a two-piece bathing suit came up from below and held up a hammer to the man. The man took the hammer and looked at it as if he didn't understand why he needed a hammer. Jeremy laughed. Hamilton laughed, too. They watched to see what the man would do with the hammer. The woman followed the man down in the cabin.

"Have you decided what you will be when you get older?" Hamilton asked, trying to take Jeremy's attention away from the hammer.

"I'm not sure, yet."

"You think you should start thinking about it?"

Across the water, one boat seemed filled with people laughing and talking over oldies music. But soon they joined the quietude, and the sun going down announcing the end of the day. Hamilton tried to remember whether they'd missed a water event. He didn't remember reading anything in the paper. A man in a sailboat heading out from the marina reached across for something and his sails unfolded. Hamilton pointed it out to Jeremy when the boat was farther out, all the sails up. From the distance, he could hear the motor shut off.

He had grown up around boats, yet his father never owned a boat. Hamilton remembered when Taylor wanted his father to buy a canoe for Hamilton and him, but his father refused, saying they didn't have time to boat. They had to work in the vineyard.

It was always about the vineyard. They had to work in the vineyard when they were twelve. If it hadn't been for their mother, his father would have had them start at ten. Even at twelve, his mother only allowed them to work a half day on Saturday during the school year. She told Hamilton's father they needed to be with friends, and this was a different time from the time he grew up.

"Dad," Jeremy began, bringing Hamilton back to the present, "You never told us what the doctor said. I want to know." He turned toward his father.

"Buddy Boy, he said I'm fine. I just had an anxiety attack, that's all."

"You don't have to stay in bed or anything? No medicine?"

"No, none of that."

"Good."

Hamilton pulled his son to him and tightened his hug with Jeremy. "Buddy Boy, I promise I won't go anywhere permanent without you. How's that?"

"That's better."

They sat quietly for a while. Hamilton's thoughts went to the discussion earlier about how his father ran to save him from a stranger. He was six or seven when he was almost abducted, and his father saved him. Jeremy interrupted his thoughts.

"Dad?"

Hamilton looked down at Jeremy.

"I'm sorry about what happened with you and mom."

"Thanks, Buddy Boy. Thanks."

"Are you going to find another wife?"

"That's a surprise question."

He thought about his need to find someone to love. "Why?" he asked.

"I want you to be happy."

"Then I'll have to do that. But I have to see to you first."

Hamilton and Jeremy walked back to Deborah's house. It wasn't hard to locate with the talking, laughing, and music drifting all the way to the bay. The smoke from the barbeque pit aroused Hamilton's hunger again, and he made another plate for Jeremy and himself.

The next morning, Hamilton found his father sitting on a bench outside the store of the old vineyard he used to own. His mother had asked him to go down to the vineyard and bring him back. Since the day he sold the place to a married couple almost seven years ago, he had made occasional appearances at the vineyard. But, since he heard the couple had sold the vineyard to a developer who would put up townhouses and single-family homes, he was there every day, regardless of the weather.

Hamilton's mother worried about her husband and asked Hamilton to sit with him, talk to him, and find out what he was thinking. She didn't want him to do anything rash.

At the vineyard, Hamilton saw his father sitting on a bench outside the store. Hamilton noticed the sign over the cabin that announced, "Wine Store," not the wine tasting cabin his father had.

"Pop, mom told me you'd be here."

"You know, when I had this place, the grapes were always plump and shiny." He pointed to a section. "Not what you see here, puny and shriveled up."

The vineyard was a mess; grapes strewn everywhere. The property was sold, and the grapes were no longer needed. Hamilton sat down, looked around the vineyard and how it was fading away bit by bit, as if someone had a huge eraser and erased one thing at a time. Soon, there would be no sign of his vineyard. Everything gone, erased, almost as if it was a mistake.

"Pop, you remember when Taylor and I were in high school, and we tried to sneak some wine out to take to a party? We thought we'd taste it first. We'd selected a bottle and Taylor hid it out in the vines somewhere. After dinner, when we were on our way to the party, we had to first, go to the vineyard to get the wine we'd hidden. We got there and looked and looked because Taylor forgot where he'd hidden it. We were there for maybe an hour combing every inch of those grounds, looking everywhere he thought he had hidden it. Then he found it. After all that looking, we got a little thirsty and opened it. Neither of us remembered to bring a corkscrew. I went to the car to see if maybe there was one in the car. It was your car, Dad, and it seemed likely to me you would have had a corkscrew, and even cups in the car. Well, I was right. I brought back a corkscrew and two cups. We drank and drank until we finished the entire bottle. We never made it to the party. We slept out here in the vineyard all night. The next morning, you found us. You remember?"

"I remember that time. I saw the empty bottle and called your mother and told her where you two were." He paused for a moment. "She almost had a heart attack. Stayed up all night after you two didn't come home. She called everyone we knew."

"We thought we were in real trouble."

"I was thankful you didn't drive and all that happened was you both got drunk and passed out."

"We slept on some grapes. When we got up, Taylor saw them all mashed up, so he tried to fix them. He tried to put them back together or something. I don't know what he thought he was doing."

"I knew that if you were here, the vines would keep you safe and warm. When you put love in, you get love in return."

"You miss it," Hamilton said.

He turned to Hamilton, "This was all I ever did."

"Pop, your wine was the best wine in Maryland."

"My father gave me this winery when I graduated from college; and if you remember, I did that on my own. He told me the day I graduated I wasn't smart enough to have a regular high-paying job, so he gave me money and told me to buy this vineyard."

"That's why you bought this vineyard?" Hamilton asked. "Good thing you did."

Hamilton's father never said much about his father.

Neither man spoke. Hamilton still had trouble finding something to talk about with his father and the fact his father was quiet now, must have meant he too, had trouble figuring out what to say to his son. Hamilton cleared his throat. George gave Hamilton a sideways glance and picked up a grape off the ground. Hamilton gave a quick glance back and then looked around at the vineyard.

"He would have beat the life out of me if I hadn't. He had already slapped me around after I told him I wanted to go to college. He had hit me my whole life. So, yes, I bought this vineyard. Turns out, this was the only thing he did for me that turned out good."

Hamilton turned to face his father. "You never told us much about your father." Hamilton, trying not to show it on his face or body, was shaken hearing how his grandfather had treated his father. What struck Hamilton was his father's voice. It was without malice or anger.

George turned away as if he was embarrassed and ashamed. "There wasn't much to tell. He used to beat me, and my two brothers, just because." He paused, threw the grape he held, on the ground. "That was the reason I kept my distance with you and Taylor." He turned to Hamilton. "Son, I love you and Taylor, and I'm very proud of you both. I need you to know that. But I was always afraid I'd do to you what my father did to me."

"Did mom know about your father?"

"She did. When your mother and I got married, I sat her down and told her everything. I told her if she wanted us to have children, she would have to be like the mother and father at times. Your mother understood."

They were both silent for a short while. Hamilton was lost for words. From as far back as he could remember, he'd wanted his father to pick him up, hug him, throw a football back and forth with him, sit him on his knee. His father never did any of those things. Now he finds out his father has always loved him and cared for him. How was Hamilton to handle this? Was he supposed to change his mind about his father—the man he needed so much, the man from whom he needed love and approval? What was he to do now? He'd always wanted to love and forgive his father. Was this now what he should do?

"I tried to set an example. I did a lot of research about how to grow grapes and make wine. I had to do it for two reasons. First, my father told me I would fail at it, and second, I couldn't disappoint my family. I had to make it a success, so I worked hard every day."

"Pop, I always thought you didn't, you know, I always—"

"Thought I didn't love you."

Hamilton looked toward a row of grapes, still growing.

"Your mother told me everything going on with you and Taylor. Before I left every morning, I asked her to tell you boys how much I loved you. I left you and Taylor notes, and went to many of your PTA meetings, and was there any time either of you won awards for games and for anything else."

"Pop, I believed Mom just said those things or did those things to make us think you cared." Hamilton stood up and walked back and forth in front of his father.

"Pop, you couldn't have come to us every morning, yourself?"

"Son, I did what I thought was best. That's what parents must do–what they think is best. I'm sorry, and I know you boys needed more, but I did what I needed to do."

"We needed you, Pop. Taylor and I, we needed you."

"I know, but that's the way it had to be."

"Pop, yesterday I found out something." Hamilton sat down.

"What? You didn't think I would just let someone take you away from me, did you?"

"I didn't know—" Hamilton began.

"Ham, after what I went through with my father, I lived in fear of something happening to you and Taylor."

"You never told us anything about your father. I don't remember visiting him or your mother and I don't remember a funeral for either of them."

"After I got the winery and found your mother, I broke all ties with my parents. I tried to get my mother to leave, but she wanted to stay with him. I never contacted them again. I didn't want him to have any influence on you or Taylor."

The two men were silent for a moment.

"Pop, I always thought you wanted to be at the winery more than you wanted to be with me or Taylor."

"It might have seemed like I put all my love in the winery, but I wanted you boys and your mother to have an easier life. I wanted you to use whatever I could give to you for your future. I worked hard to put out superb wine, establish us, establish a reputable name in the community."

"The community?"

"Yes. The community. My father was an important man in the community and had a nasty reputation. People knew he was beating on us. But back then, people turned the other way."

He paused again, and Hamilton saw, for the first time in his life, tears forming in his father's eyes.

"When I found out someone had taken you, a fear mixed with anger built up inside me. I'd never felt like that, and I knew I would do whatever I needed to do to get you back." He looked over at Hamilton. "Son, I have to believe that because I wasn't as present in your life as you wanted me to be, you both are better men. You two are great fathers."

He paused for a moment, reflecting on what his father just said; realizing he and Taylor turned out okay.

"The best wine around," Hamilton murmured.

"That's what they said. And over the years, I got several awards for my wines," George began. "You have to remember that the winery bought you the house we live in, your clothes, the bikes you boys wanted, the food we ate every day, Christmas gifts, birthday gifts and the medicine you needed when you got sick. Providing, that's also a father's job."

"Pop, the best wine around," Hamilton said again.

"All that's gone now. This vineyard, that's who I am. That's my success. When they tear all this down and put up something new and different—"

"You're not just a vineyard owner, Pop. You're also a loving husband and father. I'll bet you're good at a host of other things. You just never gave anything else a try."

His father looked at him with tears in his eyes. "You think so?"

"I know so. You just have to find something else, that's all."

"You know, you have to grow a good grape; you have to give it nourishment, feed it, love it and it'll grow for you." He gazed at Hamilton. "You have to handle each grape tenderly, even when you pull it off the vine. If you pull too hard, then you'll have a mashed grape leaving it less flavorful; and if you pull too easy, you could drop it and bruise it. You have to find that perfect middle and do it just right. That's what I learned."

Hamilton looked over at his father and for the first time understood that his father treated his grapes the way he wanted to treat his sons.

"I know, Pop. I know."

"Look at all these grapes on the ground here. When I had this vineyard, I never had any mess like you see here. The grapes are not plump enough. They need to be overflowing with its unique juice, ready to burst and offer its pleasant and dulcified taste. The bouquet should fill the air with its sweet, but pungent fragrance and fill the imagination of everyone who makes or tastes the wine. But the people here, pull them too soon." He picked up one from a group of vines on the ground. "This is wrong," he said, holding up the grape so Hamilton could get a good look. Then he cradled it in his hands, lifted it up to his nose, and inhaled its fruity scent. With his fingers, he dexterously pulled off a piece of skin and allowed it to sink into his fingers and into the palm of his hand, melting into his skin, becoming part of him. Then he tossed it into his mouth. "You have to love the grape."

His father cherished his grapes as much as Hamilton cherished his children.

"Pop, you remember when you told us to make ourselves honorable people so we could find a good wife and marry her, honor her, and take care of her and our family?"

"I wanted to pass along something to you. Advice that you could use. I just wanted you two to be careful."

"What do you mean?"

"Even though I never laid a hand on either of you, I was afraid I might have passed along something inside me that you boys could pick up."

"Something genetic, you mean?"

"Something in the genes, yes. So, I wanted you to remember that a wife and family are a gift and a privilege and if you have one, you must honor her, like I do these grapes. Your mother will tell you we both raised you boys well." He stopped for a minute, as if thinking about something in his past. "I just didn't want either of you beatin' on your children."

Hamilton had mixed feelings. He understood the distance that his father created between them. But he still needed his father. At this moment, Hamilton loved his father more than he ever had. His father had spent his life trying to protect Taylor, his mother, and him from a danger he had experienced. Hamilton wished he had understood this when he was growing up. He had no idea what he would have done, maybe nothing; maybe he was too young to understand. Otherwise, his father was a principled man. He saw that.

"You tried to tell us through your rules?"

"The best way I knew how."

Hamilton didn't know what to say to his father, whether to continue to be angry at him or happy his father saved them from a brutal life. George turned away from him and cast his eyes around the vineyard, the acres and acres that stretched from the road all the way back to where the land dipped, and the vineyard was no longer visible.

He seemed to study the grapes on the ground near him, at the vines that still had life, and those dying off to make room for the new housing project. He turned his head up to the sun and stuck out his hand as if gauging the sun's temperature, seeing it was just right for his grapes, the thing he used to do when Hamilton worked at the vineyard.

He brought his hand down. "This is not my place anymore. Soon there will be townhouses sitting on the land that once grew grapes that made the best wine in Maryland. Soon all I ever knew or did will be gone, in the past."

When Hamilton was in the eighth grade, his science teacher asked him to enter a project in the upcoming science fair. He was reluctant to enter because he didn't know what to do. He hadn't paid much attention to wines and wine making. He was often doing things he thought his father objected to. His teacher told him his grade in science depended on his project. After he decided, he told his parents he had entered the science fair and his project was not about making wine. He wasn't sure his father would even attend. Hamilton had selected wind harvesting. He won first prize for his wind harvesting exhibit. He had to explain to the audience how to harvest wind and use it for energy. He looked over to his mother and saw his father sitting beside her, a smile on his face. His father never told him how proud he was of him. However, Hamilton found a note beside his cereal bowl the next morning.

> *Your project was excellent and very important to our community. You're very creative and I'm proud of you. You are meant for something great.*
> *Your Pop.*

Hamilton always thought his mother left the note and signed his father's name. Now he believed the note came from his father.

Hamilton reflected for a minute on his father's life and how his world was changing. His father was having trouble finding his place in a world that left him behind.

"Son, I know I'm not the one to give you advice about your marriage. I never did a lot of that when you were growing up, but—"

"Pop, you just did. Thanks." Hamilton paused for a long second. "I'll be right back."

Inside the store, Hamilton selected three types of wines and brought them to the counter. It was nice that the couple continued making the same kinds of wine his father made.

"Will that be all?" the man behind the counter asked.

"Yes."

"I saw you talking to old man Maddox outside. You know him?"

"He's my father."

"Your father has been coming here and sitting on that bench every day since I sold this winery to the new developer."

"He misses it," Hamilton began. "My brother and I used to help him after school and during the summer. We used to taste it, a lot."

The man behind the counter laughed. "I caught my sons doing the same thing. Why not, the wine is free, and it's there?"

"Precisely what we thought."

The man behind the counter took his time with giving Hamilton his change. "Could you just ask him not to come here anymore?"

"Is he a problem?"

"Not for me. For him. I imagine this is very hard for him. He told me he bought this vineyard when he was twenty-two years old and just finished college."

"I'll talk to him." Hamilton picked up his bag, "Thanks," and turned toward the door.

Outside, Hamilton went to his car and pulled out two plastic cups and a corkscrew. He sat down on the bench beside his father, opened a bottle of wine and poured it in the plastic cups.

"I know, Pop. Superb wine should be served in a glass, but this is all I have."

"We can excuse it this time."

They raised their cups of wine.

"Here's to you, Pop, for raising excellent wine, and a wonderful family."

As he sipped his wine, he couldn't help but feel for his family. Unlike his father, Hamilton had invested heavily in his family, particularly with his children. His parents worked together to decide what kind of marriage they would have and how they would go about raising Taylor and him. Hamilton and HolliAnne had a marriage where they honored themselves. Hamilton was unhappy with how HolliAnne did things, and HolliAnne was unhappy with how Hamilton had to control everything. A marriage is a community of two where the two people decide on the tenets of their marriage and work together toward a prosperous future.

CHAPTER 7

Hamilton awoke when his cell chimed. Jeremy sat in a chair across from Hamilton's bed, a bowl of cereal in his hand. Hamilton sat up, grabbed his phone, and read the text message.

"Hello, sweetheart," Hamilton half whispered, while texting back.

"Hi, Dad. I am holding a ceramic plaque of ships and boats on the Susquehanna River. Do you know what that is?"

"From the gift shop at the museum?" He waited after he texted.

"You're right. It's beautiful, Dad, just like the road trip. I'm saving the cookies. I'll take a bite every time I think about that day."

"That's a sweet thing to say, sweetheart."

"Just wanted to let you know I was thinking about you. Love you, Dad. Take Care."

"Love you, too, sweetheart. Don't forget to call from time to time," he texted.

"That would be impossible."

Hamilton punched the "off" button and tossed the phone on the bed.

"Bud, how about we get dressed, and then go get you some things for school?"

At the department store, while Hamilton waited for Jeremy to decide what he wanted, he took out the letter he had been carrying around. When he had received the letter months ago, guilt hung over him like a foggy morning, gripping him, saturating him to his core. He made himself carry her letter with him, reminding himself, punishing himself. He'd already read it several times, and he now had to read it again. The letter was from his friend, the dean of HolliAnne's social sciences department. He wanted to let Hamilton know of the letter he had sent HolliAnne. As he read the letter, several words jumped out at him.

Mrs. HolliAnne Maddox, deficient in important areas of responsibility, I tried to work with her on deficiencies, past two years, HolliAnne not made improvement in any areas, assigned mentor to help. Ham, on a personal note, we've been friends for many years. I know you wanted her to succeed, and I did everything I knew and more, but it wasn't working out. I wanted you to know what happened from your friend. Kev

HolliAnne made it out of high school, but one day she got the idea to go further. One evening after dinner, Hamilton left the kitchen to study. She called him back.

"Let's talk. We don't talk much anymore. You always have to study."

"Okay. We can talk. Sure, let's just talk."

"Hon, you know what I've always wanted to do?" HolliAnne said, clearing the table. They had just moved into a two-bedroom apartment near the university and had been married two years.

"What's that?" Hamilton asked, picking up Eric's kiddie dinner plate and putting it on top of his dinner plate.

"I always wanted to be a pre-school teacher." After a moment, she continued, "Don't you think that's crazy?"

"No. I don't. But why preschool? Why not high school? Or better still, why not college?"

"High school? College? Ham, are you out of your mind? I couldn't do anything like that." She scraped the plates and put them in a big pan filled with warm soapy water and placed in the sink.

"Sure, you can," Hamilton said, wrapping up the leftover meat loaf.

"No. I can't, and I don't want to," HolliAnne said, throwing the forks and knives into the pan and splashing soapy water on herself.

"You need a college degree. After that you could be a high school counselor," he said, as appeasing as possible.

"But I want to be a pre-school teacher. Why can't I do that? What's wrong with being a pre-school teacher? That's what I want."

"No, you don't. There's no rise in that. You don't even need a degree for that. Don't you see that?"

"I can get an Associate Degree to be a pre-school teacher, Ham."

"But it's only an Associate Degree."

"Can't you ever see what I want? Why do you have to change me and turn me into something you want all the time?"

"HolliAnne, what is that? You can't do much with an associate. An Associate Degree is hardly recognized anywhere. It has no more value than a high school degree."

"Why do you need to change me? Aren't I good enough?" Tears formed in her eyes, and she wiped them. "You said I needed a goal."

"Yes, but I meant an actual goal." He had upset her, something he didn't intend to do.

"I thought you'd be happy about my goal. I don't need to rise higher. I have a husband for that. Besides, what happened to family life?"

"My goal is to complete the Ph.D. But you can earn a degree, too. And you should."

"Ham, why can't you honor my choice?"

"It's your choice. But I hope you'll see it my way and make the right decision for yourself." He left the kitchen and went to his study, a small alcove-like space off the living room.

HolliAnne took Hamilton's advice, and after she had worked in the high school for a few years, Hamilton persuaded her to apply for a counselling position at his university. She applied, and he helped her get the position. She'd been a counselor a while and had several fair evaluations. Two years later, through Hamilton's encouragement and help, she hesitated, but accepted the department chair's position at the university.

As a department chair, she often had to work long hours, she said. When Hamilton questioned her about her hours, she became defensive and accused him of not trusting her. She also spoke of how she had some difficulty with the job. He told her she wasn't trying and wanted to prove him wrong. Her comments tore through him, much like a tornado ripping across the land, destroying things in its wake. It was then he realized he and HolliAnne were no longer truly married. They had created that space between them, the kind that couples who no longer care for each other create.

Hamilton folded the letter and put it back in its envelope. Kevin had called him soon after she got the job and told him she wasn't right for the job. Hamilton asked Kevin to work with her as much as he could. Hamilton knew he had. HolliAnne always wanted to be a pre-school teacher. Maybe he was wrong in wanting her to reach higher. He had wanted his wife to be successful and thought success meant to reach higher. Success also means being excellent at what you do. She failed because he pushed her too hard, wanted her to do things his way. She told him several times her heart wasn't in it, but he wouldn't listen.

After Hamilton purchased the shoes for Jeremy, they walked through the pants section of the men's department on their way to the teen section. Jeremy stopped in front of a large poster advertising dance lessons and a picture of a man and a woman dancing. "Look, Dad. Look at this."

Hamilton studied the poster. "This is just an advertisement." He read the poster. "If you buy this cologne, you can dance like they do. They will offer you a free lesson. See?" He pointed to smaller print on the poster.

"Sign up."

"You kidding? I can't dance."

"Isn't that why you would sign up?" Jeremy asked.

"I don't need cologne."

"You don't have to buy the cologne. Just sign up and take lessons."

"I'm too clumsy."

"You took tap dancing a long time ago. Remember, when Eric wanted to learn to dance?"

"It was Anna. She wanted to learn ballet, and Eric, and I went for lessons just to keep her company. Eric took jazz dancing, and I took tap dancing."

"That's it. You can take tap dancing."

"Buddy Boy, that was a long time ago."

"Come on, Dad. Sign up."

"I'm hungry. Let's go eat."

After lunch, they took the steep steps, the only way up to the second floor and straight down the hall in the back of the building to the Hartman dance studio above the furniture store in town center. They stepped into a huge room with a high ceiling, wooden floor, and a barre and mirror on three walls. Men and women were standing around talking. One man and a woman dressed in what Hamilton thought was proper dance attire — all black — were off to the side, having what looked like an animated conversation. The woman, head down and watching her feet, took a few steps to her left and then to her right. The man watched and did the same thing.

"Hi," a bright-eyed woman rushed up and stood in front of them. "Are you here for lessons, or the job?"

Just as Hamilton was about to speak, she continued.

"I have a job opening for an organizer. I need help with keeping on track. Which one are you here for?" She looked from Hamilton to Jeremy and back to Hamilton.

Hamilton, caught off guard, stretched out his hand. He didn't know about the organizer job. That was right up his alley. "I'm Hamilton and this is my son, Jeremy."

"Nice to meet you both. I'm Francine Hartman, Franny. I own the studio. My mother's."

"Tell me more about the organizer job."

Jeremy left them to talk as he surveyed the studio.

"Come on back," Franny said, waving Hamilton to the office.

He followed her to a small, cluttered office where papers were spread out all over a gray metal desk. The many papers, books and pictures were too much for the boxes and spilled out over onto the floor. Clothes overflowed on the several chairs alongside the back wall. The papers and larger boxes took up most of the floor space where the two desks were placed. A computer box sat next to the door and Hamilton looked for a computer and printer. Papers and books, opened to pictures of dance steps, according to the captions, covered the desk and printer. Hamilton picked up the keyboard and saw it wasn't connected to the monitor. He looked to see if the computer or monitor was connected to the outlet, and it was not. Wires hung down under the desk.

"What do you want done?" Hamilton studied the entire room. "You mean you just want someone to organize your classes?"

"Partly. I know how to teach dance, any dance you want, I can do it. But I'm not good at keeping track of what people owe, communication from the community, requests from people and mostly, taxes, because taxes, well that's a huge problem for me. I just need someone to help me get this organized so I can be free to teach people how to dance." She paused for a moment. "Do you want the job?"

"Don't you want to know who I am and what I do?"

"Of course, I do. But you brought your son with you, and you're dressed nicely so I know you're organized."

"I could help for a while, get you started. You may need to hire an assistant and an accountant, but yes. Okay, I think I would like to be your organizer." Hamilton said, smiling, still wondering about the duties of the job.

"There will be a few times when you'll need to help me in the studio with the lessons. I usually get more women than men in this business. Sometimes I get classes of only women. Will that be okay with you? It won't be very difficult, and it won't be very often. The last session went well without help."

"If it's limited, maybe once or twice, okay. I'm best at organizing."

"Can you start on Monday? I'll have a place in the office for you to work by then."

"What style dancing do you teach?"

"I teach American style dancing."

"See you Monday."

"Great. I open at 10:00 a.m."

Hamilton and Jeremy left. He wouldn't have to sit around his house all day thinking about his situation, and Jeremy wouldn't have to worry about him. Jeremy could relax. He worried about the once or twice times he would need to help her. It was not that he couldn't learn to dance; it was the chaos that came with learning to dance. For him, helping someone learn dance steps would be like being in an ocean without a life vest.

CHAPTER 8

Hamilton pulled his car into the parent drop-off lane behind a row of other cars, dropping off their children for the first day of school. Jeremy looked out his window at the students running to get inside the building, squealing, and laughing, hitting each other, knuckle bumping, high-fiving, and some girls hugging teachers. It pleased Hamilton that Jeremy wasn't as excited about leaving him as the other kids obviously were excited about leaving their parents to go back to school.

"Hey, Buddy Boy," Hamilton said.

Jeremy turned to Hamilton. "Dad—"

"I want you to promise me you will go in that school, do your very best, don't worry about me, and stay until school is over, okay?" Hamilton asked.

Jeremy sat staring at the windshield. He took in a deep, lengthy breath, like someone about to do something frightful. He reached down and picked up his backpack, held it between his knees. Then he turned to his father. "Okay. I will, I promise." He opened the door to get out but reached back to hug his dad before he left.

Hamilton arrived at the Hartman Dance Studio just before 10:00 and found Franny in the office searching through boxes.

"I hope I'm not late. You said ten o'clock." Hamilton said, looking at his watch as he entered the office.

Franny turned around sharply, "Oh, my, you scared me."

"I didn't mean to do that."

"I don't know the names of the people coming for the 10:30 class. I know I had the list the other day," Franny said in a frantic voice.

"Why don't I make a sign-in sheet for you? Do you have name tags?"

"I do have that." She tossed around some papers in a drawer and came up with nametags. "See," she handed the bent package of blank nametags to Hamilton. Hamilton found what he needed to make a sign-in sheet.

The office would be a good size if it were not filled with boxes and papers stacked everywhere on the floor. The two metal desks were against each other, arranged in the middle of the office. He had to clear a desk so he could have a place to work. He looked at the mess of papers on what must have been Franny's desk but decided she would have to straighten it later.

He had learned his lesson a few years ago when he moved HolliAnne's notebook to a place more convenient, easier for her to get to. When she came home and found the notebook missing, the book where she kept her "to do" lists, appointments, reminders and whatever else she used it for, she roared throughout the house, moving from room to room, roaring louder and louder. Hamilton actually felt the house move; she roared and screamed so loud.

She also threw things and accused everyone in the house of taking her book. It was so bad, Hamilton didn't want to own up at first, but when she accused Jeremy, he spoke up. They didn't stop hearing about that book for at least a year, and when she and Hamilton had a disagreement about anything, she always brought up that book.

He found a clipboard and a pen from somewhere under another stack of papers on the desk and, with the name tags, he put them on a small table he found in the studio. He moved them all near the door.

Franny turned out to be a talker. She was like a radio, continuous talk. She had a high pitch, but an almost soprano voice that took some getting used to. It was whiny, and had a nasal-like quality, almost squeaky. At first, he tried to ask her what she wanted him to do next, but he couldn't get a chance to slip into her conversation. He tried to respond now and then to let her know he was listening, but she didn't leave time for him to say anything, like "I see," or "Yes." He tried to grunt out something while she was talking, but she seemed to misunderstand and repeated what she'd just said.

In the twenty minutes before her class began, Franny told Hamilton her mother was a famous ballet dancer who danced all over the world in Russia, Germany, France, and Brussels. After she married Franny's father, who was a cross dresser, she continued to dance, and as soon as Franny was old enough, she took Franny with her most of the time. "My life has been filled with dance from the time I could walk. I don't think I ever walked. I was like my mother, born dancing."

Franny talked about how beautiful her mother was, with a youthful face and dark mysterious eyes seeming to say, "I have a secret," or "I know a secret about you." She went on about how elegant and how respected she was. She showed Hamilton a picture of her mother she had hung on the wall. Hamilton saw a woman so beautiful and captivating, who would make any man run to her every time she beckoned him. Franny, though beautiful, was not her mother. He tried hard not to say anything, comparing Franny to her mother, and handed the picture back.

"Very nice," he said, as he looked around the room.

"Mother is now in a nursing facility," Franny said.

"I'm sorry to hear that," Hamilton said, though he didn't know her mother. "Will she be out soon?"

"She has Alzheimer's disease."

He looked up at her, curious about the word, "disease." He didn't think of Alzheimer's as a disease. It was something that happened to many elderly people after a certain age. "Well," began Hamilton, "I've completed the sign-in sheet. What would you like me to do next?" He hated to leave her comments hanging, but what else could he say?

"The place is a mess. I know it looks like I'm just moving in."

"Go on to your class. I'll start doing something with the office."

The students arrived one by one for the 10:30 class and Franny went out to ask them to sign in, take a name tag and then go do whatever changes they needed.

It occurred to Hamilton he never asked her about his salary and when he would get paid. From the looks of the office and the way she seemed to handle things, he didn't expect much. Not to mention the fact that Franny never said when her mother stopped teaching, one of the few things she omitted.

He remembered the first summer he worked for his father. Taylor was away at a camp where he was a junior counselor, so his father thought it a good time to teach Hamilton the secrets of wine making. Hamilton thought he'd be outside, pulling grapes, but his father told him he'd be inside, removing the leaves and things from the grapes.

At first, he didn't understand why his father had him work inside rather than outside. But when he saw the helpers with their clothes soaked and dripping with sweat, Hamilton was happy he didn't have to work outside. His father had given him a favored position.

Grapes do best in direct sunlight, his father said often enough during that summer. His father showed him how to test the soil to check for the pH balance. He showed Hamilton how to get the grapes to wrap around the trellis. Hamilton saw how much his father knew about grapes and wine. He saw how important the winery was to his father.

A high-pitched voice brought him back, and he turned to see Franny was talking to him.

"What is it?" He gazed at his watch. The 10:30 class was over.

"The class. They are all new. Did everyone pay? I forgot to get payment from everyone. Did you find the receipts from this class?" The look on her flushed face and her hurried speech were upsetting to Hamilton.

"Slow down a bit. I've been sorting out your papers here, putting like things together. I connected your computer and tomorrow I'll start scanning everything into the computer."

"Okay, I'm sorry. I should have realized you were already working on something." She moved to her desk.

"I'll look for the receipts from everyone in the class." He got up and got the sign-in sheet to match against the receipts. Franny went on talking again. This time, he interrupted her. "How long has it been since you took over the studio?"

"Mother had to stop teaching about a year ago. Maybe two years ago or three..." She trailed off and sat down opposite Hamilton. "I had been taking other classes and studying under people at other studios."

"So, you've had the studio since that time by yourself?"

"I guess that's right. It has been almost three years." She looked at Hamilton.

"Do you have classes all day, every day?" Hamilton looked at his watch and saw her last class ended almost an hour ago.

"Just about. But a few people dropped out."

"Have you had anyone to organize this for you? I mean before me."

"My boyfriend. But he decided he didn't want to do this anymore, and he left about five months ago."

"Did he help you teach, too?"

"No. He was just, just a drug addict." Her voice filled with sadness, and she cast her eyes toward the floor.

"What? Seriously?"

"Yes. Seriously."

"Can I — I need to ask you for your bank account information."

"You don't think?"

"Have you checked to see how much money you have in your account?"

"Why are you asking?"

"I see 'final' on some of your utility bills here. You may have to close. You certainly wouldn't want that. And if he took anything, it's a good bet you'll never get your money back."

Franny found her last bank statement and handed it to Hamilton. He gave her the balance on the statement. "Does this sound right to you?"

"No. Is that all? That's not correct."

"He left you something unless he's still writing checks. I see his name on the account. We'll have to go to the bank first thing in the morning and see what's what."

"Now, I'm scared."

"Don't be. It may not be what it seems, but it's serious. We should go to the bank anyway to remove his name from all of your accounts."

Hamilton put his things away. "I've got to get my son. I'll see you at the bank in the morning."

On his way out, just outside the door, he almost bumped into a woman pacing back and forth.

"Are you thinking about taking dance lessons?" Hamilton asked.

"Yes, I was waiting for a friend. I think she decided not to come."

"Go sign up."

"I didn't want to, never mind." She started toward the stairs.

"You don't need her. Go sign up."

"You know, maybe I will." She turned around and walked through the door. Hamilton heard Franny greet her. Jeremy's words, "sign up," worked. He should use them more often.

CHAPTER 9

The bank business didn't take long. After Hamilton explained to Franny that leaving her ex-boyfriend's name on her bank account could destroy her business, she still didn't want to have his name removed. It was clear to Hamilton she had hoped he would return; he would come back to her.

"May I see some ID, please?" the bank manager asked, leaning forward on his desk.

Franny rummaged through her bag, found her wallet, pulled out her driver's license, and handed it to him.

"Just a moment, please," he said. He rose from his chair and went through a door.

Franny looked at Hamilton and Hamilton smiled back.

In a few minutes, the manager returned. "Do you have a check with you?"

"Yes." Franny dug into her bag again and brought out a checkbook. She showed him a check and showed him other checks she had written.

"Just a moment, please." The bank manager left again and went through the same door.

Hamilton sat back in his seat and looked around the bank. He hoped that there would not be a problem, but surely something was wrong.

The bank manager returned with a form for her to complete. Franny showed the form to Hamilton. Hamilton suggested she keep her business life separate from her romantic life, even though they were the same to her. Using the form, Franny had her boyfriend's name removed from all her bank accounts. The man took the form and went back through the door. Hamilton looked at Franny and saw tears welling. He wanted to say something to her, but what? They'd just met. The bank manager came out again and told Franny her boyfriend had written several small checks, but there was a balance. He showed her what she had left. She looked at Hamilton and he gave a wide smile back.

After the bank, Hamilton and Franny left for the studio. A sadness came over her with the realization her ex-boyfriend would not be back, and Hamilton gave her the space she needed. He left the bank after her. Just before they reached the cove, with the long stairs that led to the studio, Franny stopped in front of the drugstore. She handed Hamilton the key to the studio and told him to go on up.

After he entered, he went straight to the office and got himself settled. He scanned business papers, created a spreadsheet with each class and the students' payments, and worked at break-neck speed to finish things before Franny entered. The surprise of things done could brighten her spirits; and he wanted to do that. The truth be told; he had to admit he enjoyed her chatter. Asking a million questions, looking to him for answers, enjoying her not-so-funny jokes, and getting used to the sound of her voice.

After he completed the tasks, he'd set out to do, he sat back in his chair, a smile on his face, and waited on Franny. He looked at his watch, the clock, and got up a few times to look down the stairs. He tried to be more patient, but she should have returned by now. What was keeping her?

When he looked at his watch again, a loud popping noise startled him, then again, and again. He went to the back window, where he heard the noise and saw a man in a gray hoodie running from the drugstore and down the back of the buildings to the street. He seemed to have something tucked under his arm from the way he held it up against his chest.

Hamilton ran down to the drugstore where people were running out, pushing, and screaming. He made his way in and ran down two aisles, but he didn't see Franny. Thinking she may have been trying to leave the store, Hamilton ran back to the front. Customers pushed and shoved each other trying to get out, but the police arrived and stopped them at the entrance. To the right of the door near the counter, a man knelt next to someone on the floor by the candy and gum display rack. The man moved, exposing Franny on the floor. "Franny, Franny?" he yelled as he ran to her.

"The store's been robbed." The man looked at Hamilton. Hamilton knelt next to Franny.

Holding her head, Franny tried to raise up on her side.

Hamilton took her arm to help her sit up. "Franny take it easy. Let me see your head?"

"I saw it. That robber knocked her down on his way out. She must have hit her head when she fell," the man said.

Hamilton took Franny's hand from her head to get a look at the injury. "I'll call for an ambulance," he said.

"She wouldn't have gotten hurt if she hadn't tried to stop the robber," the man said.

"I thought I could talk him into just leaving," Franny said, her voice woozy.

"She fell when he pushed her. I saw it. I'll get the police to get an ambulance for her. By the way, I'm the manager, here."

Within minutes, a police officer and two EMTs, one with a gurney, entered the store and rushed to Franny.

"Are you hurt?" the police officer asked. "I'm Officer Daniels. These two men are here to help you." Officer Daniels stepped back for the EMTs.

"Are you in pain?" an EMT asked, kneeling beside Franny.

"My leg. It hurts." Her left leg was crossed over the right leg as if she'd tried to step, maybe to keep herself from falling. She tried to move it and screamed out in pain as she did.

"Can you raise your leg at all?" an EMT asked.

"It hurts. I can't." She tried again, but she screamed out in pain.

"How did this happen?" Officer Daniels asked. He moved closer to Franny.

"I thought I could stop him. He pushed me down, and I twisted something in my leg as I fell."

An EMT pressed on certain parts of Franny's leg and when he pressed near her ankle, she cried and screamed louder.

"You tried to stop him? Did you know him?" Officer Daniels continued.

"No. I don't think so. I never saw his face."

"Why? You mean you didn't look at him?" Officer Daniels went on.

"I think he wore a mask or something dark around his face."

"Why would you try to stop him?"

"I don't know. I just took a chance."

"You also knocked your head when you went down," the EMT said. He looked at the side of her head and pointed to a big red spot. The other EMT nodded.

Hamilton hoped her head injury wasn't serious.

"Let's get her in the truck," an EMT said.

The two men lifted her and put her on the gurney to wheel her out to the ambulance. An officer from the robbery division asked to talk to Franny. Did you notice anything about him, like his voice? Did he sound nervous to you at all?"

"No. I don't think so."

"Was there anything about him you recognized, such as the way he walked, his jacket, or cap?"

"No. Nothing that I remember."

"Are you sure you didn't recognize him?"

"I don't think I've seen him before."

"Okay, you can go now." He nodded to the EMTs.

The store manager yelled. "Wait. I have your change for you." He handed her the change from her purchase. She held it in her hand.

"I had a handbag. Where's my bag?"

The store manager left for a few minutes and returned with a bag. "Is this it?"

"Yes," Franny shouted. She put the money in her bag.

The EMTs began wheeling Franny out.

"I can't go. I have my dance classes to teach." The EMTs stopped. "My cha-cha class coming up. I own that dance studio up there." She pointed to the ceiling, indicating the second floor. Both EMTs looked up.

"Franny, you need to go to the hospital to get your head and leg checked out," Hamilton said.

"But my classes."

"I'll take care of that for the day. Do you have a schedule or something?" Hamilton asked.

"On the back of the door. If you could stay until I return. I won't be all day." She glanced from one EMT to the other, but neither responded.

"We'll worry about that later. For now, go get checked out," Hamilton said again, and nodded to the EMTs.

The ambulance drove off. After Hamilton gave his statement to the police, he went back upstairs. The woman he found waiting in the hallway the day before was, this time, waiting at the door. She smiled and before he had a chance to say anything; she spoke.

"I'm taking your advice," she said.

"Good, you won't be sorry."

The others in the class arrived and Hamilton showed everyone where to sign up and pick up a nametag. He was a little nervous until he realized he wouldn't have to teach. After everyone signed in and ready, Hamilton explained why Franny wasn't there. So that the day wouldn't be wasted, he suggested they practice the steps to the cha-cha they learned during the last class.

He remembered he saw a video on how to do the cha-cha. He found it and played it for the class. He thought they could watch the video and then practice the steps and he could go back to whatever he was doing in the office. But he changed his mind. He played a little of the video and then selected two people to demonstrate. The class observed first and then practiced the steps. Then he showed the steps.

"That's not the way they did it on the video," a male student said.

"Yeah. I'm confused," began a female student, "I thought we had to do it the way we saw it on the video."

"It's time to go," another student said as he ran toward the dressing room. The others followed.

Later that evening, Franny returned from the hospital. She had made it up the steps on crutches. Hamilton looked at her in disbelief. "Is it broken?" He kept himself from asking how she would teach the class.

"A severe sprain. I can't walk on it. They thought it was broken, but it's not."

"How long?"

"About four weeks, maybe six."

"Do you know anyone who could come and teach your classes until your leg heals?" He tried not to sound as frenzied as he felt.

"I can call Eleanor, my friend. She's at the Kennedy Center, but she may not help. She has a part in a dance show."

"What about a student?"

"I know. I can get Maria. She was my best student in one of my night classes. I'll call her." She hobbled off to the office to call Maria.

The lady who he found pacing around outside and who came back that morning came out of the dressing room with another lady.

"I'm Hamilton Maddox, the helper here. We haven't met." He wanted to sound friendly, even though he couldn't get his mind off Franny.

"I'm Marilyn Chapman. This is my friend, Emma Stevens. I just wanted to thank you for the encouragement in the morning class."

"I'm happy you got something out of it. It was last minute."

"I hope you'll be here for this session. I filled out the application. Here's my check."

"And mine." Emma handed him her check. There was something about her, but he couldn't attend to that now.

He went to the office to record the checks and to get the sign-in sheet for the next class. On the way out of the office, he looked at the schedule for the time of the next class. He wouldn't have time to get Jeremy, so he called HolliAnne and asked her to pick up Jeremy and bring him to the studio.

Franny came out of the office to talk to him about the evening class. She needed him to show the steps for both men and women. Anxiety came over him and he was stricken with fear and couldn't move, almost as if some kind of malevolent power kept him in place.

He had never been able to remember a sequence of steps. Trying to teach someone to dance was a little unnerving for him. He couldn't show the cha-cha or any dance to anybody, and even though Franny said he would have to help from time to time, he figured he'd find a way to get out of it. But he didn't see how he could find his way out of this.

Franny suggested they begin by using the video to show the steps to the students. As calmly as he could, Hamilton said, "The video is an excellent substitute. I used it this morning."

Jeremy and HolliAnne arrived just barely before the class began. As soon as he saw Jeremy, Hamilton gave Buddy Boy the widest smile and rustled his hair. He had missed his son all day.

HolliAnne shook out the umbrella, raindrops darting the floor.

"Is it raining?" Hamilton asked, a bit of disappointment in his voice.

"It's nasty out there. The rain is really coming down," HolliAnne said.

"Franny has sprained her ankle or hurt her leg and won't be able to teach this evening," he said to them.

"Does that mean you—" Jeremy smiled.

"I know what you're thinking. But weren't you the one who coerced me, twisted my arm, and threatened me into signing up to begin with?"

"See how much effort it took?" Jeremy laughed.

"How can you do that? Don't you have to have a certificate or degree or something that says you're a specialist?" HolliAnne asked, a sly grin on her face.

Hamilton gave her a sideways glance. He didn't want to get into anything in front of Jeremy or in the studio.

"It's nice to see your appreciation for this art style," HolliAnne said.

"The class must go on," he said, trying to understand her comment.

"Teaching dance must not be as complicated as teaching journalism or being a dean."

"Can I help?" Jeremy asked, interrupting.

"This morning, I showed a video. It's already in there." He pointed to the large screen TV. "Can you get that ready for us, now?"

Jeremy went to the big screen TV.

"Dancing speaks the language of romance," HolliAnne said.

"Yes, it's here. It's ready," Jeremy said.

"Good. Can you operate it when we're ready?" He gave a quick glance at HolliAnne, still not understanding what she wanted from him.

"Well, try not to mess up everything. You wouldn't want to be responsible for her spraining her other ankle," HolliAnne said.

"For now, start on your homework. I'll call you when we're ready." Jeremy nodded.

At this moment, Emma came out of the dressing room. She stopped and stood in a streak of fluorescent light that angled itself across the floor. The light revealed the soft lines of her face, exposing the voice in her eyes, the tease in her smile, and the shyness in her face. Her shoulder length hair parted itself and fell across her face, creating a wondrousness, a hypnotic beauty. She held up her dance shoes. "Are these the right shoes?"

Hamilton couldn't speak or take his eyes off her. HolliAnne elbowed him. He turned to HolliAnne and back to Emma. "Uh, huh."

"Yes, they are," began Franny, coming out of the office on crutches. "They are the best quality, too."

After a moment, "Why don't I walk you out?" Hamilton said to HolliAnne. She grabbed her umbrella. He ushered her out of the door.

"Is she a dance student?" HolliAnne asked as they approached the steps. The thunderclaps were loud, and HolliAnne jumped with each clap.

"Yes." When she was afraid of the thunder during their marriage, he would hold her and stroke her hair so she wouldn't be afraid.

"Is this what you're doing now?"

"Just helping Franny for now." They started down the steps.

"Jeremy told me about Anna's trip."

"That sounds like a partial complaint is in there somewhere."

"You're good to the kids. How is that a complaint?"

"But?"

"But you weren't always as good to me."

"I know. You've told me often enough." The rain pounding on the sidewalk outside made it difficult for Hamilton to hear the calm in her voice.

"Ham, you—"

"I know. I ruined your life."

"Don't you even care?"

She stopped on the steps. He stopped beside her. They faced each other. She was so close he could feel her breath. Her eyes held a softness around the edges with a twinkle of happiness and seemed to say, "I'm sorry we couldn't work on our marriage." Her lips held a slight smile, the kind she had when she wanted something. Her breathing grew louder with a wanting expectation that frightened him.

"HolliAnne. Can I ask you something?" his voice barely above a whisper.

"What is it?"

"If you were so unhappy, why didn't you leave earlier?" He braced himself.

She looked at him as if asking what an incredulous question. The hard rain now sounding more like a soft summer rain. Then her face softened. "Because I thought our marriage had a chance to get better." Tears formed in her eyes, and she turned away.

He was sure his face had a shocked look because he was.

"But you don't care. If you're going to tell people what to do with their lives, you have to be there for them when they fail." She regained her composure and continued down the stairs.

He wanted to tell her how he didn't trust her, how he expected more from her, how she didn't come through for him, but he didn't. It wasn't all true.

She dashed off down the steps and out the door, leaving him standing there. He wished he loved her enough to call her back. He had always wanted to know what he had done wrong, how he had failed HolliAnne. But he didn't expect to hear that.

After Jeremy was five, and HolliAnne had been back to work for several months. She called him and told him she had to work late. The counselors at the university rotated sometimes. Those who worked during the day would sometimes have to work during the evening.

After he picked up his children, Hamilton got them all home and organized. He went to pick up the dinner he'd ordered before he left his office. While he waited for his takeout, there was HolliAnne at a table with one of the other deans, Vic Thomas. He wanted to greet them, but he couldn't move, just stood there watching.

Then HolliAnne reached for Vic's hand, and he took hers. When the takeout was ready, Hamilton paid for it and left. He wanted to drive away; instead, he sat in his car a few minutes trying to pull himself together. HolliAnne and Vic came out and got into Vic's car.

Hamilton was parked in the row behind them and to their right. Vic pulled out of the space and turned left down the street. Hamilton followed them all the way to a motel several blocks away. Vic got out and went into the office while HolliAnne sat in the car. After Vic came out of the motel office, he got back in his car, drove a few rows down, and parked in front of a motel room. They both got out and went inside.

Hamilton sat there for a few minutes. He imagined himself barging in, demanding that HolliAnne come home with him. He saw himself hitting Vic in the face, bloodying his nose, and giving him a black eye. He saw Vic lying on the floor, unable to get up. But after a few minutes, Hamilton drove home. He never said a word to her. But he lost trust in HolliAnne, women, and in himself.

After a few minutes, he heard Jeremy somewhere in the background, calling him. He turned around and followed Jeremy back into the studio.

"As you all can see, I have injured my leg. I mean my foot. Sorry, but there's so much pain, I'm not sure what I injured. This morning Hamilton helped by using this video. So, we'll do it again for this class." Franny nodded toward Jeremy, who began the video.

Hamilton watched the demonstration of the couple on the video, as they danced the cha-cha, in sync with one another, he expecting and she complying; she falling gently in his arms, he there to catch, he reaching up to twirl her at just the right height and moment, and she smiling and twirling according to his lead; everything he wanted in his marriage. When the demonstration ended, Hamilton glanced at Emma. She stood up and eased out of the studio.

CHAPTER 10

Hamilton arrived at the studio early to review the eight-week schedule of all the classes. He found one copy of Franny's hand-written schedule hidden under an avalanche of papers and books on her desk. The first mid-morning class had five retired women and four men, nine people, making a small class. Later in the afternoon, she had scheduled one forty-five-minute class with twelve 7, 8-and 9-year-olds for beginning ballet. Two mornings a week, she had two women in a tap dance class, and in the evening, she had eight women and two men in another ballroom dance class. She had four classes for the week and thirty-two people in all.

At this point, she could barely pay the rent on the building, much less pay him a salary. She told him, in one of their conversations, how full the classes were when her mother taught. Franny also said many of the same people signed up session after session. Now, Franny struggled to hold on.

Nevertheless, Hamilton typed the schedule, made copies of the schedule, and taped one copy on the back of the office door. He also stapled one on the bulletin board with old news and yellowed newspaper clippings of Franny's mother dancing with a man, her mother sitting opposite a man during what seemed to be an interview, and her standing behind a podium, perhaps speaking.

Hamilton took down all the pictures of her mother. He found a description of each of her classes, typed them up, and hung those on the bulletin board around the schedule. He found pictures of Franny dancing and her teaching young children dance steps, and he found a picture of Franny and her mother dancing together in the studio. He hung those pictures on the bulletin board. He downloaded news about dance competitions and places to purchase shoes and clothing and hung those on the bulletin board. Franny needed someone to get her organized, and he needed to be an excellent organizer. He wanted her to need him to organize things so he wouldn't have to do any dancing whatsoever. But Franny also needed something else.

Hamilton came out of the office when he heard the music signaling the start of class. From the clock on the wall, he saw she was starting at 10:30, on time.

Carol, who must have thought of herself as the class leader from the way she repeated everything Franny said and gave out directions to everyone, looked at Franny and asked how she would teach the class on crutches.

"I want to introduce you to Eleanor. She'll help with the class today."

"What are we doing today?" Carol yelled out.

"We will review the steps from the cha-cha, the dance from our last class."

Carol gave everyone the "okay" nod and imitated Eleanor's positions.

Hamilton leaned up against the wall and watched the students practice the steps to the cha-cha. Franny, on crutches, stood to the side. Eleanor's long thin body with its graceful curves made this dance look easy, as though even he could do it. Her solid frame with her back straight, head straight, even weight, and arm held high caused him to think about his own appearance, and he straightened his posture as he watched her step around the floor. Her tan skin and long dark hair, slightly bouncing on her back, added an elegant quality to the dance.

During class, Carol seemed to forget about her need to confirm. She seemed to enjoy learning the dance steps. Hamilton looked around and saw the other students laughing and enjoying the class. They liked Eleanor. She knew what to say, how to coax the shy ones and how to show them all what to do. She made everyone feel comfortable. He even over-heard someone say how they would practice at home and be ready for her at the next session. Others nodded.

They looked forward to her being their teacher. Her eagerness and energy were contagious, and the class seemed happy and excited about the new teacher. Hamilton would not have to worry about teaching the class. They had found a savior.

At the end of the class, Eleanor complimented everyone on their performance. The students clapped and thanked her for the session. "I enjoyed teaching and I look forward to our next session." They wanted her to return. The students left. Eleanor changed her shoes and left. Within a few minutes, Eleanor appeared at the door, distressed.

Franny saw her. "Did you forget something?

"No, I'm afraid I, I have to—" Eleanor began.

"What's the matter?" Franny asked.

"I'm so sorry. I just found out that I've been given a bigger part in the musical at the Kennedy Center. I was looking forward to working with this class."

"What are you saying?"

"I won't be able to—"

"But you can't do that. You promised you'd help," Franny said.

"I said I had a part in the show, and I thought I would get something else. I told you I'd do what I could. I'm sorry."

"I need you, Eleanor."

"Franny, I'm sorry. I won't have time to do this. You know how rehearsals can be." She started out of the studio.

"My mother, the studio, Eleanor, please stay," following Eleanor out the door.

"Franny, let her go," Hamilton said. He took her by the arm and pulled her back.

"But the studio. My mother—"

"Franny, she can't. Come on. Thanks for your time, Eleanor. Come on, Franny."

They walked to the office. Hamilton closed the door.

"I don't have money to pay someone to teach." Franny confessed when she heard Hamilton pull out his chair.

"I know. From the number of classes you have, and the number of people in each class, you can't be making that much."

"I'm not."

They were silent for a while.

"You could do it."

"I'm not a professional."

"No, you could do it."

"Do?"

"You could help me."

"Franny, I'm already helping you."

"You could do it."

"Do what?"

"I could teach you the steps and you could teach it to the class. I can handle the ballet class, but the ballroom classes are where I need help."

"I don't know anything about dancing. You gave me a choice, and I chose the office, remember?" Hamilton panicked, and began breathing hard, as he thought about his clumsiness, his inability to learn steps in a sequence, and his need not to bring attention to them, those secrets he held. He gathered his things.

"Yes, but these are beginning classes. If you don't, I'll have to close for two months until I can use my leg again and I can't afford to do that."

"You've already spent the money, haven't you?" He said while putting on his coat.

"Yes, you saw when we went to the bank."

"You'll think of something," he said. "I know you will." He turned to leave. Halfway down the steps, he turned around and went back. Franny was at her desk in tears and staring at the phone.

"Franny, there must be something you can do."

She looked up at him. "I don't know what to do. Eleanor helped because she was one of my mother's students."

"You don't have friends in the business who could do you a favor?"

"No, not really."

"No other students from your mother?"

"Most left the area to dance in a company."

"What about someone from one of your classes? Or from another studio?"

"The people from my classes were not able. Most of them just wanted to learn to dance for a cruise or wedding, things like that."

"Franny, you're not trying."

"What do you want me to do?"

"Open a directory or something. Look in your cell for names, something your mother must have used. I want you to do something. I can't do what you want."

"I don't have a directory or a list or anything in my cell phone."

"Well, I guess that's that." He turned to leave again.

"You're my only hope," Franny said in a small voice.

"I can't Franny. I just can't do this." His back to her.

"Okay. See you tomorrow."

He turned around, "Franny, think about it. Maybe someone or some idea will come to you." He paused. "There's no need for me to come tomorrow if you can't find anyone."

She gave off a helpless "all hope is lost," smile and looked down at the desk.

He started out again. When he reached the bottom of the steps, he stood there a moment as if he'd forgotten something and afraid to go back and get it. Then he turned around and started up again. When he reached the office and before he could say anything, Franny yelled,

"You'll do it?" She smiled through her tears as he stood in the doorway.

"I can't leave you all upset." He could try to help her, but how could he help himself.

Franny wiped her tears and smiled at Hamilton. For the next hour, she taught Hamilton the cha-cha. He was so busy trying to get the steps correct and in the proper order he forgot to keep his body straight, and he forgot to loosen up and allow himself to feel the steps. They worked until they were too tired to do more.

On the drive, Hamilton thought about his middle and high school experiences. He knew how it felt to be humiliated. He was humiliated when he found out that the counselors in HolliAnne's department knew she saw other men. It was because of that feeling that he agreed to help Franny with the class. It was because of his humiliation he understood HolliAnne, no matter what she thought.

CHAPTER 11

The next day, when Hamilton arrived at the studio, Franny was in the office, limping from one side of the small, crowded office to the other. She hobbled around the boxes still on the floor and hopped over stacks of books. Her apparent nervousness made Hamilton uneasy. As soon as he got in, Franny asked for a practice session before the 10:30 morning class began. While he tried to make himself believe everything would turn out okay, she left to put on the music.

On the dance floor, during the practice session, he followed her instructions, as best he could, demonstrating the basic step, step, 1, 2, 3, cha, cha. Together, they worked hard, and Franny seemed satisfied. Franny told him to take a break and relax before class. She handed him a pair of dance shoes left in the dressing room, she said would fit. He reluctantly took them and instead of telling her he would use his own shoes, he put on the pair she gave him. They were comfortable dance shoes, probably once owned by a professional dancer, and he was more relaxed.

Carey was the first to enter the studio. She went to the dressing room to put on her shoes, and the others drifted in one by one. Hamilton was surprised to see Marilyn. He thought she and Emma were taking the evening class together. At 10:30, Franny put on the music to signal that class had begun, while Emma slipped in and took a spot on the dance floor. Franny turned off the music and said they would continue the dance lessons for the upcoming weeks.

"Hamilton will show the steps as I call them out," she gestured toward Hamilton. Hamilton tried hard to form his face into a smile.

"What? What kind of lesson is that? He's not a professional. I want my money back," Carey said.

"You should have given us our money back the other day," Carol said.

"Wait, a minute. Let's be reasonable," Ronald said. "I used to be a lawyer and—"

"What? You like this set-up?" Irene asked. I don't want to pay for an amateur," she announced to everyone in the class, and turned around to everyone as if she wanted them to join in with her.

"I paid for a professional," Betty said, nodding.

"Don't you think you're not being very logical?" Ronald said.

"I think it's only fair we get our money back," Carey said, looking at Ronald.

"But she didn't twist her ankle on purpose. And it won't take her forever to heal," Ronald said.

June, Robert, Dacie, Edna, Marilyn, and Emma all stood quietly, looking as if they hadn't given much thought to how the class would be taught or who would teach it.

"I want my money back," Irene said.

Ronald wasn't finished. "Wait a minute, everyone. Before we get into something we don't need to, give it a chance. We haven't given Franny's solution a chance. Why not give it a chance before we judge it?"

Hamilton was thankful for Ronald. He wanted to help Franny, but he also didn't want to interrupt and take over like HolliAnne said he always did. It was hard for Hamilton to stand there and watch them do that to Franny. She was sweet and kind and delicate and incredibly naïve. She had a softness about her that allowed people to walk over her. The class could see her predicament and at least give a little.

"That's what I say," Ronald added.

No one spoke for a short while. Ronald turned and looked at the other classmates as if asking them to try it.

"I guess one more day wouldn't hurt. We haven't missed much time, anyway. We had a professional for the last session," Carol said.

"Let's get on with it. I came here to get some exercise, lose a few pounds," Robert said. He cast his eyes downward, as if embarrassed about how much he needed to lose.

"Okay, then. Let's get started." Hamilton began. "In the excitement that we had our second day, we might have missed something. I want to call out your name and just let me see you. That way, we can all remember your name. Also, don't forget to sign in every day." He called out the names. He just needed to match the names with the checks to make sure everyone had paid.

Franny asked everyone to get a partner. She asked Hamilton to show the basic steps to the cha-cha from the man's position first. When they began and Franny called out the steps, Hamilton was nervous and confused. He felt as if he didn't raise his feet high enough, but he was afraid to look down. When he tried to perform the 1, 2, 3, he thought he'd stepped on something, and he stumbled slightly. He fell behind in the timing and tried to catch up, but there was something on the floor that prevented him. He hadn't noticed anything earlier. He slumped in posture and had to remind himself to hold his head up, keep to the time, dance with grace. Then he heard a giggle from the group and just knew Carol was laughing at him.

Franny yelled, "Turn now, turn now," and when he took a step to turn, he tripped over his feet and fell flat on the floor.

"See, I told you we needed a professional. We're paying for one," Carol said.

"Are you okay?" Franny asked Hamilton.

"I think so. I don't know what happened."

"What happened to your shoes?" Robert asked.

Everyone looked down at what was left of Hamilton's shoes, the shoes that Franny gave him to use.

"The shoes came apart. Look at the floor," Dacie said. "Parts of his shoes are all over the floor."

"Where did you get those shoes?" Carol asked.

Hamilton turned to Franny. Everyone looked at Franny.

"They were left in the dressing room. I thought they fit him." Franny said.

"How long have they been there?" Carol asked.

"Clearly, the shoes were dry rot. You didn't notice that?" Robert asked.

"Whose shoes were they, Franny?" Dacie asked.

"I don't remember," Franny said.

"They look old. Look at the laces. You don't remember?" June asked.

"I think they belonged to my father," Franny whispered.

Hamilton tried to sit up. He unlaced the shoes and slipped each foot out of what was left of them. Robert and Dacie helped him stand.

"Okay everyone, our time is up." Hamilton said, looking at the clock.

The evening 7:00 ballroom dance class went much like the 10:30 morning ballroom dance class, except they never argued or demanded their money back. He waited to hear the same fawning that the morning class made earlier, but no one said anything he could hear. In fact, Hamilton thought they were unusually quiet and still. He didn't know what to make of it. Franny turned the music off and Hamilton, with his new black dance shoes, demonstrated the steps for the cha-cha, first several times for the men, then several times for the women. He tried not to let the mishap during the morning class bother him. He remembered his posture, his arm up and elbow out, and his head straight as he followed Franny's instructions for each direction and step.

It was when Hamilton had finished his demonstrations and the group had to practice with their partners that the confusion started. Dagmar and Frida both grabbed Miles at the same time. He got angry at being snatched at and sat down. Dagmar and Frida ended up being partners. Keith told Elise that she was doing the man's part, and she countered by telling him he needed to be a man. Albert and Aileen, the oldest in the group, were trying to follow the directions that Franny had given, and Hamilton had demonstrated earlier.

"Is this right?" Aileen asked. At that moment, Albert stepped down on her right foot. A sea of red spread across Aileen's face and she held herself stiffly. Albert continued pushing her around the floor, ignoring the obvious pain in her foot. She kept going.

Hamilton sighed in exasperation. He turned away from Aileen and Albert as he tried to hold on to his composure. Emma gave him a smile and held there for a minute as her smile grew wider. Hamilton smiled back, took a relaxing breath, and extended his hand to Aileen.

"Stop a minute. Are you okay?" Hamilton asked, looking down at Aileen's foot. "I'm okay," she said. Her face held a "thank you for caring" pose.

"Let me show you again," Hamilton said. He eyed Emma again, and she smiled again.

Albert released his wife; his hands folded, he bowed as if repeating a long prayer.

Hamilton asked Albert to follow him one step at a time. Hamilton stepped, then Albert, Hamilton, then Albert, until they had made it around the dance floor.

"Do I have to step your way? I lose my balance like that."

Hamilton caught himself. "Step so you keep your balance."

He asked Albert to dance with his wife. He showed Albert how to allow her to move rather than him push her around the dance floor.

"Thank you. That was so much better," Aileen said.

"We thank you," Albert said, his hands folded, and he bowed.

Hamilton tried to get Miles up and dancing, but the man who declared he was on his search for his one and only refused to dance with any of the women in the group. Hamilton let him sulk and went to Dagmar and Frida, who seemed to work well together. Hamilton tried to get both Dagmar and Frida to change the way they turned. He showed them his way and said it was better. When they both tried to turn his way, they smashed into each other. Frida fell and injured her right side and face. She said she was okay and got up to continue practicing.

The clock on the wall must have stopped. The class seemed to go on for centuries. When it was finally over, the students rushed out the door. Franny told Hamilton he should allow the dance students to practice their way.

In both the 10:30 morning and 7:00 evening classes for the next two days, Franny used the two videos that she had already planned to use for her classes. She stopped the videos every so often to point out and explain the steps so that the class could see exactly what the dancer was doing. She had each class member practice with a partner, and she went to every group to guide them.

During their non-class times, Franny rehearsed Hamilton. She had him use the mirror to see his form and his step. After hours of practice, they stopped and turned toward the mirror.

"I think you're ready," Franny said, smiling at Hamilton through the mirror.

"Franny, I still don't think this is a wise idea." Hamilton said. "I'm not ready for this." He turned to her.

"But you are. Look how far you've come."

"I'm no better off than when we started."

"But, Ham, you—"

"Franny, I'm sorry, but I can't do this," he shook his head several times, "I'm not a dancer. I'm not comfortable teaching dance. I'm an organizer. Find someone who can demonstrate these steps the way they're supposed to be done." The incident with the shoes weighed heavily on him.

"So, you've made a few mistakes during the practice sessions. So what?"

"So what? These people want to learn how to dance." He tried to keep himself calm and not let his fear and anxiety mount.

Franny turned away.

"Franny, can you at least try to find someone else? There must be an organization where there is a list of dancers who could substitute." He suggested that because he knew there was a list for his teachers in the event one of them needed a substitute.

She turned toward him. "There must be. But I don't know where to find it," she said in a whisper.

He had embarrassed her, something he didn't mean to do. He wanted to help Franny by trying to find an organization or by contacting another studio, but that would make her seem incapable. He didn't want to do that. HolliAnne already told him how he made her feel when he took over for her. Every time he tried to stop, every time he stepped back to let them handle it, HolliAnne, and now Franny, needed him.

Okay, Franny," he said, "I'll try it tomorrow." He said it like he understood this was the only choice. But deep down, he knew he had another choice. He couldn't do that to Franny.

The next week in the 10:30 class, Franny announced they would begin the fox-trot and that Hamilton would demonstrate the steps.

"Oh, no," Irene said. She must have thought no one heard, but Hamilton did.

A grumbling noise came from Carol, and she gave one of those "cover" coughs.

"Good," Robert began. "Good," he said, as if that would make things final.

Franny paused and Hamilton thought she had another comment, but she turned toward the music table, and music for the fox-trot emanated from the speakers. She nodded to Hamilton to center himself on the dance floor and begin. Then she stopped the music.

All Hamilton remembered was something about a box. He looked around the room for a box and then realized that the figure for the fox-trot was a box step. He lifted his arms as if he had a partner and picked up his right foot. But was he to do the left turning box? He must have begun on the wrong foot. He tried to change to his left foot, but he was too late. Franny, calling out the steps, was ahead of him. He couldn't think of how to catch up. Perspiration filled his forehead, but he didn't know how to wipe his brow since he was supposed to keep his arms up as if he had a partner. When he was to step slow, slow, quick, quick, he stepped slow, quick, quick, quick, or slow, slow, slow, slow. He couldn't remember the steps or the order of the steps. He had failed Fanny again.

"I missed a step, I—" he tried to defend himself before Franny spoke.

"Thank you, Hamilton," she began, "it's very important to remember the steps. Remember, you're doing a figure 'four' and making a left turning box. Knowing when and how to change your weight, is very important when you are turning. Keep in mind the line of dance.

The line of dance is the counterclockwise flow of traffic around the dance floor. You don't want to bump into each other."

Hamilton was angry at himself for allowing Franny to talk him into the embarrassment he had just made of himself. He wanted to escape to the office, but he wasn't a man who ran away and hid. He stood there in his embarrassment as the class members watched him and turned away from him.

He recalled the very first time he had trouble following directions or a sequence of steps. It was his second summer helping his father in the vineyard. Hamilton wanted to work in the vineyard. He thought it was a way to be with his father. His father assigned Daniel, a supervisor, to teach and work with Hamilton. Hamilton's father, George, had a reputation for making the best wine and he created ways to keep his wine superior.

One thing he did was to use what he called the "separation method." Daniel showed Hamilton how to sort out the grapes, looking for bad spots, grapes with a dull color, too soft, overripe, or too small. His job was to separate them and put them in different barrels that he should have had labeled. Hamilton forgot to label the barrels and mixed up the grapes. He put the over ripe grapes in with the ripe grapes and he did not thoroughly wash and clean the grapes.

No one realized what happened until weeks later, after the secondary fermentation. The tasters, including his father, rejected the wine, each one saying that the taste was dull and bitter. Daniel traced the problem back to Hamilton and saw the barrels were not labeled. His father could not send the wine out. From experience, George knew the wine would not improve over time. They would have to get rid of the bitter wine or do something else with it.

One night after it happened, Hamilton overheard his father tell his mother the workers would have to work overtime to make up for the error, and he wouldn't be able to pay them. The next day, in a meeting with all the workers, George brought his problem before them. The employees suggested ways they could stretch what was good to make up for the loss. But George didn't want to soil his reputation. George told his workers that he couldn't pay them for overtime.

Later, Hamilton overheard the workers say his father had to borrow the money, so he could pay everyone and for any overtime. Hamilton saw for himself what happened, the mistake he caused. He promised himself he would never let anything like that happen to him again. That was when he created his own rules, and his method of implementing his ideas, and directing, and controlling his life, and often everyone else's life. After that, Daniel assigned Hamilton another job as clean up boy.

"See you next time." Hamilton heard Franny say, when the class ended. He hurried off to the office before anyone could say anything to him.

That evening, as soon as Jeremy got home from school, "Bud, I could use your help before you start your homework."

"What's up?"

"I need you to help me with the fox-trot." Hamilton took Jeremy's coat and Jeremy sat his backpack near a stool in the kitchen. Then they went into the family room.

"The dance?"

"Will you help?"

"You want me, a nondancer, to help you with the fox-trot?"

"Bud, I need your help."

"What about my homework? Do I get a pass on that?"

"Bud."

"What's the matter, Dad? Why are you so nervous?"

"I just want to get it right, that's all." He read off the steps, and even showed the steps, the way he knew them.

"Okay. Let's do this," Jeremy said.

Hamilton and Jeremy practiced and practiced the fox-trot. After a while, Hamilton realized that Jeremy, yawning, was tired and so was he.

"Dad, you got this."

"You sure?"

"I'm sure. You got this."

After dinner, Jeremy went off to his room to do homework and Hamilton, by himself, continued practicing. Before they went to bed, Jeremy told Hamilton he wanted to go over the dance steps with him one more time.

On the next day before the 10:30 class began, Franny suggested to Hamilton that he not be the one to demonstrate the steps anymore.

"Franny, I told you I wasn't ready, but you insisted, remember?"

"Yes, but I was wrong. I used a video on the first two days. I can do that again."

"Okay. Do you think that will be okay with the students?"

"I don't know. I don't know what to do."

"Let me try again."

"But, last time—"

"I know. You don't have to remind me. I know. But I've been practicing. I think I can do it this time."

"Ham, that's okay. I'll just give them their money back."

"How? How are you going to do that?

"I don't know. I'll think of something."

"I know your situation is not what you want. But I don't think you want to give up either."

After a long pause. "Okay. Another try," she sighed.

Every class member showed up for the 10:30 morning class. How nice it would be if one or two of them could be absent. During the previous day, when everybody watched him fumble, was misery for him and them. But this morning, he had the support of Buddy Boy, and he was confident, able, and ready. Once Franny saw everyone was present, without a word, she went to put on the music for the fox-trot to signal the start of class.

After he had changed into his new dance shoes, Hamilton took his place on the dance floor. He held his head high, his arm out as if he had a partner, and with self-assurance, lifted the correct foot, this time, to begin the box. He slow, slow, quick, quick, slow, slow, quick, quick stepped all around the room as he showed the man's part first.

"That's a nice back."

Hamilton thought it was Carol who commented, but he didn't dare turn his head to see.

"You mean, butt. And it certainly is," Cary said.

Being watched, or more like being on display, made him aware of his body and its imperfections. He was happy he had dropped a few pounds over the past year, particularly around his stomach area. He could thank his stress for that. Maybe being stressed out is good for something. As he turned and tried to keep his legs straight, he tried not to think about his inability to remember directions or follow a sequence of steps and the suffering it caused him over the years.

He focused on his posture, and, as Buddy Boy said to him the night before, his feet knew what to do; so, let them do it.

"I like that side view. Could you repeat that step so we could get a really good look this time?" Carey asked.

"Wow!" June sang out. "Look at the muscle tone in those arms. Grrrrrr."

"No junk food for him," Carey continued. "Every man should take that kind of care of his body."

"Ladies, please," Robert said. He sounded embarrassed, or more like jealous. Hamilton wanted to laugh but couldn't.

"Don't be a prude. We're just trying to get a good look at the steps, that's all," Carey said. The ladies laughed.

Hamilton wasn't sure about being in this position. At first, he wanted to say something about the inappropriateness of their comments. But then, he remembered he had lost a few pounds, and he wasn't superfine, but he was fit. Sure, he needed to tighten up a bit; the gym could help, and he didn't have to let everyone know about how he had a hard time remembering the steps. But, overall, he was proud of how he looked. He tried hard not to smile or show he accepted or enjoyed their comments.

"Now, he will show the steps for the women's position. Ladies, please try to hold your comments. We don't' want to make Hamilton nervous," Franny said.

"I hope I look like that while I'm dancing," Carol said, laughing.

Franny asked Carol and Hamilton to demonstrate to the group while she called out the steps for the women. Even though he thought he looked good while demonstrating, he was a little nervous about dancing with Carol. But he should just allow his feet to take over, like Buddy Boy said. He and Carol showed the steps by dancing all around the floor, giving the students the chance to see from all angles.

Franny asked everyone to partner up and each pair would do the fox-trot. Hamilton, a little relieved he didn't have to stand out in front of everyone, circulated and helped those who needed position reminders. Several times Carol and Ronald bumped into other couples. Hamilton came over to help Ronald get back on track. Ronald had trouble figuring out his right from his left and deciding which foot to use. Hamilton could relate to that. He showed Ronald how to be less clumsy when he danced by having him bend in the waist a little. Ronald tried it, but he put more focus on his posture, causing him to misstep several times. Hamilton tried to show him again several times, but Ronald walked off the dance floor in frustration.

Hamilton turned to Carey, who watched her feet as she danced. Hamilton asked her to straighten her back. Dick stuck his elbow out, so it jabbed other people as they danced. He said he'd found a way to keep people away from him and off his feet. Franny asked them all to watch out for the line of dance, the flow of traffic around the dance floor.

Just before it was time to go, Franny turned the music up and, in the remaining time, the couples danced until it was time to go. When the class ended, Emma and Marilyn walked to the exit, where Hamilton and Franny stood to say goodbye as the students exited.

"Thank you. It was a very nice class," Emma said on her way out.

"Yes, it was. You did a marvelous job keeping the class together," Marilyn said. She glanced at Emma.

Hamilton let out a long sigh after everyone left. He and Franny went to the office. Franny closed the door.

"Ham, we need to talk."

"I know, I didn't mean for Ronald to walk off like that."

"I'm sure you didn't. Maybe it would be better if you didn't tell everyone your right way to do things." She said, while pulling out her chair.

"I didn't realize I was doing that," he gazed at her.

Franny didn't look in his direction. "We just can't have people running off like that."

He recalled a time when a student reported a journalism teacher to him. The student said that the teacher harassed him and bullied him. In his conference with the teacher, Hamilton deduced that the teacher made a rude comment, but the teacher's actions and comments weren't to the extend the student had reported. Hamilton told the teacher he would not put anything in his personnel record, but he couldn't do that to students. Hamilton, after speaking to another teacher, took the student out of that class and put him in the other teacher's class.

"I understand. I can leave if it makes things better."

"Leave?"

"That'll make things better."

"What good would that do?"

"Franny, this is your business. I don't want to interfere with your business. If I'm in the way, then I have to leave."

"First, I don't want you to go. Ham, everyone here, likes you. You've brought a lot of energy to these classes. But no one here wants you to control how they dance. Dance is a free spirit effort, a personal expression. Show them and allow them to do the steps, but their way." She paused, watching him. "I know you can do it," she smiled.

"Okay. Right back at me, huh? Their way. I show them and let them do it their way."

As he left the office, Hamilton thought about HolliAnne and how she felt under his control, the same way he felt now, demeaned, humiliated. After agreeing with her about how her parents treated her, controlled every moment of her life, he treated her the same way.

Anita told him she would eventually have to open her heart to someone else. Hamilton wanted the same, but he could see now that it would be difficult for a woman to open her heart to him. He had to stop trying to control himself so he could stop controlling others. HolliAnne was correct when she said to him no woman would want him controlling them. If he wanted a woman and wanted to be happy, he would have to allow her to be her own person.

CHAPTER 12

Hamilton decided Franny needed to improve the visibility of the studio to increase her enrollment for her winter session. As her organizer, he made plans for an open house where the students would invite friends and earn a discount if the friend signed up. He made plans for two dance parties for the year. He called an art student whom he knew needed jobs to build his resume and asked the student to paint a small picture of a man and woman dancing together on the window downstairs next to the entrance of the studio. He also asked the student to paint a short list of the dances, the studio phone number and a black arrow pointing toward the stairs. The student asked for ten dollars and when it was complete, Hamilton, being satisfied, paid him. Franny was sure to like what the student did. She liked the changes in the bulletin board, she would like these other changes.

He heard her returning just as he had completed the description for the open house, but it was almost time for her 10:30 class. Since he wanted to surprise her, he would wait until class was over to tell her about everything he'd done.

On this day, the 10:30 tap dancing class included two people, Sofia and her aide, Gertie. Sofia was full of smiles. She repeated throughout the lesson she was just happy to move her feet, even if she had to have help.

Franny sat in a chair facing Sofia and gently placed her hands on her right foot. "I will turn the right foot just a tiny bit to the right." With Sophia's help, Franny turned her right foot to the right several times. "Good, Sophia, you're doing fine. Let's do it one more time."

Then Franny let the right leg rest and lifted her left leg to turn her left foot. Then she guided Sofia into standing and showed her how to balance herself. Several times, Sofia reached out to Gertie to keep herself from falling. Hamilton stood by the office door, watching Franny. Franny had a loving way about her as she tenderly lifted Sofia's leg or her foot, encouraged her to stand and move her foot on her own. Hamilton smiled.

"I know I won't be tapping on stage or doing anything like that, but my entire life, I always wanted to learn to tap dance," she held onto Gertie and Franny while moving her right foot forward.

"Why didn't you take lessons?" Franny asked.

"I never seemed to have the time," Sofia said. "But it's not too late." In a small move, she slid her left foot forward.

"No, it's not too late."

"The doctor said I could do this." Sofia said.

"I called him like you suggested. I hope you don't mind."

"No. I asked you to. What did he say?" They turned around, and Sofia, with Franny and Gertie, walked back to her chair.

"The same thing you said. He was very encouraging. He said you can move your right side much better than your left side. I asked him what exercises I should do with you, and I told him you wanted to learn to tap dance. He said the stroke inhibited your left side, but if you continue these dance exercises, you can gain back some movement, and maybe do a little tapping someday." Franny smiled at Sofia.

"That's what he told me. Did he tell you how old I am?"

Franny smiled. "Yes, he did, and I think that's the nicest thing." Gertie got her chair.

"I regret I had to wait until I turned 89 years old and after a stroke to take tap dancing lessons, I've been wanting to take all my life." Sofia sat.

When the class ended, Hamilton helped Franny walk them out of the studio and he lifted Sofia down the stairs to her wheelchair waiting at the bottom of the steps.

"That was nice what you did out there," Hamilton said when they entered the office.

"Oh, yeah. Can you believe that no one else would take her? She's such a dear person."

"There aren't many people who could do what you do for her."

"She said she called three studios, and everyone said they couldn't do it. They said she needed special classes or something. I don't understand how people can be so thoughtless and mean."

"How do you know what to do?"

"I asked the doctor, and he sent me some exercises for her. I try to make them into tap steps as much as I can." She sat down at her still messy desk.

She was in a caring mood, and now would be an opportune time to tell her. "Speaking of dance, let me tell you what I've done so far." Hamilton told Franny about the flyers, announcing the location of the studio and the dance styles, the dance party, the idea that the students could get a small discount when they got a friend to sign up. He sent a flyer advertising the studio to the community newspaper. He also mentioned that he saw from the applications that one of the class members worked at a radio station at night and he could ask her how to make a community service announcement on the radio.

He just knew Franny was as joyful about his ideas as he was. But, with her bug-eyed glare, her mouth open and forward lean, she seemed more shocked than anything else. Maybe he didn't explain it right. He opened his mouth to start again when she sat back in her chair, arms down and out on each side as if to say, "I've given up," and her mouth still open.

"Oh! Oh!" she finally said.

This wasn't going the way Hamilton thought it would. He expected her to be more jubilant, thanking him for the time and ideas. But she was just sitting there, staring at him.

"What's the matter?" He stood facing her, slightly bent, and with his hands on his chair.

She closed her mouth and turned her head downward. She picked at something on her black dance pants and then looked up at him. "Nothing."

"Yes, there is. You don't seem happy." He sat down. "Don't you think you need to do these things? You also need to take on more classes, but of course, after your leg heals."

"My mother. We have plans."

"You and your mother will work together? How Franny?"

"I know there are several things we need, but..."

"There are no 'buts,' Franny."

She turned away from him.

"You asked me to help you. You wanted to get organized."

"I know. I know."

"Are you afraid to do this?" He waited a moment. "Which things should I take off the list," he began. "You don't have to do everything."

She looked at him as if to say, "You don't understand." Then, "It's not that."

"Franny, what is it. I thought I was doing the job you asked me to do. I thought this was what you wanted. Tell me what's bothering you."

"How am I supposed to pay for all this? I mean the advertisements, the discounts. The rent on this studio is paid up for a few months, but where do I get money for everything you're asking?"

"The advertisements are free. I printed the flyers from here. I paid the student for the drawing on the window downstairs. It was only ten dollars."

She stared at him.

"What's the matter, Franny?"

"You're right. The reason is that you didn't ask me. It's like you're taking over my business."

A bomb exploded within him. The smoke and gases from the explosion pulled him down, weighted his feet, and drilled a gigantic hole in the floor. He sank down deeper and deeper into the hole. He tried to speak, but all he could do was whisper, "I don't mean to do that."

Franny's stare made him helpless, and he was lost for words and actions.

"I don't want to be offensive," she said.

Hamilton couldn't respond.

"Why don't we both go home and think about things and then start again in the morning. Okay?" She said.

"I don't mean to do that, Franny." He stood to leave.

"We'll start again in the morning. See you early so we can practice before the class starts." She tried to chuckle, but a groaning sound came out instead.

He recalled a time he saw HolliAnne and one of the other professors together.

He was at a stoplight on his way home from the university. HolliAnne said she had to work late again. It poured that afternoon. Buckets of rain dropped from the dark sky and ran down his windshield, making it hard for him to see what was in front of him. After he made it through the light, he pulled over to the curb and parked his car to wait for the rain to ease up.

When the rain slowed down, he saw HolliAnne and Brandon Winters dashing out from under the awning of a restaurant and headed toward a car parked in front of the restaurant.

At first, he swore he had seen someone who looked like his wife. The woman was HolliAnne. He couldn't understand why HolliAnne was coming out of the restaurant with Brandon. Hamilton looked around for HolliAnne's car but didn't see it. When they got to his car, Brandon opened the passenger door and let her in. He then went to the driver's side to let himself in. Hamilton thought he was just giving her a ride home; it was raining hard. He wanted to get HolliAnne's attention to let her know he could drive her home. Instead, he waited. At that moment, Brandon leaned over and gave her a kiss. She reached over and put her arm around his shoulder.

Hamilton slid down so he wouldn't be noticed, but he could see everything. They continued to kiss. The way they were going at it, Hamilton suspected that this was not their first kiss. Hamilton had wanted her to kiss him like that, but she never did.

After what seemed like a miserable eternity, Brandon started the car, pulled out, and made a U turn while laughing and nodding. Hamilton got a glimpse of the smile on HolliAnne's face as the car passed by him. He ducked down, making it look like the car was empty. He went home and waited for her. She got home much later than she'd told him she would.

His way of making people, especially his wife, feel inadequate by taking over and doing things for them he could see was wrong. He saw how Franny was hurt and how she tried not to show it. He tried to control her, tell her what to do about the way she advertised her business and in doing that, he undermined and demeaned her. When he did that to HolliAnne, she fixed her situation by seeing other men.

When Jeremy got in the car, he showed Hamilton his test papers, one in math and one in English. He had earned an "A+" on each test.

"I promised you I would do my best."

"You sure did, Buddy Boy. You did great on these tests." He pulled away from the school and headed home.

After they got inside the house and settled in, Jeremy asked, "Dad, remember the other day you said I should start thinking about what I wanna be when I grow up?"

"Yes." Hamilton said with caution. He collected the newspapers from the floor.

"I thought about it and I wanna be a priest." Jeremy took the empty cups and glasses from the coffee table to the kitchen and put them in the sink.

Hamilton sucked in air. "Sure?" The news was shocking to him, but he couldn't show it.

"Yes. That's what I wanna be." Jeremy stood between the kitchen and the family room, a serious look on his face.

"Okay, then." He wanted to support Jeremy in whatever he wanted; even though it was difficult for Hamilton to support a cause he didn't believe in. He didn't stop Eric or Anna, but neither of them wanted to be a priest.

When Taylor, Hamilton's brother, announced that he wanted to become a priest, Hamilton wanted to know why. He never understood why Taylor wanted to be a priest; why he thought being a priest was a productive profession. Taylor began talking about God in high school and took classes in religion in college. But Hamilton could never bring himself to tell Taylor that he didn't believe in God. Hamilton never understood this concept about handing over everything to God or the fact that God directs our lives. Hamilton thought that kind of talk was a bunch of absurdities. He directed his life. He decided to get his Ph.D. He decided to marry; he decided to teach. God didn't do any of these things. Hamilton has had to do everything in his life himself. He thought it was silly to even entertain ideas like that. But Hamilton loved Taylor, and he allowed Taylor to believe that he believed in God.

He looked over at Jeremy. "Why Bud? Why do you want to be a priest?"

"Dad, I love the Lord. I feel He wants me to do more with my life. I have a strong feeling He's calling me to pray and spread the Gospel."

"What does that mean, spread the Gospel?"

"It means to tell others through sermons and actions by helping people, showing everyone God's love. I want to help the needy and do right by everyone. The Bible tells us to love each other, no matter who."

Hamilton was surprised to hear his son talk like this. He didn't know Jeremy was so deep into religion. "Bud. Is this what you've been learning in Sunday School?"

"Yes. And I read the Bible."

"I didn't know you were so passionate about being a priest."

"The more I learn, the more I love God and the more I want to be a priest."

"Bud, keep in mind that you could change your mind when you get to high school and then college. You'll have more choices as you grow." He wanted to say more, but he didn't. He was afraid he'd turn Buddy Boy away from him. He couldn't tell him not to become a priest and he couldn't tell him why.

With the way his life was going, how could he believe in God. Why is there a need to believe? What does God do, anyway? He could think of nothing God ever did for him. If there were truly a God, why didn't He show HolliAnne how to love and how to love him? If there were truly a God, why didn't He stop HolliAnne from giving herself to other men?

CHAPTER 13

The days with frightening thunderstorms and tornadoes of September were fading out, and October, with cooler temperatures during the early mornings, teased the earth. The afternoon's sun, with its distant reach, withdrew its heat and cast long shadows between the trees and buildings, announcing the nature of fall. No matter what, time never stops; ready or not, the next day always comes. Though life seemed somewhat grim early on, Hamilton looked forward to the next day, the next season. But he didn't expect so many things at the studio and at home to occur all at once.

The morning began with Officers Daniels and Wendt, who visited the studio.

"We just wanted to let you know we apprehended the man who robbed the drugstore downstairs."

"That was quick," Franny said.

"You don't have to be afraid. You can just go about your business as usual," Officer Daniels continued.

Franny's face was filled with fear, the fear that one would have when the truth comes out. She should have been relieved.

After the officers left, Franny and Hamilton decided on a working relationship style.

"I know you're looking out for me and everything. I shouldn't have gotten so upset with you yesterday."

"You were right. I should have conferred with you. You're the owner. I'm only part time. Would you—"

"You had excellent suggestions. What were you thinking for the dance parties?"

That afternoon when Hamilton picked up Buddy Boy, he told his father he had come to a decision.

"I want to help teach the new acolytes. Last Sunday, my teacher, Fr. Gray, said that more boys and girls wanted to be acolytes. He asked some of us to help train the new people and show them what to do. The meeting is Saturday morning."

A smile danced across Hamilton's face. He loved how Jeremy was so certain about what he wanted for himself. "We will do that."

After the third week on his new job, as office organizer and assistant dance teacher, Hamilton felt like a new man. Franny's directions, while he demonstrated the American style swing several times, strengthened his resolve. He always liked the swing, the version he knew, the American swing. It was light and fun, and dancing the swing always put him in a joyful mood. Of course, that was when he did it his way. For these classes, he learned to swing the correct way. Even so, he sat up straighter in his chair when he was on the computer at the studio and added dance steps as he moved about at home.

The fifth week, he showed a little superiority in his movements. He felt like a dance teacher, as if he had been dancing all his life. Added to his feeling was the fact that Franny's leg didn't seem to heal, like the doctors told her it would. She continued to wear her boot just as much as she did when she first sprained her foot or twisted her ankle. She complained about the pain now and then, but she showed no signs her foot or leg, or ankle was improving.

Hamilton was a little afraid about what would happen when Franny would have to teach the classes herself. He had already replaced the flyers in the stores downstairs several times, and more people signed up for the winter session. Hamilton scheduled classes for Franny throughout the day, concentrating on that sizeable gap she had in the afternoon, as much as possible.

After the rumba, they began the tango. In the 7:00 evening class, as he showed the steps to the tango, the women took him more seriously, and the men pulled him to the side and asked for private practice.

Everything was going well for Hamilton until one evening, when he was showing the tango before they practiced on their own.

"You're almost looking like a real dancer, there Hamilton," Miles said after watching Hamilton show the steps to the tango.

Hamilton held his back straight and, with a slight tilt of his head, gave Miles a smile.

"Yes, quite nicely done," Albert said, bowing, with his hands folded in prayer.

Aileen nodded, hands folded, as if she had just finished her prayer. She looked down at her feet and moved closer to her husband.

"What's the question?" Dagmar asked. "I missed it. We were talking."

"We were all saying how much Hamilton looked just like he's been dancing all his life."

"Not quite," Frida said, giving Hamilton a once over.

"Oh, come on now," began Miles. "Course he does have that funny little thing he does with his feet, an extra step or something. Something funny is going on with you and stepping." Miles said, pointing to his feet.

"Yes. What is that?" Elise asked. "I've been trying to do that but can't quite get it right."

He stopped dancing. "Extra step? Something funny? I didn't know I did anything different," Hamilton said, embarrassed. All along, he thought he was improving. So that he wouldn't look so clumsy, he must have subconsciously added something.

One afternoon at the vineyard, during those years when he worked for his father, the grapes were a funny-looking yellowish orange or brown color. Hamilton washed them; maybe the color would change. His father said grapes were like people. They're not always perfect and you can't change them. Hamilton couldn't remove the color by washing them. That was the color. Some things were the way they were. A person can accept what's given to her/him or not. But not accepting does not change what's been given.

CHAPTER 14

Hamilton arrived at the studio, but it was closed. Franny had not arrived yet, and it occurred to him he had never received his own key. He had returned the one she had given him to open the studio on the day of the robbery. He took out his cell phone and tried to call her, but she didn't answer. He went back downstairs and headed toward the drugstore.

Franny came out of the drugstore and turned down the sidewalk in the opposite direction. Hamilton hastened his step to call out to her when he noticed she didn't have her crutches or her boot on, and she walked without a limp. She walked to the end of the shopping center and turned the corner. He went back to the studio and stood outside until she finally arrived, her boot on.

As she opened the door, "Good morning," he began, "Isn't it a beautiful day?" He couldn't think of anything else to say. It was either the beautiful day or let her know what he had just seen, and he didn't think that was a good idea.

In the office, Hamilton sat down at the computer and powered it up. Franny picked up some papers and began arranging them on her desk.

"This day reminds me of the time my mother had to dance in France," she began, her voice filled with sadness. "It was a beautiful day for a beautiful dancer."

Hamilton heard her sadness. It was as if she was thinking back, a once happy memory that now made her sad. "Why does this day remind you of that time?"

"I don't know. Maybe it's the weather."

"I'll bet you dance just like she did." Hamilton said. He opened to the web page he'd started creating.

"Oh, no. My mother was the best. She danced in Prague, in Paris, in Barcelona, Naples, Canada, New York and almost every place in the states and all over the world." Franny moved to the couch.

"It must be very difficult for you, trying to follow in her footsteps."

"Nobody could compete with her," she said in a half-whisper.

Hamilton gazed at her boot. "That must be uncomfortable," he said, nodding at the boot.

"Sometimes, but I need it."

"Have you tried walking without the boot?"

"It hurts a lot."

"What has the doctor said. He must have given you exercises or something."

"No. He said it'll heal better if I don't put any weight on it."

"You've never tried to walk on it? You've not tried to strengthen it?"

"No. I need the boot."

"You mean you need it to help your foot?"

"Yes, of course."

"Franny, this morning," he began. He faced her, eye to eye, gave a half-smile. He had to tell her.

She held a youthful innocence on her face.

"Franny, when you...," he began again.

"I mean, this morning...." He saw the swell of tears in her eyes. "I mean, of course, I—"

"Yes?" she said, the tone begging him with all the life she had not to ask the question.

"I mean, when did you take lessons?"

"Whenever she went anywhere, she took me and when she rehearsed, I took private lessons from her trainer." She sounded relieved.

"You've been taking lessons almost all your life?"

"Just about." Franny said. The two hardback chairs needed rearranging. She got up and placed one on each side of the room.

"Where have you danced, other than here, I mean?"

"New York. I was with a company in New York for several years. When my mother retired and opened this studio, she asked me to come here."

Hamilton stopped typing.

"Then she was diagnosed with Alzheimer's?"

"Yep." She slammed herself down on the couch and laughed. "This couch sinks in. Anyone who sits on this couch might not want to get up."

"Your studio, it's called Mazzie Hartman, your mother. You're operating under your mother's name?"

Franny stood up, hopped toward the door, and then turned around. "Yes, what's wrong with that?"

"I'm just asking for the website. I should put it on the website, right?"

"I don't see why not. It's still my mother's studio. You think I have to change it just because she's in a nursing home?"

"I don't know. I don't think so."

"I don't know what else to do," Franny said, and she left the room and the studio.

He didn't mean to push her so hard, but something was seriously wrong. He looked at the clock on the wall and saw it was time to begin class.

Marilyn was the first one of the 10:30 class to arrive.

"I have brownies," she chanted, holding up a bag. She handed them to Hamilton, standing just outside the office. "I made these brownies for you, Hamilton. I hope you will enjoy them."

Without waiting for a response, she went to the dressing room to change her shoes. When she came out, Hamilton had put the brownies on a table in the back and changed the music to note the start of the day's lesson.

"Today is waltz day, and I remember a few steps from long ago when I danced the waltz." Marilyn clumsily took quick steps, nodding her head the entire time.

"Looks like you're off to a good start."

"I don't remember everything, but I remember this part."

Carol, Robert, and Elise waved to Hamilton as they arrived and then went to change their shoes. Franny returned. The group assembled in the middle of the floor.

"Okay, today we begin the waltz," Franny spoke out to the group. Hamilton walked to the front and stood next to her. He demonstrated the steps as Franny called them out and then the students selected a partner for practice. After watching the students, Hamilton stopped

Carol and her partner to show them how to correctly bend the knee for the first step.

"But I'm already bending my knee."

"Yes, but you're not doing it right."

"This is the way I have to bend my knee."

He showed her how to do a deep knee bend. She tried it.

"Very good," he said. He pulled away when he realized he was trying to get her to do things his way. He felt good that he recognized it. Hamilton went to help Marilyn. He explained to her she was not turning enough to make the circle. He showed her how to step under so she could follow Emma, her partner, around the floor. Marilyn tried to take an even wider step. She lost her balance and fell to the floor.

"I think we should call an ambulance," Hamilton said.

"Do you hurt anywhere?" Franny asked.

"I'm okay," she began. "I tried to stop myself from falling, but I couldn't." She tried to get up. "I don't need an ambulance."

"Can you stand?" Hamilton reached for her to help her up. "Are you sure you don't want to go to a hospital?" Emma took Marilyn by the other arm to help her stand. Emma's hand touched Hamilton's. Hamilton turned his head toward Emma, then spun back to Marilyn.

"I'm okay." On her feet, she tried to take a few steps. "My hours at work changed and I haven't been able to eat right. Maybe that's it."

Hamilton turned to Franny, his back to the group, and spoke in an inaudible voice. "I have to walk her to her car."

When Hamilton returned, Emma showed the steps as Franny called them. Hamilton watched her. Emma turned to him and smiled.

In the office, Hamilton took a chance with Franny.

"Franny, why don't you take your boot off?"

"I can't do that. My leg hurts. I'm a slow healer." She turned and limped to the office.

"You haven't tried. Take your boot off and let your leg breathe for a while," he said.

"But—"

"Here. Sit down on the couch. Let me have your foot. I'll take the boot off for you."

Reluctantly, Franny sat down and rested her foot on Hamilton's lap. He undid the Velcro strap on the boot and eased the boot off. He set her foot on the floor and got one of her black dance shoes she kept in the office. He put her foot back on his lap and saw the foot was not swollen. He stretched the shoe, still looking for any swelling anywhere on her foot. It occurred to him that Franny said her foot and leg hurt. She couldn't make up her mind what was wrong. He put the dance shoe on her foot and fastened the strap. "Stand up," he said.

Franny stood up. She bent down to look at her foot, and tears ran down her face.

"Take a step, Franny."

"I can't," she said. She stood with all her weight on the other foot.

"Just one tiny step."

"I can't" she said again, tears still flowing, and she held out her arms to balance herself. Most of her weight still on the other foot.

"You've made a lot of progress. The shoe fits, and you stood. Maybe tomorrow we can work on taking a step." He didn't know what else to do.

Whenever HolliAnne or Anna cried, it would just go right through him. He couldn't stand the idea he couldn't help them and whatever bothered them was so bad they had to resort to tears. He found the best thing to do was to back away. This was one reason why he had to control his environment. When he didn't use control, things would go awry, and he would have to back away. When he backed away, he thought of himself as a failure; whatever bothered them was beyond his capabilities.

A man was supposed to protect his wife and family. He was supposed to keep sadness away from his wife and daughter so they could live a happy life. When he couldn't, he failed his family. Franny needed him. But he wanted to stop controlling. Wasn't that what everyone wanted him to do? He continued to fall into the muck he tried to dig himself out of. He couldn't fail her. He had to help her without controlling her.

CHAPTER 15

The following day, just as the 10:30 class was finishing, Hamilton got a phone call from Jeremy's school. He rushed to the school and headed in to see Christine White, the principal. HolliAnne and Todd Wilson sat in front of the principal's desk. Jeremy sat on the end next to Todd. HolliAnne sat on the other side of Todd.

"Stop lying, you know it's yours, you had it." Todd said, as Hamilton entered the office. Jeremy, in tears, squirmed about in his chair.

"Quit your crying. You're a baby? Huh?" Todd said, in a high, angry voice.

The principal, Christine White, stood when Hamilton entered the office and Todd said, "Man up, you know it belongs to you."

"What's this all about?" Hamilton asked. He stood behind HolliAnne. "Buddy."

Jeremy got up and stood beside his father. Relief came across his face, and he wiped at his tears.

Hamilton looked at Christine White. "What is this about?"

"We got the news this morning that drugs were being bought and sold on the premises. Since this is a middle school, it's my decision as to whether the police are needed. Before I involve the authorities, I thought it best to do a locker sweep first. When we got to Jeremy's locker, we found this inside." She held up a sandwich style plastic bag with a greenish brown leafy substance that filled about one third of the bag. "I asked to have Jeremy come to my office to talk about it and called his mother and you. Jeremy denies it is his but won't tell us who it belongs to."

"This is a surprise. Why am I just now hearing about this?"

"We just received this information this morning. We haven't had anything like this in a long while."

"How do you know what that is? Hamilton asked, pointing to the plastic bag.

"Well, I just—Christine began.

"Assumed?" Hamilton said.

Hamilton turned to his son and put his arm across his shoulder. "Buddy, is this yours?" He pointed to the plastic bag containing the greenish brown leafy substance in Mrs. White's hand.

"No, Dad."

Todd let out a sigh.

"Mrs. White, Jeremy said it's not his and if he says it's not his, then it's not."

"If it's not his, then whose is it, Jeremy?" she asked.

Jeremy didn't respond.

"Are you holding that for someone?" Mrs. White asked.

Jeremy didn't respond. He kept his eyes glued on the floor in front of him.

"Do you think someone found out about the locker sweep today and put it in your locker? You know the person who did it, just tell us," Mrs. White probed.

"Stop right there," Hamilton began. "This is a middle school. What's happening here is unbelievable. I don't send my son here to snitch on anybody, I send him here to learn. I expect you to provide a school where he can freely do that. You're asking him to do your job for you. You know who this stuff belongs to. You know exactly who it is. You go pick him up and make him confess, but don't make my son do something against his will and against our beliefs."

He turned to Todd. "Don't you ever," Hamilton bent down a little, pointed a finger on his chest and pushed his finger into him, "ever in your life, talk to my son like that again. If you do, I will ask the court for a warrant against you if you come within five feet of Jeremy again. You'd better understand that."

Todd gave an irascible glance at HolliAnne.

"Mrs. White, we have to leave now because only Jeremy's parents should be present at this meeting. We will talk later." He turned to HolliAnne and Todd. "I will let his mother know any decisions we come to during that conversation. For now, I'm taking Jeremy home. He will be back tomorrow for his classes, as usual. Let's get out of here, Buddy Boy."

In the car, on the way to the studio, tears ran down Jeremy's face. Hamilton pulled the car into a nearby parking lot of a small shopping center and cut the motor. He unbuckled his seat belt and turned to Jeremy, his back against the door.

"I, it, so embarrassed."

"You don't want to tell on the person?"

"It's not that."

"Buddy, if you know who did that, you need to tell."

"I don't know."

"Your principle seems to think you do. Why?"

"I don't know."

"Are you afraid? How many are there? If you're afraid they may do something to you, you need to tell me."

"No, Dad. It's none of that. It's that I don't know for sure."

"But you have an idea. Buddy, don't you think you have a responsibility to keep the place where you learn free of this kind of activity?"

"I don't believe that."

"What do you mean?"

"I mean, I don't believe that it's my responsibility."

"Sure, it is. You attend school there. It is your civic duty. It's everyone's right to live in an environment that provides safety and freedom from criminal activity."

"Yes, but the adults are responsible for keeping us safe. Not us; not in a middle school."

"No, Bud. It's everyone's responsibility to help keep the environment safe. If you know something, if you know who put that in your locker you need to tell your principle and let her know, now. She needs to know now."

"I'm not sure who did it. I can't just give out a name without knowing for sure, just to save myself." Jeremy unbuckled his seat belt. He looked over at his father. "This is bad, isn't it?"

"It's bad." Hamilton said. "It could get worse if the person does it to you again."

"I'm just not sure who did it."

"Maybe they think you know who did it."

"And if I don't tell, they could do it again?"

"They will think they could."

Jeremy looked at his father; fear filled his eyes.

"Bud, taking drugs of any kind, that's serious. It's also dangerous and against the law. By stopping this, you could save someone from becoming an addict, overdosing, being beaten or killed during a drug buy. This is urgent."

"What if I just name someone and that person had nothing to do with it? What's going to happen to me?"

"If you think you know, but don't know for sure, you have to tell Mrs. White who you think it could be, tomorrow."

"But, Dad, it's not right to accuse someone like that."

"You have an obligation to the students in your school. It's everybody's responsibility to help, not just the adult's responsibility. You guys do things we don't know about. You can't do things in secret and expect us to know about it when something dangerous happens."

"You're asking me to accuse someone to help society?"

"Your society, your school environment."

"I still don't think it's right. It can't be society over a person."

"Bud, I understand how you think about this, but I'm asking you to put that aside for now. I'm saying to you if you know or think you know who put that in your locker, then you have an obligation to your school, and for the safety of everyone in that school, to tell your principal, Mrs. White, what you know."

Jeremy looked at Hamilton, then cast his eyes downward.

"Do you understand?"

"Yes, Dad. I understand."

"Good, then talk to Mrs. White and tell her who you suspect. It's the right thing to do."

"You were right when you said she knew. If it's the two kids I'm thinking about, they've gotten into other trouble before, but I don't think they're involve in this," Jeremy said.

"Before? How long has this been going on?"

"There was one other time. But that was two years ago at the beginning of the school year. It was my first year."

He needed to be stern with Jeremy, but he also thought about Anna and how she would stand up for herself when she knew she was right. He didn't want to stop Jeremy from doing what he thought was right.

Both quiet, they sat together for a short while.

"Bud, think about what we just talked about. I hope you won't let this stop you from having your food drive for the homeless."

"No. I would like to have one for Thanksgiving and Christmas."

Later, Hamilton called Christine White. "First, let me apologize for the meeting getting out of hand," began Mrs. White. "I had no idea that Mr. Wilson would speak to your son in that manner. I thought Jeremy's mother would have stopped it, but you walked in just in time."

Hamilton explained to her that Jeremy would talk to her at school. He told her that Jeremy didn't know who put that stuff in his locker, but he could guess at it. He said she also knew who they were. Mrs. White said she had an idea, and she would start from there. Hamilton asked her to protect Jeremy since the boys may think Jeremy told on them. Mrs. White would do that. He also told her that Jeremy wanted to do the annual food drive for both Thanksgiving and Christmas. "I was hoping he would. The students love him," she said.

"We are a good team, you and me," Franny said to Hamilton as the 7:00 evening class members were leaving and heading down the steps.

Hamilton wanted to say something about her injury but didn't. After all, he needed her to know it was the eighth week and a sprain would have healed by now. But he couldn't find the words.

"Yes, we make a good team," was all he could get out, and that made him feel more like a traitor or an enabler than a friend.

"While you were away, I went to see my mother."

"That was nice. How is she?"

"I can see some improvement in her. I told her all about you and Jeremy and she would like to meet you."

"She's a little more alert and talking?"

"Oh, yes."

"That is improvement."

"I told her we'd come tomorrow. Is that okay with you?"

"Sure." Hamilton said reluctantly. This conversation made him very uncomfortable.

CHAPTER 16

The next morning, during breakfast, Jeremy told Hamilton that he had already signed up for junior varsity basketball. Tuesdays and Thursdays were practice days. Hamilton was a little nervous about this. The boy who put the marijuana in his locker could very well try to harm him, and basketball practice would be a time for that to happen. Hamilton told Jeremy to tell anybody who asked he was sent home and he couldn't say who put that in his locker because he didn't know.

After Hamilton put toast, scrambled eggs and bacon on Jeremy's plate and was dishing out scrambled eggs for himself, his cell phone rang.

A smile sprang out and grew across his face when he saw it was Anna, and he answered the phone. "Hello Sweetheart. How is everything going?"

"Everything is fine, Dad. I just called to remind you that I changed my schedule. I didn't want you freaking out or anything."

His smile vanished.

"You changed your schedule? I don't remember you telling me that." He tried to keep his voice even and remain calm. He sat back on the stool, took a deep breath.

He recalled the time when he put Anna in the Honors and Advanced Placement Program in high school. He just enrolled her. He didn't ask her what she wanted, whether she wanted to be in the program. When Anna found out, and only because her counselor handed her a new schedule, she was outraged. She insisted she didn't want to be in the program and refused to go to her new classes. She told her principal to remove her from the program. After a meeting with Hamilton,

HolliAnne, the counselors, her teachers and the principal, Anna participated in the program, but she made it clear the only way she agreed was because she was asked what she wanted. Anna demanded dignity and respect from him, the thing he did not freely give to his daughter. He disliked himself for disregarding her. She stayed angry with her father for the next day until he bought her a pint of her favorite ice cream. She had to give in then.

"I had a conflict with the times of two classes. They were too close together, so I went to see the counselor. She told me my schedule was too heavy and I could take a class in art to lighten my load. But she wanted me to drop a class. That would have made the schedule easier, but I didn't want to drop a class. The counselor suggested an art class, and I thought it would be nice. So, I added the class. It's only one day in the early evening. I thought it would be good for me. She also dropped me from one of the earlier classes and enrolled me in a later one. That also made it better for studying."

"Are you sure? I thought we did a nice job arranging your schedule. I thought we looked at the times and how much time you needed between classes." He looked down at his scrambled eggs he no longer wanted.

"We did, but we didn't know the location of the classes. The classes are too far away from each other, and I need more time between them. I didn't want to drop the science class. I want to get that out of the way. The art class is new and interesting and a nice break. I just wanted to tell you what I did, Dad."

He wanted to let her know how left out he felt, how useless he felt at this moment. But he could see how independent she was, making her decisions based on what was good for her. He couldn't say one word, and he held back for a moment longer.

"Dad, we, you rather, put a good schedule together. But I saw an opportunity. I hope this is okay with you."

He closed his eyes and took a deep breath. "Sweetheart, I'm just thrilled that you are such an independent young lady," he got out the half-lie, half-truth. But this, he realized, was no longer his.

"Dad, Thanks. That makes me feel good. The counselor and I changed one class for next semester, but other than that, she said that the schedule was perfect. That was because of your help. I'll let you know more about that next semester. How are things with you and the dance studio?" She gave off a chuckle.

"I'm still there." He didn't want to move to a new topic, but he didn't want to control his daughter. She had made it clear to him several times she was capable of running her own life.

"Dad, you overwork yourself. Take it easy for a while."

"I will, Sweetheart. I will."

"I guess you'll go back to work in a few weeks."

"I may or I may want to complete the sabbatical."

"Knowing you, you will go back to work sooner than that. But dad, try not to worry about everything. And please don't worry about me, well, maybe a little."

"Have you called Eric, yet?"

"See. Now you're worried about that. Yes. I did."

"I worry about you, but it's a different worry, now."

"I know, Dad."

Since her junior year in high school, he and Anna had gotten along better. She was becoming independent and self-sufficient. Before then, she argued with him every time he tried to do things for her. One day, when she had had enough, she screamed at him, "Stop trying to control me. Stay out of my life." He thought he was showing her love. She thought he was trying to control her. After that, he was very careful with her. He never intended to push her away. And since then, they hadn't argued about her life as much. "I love you, sweetheart. Take care."

During the 10:30 morning class, Franny had more energy and zest than she had since Hamilton began working at the studio. When the class ended, she was ready and standing at the door waiting for him so they could go see her mother. Hamilton hadn't forgotten about the visit; he just didn't know what to expect. The news earlier indicated a down pour and Hamilton didn't think it safe to leave the studio. Franny insisted.

He drove them to the Caring Hearts Nursing Home across town at the height of the downpour. It was raining so hard that Hamilton tried to pull over to wait for the rain to subside. But Franny became frantic and urged him to keep going. "We can make it. I can see. I'll see for you," she coaxed. Hamilton continued through the heavy rain but cut his speed.

"There, there, it's over on the right. Turn into the parking lot, here." She pointed. Hamilton turned.

"See, I told you we could make it." Like a happy little girl, she jumped up and down in her seat as they pulled into the parking lot and parked.

As soon as Hamilton cut the motor, the rain eased up. Franny jumped out of the car, forgetting about the weather, her leg, or ankle or whatever it was, and boot and all, and dashed into the home. Hamilton tried his best to keep up with her.

When she entered, she waved to the lady at the desk and took two visitor passes for them.

"You'll need name tags," the lady behind the information desk said.

Hamilton took a tag from Franny and put his name on it while Franny finished her tag.

They got on the elevator and went to the second floor. When the elevator stopped, Franny got off, turned right, and hobbled down the hall to her mother's room.

Mrs. Mazzie Hartman was dressed and sitting in a chair facing the window, her back to them.

"Hi, Mom. I'm back." She sang out as she walked to her mother and gave her a kiss on the cheek. "Why are you sitting in here? Let's go out on the veranda. The rain stopped and the sun just came out. Let's get a little sun. Would you like that?"

When Franny turned her mother around, Hamilton's face turned white as if all the blood had drained from his body. He could not move. After a few moments, he tried to put a smile on his face to mask the shock. Mrs. Hartman stared out with vacant, glassy eyes. She didn't move or blink and she didn't seem to breathe, except for a soft inhale and exhale.

She held the face of a once beautiful, youthful, vibrant woman who had grown wise and old over time, much like a faded ruby rose. Her look saddened him, and once again he realized how short and cruel life-the essence of time—could be. Her hair was colored a medium brown and styled in the way he had seen in her pictures–a shortcut with waves around the ears. Not one strand was out of place. She wore a dark green satin gown that must have been one of her dance dresses, now too large for her emaciated body. On her feet, a pair of black ballet shoes. She wore a single strand of pearls around her neck and what he thought were diamond and emerald rings on her right hand.

"Franny?" Hamilton said.

Franny turned to look at Hamilton with a "Please don't do this" look.

"Hello Mrs. Hartman. It's nice to meet you," Hamilton said, complying.

Mrs. Hartman didn't move or blink or do or say anything.

"Mother, I brought him like I told you I would," Franny went on.

Franny put a big heavy-looking blanket over her mother. She got behind her mother's wheelchair and pushed her down the hall to the glassed-in veranda. Hamilton followed.

The warmth of the sun seeped in through the glass. Outside, the brown and yellow leaves and branches offered them protection from the fullness of the afternoon sun. Hamilton observed the other residents in the nursing home sitting in wheelchairs or on cushioned chairs, glassy eyed and vacant stares. Franny pulled the blanket up to cover Mazzie's shoulders to protect her against the slight chill in the air, she said. Hamilton unbuttoned his coat. The nursing home was nestled back in the woods, that guarded them against the weather and surrounded them with a resplendent view of nature. Hamilton watched a deer chomping on something green.

Franny told her mother about the fact that she was going to give up the apartment and she was now sleeping in the back room of the studio. Hamilton was surprised to hear that. Franny told her mother how her leg wasn't healing and how it hurt. Mazzie slightly turned her head toward Franny.

"Mom, you know what I think about a lot? I enjoy thinking about the time you had to dance at the Austrian Embassy."

Mazzie let out a quiet grunt but continued to stare.

"It was decorated so beautiful with live flowers and green plants all around and you were on stage with your partner, Tim, just dancing all over the place. When you and Tim were practicing, I heard you tell him some of the dance steps were different and more challenging. Mom, you performed them with grace and a skill beyond anything anyone had ever seen. You remember? They had the lights cut down, and all eyes were on you. Your form was so perfect, and you were so elegant with your dark hair styled in a perfect ball." She touched her mother's hair. "You looked like you loved to dance, Mom, you looked like you were made to dance." Tears filled Franny's eyes, and she stopped talking for a moment.

Mazzie grunted again but didn't move.

"That sounds like a nice memory, Franny," Hamilton said to fill the silence. He regretted he couldn't think of anything better to say.

Franny continued as if she didn't hear Hamilton. "Mom, some students dropped out when you left, but a few of them stayed. I do the best I can. Hamilton," she pointed to him, "helps a lot. You'd be surprised at the difference he makes, especially with my leg and everything."

She paused for a moment to fiddle with a curl on her mother's forehead, as she must have done when she was a young girl. "I guess we should get back. Hamilton and I have a class in a little while."

Hamilton followed as Franny rolled her mother inside and down the hall and back to her room. She faced her mother toward the window.

"Mom," she began, tears filling her eyes again. "I love you and I miss you so much." She let out a loud sob. "I'm trying, Mom, I'm really trying. I wish there was some way for you to get better." She kissed her mother, turned, and walked out of the door. "Goodbye, Mrs. Hartman," Hamilton said, and he followed Franny out.

Neither of them said a word as they drove back to the studio. He felt Franny peeking at him, and he took a sneak peek at her; but they did not speak.

Hamilton wished he had never come to visit her mother. He found out too many things he didn't want to know. Her problem was apparent, but he didn't know what to do about it. Her mother could die any day. He had no idea Franny was living in the storage room next to her office. She talked so much about her mother, but she never talked about what was happening to her. He should have guessed something was wrong. And her leg not getting well, it was only a sprain. Many people sprain their ankle and walk okay the same day. She has had this boot on for eight weeks. She claimed the leg or foot, or whatever, still hurt and she was in pain daily.

Hamilton questioned whether the robber knocked her down. Maybe she just fell and claimed he did. Everything ended when the police caught the man. That must have been a stroke of luck for her. He couldn't pretend like everything was okay with her. She struggled with her fear. Franny deserved her own life. She needed to be her own person. "I'm trying, mom. I'm really trying." Hamilton wondered how many times she said that to her mother.

"I'm glad you met my mother," Franny said.

"Me, too." He was awakened to the fact that before he could have the love he wanted and needed, he first had to make himself a good person. But under the circumstances, he thought it would be acceptable for him to lie this time.

CHAPTER 17

The next day, when Hamilton arrived, Franny was not at the studio. She left him a note saying she was downstairs at the pharmacy. He couldn't get out of his mind that he knew more about her mother than he did her. He understood Franny wouldn't want to stay in their apartment alone. Franny was her mother, and without her mother, there was no Franny.

Hamilton was curious about what was inside the boxes she still had stacked in the office. He took down the box on top of one stack. Maybe he shouldn't do this. He was never one to intrude on anyone's personal life or go through their things. He never snooped on his kids to find out what they were doing or tried to get into any secrets they may have been hiding. Whatever was in the box belonged to Franny; he had no business looking in it.

He looked around at the other boxes, thinking if he saw one already open, he would assume it would be okay to look in the box. After all, it was open. But none of the boxes were open and none were taped or sealed, either. They were just closed by the crossing of the flaps. He didn't know whether that was worse or better. If she'd fixed them that way so she could open them easily, then couldn't he just take a peep inside?

He touched the top flaps of the box on top, the one he had placed on the floor. A loud slamming-like noise came from the hallway. He stopped and waited. No one entered the studio. If he opened the box and Franny had just things from the studio, nothing personal, then it would be okay for him to see those things. He was Franny's helper, and his job was to help her get organized. At any rate, he needed to see. If he invaded her privacy, then he would have to close the box. He would have to move quickly.

He slid a flap from under the flap, holding it down, and both flaps opened to the contents in the box. It was filled with photo albums of Franny's mother at ballet performances, on stage and on TV. Near the bottom were necklaces and other jewelry that looked expensive to Hamilton, though he didn't consider himself a jewelry expert.

He opened another box and the noise from the flaps seemed extremely loud, and he tried to remain calm while slowly opening the box. He found her mother's expensive-looking black and gold evening gowns and tailored suits and dresses with designer labels. The many dresses and suits were squashed down in the box, packed tightly, one on top the other and the bows and flowers and other ornaments on some were crushed. He held up an obviously tailored two-piece gray and white suit and a navy-blue silk dress. For a moment, the passing of time, an era gone by and the fact that our things can outlast us, brought him sadness.

A third box, heavy when he tried to lift it, and almost toppled over as he struggled to lift it, held china and silver items. Franny must have rolled it in on a cart or something. He inspected a china cup and saucer edged in gold. He felt like a spy, and he could no longer intrude. He was too worried she'd come in on him. He put everything back in place, or at least he thought he did. Then he closed all the boxes, and put them all back, stacked like she had them. Nothing came out of his intrusion.

He opened the door to the storage room, where Franny told her mother she was now living. He peeped into the storage room and saw more boxes, a single bed, small dresser, and TV. He hadn't noticed she was living in the storage room. When she left the door open from time to time, he saw the bed, but he never thought anything of it. He was too busy thinking about his own life; he didn't pay attention to Franny.

There was a door on the other side of the room that led to what he thought was a bathroom. The door jamb was filled with holes from the top to near the bottom where the door had once been nailed shut. He opened the door. It led to a small washroom, which led to the shower room in the dressing room, where the dance students changed and showered. Franny must have removed the nails when she decided to live in the studio.

Hamilton sat down at the computer. He worried about Franny, and what she could be planning. He had asked her to continue the spread sheet he started for her expenditures. He had asked her for her current bank balance, but she told him she didn't know it. She promised to get it for him or put it on the spreadsheet herself. He had fixed the spreadsheet so that with every deduction or addition to the account, the new balance would appear.

She should have updated the spreadsheet, like he suggested. He brought it up on the computer and saw nothing had changed. He wished now he had taken more control, but wasn't that his problem; at least one of them, according to HolliAnne? A slamming noise as if someone was coming up the steps to the studio grew louder and rattled him. He closed out the spreadsheet and looked around to see that everything was in place.

"Good morning." Hamilton said. He pulled up the website to see if anyone had signed up for the next session. Three people so far and he made a mental note to email them information about the classes.

"Good morning." Franny's limp was more pronounced as she made her way into the office.

"Everything all right?" Hamilton asked.

"Just fine," she said.

"Let's get started," Hamilton said. He went to get the music ready for the 10:30 morning class. The other members took places on the dance floor. Franny limped onto the dance floor.

"Why are you limping like that?" Carol asked, her face and brow squinted.

"Yes, your limp seems to have gotten worse. Have you seen a doctor?" asked Irene. "You really should go back to your doctor."

"You have insurance, don't you? You could just go back for a check-up," Carey said.

"Are you sure he didn't misdiagnose you?" Ronald began. "Maybe you should see a lawyer."

"Everyone. I'm fine."

"You don't seem fine," Robert said.

"You really should talk to your union rep and ask for the union lawyer. If you belong to a union, that is," Ronald continued, "It seems like you've been wearing that boot much too long."

"You've had that boot on since the second day. You should have someone look at it," Carol said.

"I can call my law office and find you an attorney, if you like," Ronald said.

"I think I might have re-sprained it coming up the stairs yesterday."

"Franny says she fine. Let's get started, okay?" Hamilton said. He started the music and motioned for Franny to begin the instructions for the waltz. Then he cut the music.

Franny was not just good at giving instructions; she was also a better dancer than she credited herself and he had to help her see that. The problem was, even though she'd done a good job teaching him, she'd done it without dancing, and he had not actually seen her dance. His first day when she showed them the steps and told them the different dances they would learn, there was no reason for her to dance. She just showed them some of the steps. But she had worked with her mother for years. Certainly, she was a better dancer than she thought she was.

"Ham? Are you ready?"

Hamilton positioned himself in a ready stance.

"Watch for the steps, now, everyone," Franny began. Hamilton followed Franny's instructions for the basic progressive steps.

At one time, Hamilton had wanted HolliAnne to learn to waltz with him. She often said they never did things together, so he suggested they learn to dance. But she didn't want to learn to dance. However, she went with him anyway. If she had learned to waltz, she would have enjoyed it and would have wanted to learn other dances.

But that never happened. All she did was complain about him stepping on her feet, which he would not have done had she moved them. She also complained about how he turned her, which he would not have had to do had she followed his lead and the instructions and turned in the right direction. So, they never learned to waltz. He went back to the class for the next week but dropped out after that week. It wasn't as interesting without a partner.

At the end of class, Franny announced that on the last day of class, she would ask each person to lead a dance. "Practice, so you can be a magnificent leader," she said.

The dancers went to the dressing room to change.

When Marilyn came out of the dressing room, changed into her street shoes, she asked Hamilton if she could speak to him in private. They stepped to the other side of the dance floor.

She looked down at her feet as if something were wrong with her shoes and she could figure it out by staring at them.

"Would you like to go to lunch? Now? That is unless you have plans."

"I don't—I—lunch — yes, okay." Hamilton tried to step away, but his feet wouldn't move.

"There's a nice restaurant a block from here," Marilyn said.

"Okay."

The waiter brought them a menu and then filled their water glasses. Hamilton ordered the salmon salad, and Marilyn ordered a hamburger.

He rearranged his water glass, lined up his silverware, and centered the candle that was already placed in the center of the table.

"I think I made you uncomfortable," Marilynn said.

"A little. This is all new to me. I'm newly divorced." He looked up at her.

"Oh. I didn't know. Should I say I'm sorry? About the divorce, I mean?" She smiled.

He chuckled. "If I were a sensible person, I'd say yes to that." He paused. "What about you?"

"Am I divorced?" She gazed at her water glass. "No. I dated a man for ten years. We finally got married, but I found out he was seeing someone else. And one day he left."

"Marilyn, I'm so sorry."

"We were into our first year of dating when he asked me to marry him. I didn't give him an answer, but we kept dating. I guess he thought I would change my mind. We lived together for about six years, and it seemed like we were married. I didn't think more of it. But he asked again. At first, I told him I didn't see a need. I liked what we had. The next day I changed my mind and a month later we were married in a small ceremony. Four years later, I came home from work and everything he had was gone. He left a blank sheet of paper on the bed, signed, and dated.

Hamilton sat forward in his chair and reached for her hand; but he didn't intend to take it. As she sat back in her chair, he slipped his hand from hers.

"You're the first person I've told, but I don't want to burden you."

"I have to say, though, you are the best student in the class. You've picked up those steps faster than the others." He had to change the subject.

"I have plenty of time to practice. I live alone and I work almost alone. There's not that much to do at the radio station."

At this moment, HolliAnne, looking as stunning as ever to him, and her boyfriend, Todd, walked into the restaurant. Hamilton was surprised to see HolliAnne, but then remembered they were in her kind of restaurant, upscale, with white tablecloths. Hamilton was a little nervous. He thought about how Todd spoke to Jeremy during the meeting at Jeremy's school. But HolliAnne and Todd walked past their table without noticing him.

Hamilton watched as the host seated them. As Todd pushed her chair in, HolliAnne looked around the room like she always did when they went out to eat, like she thought she was a celebrity and she looked for her fans and followers. HolliAnne saw Hamilton. She leaned in and said something to Todd. Then, got up from their table and came to Hamilton's table. She pulled back an empty chair and sat down.

"Ham, I called Jeremy, but he won't talk to me." HolliAnne began talking as if Marilyn weren't present.

"Marilyn, this is HolliAnne, my ex-wife."

HolliAnne gave a quick turn to Marilyn. "Hello," Then she turned back to Hamilton. "Can you ask him to talk to me?"

"What do you want me to say to him? He's hurt, HolliAnne. You and Todd accused him of something he wouldn't think of doing."

"I want to tell him how sorry I am."

"You let Todd talk to him—"

"I know, and I want to apologize for that, too. Todd and Jeremy" she turned to face Marilyn as if she suddenly remembered Marilyn was at the table with them, then turned back, "well, you know all that."

"Why don't you come by tomorrow, bring him your homemade cake he likes, and we'll talk to him."

"Thanks, Ham."

When she leaned toward him to get up, Hamilton thought she would give him a "thank you kiss," and he pulled back away from her. "HolliAnne, it would be best if you came alone."

"I understand."

Hamilton watched as she returned to her table. It seemed strange that Todd, who outright accused Jeremy, didn't bother to come to apologize.

"Was that about your son?" Marilyn asked after HolliAnne left.

"Yes. My son is one of the nicest thirteen-year-olds to walk this earth and his mother and her boyfriend can't get along with him."

After lunch, Marilyn asked Hamilton to drop her at the radio station for her producer's meeting. Marilyn was comforting. Even though she was hurt, she was also progressing her life; watching what she said, watching where she stepped. He could see them as friends. They were searching for the same things.

At the dance studio the next day, Hamilton searched for Franny, but like before, she was not there. He searched for a note but couldn't find one. He tried to remember their conversation from the day before and whether she told him she would go back to see her mother.

Since their visit to her mother, Franny wasn't as talkative as she'd been. In fact, she'd become downright quiet at times. He was sure it had something to do with him meeting her mother and witnessing her mother's present condition. He knocked on the door to the storage room, and no one answered.

He had finished responding to the inquiries on the website and was closing the computer when Franny came into the office.

"You think something's wrong with me, don't you?" She sat down in the nearest armchair. She had been crying.

"What's wrong Franny?"

"My mother. She will never recover, will she? Her doctor wants to talk to me about her prognosis," Franny said.

"When?"

"Tomorrow. You think I'm crazy, don't you?"

"Franny—"

"I know you do. The people in the class think something's wrong with me, asking about my leg."

"Is that what you thought they were saying?" Hamilton asked.

"They think I'm some kind of kook."

"What do you think, Franny?"

"I miss my mother so much. I never thought...." Tears crowded her eyes and overflowed. They ran down her face.

"What do you have to do, Franny?"

She looked down at the boot on her foot.

"The other day, we took that boot off and you could stand. Why don't we practice now?"

Franny stopped crying, wiped her face with the back of her hands. She reluctantly took the boot off. She rubbed her foot and winced a bit as she did. Then she stood. She grabbed onto the metal chair next to the desk. Hamilton tried not to help her.

"Can you walk? Try to take a step or two." She took a step but continued to hold on to the metal chair. She took another step and grabbed onto the desk, then back to the chair.

"How does it feel?" Hamilton asked.

"Funny. And it hurts a little." She paused and put her hand on her foot. "No, it hurts, it hurts." She said it like she'd just remembered her foot was supposed to hurt.

"Try to take a step without holding on to the chair. You can do that. I know you can."

She took another step, holding onto the chair and then let go. Her weight was on her good leg.

"That's good. Now take a step. Just take a step. Don't hold on to anything, just take a step," Hamilton encouraged.

Franny stood up straight. She put her weight on both feet. Then shifting her weight to the good leg, she lifted her sprained foot or leg and let it down easy.

"Good, good. Bring your left leg forward."

She brought her left leg forward.

"Good. Now take another step," Hamilton encouraged.

From the look on her face, she had, without realizing it, taken a step away from the chair and away from the desk. She tried to take another step but broke out in tears again and hopped over to the armchair where she could sit down. "I'm sorry, Hamilton. I just can't do it."

He wanted to throw that boot away and make her walk. She didn't need the boot. He saw her walk without it. But he couldn't do that. She had to wear her boot for now. She would see her own value soon.

CHAPTER 18

The final day of classes arrived. Even though time seemed to drag, it had sped by. Hamilton could hardly believe that a few months ago he was sitting in a courtroom getting a divorce and wishing his life would not take that turn. But he found he had no control, hard for a man who had a well-ordered life, and who had to control things.

During those months, he hadn't had time to think about his life, his divorce and where he was headed. Unsure, for a man who believed in working hard moving up the ladder. Over the years, he had moved from student to dean. He proved himself by doing whatever it took to do a better job. Some of the other vice presidents even said they wouldn't be surprised if he became a vice president of the university next. But here he was now, immersed in the traumas of a divorce and what he thought was a heart attack, but thankfully ended up being stress, that led him to a leave of absence where his shortcomings were unsheathed.

"Hey, Buddy Boy," Hamilton said when Jeremy came to breakfast. Hamilton put a glass of orange juice, a bowl of fruit, and an empty bowl on the counter in front of Jeremy.

"Morning, Dad." Jeremy said. "Cereal day. Good."

"You all set for today? You finished everything?"

"I got it all done."

"Why didn't you tell me your mother called?"

Jeremy looked as if he had been caught with his hand in the cookie jar.

"Bud?"

"I don't know. She was just going to accuse me and tell me I should tell who put that stuff in my locker."

"Buddy Boy—"

"Dad, she thought it was mine. She wasn't listening to me, she just kept accusing me. She and Todd said they knew it was mine."

"She hurt you. She didn't believe you."

"She always takes his side. They never listen to me. Todd accuses me of everything. If the lights are on, I did it. If something was moved, I did it. Mom believes it all, too. She never tells him I didn't do something; she always takes his side and asks me why I did it."

"Does he get violent with you like he did in the principal's office?"

"Sometimes she tries to shut him up, but he just keeps on."

"Is that all he's done? Yell at you?"

"He hasn't hit me or anything like that if that's what you're asking."

"Buddy Boy, you should have told me your mother called."

"I was afraid you'd get mad and remember what the doctor said about stress."

"You didn't think I would want to make that decision?"

"I'm sorry, Dad."

"No secrets, okay? Let's not keep secrets. I want to trust you."

"I know."

"Your mother's coming this evening after school."

Jeremy faced him and dropped his shoulders like a man giving up when he knows he's been beaten.

"She's coming alone, and I'll be right there. Okay?"

Jeremy let out a smile that said, "I knew it."

"Now let's get out of here before you're late for school."

When he entered the studio, Marilyn was already there and practicing, watching herself in the long mirror. "Dance with me," she said just before Hamilton got to the office. He nodded, put his things down in the office, changed his shoes to the new ones he bought, and was ready to help Marilyn.

"What are you doing?" Hamilton asked.

"You mean you didn't recognize it? The fox-trot," she said and laughed.

"Don't call the steps or count out loud," he said.

"Right," she whispered.

"Ready?"

They slow, slow, quick, quick stepped around the studio, holding their bodies the way Franny told them. He moved with straight legs and took long steps. She moved with him, floating around the studio like clouds drifting across the sky. Her head was tilted in the right manner, and he felt the warmth of her breath on his neck as she exhaled. His hand on her back, he could feel the excitement and confidence in her body as she moved toward him, away from him and again, toward him. He liked the way her body talked to him, beckoned him, teased him, the style of the fox-trot. The other students poured in, and Marilyn and Hamilton brought their practice to an end.

In the middle of class, the office phone rang. Franny paused to answer it while Hamilton continued with the class. After a few minutes, Franny returned and carried on with the class. "It's now your turn to show what you've learned," she said, looking straight ahead. No one seemed to notice her vacant stare, except for Hamilton.

At the end of the final session, all the students, on the way out, said they had signed up online for the next session and they enjoyed the lessons. Hamilton asked Marilyn and Emma if they had signed up and they had. Marilyn would have to join the morning class since her hours had changed at the radio station. Emma said she had to sign up for the evening class, but she may have to change. After everyone left, Hamilton hurried to the office to ask Franny about her phone call.

"That was my mother's home. They said I needed to come right away."

"Why didn't you say something?"

Franny didn't speak. She faced Hamilton, but she didn't say anything.

"Let's go," he said.

"The nursing home called because they expected my mother to pass any minute and they thought I'd want to be present to say my final goodbyes," Franny said as Hamilton drove them to the nursing home.

After they arrived, Hamilton went into the room with Franny. Franny looked down at her mother lying in the bed, arms at her sides. She said they should pray silently. Hamilton's attention was on her mother's shallow and audible inhale and exhale. He held his breath when she missed an inhale or exhale. He had never seen anyone die, and he was uneasy. But Franny needed him; and he couldn't let her down. It was just the two of them now. They were there for most of the afternoon, only leaving to take turns to the restroom. He needed to ask her for the name of the funeral home where they would take her body, but he couldn't bring himself to get the question out.

He cast his eyes all around the one room her famous mother had lived in for the past three years. The closet still open, someone must have forgotten to close the door, got his attention. Her satin evening gowns, rich in blues, greens, lavenders, and blacks, elegant and gorgeous, hung on the rack with a space between each gown. Her white ballet shoes lay discarded on the shelf above the rack, one turned on its side. He looked for the black pair she had on the day he met her. They lay empty and lost on the floor next to her bed. Franny had fixed the room and closet as if her mother would return and use these things again. He moved to the pictures of her mother as a beautiful youthful woman, dancing on a stage. He wondered what she thought about while she danced. Was she concerned about making the next turn, or how she looked sailing through the air or whether she executed her step exact enough for her to successfully complete a series of turns? Or maybe she just let her body take over. He wondered if she was thinking anything now, whether she had regrets, sorrows, satisfaction, glee. Or was she thinking she led a satisfied life. Hamilton looked over at Franny and hoped she would accept the loss of her mother; live her life without her mother.

By late afternoon, her mother had not yet passed, and they left. Franny had to get ready for the last evening class. Hamilton left to get Jeremy from school.

"Did I tell you I made the junior varsity team?" Jeremy took out his schoolbooks and placed them on the table in the family room.

"That's great. I want to see you play." He looked over at Jeremy. He hadn't expressed an interest in basketball until recently. Who was he trying to impress? Hamilton picked up clothes and handed them to

Jeremy. He then dusted the furniture and straightened the pillows on the sofa and armchairs.

"Your Sunday school teacher emailed me saying he had contacted the homeless shelter and they are expecting you guys to make food and serve it on Saturday. Hamilton straightened the furniture, put the chairs and tables back in their original places.

"I volunteered last Sunday and signed up. Is it okay with you?" Jeremy put the footstool in front of Hamilton's favorite leather chair.

"Buddy Boy if you want to. I'll try hard to get along without you." He ruffled Jeremy's hair. Jeremy couldn't duck out of the way in time. Jeremy didn't like him rustling his hair like he used to.

The doorbell rang, and Hamilton went to let HolliAnne in.

"Buddy Boy. Your mom is here." He ushered HolliAnne into the living room and she went to the armchair she always sat in, the one she used to call her chair. Hamilton didn't like the idea she thought she still had a place in his home, but he tried not to show her how he felt. Jeremy entered the living room looking hesitant. He gazed around the room and took a seat next to his father on the couch opposite HolliAnne.

"It's just the three of us. Your mother wants to talk to you."

"Jeremy, I don't want you to get mad at your father. I asked him for this meeting, okay?"

Hamilton looked down at his shoes to avoid contact with Jeremy. Even though Hamilton thought she only said it to make herself look better in Jeremy's eyes, he needed Jeremy to accept his mother.

Jeremy didn't answer.

"I just want you to know that I am so sorry about what happened, and the way Todd talked to you. He was out of line, and I told him so."

"You told him about how he spoke to me?" Jeremy said it like he didn't believe her.

"Yes, I did. He admits he was wrong. But your father and I thought it was best that only I come today. I just want you to forgive me. I should have believed you."

Hamilton's thoughts went to the afternoon when he was in the restaurant with Marilyn, and he saw HolliAnne and Todd. Todd never came to the table to apologize.

"Mom, you do that all the time and it's gotten worse with Todd around. For some reason, he just doesn't like me. I try to make him like me, but he just doesn't."

"I know, and I don't like it. I just want you to know that if anything like that ever happens again, I won't involve Todd."

"I've fixed that. I reminded the school and church that Jeremy lives with me. I'm the custodial parent. I've also filled out papers, again at church and at school, so that both places know to call me. The secretary, when she called, said they had made a mistake and called you first. But that won't happen again."

Jeremy sat back on the couch, a smile dancing around his mouth.

"I want us to be on friendly terms, Jeremy. I want you to call me when you need something, talk to me about things when you need. Understand? I want us to be mother and son, again."

Hamilton wanted to challenge the word "again," but he didn't. She couldn't believe she and Jeremy ever had a mother and son relationship. Did she tell her coworkers she did, and did she tell that to Todd?

"Jeremy, I would like for you to move in with us."

Hamilton stood. "What are you trying to do, HolliAnne? You can't just come in here and do that. Remember our divorce decree. My son is not some pawn on a chessboard that you can just move around at your pleasure. I gave you a schedule, times when you can see Jeremy. Abide by that schedule."

"You gave me a schedule you created. As usual, you didn't bother to consult me."

"The schedule I gave you considers Jeremy. You need to follow that schedule. There's nothing on that schedule about Jeremy living with you."

"It would be better if Jeremy lived with us, that's all."

He walked to the door and opened it for her. "It's time for you to go."

"No, Ham. Jeremy shouldn't be here with your health problems the way they are. What if you have to go back to the hospital or have an operation or something?"

"I'm fine and when were you ever concerned about my health?" He paused for a moment. HolliAnne used to change the subject when she found it difficult to think of something to say when they argued.

"I've always been concerned about you. I just didn't think you cared"

"Not this way." He shook his head.

"You know I don't have a job, anymore," she said, as she tried to hold back tears.

There she goes again. She wants him to feel sorry for her. "I tried to help you. I tried to get you to reach higher. But you refused. You'd still have that job now, if you'd done what I asked, but you didn't."

"I tried, Ham. I did. You know that." Tears running down her cheeks.

"No, you didn't. You didn't want what I thought you could have. You always wanted to be a pre-school teacher, now go be one."

"I've applied for a few jobs, and I wasn't accepted. You know why? They said I was overqualified. You've fixed it so I can't get a job anywhere. I just can't win."

"Jeremy is staying here, HolliAnne. You may see him according to the schedule I gave you."

"Jeremy—"

"Mom, I have my own room here where I can study and a computer where I can look up things when I need to. At your apartment, I only had that storage area. When Anna went to New York, Todd took the storage room back. He said he needed it for his study."

"Goodbye, HolliAnne," he said louder than he wanted to.

HolliAnne left, and Hamilton was happy to close the door behind her.

Hamilton's face was red, and veins popped up, almost ready to burst. His hands were balls of fists. He tried to calm himself and breathe in and out, slowly. She and Todd must have problems, but he couldn't let that involve Jeremy. HolliAnne wanted the divorce. The fact that she wanted Jeremy to live with them must mean she needed Hamilton to support her, but it would end up being support for her boyfriend, as well.

When Hamilton and Jeremy arrived at the studio for the 7:00 evening class, he found Franny at her desk, crying. She had a crumbled tissue she was still using to wipe her tears. The door leading to the storage room was open and Hamilton got another glance inside.

"Bud, can you start your homework? The table in the back by the dressing room is all cleared off."

"Okay," Jeremy said as he walked toward the table in the back.

"Did the nursing home call?" Hamilton asked.

Franny nodded as she continued crying. She tried to stop but continued with loud, hard sobs. "They asked me where they could send her body," she struggled to say.

"Where did you tell them," Hamilton asked.

"I don't have a place. I was hoping, hoping. I don't know what I hoped."

"Let's find a place. Do you want a burial or cremation?" He sat down at the computer.

"They gave me two recommendations." She handed her notes to Hamilton.

"Franny, burial or cremation?" Hamilton took the notes and called both places. He got a cost for cremation and one for burial.

"Can I have her cremated if I want a church service?" Franny asked after he hung up.

"I'm sure you can. Many churches have crematories. What's the name of your church? Call them and let them know."

"I'll get it for you. I didn't attend much, but she did."

"Franny, why don't you get everything together? Her church name and number, call them, talk to them about cremation and call the funeral home and have your mother taken there. Jeremy and I can handle your last class."

"But I don't know. ... Can you, do it?"

"Franny. I can help you. I'll be glad to, but you must see to it. You can ask the funeral home to have a small service for her. But you need a funeral home that will cremate her if that's what your mother wanted."

Hamilton went out into the studio to the last day of the evening class. He could do what Franny wanted. One day, she will look back on this time and he wouldn't want her to question why, after a lifetime of love and devotion to her mother, she didn't see to her burial.

CHAPTER 19

At the studio, Hamilton found Franny sitting behind the desk at the computer, squinting at the monitor, one finger tapping the keys. He was surprised to see her so early and on the computer.

"Hi," she said without looking up, eyes moving left to right across the screen. She sat on the edge of the chair with her face close to the screen like an amateur dancer, not wanting to miss the cue.

"Morning," he began, "how did you sleep?" He sank down in the couch.

She was garbed in her bedclothes. "I didn't. Well, off and on." She paused. "I got up to look at the website you wanted me to see the other day." She turned her head. "Thank you for this. All these pictures of my mother and the places where she danced. Ham, it's a nice tribute to her."

"She's your inspiration."

"Yes, she is. And you added three new classes to next session."

"Franny, I need you to talk to me."

She turned to him, then turned her head downward. "I decided to have her cremated. I called one of the funeral homes and they said they would get her sometime this morning." She glanced at Hamilton, and then looked away. "Would you go with me to the home? I just want one last look at her before they take her."

"Sure."

Hamilton and Franny stood there in the refrigerated room of the nursing home, where her mother's body lay, and where the frigid air settled on his arms and back, causing him to cross his arms to ward off the chill. He looked down on the once worldly renowned ballerina, Mazzie Hartman. An empty, sick feeling overtook him, as if he had missed out on something he would never retrieve, much like a married man who missed his wedding anniversary. He wished he had met her. He tried to think why he hadn't at least heard of her; and what he had done so important in his life, he missed seeing Franny's mother dance. He wished he could have seen her in the news wearing one of her designer suits in an interview, answering questions about where she had been and where she would go. For some unknown reason, Hamilton wished he could have seen Mazzie on stage everywhere, with her dance partner, taking those daring ballet movements and steps Franny described to him. The steps where she, with her white ballet slippers, twirled and flipped and split and moved her body in every inconceivable and conceivable way. He wished he had known why she loved ballet so much, and he wished he had known her as she danced with so many worldly and renowned people and ballerinas. For Franny's sake, he wished he had known her.

When two men from the funeral home arrived, Franny handed them an envelope, and they put Mazzie Hartman on a stretcher and took her body out the back door of the nursing home.

Afterward, Hamilton and Franny went up to her mother's room, where they put her mother's clothes, jewelry, cosmetics, and other things, in plastic bags and like vagabonds—transient people, people who move from place to place — carried them to his car. Hamilton opened the trunk for Franny. He tried to take her bags and put them in the trunk for her, but she pulled away and put them in herself. Franny had used her injured foot and ignored her mother's failing health to reject the idea her mother would never come back, and Franny would have to carry on her life without her mother.

At the studio, Franny took the plastic bags and put them in the storage room.

"Franny tell me why you live here. What happened to your apartment?"

"Nothing happened to it. I still have it. But I want to sell it." She got a bottle of water for herself and handed Hamilton one. "It was just hard for me to stay there without her."

"You two were extremely close. When did she teach you the ballet?" Hamilton sat down on the couch.

"When I was about eight. She tried to teach me, but I was awkward, so she got me a teacher."

Hamilton took a sip of his water. Then he looked at her as if he wanted her to say more.

"I started picking it up better when I was about ten or eleven. I was a late bloomer. I just wanted to be like her. I would watch her, her movements, her body, her love for ballet and that's what I wanted." She smiled, an almost laugh. "When I told her I was ready to learn, she was so happy. She asked my teacher to double up on the lessons."

"Did you want to be a ballet dancer?"

She seemed stunned by his question. "It took me years to develop a passion for ballet. My mother had it for as long as she could remember. And when I did, we had something in common and she loved me. I mean, she loved the idea that we both loved the ballet."

"Did you?"

"What?"

"Did you love the idea that you two had ballet in common?" He took a sip of water.

"Of course." She gave him a look of incredulity.

"What else did you two have in common?"

"That's mostly what she did. Ballet consumed her. Everything was ballet," she whispered.

"What about you?" He faced her, eye to eye. "Did you feel left out?"

Franny got up from the computer, went toward the storage room, and returned to her seat at the computer. She took a sip of water. "Sometimes," she held a quiet smile, staring into the emptiness, "but my mother was a prominent ballerina—"

"I know, Franny. You've told me that before." He sat back on the couch.

"But why—"

"I don't mean to upset you. Your mother was a world-renowned ballerina. Tell me about Franny." He heard her trying to control her voice.

"What do you want me to say?"

"You said that your mother was consumed with ballet. Maybe you thought she didn't have time for you unless you liked ballet, too." He knew the ground he was treading, but he needed her to face the truth.

Tears rolled down Franny's face. "I know she loved me. I know she did."

"I'm sure of that, too, Franny. But we're not talking about your mother, we're talking about you. Did you think that?"

Her lips opened as if she wanted to say something. Then she closed them. After a moment. "Yes, I think so. Maybe when I was little, I did."

"You were eight. You wanted to play with the other children, go to school, maybe."

"I remember asking my mother if I could go to the elementary school in our neighborhood. When she had to leave to perform, she always took me with her."

"You had little chance of being with other children."

"Not much."

"But your mother was proud of you after you started catching on, right?"

"Yes. And when I got older, we danced together, many times," she said, more excitement filling her voice.

"That must have been nice. Everyone congratulating you both."

"Mostly her. I wasn't as good as she was. I couldn't even come close to her. We danced together, but only at dance studios, introductory performances, high schools, and things like that. I was never good enough to dance in places where she danced."

"When your mother opened the studio, she taught the dance classes and did you teach, too?"

"She let me teach sometimes. I had more patience with little girls than she did. She always said that. But I called out the dance steps while she danced them, and I selected the music. She always said I had a good ear for music," she said smiling.

"When did you stop dancing?"

She turned to him. "How did you know that?'

"From you, just now."

"My mother wanted this studio. I just wasn't as good as she was. That's all there was to it."

"How do you know?"

"That I wasn't as good?"

"Yes. You've said that I don't know how many, but many times. How do you know you weren't as good?"

"She never said that if that's what you mean. But I could tell she thought it often enough. I was clumsy. Sometimes I couldn't remember the routine and my feet just wouldn't go in the right direction. She didn't have to say it. I knew it."

"But you are good at one kind. It's not ballet."

"What kind is that?"

"You're good at ballroom dancing. I saw you my first day." He paused to decide whether he should go on. He'd gotten this much out of her; he just had to go on with it and say the other things on his mind.

"Can't you see you've been trying to carry on something your mother wanted for her? Ballet was her. But it's not you. You're good at ballroom dancing, Franny, and from what I've seen and been through these past eight weeks, I can tell you they are two very different things. Your mother is gone, now. You can honor her by being the best ballroom dancer and teacher you can be."

"It's funny that you're saying all this. I've been thinking about that a lot since my mother, but I thought reducing myself to ballroom dancing would be an insult to her."

"I hope you don't believe that."

"I understand, Ham."

"Now you have to do one more thing."

She gave him a stunned look, as if she knew what he would say, but hoped that he wouldn't.

"Take off your boot and give it to me."

She sat down, took the boot off, handed it to him, and massaged her foot. There was no swelling and her foot looked like a normal foot, as far as Hamilton could tell.

"Try to stand," Hamilton said.

She stood up and walked around the room without limping. "A ballroom dancer, you say?"

"A really talented ballroom dancer."

She turned to him and smiled.

"I'll help you move back into your apartment when you're ready. You can let me know what you want to keep and what you want to give away."

As he turned to leave the office, he bumped into Marilyn and Emma.

"We wanted to bring you our checks for the winter session," Marilyn said.

"You could have done this online," Hamilton said.

Emma handed him her check. "Thank you." She left.

He watched her walk away as Marilyn said, "I know I could have, but I thought if I came in person, I could talk you into having a late lunch with me," Marilyn said.

Hamilton gazed at Franny. "That would be nice, but we're not finished here."

"That's okay, you go ahead," Franny said.

"You can pick the place this time," Marilyn said. She made it sound like a game she played to find the best restaurant.

He wasn't sure how to take Marilyn. She seemed to pop up like she did minutes ago. When she arrived, he didn't hear her come in, yet when he turned around, there she was. He almost bumped into her. She was like that, just showing up at the oddest times. She had a beautiful face and at times she was almost childlike when she said she needed help.

During lunch, they talked about her job at the radio station before he asked, "Do you have plans for Friday?" She had to look at her calendar. He liked her and wanted to find out more about her.

He knew this was not a risk-taking opportunity, but he was getting closer and closer.

CHAPTER 20

Hamilton and Jeremy entered the side door off the parking lot of St. John's Episcopal Church to meet the other youth members who had also volunteered to make lunches for the homeless men's shelter. Hamilton's face was lit up like a Christmas tree and a long smile from left to right was displayed across his face as he followed his son to the kitchen, where the youth group was to meet. Ben, the youth leader as well as Jeremy's teacher, had already determined the menu. They bought turkey burgers, veggie burgers, hamburgers, and makings for a salad. Several bags of groceries sat on the long metal tables used to prepare food. Three boys and two girls were unloading some of the bags and separating the vegetables, the meats, and rolls into groups on separate tables. Ben asked Jeremy to get bowls and strainers from the pantry. Ben told Hamilton that the group would make the lunches and then take them to the shelter. Ben also said that the shelter already had servers and if the kids weren't needed, he would take them for pizza.

Hamilton nodded.

"Robert's parents volunteered their home for movie night for the kids after pizza," Ben said, and he gave Hamilton Robert's cell phone.

Hamilton turned to leave. Jeremy, his youngest son, now growing beyond his world of thinking about himself and into a wider realm, the community. Jeremy needed the space to maturate toward that end. HolliAnne would be sorry later when she realized she had missed so much of his life.

Just before he reached his car, Hamilton's phone rang. He smiled when he saw the number.

"This is a pleasant surprise."

"I'm returning your call, even though I don't have to." Eric said, laughter in his voice.

"You get a check mark for that," Hamilton said, and laughing. "How's it going? Classes going okay?"

"I love my classes. One of my psychology classes started out being a little tough, but I got my average up, way up."

"That's my boy. Your car holding up?"

"I don't drive. Usually I walk."

"That must mean you're doing a lot of studying."

"I'm very familiar with the library." He paused for a moment. "As you often told us, you lived in the library when you were in college."

"That, I did."

"Dad?" He paused again. "I may not be home for Thanksgiving."

Hamilton didn't respond.

"Paige and I started seeing each other exclusively, now. She wants to get married and wants me to meet her family on Thanksgiving."

A sick feeling sat in the pit of his stomach, like the times when he had to interview for his jobs at the university. During those times, his voice tremored, and his nervousness showed in his shaky hands. This time, he cleared his throat and composed himself.

"Married?" He tried to say it calmly, as if it were a matter of fact. He paused, trying to figure out what to say next. Then, "That's a big step, son. I know you know that. Is there any reason you have to get married before you graduate?"

"She wants us to get married and start a family."

"Is that what you want?" Eric didn't respond, and Hamilton took advantage of the opportunity. "Wouldn't getting married make it harder for you to provide for your family? And if she stops now, will she ever finish?"

"She doesn't see it that way."

"What do you want?"

"I want to graduate first. Think about marriage later. I want a Ph.D. I understand your thinking; getting married now would make things more difficult."

"You're right. You have your answer."

"I'll let you know about Thanksgiving."

"You wouldn't want to miss out on Buddy Boy's birthday."

They laughed.

"Dad...."

"I will, you, too."

"Love you, Dad."

"Love you, too, Eric." Hamilton was proud of himself for not telling his son what to do; for not controlling his son.

He knew this day was coming but hadn't expected it so soon. Even though he was filled with joy, he didn't think they should get married. He was thankful that he was close enough to Eric that Eric would think to call him before anything happened, like taking off and getting married. He wanted Eric to know he supported him and encouraged him as he passed to the next life stage — graduating from college and living his own life.

Franny, when Hamilton arrived, was ready and waiting in the office. He had taken his black jacket out of the car and put it on over his white shirt and dark gray pants. Franny was dressed in one of her mother's black ankle-length gowns with a wide pleated skirt and sequins around the neckline. She donned a small black box-style hat with a veil that covered her face and reached down to her nose. Hamilton was a little skeptical when he saw her, especially after the conversation from the day before. Her face held a frightened look when she gazed at Hamilton. Not knowing what else to do, he smiled.

"I just got the idea to put this on. So, I did." She looked down at herself. "Is it too much for her service? What do you think?" She sounded and seemed uncomfortable.

"It's a beautiful dress," Hamilton began, "You look nice in it." He could just kick himself every time he said something encouraging and he shouldn't have.

"I thought it would honor her." She twirled around in the dress and suddenly she appeared as a child, seeking approval from her mother. As she continued to twirl, he saw her as an adult, a dancer with her head and back straight as she faded into another world. And he saw himself as a child, and as an adult, wanting his father's love like Franny wanted her mother's love.

"Are you ready?"

With her question, he brought himself back to the present.

Franny said her mother had no other friends but the ones in the nursing home. She had been in that home for about the past three years, according to Franny, and the friends she had who were not in nursing homes stopped coming after the first six months. "The people at the nursing home said that's what normally happens," Franny said.

The church provided a protestant service for her mother. Only Franny and Hamilton attended. After the service, they walked to the church owned mausoleum. Franny cradled the urn, all that was left of her mother, as they walked to the crypt. She placed the urn inside. The priest asked her to step back. He closed the vault and locked it.

Later, Hamilton drove through the parking lot of the radio station looking for a parking space. He parked in the last visitor's space, got out, and headed for the entrance to the station. Marilyn was waiting in the hallway for him when the elevator doors opened to her floor.

"What is this surprise?" she asked, getting on the elevator.

Hamilton punched the button for the first floor. "Do you like art?" he asked before he took her to some place she didn't like. It wasn't too late for him to change if she didn't.

"I love art," she said.

Hamilton relaxed a little. "An artist friend is having a showing this evening. I thought we could go. He'll be there to discuss his pieces, and they have food and wine."

The modern-looking gallery with its recess lighting, plain white walls and wood floors was crowded with men and women of all ages and ethnicities standing around eating, drinking, and talking. The only things missing were seats. In the exhibit rooms, few people were looking at his friend, Calvin's, art pieces that hung around the four long walls, their titles, and a short description, along with the prices just below them. Hamilton often thought art gallery openings seemed more like social gatherings where people got their dinner and caught up on what's been going on in each other's lives. Marilyn made her way through the crowd to a painting.

Hamilton stood next to her as they admired the picture of a flower. He turned his head in all directions, trying to get a better view. "What kind of flower is this?" he asked. He turned his head again. At first glance, it appeared to be an orchid, but taking a harder look, it had the appearance of an animal, maybe a wolf, then it seemed to change to a bird, then, the picture seemed more like some kind of fruit.

"That's scary, huh?" Marilyn said.

"It's different."

"Look at the price," Marilyn said.

They moved down the wall and studied each painting, as if there would be a test later. He liked the way she looked at him, big-eyed and excited as she tried to explain each painting and why she thought Calvin painted it. Her eyes had a happy sparkle and reminded him of Fourth of July fireworks — the beam revealed her happiness being with him. She seemed closer to him than she was, and he could feel her slight turn to him. Her perfume was intoxicating as she reached across him to point to something in the picture they'd stopped to view. When she brought her hand back, it brushed against his arm and for a moment he was enlivened, renewed. The spark of life that made him realize the darkness in which he had enshrouded himself had also closed him off to the romantic world. A slight perspiration broke out around his temples and, recognizing his nervousness, he excused himself and went to get them wine.

Hamilton returned with the wine and handed her a glass. The last painting on that wall depicted a man and woman sitting on a park bench while children played ball on the grass in front of them. For some reason, he thought of HolliAnne. He and HolliAnne were invited to an opening at an art gallery just before she took the counselor's position at the university. She knew her way around the gallery and Hamilton thought she'd been there before. The artist seemed to know her and addressed her by name. She never introduced Hamilton to the artist. Later, when they were home, Hamilton mentioned to her she never introduced them. She said she thought she had. He asked her if she'd been there before, and she said she'd passed it from time to time on her way somewhere. Her responses never sat right with him.

"Doesn't this picture make you think about your childhood?" Marilyn asked after they moved to the next wall, bringing him back from his thoughts.

He took a sip of wine.

Calvin found them. Hamilton introduced Marilyn to Calvin.

"These are different," Marilyn said.

"You're very good," Hamilton said. "How in the world did you capture this using oil? That must have been difficult. Like the orchid over on that wall?" He pointed to the first wall.

"Oil, to me, is the most challenging. Once you put it on the canvas, it has to be correct or as exact as you need it to be because it is so difficult to correct an error."

A woman, whom Hamilton took to be someone in charge, came to pull Calvin away. Someone was ready to purchase a painting, and it was customary for the artist to talk with them. While they were looking at the pieces of sculpture in wood, a woman passed through the crowd.

"Number 71? Number 71."

"What does that mean?" Marilyn asked Hamilton.

"I don't know. Unless...." He took out the two tickets he bought. After looking at the numbers, he handed one to Marilyn.

"This says 71."

The woman must have overheard her. "71?" She asked, "Then you're the winner." She left.

"Winner? No, Hamilton, you bought two tickets. This is your ticket." She tried to hand it back, but Hamilton refused to take it.

"No. It's yours."

The woman returned with a print. She handed it to Marilyn. "Calvin will sign it for you if you would like." She pointed to where Calvin stood talking to a man and woman. Hamilton took her elbow and directed Marilyn to Calvin after the two people stepped away.

"Guess what happened?" Hamilton said to Calvin.

With a big grin on her face, Marilyn handed Calvin the print.

"I'm thrilled to know you won this." Calvin took the print and signed it.

After they finished admiring the paintings in the museum, Hamilton took her to the dinner he had promised. Marilyn didn't know it, but through her easy manner and friendship, she helped him be more at ease.

He pulled up to Robert's house, where Jeremy waited outside. A girl came out and kissed him on the cheek.

In the car, Hamilton turned to Jeremy. "Who was the girl?"

"That's Sarah."

"She's also in your class at school."

"Yes. And Dad, you're right. I like her. Don't tease me about it."

"What's wrong?"

"She has a boyfriend."

Hamilton had to remind himself that Jeremy was thirteen. He was thankful Jeremy was interested in doing something important with his life. He thought about Franny and realized that he wanted Jeremy, his Buddy Boy, to grow up being Jeremy rather than a replica of him. He had to give Jeremy the space he needed to grow and be who he wanted to be.

CHAPTER 21

November, the entire month, was all about Thanksgiving for Hamilton. The Thanksgiving holiday and the fact that Thanksgiving occurred during fall, his favorite season, couldn't have been a more perfect gift for him. He loved the colors of leaves changing from greens to earthy reds, oranges, and browns. He liked to see the trees emptying themselves of leaves and limbs as they prepared themselves for the chilly and icy winters. When he was a boy, he would try to catch the leaves as they fell. He loved the hint of the impending purity and sterility of the air.

On Thanksgiving, he looked forward to an entire day where he and his family would spend most of the time in the kitchen cooking and running to the TV to see the next play of their favorite football team. Then, when a score was made, high fiving each other or when one was not, yelling at the TV, giving directions to the players. This year, his brother, Taylor, and his wife, Alice, would join them in the afternoon, along with HolliAnne.

This year, he was eager to see his children, who had been away longer than they ever had. He wasn't used to it. It was hard for him to concentrate on the dance studio; planning for his Thanksgiving weekend crowded out other thoughts. Preparing for Thanksgiving was something he found pleasure in doing.

At the studio, many of the class members signed up again for the same classes for the next session. A few new people enrolled in each class and two new morning classes of senior citizens were added. Hamilton told Franny the new people had indicated on their application, the one Hamilton created, that they had heard about the classes from the flyers, a member of the class, or searching online, a testament to his hard work.

During the previous session, Hamilton had used his own clothes to dance in, but after the shoe incident, he not only bought new dance shoes but also a new black shirt and black pants. He wanted to look like the instructor on one of Franny's videos. Franny told him dressing in black was standard in dance. "Personally, I believe the students can better see how to step. The attention is not on the clothing, but on the instructor's feet," Franny said.

On the first day of the new session, Franny told each class, except for the individual tap student, the dances they would learn and how they would learn them. She let them know about the rules of the studio and discussed class rules. She also told them what they should wear and the shoes they needed. She gave the class several places where they could get comfortable clothing and shoes.

During the last fifteen minutes of each class, Hamilton told the group he had been in contact with Kurk Collins from another dance studio. Kurk challenged them to a "dance-off." Hamilton said he and Franny accepted it. The dance-off will be held during the last week of class. Members from each class will dance with their partner. "You and your partner will select a dance you have practiced and perfected and then compete with dancers from Kurk's studio. We have agreed the dances will be fox-trot, tango, rumba, waltz, and swing. There must be at least one couple or team from each studio for each category," Franny said. Hamilton had prepared a sign-up sheet for the members to sign up to schedule their dances.

After hearing about the dance-off, Carol, in the 10:30 class, who still saw herself as the leader of the group, said, "I don't think we should have a competition. I didn't join this class to compete against anyone, I just want to learn how to dance."

"The dance-off sounds okay to me. If it's just between two studios. I don't see any problems with this idea," Ronald said.

"I think it's okay, as long as no one gets hurt," Carey said.

"Sounds like a lot of work to me," Robert said. He refused to give up smoking, which was why his wife wanted him to take the class and, according to his wife, he had trouble getting up the stairs in his home. Hamilton hadn't seen him climb the stairs to the studio and didn't understand how he made it up if things were as bad as his wife indicated. Maybe he rested every two or three steps.

"I think it's a wonderful idea, and I'm all for it," Marilyn said, standing next to Emma and smiling at Hamilton.

"This is a splendid idea, and you should dance with some purpose in mind. Everybody, go home and think about who you want for a partner and the dance you want to do," Franny said. She looked up at the clock on the wall. "Hamilton and I have just enough time to show the dances you will learn this session."

Hamilton kept in mind the body posture he learned from the last session and made it all look easy and comfortable to the group and the new members. He and Franny stepped together and turned at the right times. She followed his movements. Franny didn't have that easiness enabling him to relax, so he didn't have to concentrate so hard on the steps. She was not as smooth as he had hoped, particularly after telling her how good she was at ballroom dance. Her movements were just movements and made him feel uncomfortable.

Suddenly, Franny pulled away from Hamilton and went to cut off the music. "That's all for now. See you next time." She said it in a funny voice, one he thought sounded more like how her mother would have sounded. Hamilton gave her a quick glance.

"I see you have your boot off. I'm glad to see your foot has healed," Carol said as she left.

"Good to see you back in the swing of things," Ronald said, with a laugh.

Franny smiled.

Some members of the new 7:00 evening class came in early while the returning students piled in just at the start of class. He and Franny handled the class the same way they handled the earlier class. They demonstrated the dances they would learn in the class. At the end, he announced the "dance-off" in the same way.

"A dance-off?" Johnny asked.

Hamilton explained the dance-off to the group.

"But we only have three men," Jane said.

"You can choose anyone. It doesn't matter," Hamilton said. "More women than men sign up, anyway," He repeated what Franny said during the first session.

"I'm not dancing with a man," Johnny said.

"Select your own partner," Franny said.

"We'll have a sign-up sheet at the next meeting, so go home and think about it. Select a dance you just saw us demonstrate. You will need to select a partner and you both should sign up together," Franny said.

The next 10:30 class, Franny was ready when Hamilton arrived. She was dressed in an ankle length, off the shoulder, black one-piece dress with long sleeves and a wide skirt. A satin belt was tied with a bow around her left hip. Her black shoes were held on by a strap and fastened across the top. Her hair was pushed up in a bun and her heavy make-up made her face look as smooth as a doll's face. Her lips were painted a dark shade of red. Hamilton stopped in his tracks, slightly shifting from leg to leg, eyes glued on her. She looked exactly like her mother from the pictures he had seen of her.

When he regained his senses, he opened his mouth to speak. A low growl-like sound rose out of his throat.

"Is that how you dressed before?" Hamilton asked, clearing his throat.

"Before what?"

"Is that how you have always dressed, I mean?"

"Yes. Almost. Just about. Except I didn't wear make-up like this. But since I had it, I thought I'd use it."

He stood there, shifted from one leg to the other, as he tried to think of something kind to say to her. Dressed as she was with the heavy make-up, she was not the Franny he knew.

"Don't you like it?" Franny asked.

"The new you, huh? I better get changed," Hamilton rushed off to the office.

The class began this time with the fox-trot. Franny called out the steps as she and Hamilton danced them together.

"Look at Franny's new look. You look like a professional dancer with that make-up on," Carol said.

"I love that dress," Carey said.

Franny smiled, while Hamilton inspected the floor between his feet.

Later, during the time they practiced their dances, Emma asked Hamilton to practice with her. This came as a surprise to him since their communication so far has been a smile. He smiled, put his arm around her waist, clasped her hand, and couldn't move. "What are we doing? I mean, what dance?"

She smiled, "The waltz."

The two of them danced around the studio and, one by one, the class members gathered around to watch these two glide and twirl and step around the dance floor. They made it look easy.

"Why don't you two be partners for the dance off?" Carol said.

"You dance well together," Dacie said. She rarely spoke, and when she did this time, everyone else nodded in agreement.

"Well then, we should," Emma said, looking at Hamilton for his approval.

"Legally he can since he's not a professional dancer like Franny. So, it'll be okay," Ronald said.

"You're right. It's okay," Franny said, disappointment sounding in her voice.

"Okay, then I guess we'll compete together, Hamilton said, hesitation in his voice."

When the class ended, and everyone left, Hamilton followed Franny into the office.

"Are you sure, my dancing with Emma will be okay with you?" Hamilton asked.

"Sure. Why not?"

"I thought since I help you it would be inappropriate. But if everything is okay, then I'm okay with it." He was both relieved and disappointed. This woman, Emma, had some kind of hold on him.

"I thought about that, but Ronald said it was okay."

"Aren't there some rules or guidelines for things like that?"

"I don't know. I'll find out."

Hamilton nodded, then sat down at the computer to check the website for any contact.

"What do you plan to do with your mother's things? Have you thought about it?" He eased it out, trying not to offend her.

Franny sighed as she sat down on the couch across from Hamilton. "I have to get rid of her things, don't I?"

"Why would you want to keep them?"

"I don't know. Memories, I guess."

"Franny, show me things that belong to you. Something you bought for yourself."

Franny faced Hamilton like a dancer on stage, waltzing to cha-cha music.

"I know somewhere inside you the real Franny is dying to come out. I can't wait to meet her."

"I have some boxes. I'll pack up her things tonight. Will you help me and go with me to take them someplace tomorrow?"

He just wanted her to put on a dress that represented her and wipe off the make-up and release Francine Hartman.

Franny's apartment was in an older, well-kept stone building surrounded by trees. It reminded Hamilton of one of those grand apartments rich people in the movies or on TV live in. He walked in and stood in the foyer on a marble floor, a crystal chandelier suspended from the ceiling. Franny took his coat and hung it in the closet. She then led the way into the connecting rooms on the first floor. The moment he stepped into the living room, he saw the apartment was all Mazzie. The apartment, furnished in an earlier time period, held all her mother's furnishings. No one as young as Franny would buy furniture of that type or quality. Young people today are more minimalist and buy less expensive, less bulky furniture. He looked over at Franny and realized he had no idea how old she was, though she looked about late twenties, to mid-thirties.

The rooms were open and spacious, with hardwood floors, and long windows in the living room running almost from the ceilings and ended in a window seat that connected the three windows in the living room and adjoining dining room. The long brocade drapes were tied back and let in the light. The view from the window was of the Potomac River and the towpath.

"When I was younger," Franny turned toward Hamilton, "and whenever we were here, I would sit in this window seat for hours watching people in their boats or people walking or running on the towpath. Everybody was always going somewhere."

He understood her sadness; he understood her loss, in a world that swirled around her. No time for the weary, those hungry for more, or those regretting. The world just kept moving.

Hamilton ran his hand across the dining room table. The polished hardwood table had that stately appearance with intricate carvings. The cabinets had gold handles. A lacquered grand piano sat catty-corner in the living room near the first window. Many framed pictures that told of her mother's life, covered almost the entire top of the piano. Hamilton picked up several pictures of movie stars, congressmen, and women, some shaking her mother's hand. There was one of her mother's ride on a camel, another of her mother seated in a small plane, another of her mother waving from a yacht; many pictures of her mother dancing, and several of Franny's father, Franny pointed out. The piano, shiny and black as if it had just been polished, was closed. He never heard Franny say she could play. He would have to ask her.

Hamilton stepped into a large-size library with books that filled the shelves of the four walls from top to bottom. On one wall, the shelves surrounded a huge stone fireplace. A beige leather couch with a small table positioned in front of the fireplace. Two leather armchairs were on either side of the couch. A desk and chair were in front of bookcases on one wall. Hamilton was surprised and took a book off a shelf to see if it was real. How would her mother have had the time to read all these books? He flipped through the first pages and tried to read the signature.

The kitchen had dark wood cabinets across the longest wall with a more modern-looking refrigerator and bakers-style stove. Hamilton couldn't imagine the number of parties, receptions, dinners, celebrations, and the many other events that must have taken place in their apartment. The apartment—the place where Franny had changed herself so she could be more like her mother. There was something different about the sadness of the passing of Franny's mother. Hamilton felt it at her funeral, and he felt it again in the apartment. It was not like someone would be missed, but it was an unconventional missing. It was almost like it was the loss of Franny.

He followed her to an upstairs loft that jetted out over the entrance way below. On one side of the loft was a sizeable room with movie-style seating and a movie-size screen TV. A door was left ajar that led to a bathroom. Hamilton couldn't see much other than the tub with claw feet.

"See," Franny began, "I have too many memories."

Hamilton nodded.

She led the way back down the stairs to her mother's room, a room larger than any bedroom he'd ever seen. He picked up a green satin dress that laid across a footstool to the right of the king-sized bed. He pictured Franny's mother in the dress, entertaining important people, and financial supporters in the world of ballet.

Franny slowly began taking her mother's clothing out of the large walk-in closet. Many formal gowns and dresses and suits had already been placed on the bed and across the backs of chairs. In their time period, the dresses were of expensive taste and quality, but in the casualness of today's society, those dresses would be out of place.

"I thought I'd keep these," Franny pointed to the dresses on the chair, "and take these to a homeless shelter or someplace."

Hamilton didn't think that was a wise idea, since homeless people needed more practical clothing than those beautifully made elegant dresses and suits. He pulled back a few of the dresses Franny had laid out, and saw mink coats, and wool and silk shawls and scarfs.

"Maybe you could take them to a vintage store. A place where people want items like these. Do you have boxes, large plastic bags or something to put these in?" He looked around the room for boxes or bags. "We could pack up what we can and take those to someplace that will accept them." Even though he thought he had been in every room in the apartment, he wanted to ask to see her room. But he didn't want to push it and she didn't take him to her room.

Franny went to get large plastic bags while Hamilton looked around the room. Two bedpans on a chair, a wheelchair in front of the long window, a TV tray and several medicine bottles were on the nightstand. When she returned, they separated the things they could give away from the other things.

"Franny?" he began putting a box together to put things in. "You kept all her things?"

"Yes," Franny said it so softly Hamilton almost didn't hear.

"You said she was in a nursing home for about two or three years, but did she wear any of these things before she went to the home?"

Franny faced him, like a suspect in an investigation, finally admitting the truth. "She was ill for about two years before she went into the home. My mother suffered from dementia, and she had it longer than I wanted to admit."

"Franny, I'm sorry. I know this is difficult for you." He had never seen her like this before. She was always so fragile, so unwilling to face the truth. Franny went to the closet and pulled out several handbags and purses. She opened them before dropping them into the box. "Oh, my. Look at this. There must be, ten, fifteen thousand dollars here." She pulled out another bag and found more money. "Ham, my mother had thirty thousand dollars in these handbags. What should I do with this money?"

"You could put that money in the bank. Won't you need it for rent or something?"

"I guess you're right."

"Can you afford this apartment? It must cost a fortune to live here."

"It might. But my mother, in one of her more lucid moments, took care of everything before she went to the nursing home."

"I see. So, you can stay here for a while?"

"Yes. Another year. Or until the company sells the building."

"Then, you'll have enough time to make some decisions." He picked up a dress but put it down on the bed. "Franny, did your mother leave you anything? A trust fund or an inheritance?"

Franny looked up, surprised.

"Did she have a lawyer?"

"Yes. He's been keeping up with her nursing home stay."

"You may need to contact him."

They took the boxes and bags of clothes and coats and everything Franny wanted them to take out to Hamilton's car. They filled his trunk. Hamilton opened the car door and got in. After he started the car, Franny got in. She leaned over and kissed him on the cheek.

"What's that for?" Hamilton asked, smiling.

"For being so nice."

As he pulled out of the space, he was reminded of the time when he became dean. He and HolliAnne were invited to dinners and receptions by the president of the university, senators, CEOs of corporations, even the mayor. Hamilton didn't like to solicit help for the university like that and sometimes he wouldn't accept the invitation. But HolliAnne wanted to be among the big named people, and she encouraged him to accept all invitations. HolliAnne always had to buy a new dress. She said she couldn't wear the same dress twice. None of her dresses were as elegant or beautiful as the dresses he just helped Franny pack away.

A little after HolliAnne initiated the divorce, Hamilton's lawyer made discoveries about her. She had relationships with three other men. But during that time Hamilton made some discoveries about himself. It was hard for him to accept the fact that she started seeing other men. He lost trust in her. He accepted the blame for that by telling himself he needed to be a more devoted husband. He knew he had to face the truth about himself. He didn't make himself an honorable person. He was controlling and even though he knew she didn't know how to feel love, or show love, he didn't show her how to love him. He didn't know how to do that.

He wished now he had not ignored what he saw and knew. He wished now he had demanded that he and HolliAnne sit down and talk things out. He wished now he and HolliAnne had made a change for the other and for their children. He turned HolliAnne away from him and he had no idea how to fix it. It was true. He and HolliAnne had not loved each other from the beginning and fixing things could have led to a divorce. He wished now he had been honest with himself and HolliAnne.

After dropping off the clothes, Hamilton and Franny reached the studio just as the members were coming in for the evening class. When the class members changed, Hamilton started the music. Since Franny no longer needed her boot, she could now stand inside the circle as the class danced around her. That way, she could see who needed help. The dancers warmed up with their partners by practicing the steps from the previous session. Franny clapped and kept time. "Head up Keith," "Stop watching your feet June," "That's its Aileen." Hamilton turned in her direction. She had begun to make a change. He noticed it when they were cleaning out her mother's things and she faced the truth about how long her mother was ill. Soon, Franny will find herself.

"Let's start our next dance," Franny said.

Franny called out the steps for the tango as Hamilton demonstrated. At the end of the demonstrations, he and Franny danced together to show the class how the tango looked with a partner. Franny must have practiced. Her movements seemed more fluid, and the flow was better. Maybe since she gave away some of her mother's clothes, she also broke the connection that tied her to her mother, and she was free. When it was time for them to get partners, Hamilton partnered with Frida.

Later, while sitting in his favorite chair at home with a cup of coffee, Hamilton thought about HolliAnne. HolliAnne said he sometimes choked the life out of her. He saw what she meant through Franny and her mother. Her mother had controlled every aspect of Franny's life. Frannie gave up her life, her soul, to her mother. HolliAnne fought against him throughout their marriage. Hamilton was sorry he controlled HolliAnne's life and took away her ideas, her sense of self-worth. He was thankful his daughter, Anna, was strong enough to stand up to him and refused to let him control her. He wished he could find a way to apologize to HolliAnne.

He had promised Anita that he would "get back on the horse." But for him, it wasn't that simple. He saw, however, that he was making himself a better person. He needed to finish that first.

CHAPTER 22

On Thanksgiving Day, Hamilton and Jeremy straightened the house again, even though the day before, they shopped for food and cleaned the house. They went through the entire house, making sure everything was dusted and put back in their places. After all, it was Hamilton's turn to host the dinner and his parents were coming. He was comfortable he had picked up a birthday present for Jeremy a week ago and had it well hidden in the house.

On the table in the hallway, he picked up the key dish Eric made in high school, which reminded him of the time during dinner Eric announced he wasn't going to college. He was in ninth grade. Hamilton asked him what he wanted to be when he grew up and Eric didn't know. Hamilton asked if he was interested in things like plumbing and HVAC work. Eric laughed and said he didn't know what HVAC was. "Are you kidding?" he asked, laughing when Hamilton told him. Hamilton asked about being in sales and Eric said he had no interest in that. For the next several days, Hamilton pointed out careers and occupations to Eric and helped him see his talents and interests.

Two years later, when Eric was a junior in high school, he announced he wanted to be a psychologist, but he hadn't decided what kind. Hamilton had convinced him he needed a college education. Hamilton held the key dish, enclosing it in the palm of his hand, and then put it back in its place.

Thanksgiving Day was also Buddy Boy's birthday. Hamilton had always told Jeremy Thanksgiving was a time with special meaning for him. Jeremy was born on Thanksgiving Day, and even when his birthday didn't fall on Thanksgiving Day, Hamilton was thankful for Jeremy.

Eric and Anna arrived early in the afternoon, which gave Hamilton more time to get the turkey seasoned and begin preparing the vegetables and bread. After they arrived, and when she saw the worried look on Hamilton's face, Anna said she got a ride close to New Jersey, so Eric met her there and they drove down together. They arrived with presents for Jeremy, and he was ecstatic to see them.

Hamilton spent some of the afternoon in the kitchen cooking while Eric, Anna, and Jeremy watched football in the family room. Hamilton would go back and forth as he heard them rooting or giving orders to the TV, getting angry at some of the plays, and coming to the kitchen to help him. When they tried to help, Hamilton gave them more to do this year than he had in the past. Usually, he would give them something quick and easy to do, like hand him a pot, or a spoon, and then told them he and HolliAnne had everything under control. This year, he asked Eric to wash the green beans and season them and asked Anna to help him cut up the potatoes and asked Jeremy to season the turkey while he made the stuffing. This year, he wanted them around him more. Jeremy had missed them too, from the way he hugged Eric and Anna, though he hadn't shown how much he'd missed them until now. But kids are like that.

The arrival of his brother, Taylor, and his wife, Alice, along with his parents, George, and Mary, brought his attention back to Jeremy. Jeremy was ready to open his birthday presents.

Eric gave Jeremy biking shoes and a biking kit containing a small pump, an inner tube, and patches. Anna gave him a pair of biking gloves and the right socks, she said, to wear with his shoes. George and Mary gave him a helmet and sunglasses. Jeremy's face showed he was a little disappointed with his gifts.

"There's nothing like sprucing up the old to make it look new," George said.

Hamilton peered over at his father. Since their conversation at the vineyard, Hamilton wasn't as apprehensive or defensive toward his father as he once was.

"That's right," Mary said.

"I remember I had to do that with my old bike. Didn't I, Dad?" Taylor said.

Then Hamilton rolled a dark blue Diamondback boy's Haanjo Trail Road Bike into the family room. Jeremy, eyes lit up like high beams when he saw the brand-new bike, stared in stunned silence.

"That's your present," Eric said.

"Dad, is this for me?"

"I know it's what you wanted."

"Boy! What a beautiful bike, Jeremy." Taylor said.

"You got all the gears you need," George said while inspecting the bike, and a wide smile on his face.

"Be sure you keep that helmet on and wear it the right way," Mary said.

"I can finally get rid of that bike that's too little for me?"

"Yes, you can. Go try it out?" Hamilton said.

"Come on. I'll go with you," Eric said. He went to the garage to get his bike where he'd left it.

After they left, the others continued preparing the Thanksgiving dinner. Hamilton rubbed the turkey with olive oil again and put it into the oven.

"Why didn't you just give Jeremy Eric's old bike?" Anna asked while cutting the white potatoes into small squares.

"You each got a new bike, why shouldn't he?" He opened a bag of ready-made stuffing and poured it in a bowl. "Besides, I don't believe in hand-me-downs." He added a roll of Italian sausage and chopped apples to the stuffing and mixed it all up, separating the sausage into tiny pieces as he mixed.

Mary prepared the vegetables from their garden, she was proud to announce, and made a casserole and several other vegetable dishes. George brought in several bottles of wine and poured everyone a glass, except for Anna.

Eric and Jeremy, back from their bike trip, entered the kitchen, both breathing hard from strenuous activity.

"How was the new bike?" Hamilton asked.

"It's a nice, smooth ride," Jeremy said.

"It feels sturdy, too," Eric said.

"So, you rode it?" Anna asked in a way that sounded like she was left out.

"Well, yeah. I had to make sure it was safe enough for Jeremy. What kind of brother do you think I am?"

"He almost wouldn't get off," Jeremy said, laughing at his brother.

"Just making sure, that's all."

"Anna, it looks like we missed out," Hamilton said.

"If you want to, you can ride it now," Jeremy said.

Anna looked at Hamilton as if asking permission.

"Go ahead. It's okay."

After Jeremy and Anna left, Hamilton turned to Eric. "What about you and—"

"We took your advice," Eric began, cutting Hamilton off. "We talked about it and decided to finish undergrad first."

"Good. Is she still at Princeton?"

"Yes. She's still a freshman."

"I would like to meet her whenever you're ready."

"I know. What about you? What are you doing with yourself these days?"

"Dancing, that's what he's doing. Having fun dancing," George said, entering the kitchen.

"Dancing? You?" Eric said, smiling.

"After Buddy Boy talked me into helping at a dance studio, I've been doing that on my leave."

"Do you remember when we took classes at a dance studio?"

"I think about that often."

"I was a clumsy kid. I don't remember why we went."

"We went to help your sister. I'm finding it to be fun."

Later, when Jeremy and Anna were back and the food was ready, they all sat down to eat. First, Jeremy spoke. "Before I say grace, we should all say what we're thankful for."

Anna told about her need to be a journalist and the fact that she loved the idea she would make government facts known to the public. Her idea was to keep the public informed. She was firm on the idea that the public had a right to know about the things affecting them. Eric wanted to help people overcome traumatic events in their lives. Jeremy expressed his need to be a priest and lead everybody to God. He loved the Lord and thought everyone else should. Taylor said he wasn't surprised about Jeremy. George and Mary were proud of their new garden, where they grew vegetables and sold them at market stands in town. Taylor and Alice talked about the new ministries happening in Taylor's church. Alice said her grown children were ministering in other countries and not able to come this Thanksgiving. Taylor said he wanted Jeremy to do more in the church, maybe become a reader and later, help serve during communion. Hamilton told them about the dance studio and his leave ending soon. Jeremy said a blessing, and the eating began. The conversation around the table continued with questions to Jeremy about his wanting to be a priest, to Eric about his classes in psychology and George and Mary's garden.

The day sped by too fast for Hamilton and before he knew it; it was late evening. HolliAnne called to say she couldn't make it to dinner; she was sick. Hamilton said she sounded horrible on the phone but wished her a speedy recovery.

The next day, Hamilton took his three kids on a bike ride in Pennsylvania. They rode through "Amish Country," a section in Pennsylvania where many Amish people live. Jeremy raced a man and boy riding in a one horse-drawn buggy down an unmarked road. The four of them waved to the man and boy in the buggy as they passed and continued down the road until they came to an Amish Farm. A man dressed in black pants, a white shirt collar and black tie peeping out from under his black overcoat, stood in front of the driveway leading up to the farmhouse. Jeremy waved to the man as they all passed by, and he and Hamilton led the way to the Amish Diner on the edge of the small town. After dinner, Anna insisted they visit the Amish Museum.

On Saturday, the four of them decided everyone would make their favorite breakfast item before they left, when HolliAnne showed up. She said she felt better and wanted to bring breakfast. Eric helped her take the items out of the bag. There was a certain disquiet over the room. The sounds of silence permeated the atmosphere. Not knowing what to do, Hamilton put the bacon, bread, sausages, and home fries back in the refrigerator. Anna got plates and Jeremy got forks and spoons and placed them on the counter. After the food was all laid out, HolliAnne said, "Help yourselves."

"This is great," Anna said. She smiled at her mother.

"HolliAnne, I wish you'd called first," Hamilton said.

"Yes. Anna and I have to leave in a few minutes," Eric said, while stuffing the food down as fast as he could. "The scrambled eggs are really good."

"So soon?" HolliAnne asked. "I just got here."

"The breakfast is great. Mom, thanks. But I promised Paige I would spend time with her."

"I have a paper to finish before Monday. The hash browns are sooooo good," Anna said.

"Stay a little longer," HolliAnne pleaded.

"I can't. Paige's family is expecting me."

"I have to finish my paper," Anna said.

"The paper can wait."

"I've never turned in anything late."

"Okay. I guess if you must, you must," Hamilton said.

"My friend's mother is picking me up in a few minutes," Jeremy said, eating hurriedly.

"The kids are all grown up. I hate it, but I understand," Hamilton said, turning to HolliAnne.

HolliAnne turned to Hamilton.

CHAPTER 23

When Hamilton arrived at the 10:30 morning class on Monday, he was enthusiastic to see the members were hard at work practicing for the competition. Hamilton passed by the bulletin board, where the men had already placed bets on who would win. The women had a chart showing the amount of weight each woman lost, and who would look best in their dress. Carol said she got the idea when she saw Franny come in dressed like a professional ballroom dancer. She thought they should do the same.

"Does this belong to anyone?" Dacie held up what looked like a black scarf.

"That would look nice on you, Hamilton," Carey said.

"Yes, it would. You need something like this," Dacie said.

"Unfold it," Carol said.

Dacie unfolded it. "It looks more like a sash. But it has a big hole in it and what's this yellowish stain?"

Franny walked out of the office. "Where did you find my dust cloth?"

Dacie laughed. "Dust cloth?"

"We thought it was a sash," Carey said, handing the cloth to Franny.

"Well, I still think Hamilton would look nice in a sash. In fact, he should have one for the competition," Marilyn said.

"I agree," Ronald said.

"I will have a sash for you for the competition," Marilyn said.

On the next day, just before the 10:30 class began, the office phone rang. The call was for Marilyn. The woman on the other end was from the Clear View Mental Hospital and left a message with Hamilton saying Marilyn's son had suffered an injury and they needed her to contact them immediately. The woman said she hated to call, but she tried Marilyn's cell, and Marilyn hadn't answered. Marilyn left this number and her work number as emergency numbers. Hamilton promised to deliver the message.

Hamilton didn't know Marilynn had any children, but someone called her about her son. She didn't owe him an explanation, but he couldn't help feeling somewhat deceived by Marilyn. He turned around in his chair to Marilyn standing in the doorway.

Hamilton got up to greet her, but she greeted him first. He told her about the call from the Clear View Mental Hospital. He handed her the message. She took it but had a confused look on her face.

"Would you—"

"Thank you," she said over her shoulder as she turned to leave.

In a few minutes, she returned.

"Hamilton, could I talk with you a minute, please?"

"What is it?" he asked.

"It's about the phone call."

Franny got up, mumbling something about sorting out the music and excused herself. She gave Hamilton "the look" on her way out the office door.

"The woman apologized for calling, but she tried calling you on your cell. You didn't answer," he began.

"It's not that. It's about my son."

He waited.

"I never told you I had any children, and I don't."

"But the woman said it was your son," Hamilton said.

"I know. He's not my son. He's my husband's son."

"Marilyn, you don't have—"

"I know I don't, but I need to talk about it. For years, my husband was seeing someone else. Lucas is the product of that relationship. When

I found out about it, I tried to leave, but I couldn't. I stayed, hoping things would change. The woman he was seeing died years ago. And later my husband died. Lucas has no one to care for him, or to make decisions, or pay for his care. I took it on."

"Marilyn, I—"

"I just wanted you to know I didn't lie to you. I would never do that." Marilyn turned to leave the office.

"Marilyn..." He stood to talk to her. Then changed his mind.

When the lesson began, Hamilton got another taste of what happened in dance classes. Franny never told Hamilton fights and arguments would break out. He wasn't sure how to handle them.

Irene didn't like the way Ronald snatched her around. Irene wanted to be turned the way she saw Hamilton turn Franny. Carey and Carol couldn't decide who would take the man's role. Both ladies seemed to want to lead; and June had a problem with Robert's odor.

"Do you have to smoke just before dance class?" June asked. "Doesn't that defeat the purpose of exercise?"

"I smoke because I'm nervous," Robert yelled back at her.

"Well, maybe after you've smoked you could clean yourself up before you come around people. I don't have that nasty habit and I don't want to smell like smoke."

"Calm down everybody," Franny said.

"It looks like we need Hamilton and Marilyn," Dacie, who rarely spoke, said. Her partner Brenda, a new quiet lady nodded in agreement.

"I can't—"

"I think you'd better dance," Franny said.

Hamilton went to Marilyn. "Okay?" he asked.

"I think so. But don't do anything you don't want to do.

"What dances?" he asked.

"I like the tango, waltz and cha-cha."

"Let's begin with the tango." Smiling, he took her hand and the two of them bowed before the group. With his hand, he signaled for her to move in front of him, the two of them taking easy, wide steps, and they danced. As they twirled around the dance floor, the class members admired their smooth rhythm, dramatic turns, talented head moves, Marilyn's sensuous and suggestive smile, and Hamilton's perfect timing.

"They have been practicing without us," Carol said.

"Look how good they are," Carey said.

Hamilton took a sly peek at Marilyn and saw her smile and how happy she seemed. He turned his head a little more toward her and her smile widened. When he put his arm around her and drew her to him, he felt her relaxing more and more as they danced. At one point, when he pulled her into him, she stepped closer to him where her torso touched his and she seemed to give her hips more sway, the sway the tango required.

"I think they lied. They're not beginners," Ronald said.

"I told you, you had your step wrong. See how he's doing it?" Irene, Ronald's partner, said. When they finished, Hamilton and Marilyn stood apart, eyes on each other. To him, he showed the steps of the tango. But he could see that it meant more to Marilyn. He bowed to the group.

The 7:00 evening class had just as many problems as the morning class. Hamilton wondered whether the competition was a good idea. Lewis, a new guy this session, made it clear the only reason he joined the class was to find himself a girlfriend or a wife, and he didn't care about the competition. Jane was left without a partner for the competition. Lewis' remarks offended Miles because Miles thought of himself as the "Romeo" flirting with the ladies in the group. Albert and Aileen apologized for every mistake they made while practicing and in keeping with their personalities, they also apologized for every mistake other class members made as well. The competition was causing more problems than he thought. He originally thought everyone would learn the steps and relax and have fun. But these people had to turn it into something personal. Some things are just out of his control. He smiled

when he looked at the big clock on the wall and saw it was time to end class.

The third ballroom dance class, newly formed for this session, elected not to compete. They said even though there were six people in the class, they weren't good enough to compete. They all agreed they just wanted to learn the dance steps. Their decision disappointed him, but Hamilton was thankful. He didn't convince them otherwise–something he would have done in the past.

CHAPTER 24

Jeremy whizzed by Hamilton as they rode their bikes on the trail that ran around the lake at the university. The late November Saturday afternoon became a gift and instead of snow and temperatures below 35 degrees, sunshine and milder temperatures surprised everyone.

"Are you passing me?"

Jeremy laughed.

"Okay, you asked for it." Hamilton pushed hard to pass Jeremy. On his new bike, Jeremy sped up more to keep Hamilton back. Hamilton pushed harder and overtook Jeremy. He continued speeding until he was way out in front. Jeremy changed gears, peddled harder and spun as fast as he could. The bike was fast, and he caught up to Hamilton. Hamilton slowed down a little and allowed Jeremy to overtake him. Jeremy continued to push hard. "Yahoo," he shouted as he, at a high speed, zoomed by Hamilton. "I won." He slowed down to catch his breath. "I love this bike."

"You're getting good. I had a hard time trying to pass you that first time," Hamilton said, still panting and now sweaty.

"Getting good? Did you say getting good?"

"Well, of course, I'm the best," Hamilton laughed.

"You didn't let me win, did you?"

"Now, why would you ask that?" Hamilton led the way as they continued their ride around the lake. He gave a half smile to himself and pointed to a bench by the lake. They took off their helmets, loosened their jackets, and sat. His youngest son was now an official teen, at fourteen. This was the last time he could "let his son win." From now on, Jeremy would have to win on his own.

"How are things going at school?

"You know my grades are good, so you must mean about the locker incident."

"You haven't said anything. Does that mean that no one is trying to get back at you?"

"Aaron asked me about what happened and what I told Mrs. White. I told him, the same thing I said to you and Mrs. White."

"What was that, Bud?"

"I couldn't say who did it because I didn't know, and I didn't want to accuse anyone unjustly. Dad, I know you wanted me to say who I thought it could be, but when the time came, I couldn't do it. I had to do the right thing for me. I'm sorry, Dad."

"Why would you do that after I told you the best way to handle it?"

"I thought about Todd and how he's always accusing me of doing something I didn't do. It helped me see the injustice of accusing someone without certainty."

Hamilton swallowed hard. "Your friend, Aaron, left it like that? What you told Mrs. White?"

"Not at first. I think he thought I was lying. But I told him I didn't go to my locker after lunch. Aaron said he remembered me telling him that." He looked over at his father. "Dad, are you upset with me for not doing what you asked?"

"Buddy—" Hamilton began.

"Dad, I know you want me to do things your way, but I had to do this my way this time."

"I wish you'd taken my advice. I see nothing wrong with what I told you to do."

"I know. But I don't believe in getting people in trouble just because I think something. I need it to be true. You've always taught us to do what's right and to think for ourselves. That's what I did."

"Then, you're happy with your decision?"

"I am."

"Did Mrs. White find out who did it"

"Yes. It was not who I thought."

"Then you were right."

"I was right."

"What happened to him?"

"He was expelled. I knew him. He was having trouble at home, but I never thought he would do drugs, and I never would have thought he'd be the one to put it in my locker."

"Buddy, I understand your position and I'm very proud of you. You do what you feel is right and stick by it." Hamilton paused a second, "It takes a good heart, and loyalty to do what you believe is right."

He remembered a time when neither he nor HolliAnne did what was right by each other. After Jeremy was born, and before she left the hospital, HolliAnne had a tubal ligation. Hamilton didn't know about it. At the time she signed the consent form, Hamilton was in a meeting convincing the board members that the lake and a trail around the lake were needed for the faculty and students at the university. HolliAnne didn't consult with Hamilton, she just gave the doctor permission to tie her tubes. Hamilton didn't consult or let HolliAnne know what he was doing about his idea for a lake and bike path. He spent an enormous amount of time drawing up plans and trying to get them approved. Hamilton didn't find out about the tubal ligation until the doctor's unpaid bill came to him at the university. HolliAnne's insurance paid some of it, but she decided not to pay her portion and Hamilton received the bill. When he saw the itemized procedures on the bill, Hamilton went to the hospital to speak to the doctor. The doctor was not available. Hamilton then went to talk to HolliAnne. She told him three children were enough for their family. A tubal ligation procedure was best.

He regretted not making her a part of the creation of the lake and bike path. He should have taken her to the place where the men removed trees, showed her where the lake would be, and he should have had her share in his excitement. They should have celebrated together when the lake and trail were completed. But he didn't. He hoped she regretted not making him a part of her decision to have her tubes tied. They were both wrong.

"Dad. Guess what?" Jeremy asked as they were putting their bikes on the back of the car. "I'm scheduled to serve Christmas Eve and on Christmas Day."

"Good news. I've been waiting to hear that," Hamilton said.

Jeremy turned to his father and let out a wide smile.

"How did your food challenge go?"

"It's not over yet. So far, we have more canned goods than we got for Thanksgiving. But we haven't reached my goal yet," Jeremy said.

"You will. I know you will." He stared at his son, this miracle of extraordinary qualities. Suddenly Hamilton felt incomplete.

"The youth group wanted to make ice cream floats for the church members who bought something from Mr. and Mrs. Charles's boutique."

"Who else will be there?" Hamilton asked, regaining himself.

"Dad...."

"I see."

"I have basketball practice right after school. Amanda said her mother could pick us up and take us to her house and then to church to meet the others."

Hamilton's heart swelled with pride listening to his son and his herculean ability to make cogent decisions and stand by them. His son, whom he thought would be the weakest, was the strongest; the youngest, now the oldest; the most incapable, now the most able.

A few months ago, Jeremy didn't want to go anywhere without his dad. At that time, he followed Hamilton around everywhere he went. He didn't want to go to school because he wanted to be with his dad. Now look at him planning the evening. Could he still call his son Buddy Boy? Or would Jeremy demand to be called Jeremy from now on? Hamilton cleared his throat, "Who else is going?"

"Most everybody in the youth class I think."

"Text me all the information."

Later, when Hamilton arrived at the studio, the students in the 7:00 evening class had committed themselves to working harder at looking more like dancers. As soon as Franny began class, they swamped her with questions about technique. Hamilton pulled back.

"We know the steps," Albert said. He turned to look at everyone for affirmation. The others nodded.

"We want to know how to perfect the body movements," Aileen chimed in.

"We just need to look more artistic and less clumsy," Albert agreed.

"Yes!" others echoed.

"Walk us through that head movement that you both do," Dagmar said.

"I need to do more with my elbow. Can you show me what it should feel like?" Aileen asked.

Aileen and Albert were older than the others, and the most enthusiastic dancers in the evening group. Hamilton asked Albert and Aileen to show everyone the steps to the fox-trot. Hamilton and the class watched the two of them as they danced around the dance floor. They almost looked like professional dancers. Aileen no longer criticized him as they danced. She was more elegant than anyone could have imagined. Hamilton believed these two people were once professional dancers but were too modest to say anything to anyone.

They had grown to be the best couple in the group. Hamilton liked the air of confidence the two of them had when they danced together, and they looked like they were in another place where happiness was the color of grass and love the color of the sun's warmth and where lilies, daisies and mums all blended together in nature's harmony. Their faces held a peaceful, contented look as they circled the studio, unaware of anyone or anything, creating their music with a rhythm of their own. When they danced, they were transformed into unfamiliar people, and it was during their dancing Hamilton understood their special kind of love. Albert and Aileen needed each other. He didn't think he and HolliAnne ever had anything like what he saw from these two people when they danced together.

He turned to Franny, and they glanced at the other students in the class. Everyone seemed fascinated by Aileen and Albert and how they danced. After watching them, Lewis said he had changed his mind about his reason for taking lessons. "I really want to learn. But there is no way I could ever be as graceful as Albert," he confessed.

The evening 7:00 class also came to an agreement. There was much for them to do if they wanted to win the competition. They agreed to stop their disagreements and get to work. "There are twelve people in the class, and everyone had a partner. There are no excuses," Hamilton said. The evening class became more serious about winning and they separated themselves; each pair headed into their place around the dance floor and began work on their steps. Franny played the music for each couples' selected dance and when their music was on, they would dance. When they were not dancing, they were practicing turns and steps.

Just before Christmas, the evening class was looking better, and Franny thought they had a much better chance of winning now that they were serious.

The evening class had also gotten into the habit of meeting at the bar at the end of the shopping plaza for a beer after class on Fridays. Dorcas invited Hamilton to join them at the bar whenever they went. Hamilton had declined, saying he had to pick up his son. But on this Friday, Hamilton was without an excuse.

"It's just at the end of the shopping plaza," Dorcas pointed in the direction of the pub, "I hope you'll come this time."

After he left the studio, Hamilton walked down to the pub at the end of the plaza and found Dorcas, Johnny and Jane sharing a table. A waitress came with beer for the three of them and Hamilton asked for a beer as he sat down. Johnny and Jane carried on a conversation between them, which left Dorcas alone.

"I've never been in here. This is nice." Hamilton said, looking around the room. He could think of nothing else stimulating or motivating, or at least of some minimal interest.

"It's a nice change," Dorcas said.

"Is this your first dance class?"

"I took a class years ago. I always wanted to come back, but you know, things get in the way."

A sharp sound, as if someone turned on a radio, blasted through the room like a bolt of lightning that sent a shudder through him. A long, loud squeaking sound came up again at the same time a man picked up a mic from the floor. He announced the band coming onto the makeshift stage erected on one end of the restaurant.

"I forgot they have a band here on Fridays," Johnny yelled over to Hamilton.

Hamilton nodded and let out a sigh of relief.

"Maybe we can get a chance to dance," Jane said.

Dorcas smiled at Hamilton and cut her eyes down. Albert, Aileen, Keith, and Elise arrived and stood around the table. Dorcas moved her chair closer to Hamilton. Keith and Lewis found chairs for the group, and they all crowded around the table. The band, for its first set, played jazz. When they began, Hamilton relaxed. He wouldn't have to dance. The class members listened to the band's peppy music. No one from the class got up to dance. They sat bobbing their heads to the music, drinking beer, and tearing into their fries and burgers. When the band ended its first set, Hamilton finished his beer and stood to leave.

"Can I give you something before you go?" Dorcas asked Hamilton.

"What is it?"

"I like to bake and cook. It's a hobby of mine." She reached inside her handbag and took out a folded, brown paper, lunch bag and handed it to him. "Could you taste this for me?"

"What is it?" He sat down.

"It's a dessert that I'm trying out."

He took the bag from her and started to unfold it.

"No, please. Take it home and try it. I just brought enough for you."

He refolded the bag. "Aren't you going to tell me more about the dessert?"

"Can we just leave it like that? I like to make desserts and just cook. I make things up and try recipes. Sometimes well, many times, I change the recipe to something different. Could you taste this for me and let me know how you like it or what I can do to make it better?"

He wanted to make a comment about how small she was for someone who cooked, but he knew better than to say anything. He didn't want her to think he had noticed her, her long slim body that sailed around the dance floor slicing through the air like an eel. Her head held up and tilted like a queen who had just handed out orders and looked to see who dared not follow them, her feet in perfect time and step, moving her forward, backward, and side to side. He couldn't let her know he had noticed her in any way. He accepted the bag and left.

CHAPTER 25

"I couldn't wait for class. I am eager to hear about what you thought of the pie. Did you like it?" Dorcas said, entering the office of the studio. She rested on the doorjamb as she was almost out of breath. She held a cautious smile.

"You must be worried. You ran up the steps?" Hamilton asked, getting up from the computer to greet her at the door and offer her a chair. Franny stood behind him.

"I did. I am eager to hear what you think. But I'm a little worried also," Dorcas said. Her smile changed to a playful grin.

"What's it called?"

"It's chocolate pistachio pie. It has a dark chocolate custard, and a cocoa flavored crust. Did you like it?"

"I loved it. It was the best dessert I ever had."

"No changes or anything?"

"None needed."

"That's a relief. Now I can call my friends to confirm dinner." She left the office. Hamilton turned to go back to the computer. Franny shrugged her shoulders and went back to her planning. After a few minutes, Dorcas returned and stood in the doorway, with a confused and disappointed look.

Hamilton looked up. "Is everything okay?" he asked.

"The pie. I had invited a couple over for dinner, and my friend said they couldn't come."

"An emergency?"

"She said her husband got his dates mixed up. They can't make it tomorrow."

"I'm so sorry, Dorcas."

"I bought the food and the ingredients for the pie, I ...." Slowly, Dorcas turned to leave. She stopped herself and then turned around. "Hamilton, would you have dinner with me tomorrow? I'm serving the pie."

Franny went into the storage room, mumbling about needing to get her dance shoes, the ones already on her feet. These kinds of things were always tricky for him. Dorcas, as graceful and beautiful as she was, stood in front of him on the verge of tears asking for something, and he didn't know how to say "no."

"Dinner. What time is dinner?"

"Tomorrow about six?"

Hamilton nodded.

"Okay, then. Tomorrow at six for dinner." She gave him her address and phone number in case he needed it. He smiled and took the paper from her with great reluctance.

Hamilton drove to Dorcas' house and parked in front. The house was a small one level ranch-style house. He sat in the car, debating about whether to get out or drive off. He was long past the age where taking a woman to bed was important to him, or his only goal for the evening. He wanted to enjoy a woman. When he was ready, he wanted a solid relationship, one that would last. A relationship with Dorcas wasn't what he wanted. Calling at the last minute to say something came up was not the right thing to do, either. Besides, Dorcas was already disappointed about her friends not being able to come; he couldn't do that to her. He picked up the plant he bought earlier, got out of the car, and knocked on her door. She answered immediately, and he was caught off guard. She must have been watching him from the window and would have seen him drive off. He felt good that he went in.

When he entered, he handed her the plant. She took it and stepped aside. He was introduced to Dorcas' artistic talents exhibited throughout the living and attaching dining rooms. She had many pieces of watercolors, silks, pastels, and oil paintings covering all the walls in both the rooms. Artists designed some of her furniture, and she pointed out the signatures on the tables and chairs displayed in the living room. The furniture was a conglomeration of antique, very modern, and contemporary styles by unique artists, and every piece seemed to fit well with the other pieces. Hamilton sat down on the striped, pale lavender satin couch. When he felt the satin fabric and how soft it was, he sat up straight and tried not to move. HolliAnne wanted him to buy a couch much like Dorcas's when they were furnishing their family room. Hamilton said it wasn't practical, and they bought something else.

"Can I pour you a glass of wine?"

"Sure." Hamilton followed her to the kitchen to help with the wine. Then they sat down to a meal of veal parmesan made like he had never tasted before, where the veal so tender it slid down his throat and the cheese so pungent, he could identify it, and the sauce - the bow tie that brought all the flavors together - exploded in his mouth. It was like the food of the gods, and he had to control himself from eating too much. The food was meant to be devoured. At last, when he realized he was so consumed with the meal he forgot about her, he asked, "How did you get into cooking?" He wanted to ask something different, but the dinner was on his mind.

Dorcas told him about how she loved to mix different foods and ingredients and come up with something good and unusual. She told him about all the classes she'd taken, and she had had a cooking show on a cable network. Hamilton told her his father had a winery, and he worked there when he was in high school. He told her some funny things he and his brother did and how they sneaked wine and got drunk.

The last part of the evening, when they were having the dessert, his nerves took over and light beads of perspiration formed on his forehead. At that moment, he decided to go where the evening took him, but he didn't want to have Dorcas think they were starting a romance. He watched for cues as to what she wanted from him; those flirtatious comments with eye blinking or sometimes winking, or something. But he didn't see any of those things. Or maybe he just didn't recognize them. It seemed to him Dorcas just wanted someone to share her dinner. He gazed down at his watch. It was time for him to get Jeremy.

"Can I help you with the dishes?"

"I never ask my guests to help clean up."

Good. She thinks of him as a guest. "Thank you," he began, making his way to the front door. "Your friends don't know what they missed. The dinner was scrumptious." He leaned down and kissed her lightly on the lips, his eyes closed. He opened his eyes; aware he had just kissed her on the lips. He kissed her again like a father kisses his daughter and left.

On the drive to get Jeremy, Anita, the woman from Hawaii, popped in Hamilton's thoughts. He wondered how she was doing and remembered the promise they made. Tonight, he took a risk. At least he thought of it as a risk. His heart was not involved, but he took a step outside his box. He wondered whether Anita had.

On Monday in the 10:30 morning class, Emma surprised Hamilton by asking him to dance with her. When he heard his heart beating and pounding and felt the vibration throughout his body, he thought he was really having a heart attack this time. He didn't know what he said, but he felt like someone on high, looking down on him. He took her hand and led her to the center of the dance floor. He pulled her to him, and they began their dance.

The class members were fascinated by how these two people worked so well together. They were like a river; he was the ripple, and she was the tide. They stepped together, and when he signaled her to turn, she turned with the grace and beauty of an eagle soaring through the sky, dipping, and rising, and turning over trees and rivers and mountains. When he demonstrated with others, the magical energy that turned them into a symphony of distinct sounds was not present. But when he and Emma danced with each other, they were complete, all-encompassing, perfection. They hardly looked at each other; each turning and moving at the feel of the other.

"I think we need them to dance in the competition. Don't you think so?" Ronald said. He turned to everyone in the class, looking for group acknowledgement.

"You two are the best," Brenda said.

Her partner nodded in agreement.

Carey and her partner, Carol, clapped, the others clapped.

Robert clapped and started, "Dance, dance, dance." Everyone joined in.

"It's the only way our class can win anything against that other class." Ronald continued.

"How would you know that?" Carol asked.

"Yeah, Ron. How would you know that?" Franny asked.

"I, uh…"

"I didn't figure you for a spy," Brenda said.

"Did you go to that studio and watch them?" Carol asked.

"Why not?" Robert said.

"Look, everyone," Hamilton began, "let's not accuse anyone of anything. Besides, I don't want to know anything else."

"Yeah, I agree. And even if he did, Robert, is there anything we should know?" Franny asked.

Everyone laughed.

"Let's get back to work," Hamilton began. "Just so you know, as an employee of the studio, I can't compete."

Dacie's face changed from disappointment to a slight smile like a sultry summer day with heavy rains and the sun comes out before the showers have ended. Marilyn had a look of expectation, as if she already knew Hamilton could not compete. Franny's face held a look of confusion and, in all the commotion about Emma and him dancing together, he never once thought about how Franny thought about it. Even when they were alone together in the office talking about the classes, the students, about Jeremy, her mother, her ex-boyfriend, never once did he consider how she felt about the morning and evening classes, both wanting him to dance. Coming out from under her mother was still a little scary for her, and maybe she held a little jealousy inside her, like a faint spray of perfume, the scent hard to detect.

It was because of his dancing with Emma that the morning class ramped up their moves. They were running out of time. They also admitted that some people weren't as far along as others.

The following evening, before the 7:00 class, Hamilton heard a soft knock on the door. He and Franny turned to the door that was now ajar.

"This cake is for you," Dorcas said, holding the cake out to Hamilton, "and for you too, of course, Franny."

Hamilton looked at Franny, and Franny took the cake.

"We can put it out here so everyone can have some," Hamilton said, standing next to Franny. Franny took the cake out of the box and saw it was a chocolate fudge layer cake. Hamilton found a small table. Franny placed the cake on the table. She found paper plates, and a knife and forks and placed them beside the cake. Dorcas rushed off to change her shoes.

During the next 7:00 class, Dorcas brought in her famous Pistachio Pie, the kind she gave to Hamilton to taste for her.

"Hamilton, before class starts, we need to go over a few things," Franny said, pulling him to the office. She closed the door. Franny brought to his attention that Dorcas had been bringing cakes, cookies, and brownies over several sessions. He hadn't noticed or given it thought until Franny mentioned it.

"She likes you."

"Who? Dorcas?"

"She likes you."

"As a friend. That's what we are."

"No. She doesn't think so."

"What am I supposed to do about it?"

Franny hit him on the arm, then shook his arm, as if waking up a friend from a deep sleep. "She likes you," she repeated.

"I don't—"

"Do you like her?"

"Franny, we have work to do."

"She likes you."

"She's just being friendly."

"Let's see. Didn't you two go out to a bar or something?"

"No. She asked me to go with the class to the pub after class one Friday."

"And don't forget that dinner she invited you to, and you said yes to," Franny paused. "Do you like her?"

"Yes, I like her. She's a member of this class. I want to keep it professional."

"You have to say something to her."

"What?"

"If you don't like her romantically, then you need to tell her. She can't continue to bring food. It just doesn't look right. And you can't allow her to do that to herself."

He looked at Franny, searching for the Franny he knew, the one who talked too much with nothing to say and who gave out advice that wasn't relevant. This was someone else giving him sage counsel. She had changed.

After class, Hamilton asked Dorcas to dinner with him. They went to the pub at the end of the shopping center, the same one from their Friday night after class pub. The place was a different place during the work week. In fact, it was more a restaurant than a pub. It was quiet and filled with people from the businesses in the surrounding area dressed in business suits and ties. Beethoven was softly playing in the background. There was even a different menu from the fatty, salt laden fries, onion rings, greasy burgers and tacos on Fridays and Saturdays.

When they were seated and had ordered, Hamilton opened the conversation with more cooking questions.

"I have to cook because I write cookbooks."

"How long have you been a writer of cookbooks?" He wished he had more experience with this kind of social interaction. But he just didn't know what to ask or say sometimes.

"For over fifteen years. I used to teach cooking at a high school. Then I had a cooking show on TV. I have several awards for my pastry."

"The Blond Brownies were out of this world. Award worthy."

"I didn't think you had any. You haven't said anything."

"I've had some of everything," Hamilton said, but not entirely the truth. He had gathered up a few of the leftover crumbs from the brownies. Since his conversation with Franny earlier, he could see that she brought those for him. But he rarely ate sweets.

"The problem is, I have to watch my sugar intake, so I don't eat many things containing sugar." He was aware he made it sound like doctor's orders, even though it was something he did for himself.

"I'm sorry I didn't know."

"Dorcas, I just wanted you to know I enjoyed the dinner we had, and now this evening, but soon, I'll have to leave."

"What are you saying?"

"I'll go back to my old life, old friends."

"But we can still have dinner and lunch and see each other, can't we?"

"I don't see how that would be possible."

"We won't continue in the time you have before you leave?"

Hamilton didn't respond. He had to rearrange his fork and spoon.

"I should have known there was someone else." Dorcas said.

Hamilton looked up at her. He was not good at this. He was with HolliAnne for so many years that he'd forgotten how to end things. Even though, in this case, he didn't think there was a real beginning.

"It's about me. I'm still sorting things out for myself."

"I could help you with that."

"I need to do it for me."

After a moment, he summoned the waiter and gave him the sign for the check.

Outside, Hamilton walked Dorcas to her car. Once she pressed the button to unlock the door, he opened the car door for her.

"By the way, I'm hoping you and Brenda win the contest. You two have my vote."

She smiled back at him.

He walked toward his car. He wanted to be honest with her, without upsetting her or hurting her in any way. He thought for a moment and wondered whether this counted as risk taking. He felt better about himself.

At the studio, the next morning, Hamilton rearranged some items on the bulletin boards.

"What's this?" Franny asked, coming out of the office. She stood beside him.

"Just doing some rearranging."

He gave a sideways glance at Franny, but he didn't say anything. He knew she wanted him to tell her what happened with Dorcas. "Do you have to stand so close?"

"Do you have to make me ask? What happened?"

He turned to Franny. "You were right. She was interested. I explained to her I'm not ready for a relationship at this point."

"You tell that to everyone, Ham. When will you be ready?" Franny asked.

Her question startled him, and he tried to think of an answer for himself. When will he be ready? He wasn't ready, but after his experience with Dorcas, he was making progress.

He watched Franny's back as she walked to the office. Franny didn't seem to need him anymore. Once she got free of her mother, she was surprised at how she could manage by herself. Perhaps her progress was coming too fast. He hadn't heard her say a word about her mother since she gave away all her mother's clothes. He hadn't heard her say anything about the furniture and guessed she'd kept most of it. She entered the office, turned around to Hamilton and then sat down at her desk, the one that used to be his. He not only gave up his position at the desk, but he had her take over the website and the spreadsheets and everything else she needed to do on the computer. His place now was in a chair at the small table facing the wall. Franny had also taken her things out of the storage room and returned the storage room to its proper use.

Months ago, he had promised Anita he would take risks. But he hadn't. Sure, he took out someone whom he liked and accepted a dinner invitation. But he wasn't risking his heart. When will he be ready? In helping Franny, he saw himself. He saw how he controlled people and he saw what he did to HolliAnne through his control. He risked changing himself from a controlling person to someone less controlling. He saw how Franny's mother controlled her and what it did to her. For him, these situations weren't romantic and didn't involve his heart romantically. What about his romantic life? When will he be ready? He hoped Anita fared much better than he. That is, if she kept her promise. He wished he could ask her.

CHAPTER 26

The days leading up to Christmas were threatened with snow. Hamilton had always enjoyed snow. He loved to wrap up his children in warm clothes with scarfs, hats and earmuffs and watch them build a snowman in the front yard. Or watch them play in a snowball battle while he shoveled the driveway and walkway. When he had finished shoveling, he would join them in doing more to the snowman or the four of them would lie down in the snow and pretend to be snow angels. After his children tired out, they went inside where HolliAnne had hot cocoa and served the gingerbread Josie made every year for everyone in the office. Every winter he would hope for snow.

When Eric and Anna were in high school, things changed for Hamilton. Eric wanted to shovel the snow for two elderly women who lived one street over, and Anna went to check on the neighbors who lived at the end of the block; things he asked them to do when they were in middle school.

On this first snow day, while Hamilton and Jeremy were driving home, the dainty intermittent snowflakes teased the ends of the bare tree branches, streets, and sidewalks with light velvety flakes, leaving the city flickering like a neon sign blinking off and on. Hamilton heard the phone ringing as he pulled into his driveway.

"Dad, the phone. I can get it." Jeremy jumped out of the car.

"That's ...." he began. But Jeremy was out of the car and headed inside before he could finish.

"Mom, I would like to, but I have to serve on Christmas Eve and Christmas Day. I should just spend Christmas eve here."

Hamilton could hear Jeremy's raised voice when he entered the house. As he took his coat off, he walked to the family room and stood by Jeremy, listening to the one-sided conversation. Hamilton held out his hand, asking to take the phone. Jeremy held up a hand as if to say, "Just a minute." Hamilton turned to pick up the extension in the hall but changed his mind.

"I know. Yes. I understand. But I have to be there early for both services."

"I do want to see you and Todd on Christmas. And What?"

"Mom, I know, I know. I spent Thanksgiving with dad, but you don't understand, I–."

The frustration and building anger in Jeremy's voice bothered Hamilton, and he took the phone from Jeremy. Jeremy turned and ran upstairs.

"HolliAnne–" She cut him off, but he didn't give her a chance to speak.

"I signed Jeremy up to serve, and he wants to do it. We're not changing that. I gave you a schedule, remember?"

Jeremy returned with his backpack.

"I don't care, HolliAnne. This is something Jeremy wants. Rearrange your day. He'll be there later in the afternoon, like the schedule shows."

Jeremy opened the back door. Hamilton continued talking as he kept an eye on Jeremy through the family room window. "You don't understand. We're not negotiating. He'll ...." Jeremy, on his bike, rode on the slick grass along-side the house to the front and out to the snow-flaked street. Hamilton slammed the phone down and ran outside.

"Bud," he called out several times. Hamilton, without a coat, ran to the end of the block, but no Jeremy.

He stood on the corner walking around in circles, exasperated, the snow falling on his head and shoulders. He ran back to the house, got his coat and keys, and drove to the places where Jeremy usually went. He drove to the park, but it was empty. A light layer of snow covered the grass. He drove to Amanda's house; but didn't see Jeremy's bike there either. Frantic, Hamilton drove to the home of his best friend, but there was no sign of Jeremy there. Hamilton relaxed a little and drove to the church. Jeremy would go there. He pulled up in front of St. John's church but couldn't tell anything from the front. The smooth snow carpet was untouched. Lights were on in some parts of the church, but from the window where he was, there was no activity inside. He drove around to the back to the parking lot, and there, Jeremy's bike was up against the brick wall.

Hamilton got out of his car and found his way inside and to the sacristy. Jeremy at the railing knelt with his hands folded in prayer, whispering, crying, and praying.

Whenever Eric or Anna cried about something they didn't get or something that caused them frustration, Hamilton didn't have the same depth of worry as he had for Jeremy. He always believed Jeremy knew his mother didn't want him. Now, watching his son at the Altar in prayer crying pained his heart. His son, in tears for this silly, selfish reason, just ripped him apart. He grabbed his chest and rubbed it as he tried hard to keep his tears from gushing out. Hamilton knelt beside Jeremy at the railing. He put his arm around his Buddy Boy and Buddy Boy sank into the cradle of his arm.

"I'm sorry. I was so mad I didn't know what to do, so I came here."

"You had me worried about you, Buddy Boy."

"I'm sorry."

"We used to talk. We aren't doing that anymore?"

"I don't want to start fights between you and mom."

He took Jeremy by the shoulders. "Buddy Boy, you are not responsible for us. You have your relationship with your mom and one with me. I have my relationship with you and one with your mom. They are different. But you have no responsibility in how we behave or what we say to each other. I need you to understand that, okay?"

"Okay."

Hamilton pulled his son to him and wrapped his arms around him. They stayed like that, holding on as tightly as they could to each other for a long time. From the day he was born, all Jeremy wanted to do was please his parents, mostly his mother. Hamilton wanted HolliAnne to wake up and see how hard Jeremy wanted her love. But all she wanted was something for her. When Jeremy gave her his love, it was the wrong time, or the wrong amount, or expressed in the wrong way. Whatever

Jeremy tried to give her was always wrong. Hamilton hated to see his son go through that rejection, and he did whatever he could to make up for it. As much as he tried to control everything, he could not control her lack of love for her son. No matter how hard Jeremy tried to earn his mother's love, she couldn't give it. In all the trying, he couldn't help his son, and he couldn't get HolliAnne to see what Jeremy needed.

"I don't want you to be upset with me," Jeremy said, pulling away.

"I'm not upset. I'm glad I found you."

Jeremy looked around the church and at the cross.

"I know. You can't miss it. You have to serve, and you will."

"She said it was okay?"

"Actually, we didn't get that far. I hung up when I saw you walk out the door. Your mother, well, she'll just have to accept what you want to do. I'll talk to her again, okay?"

Jeremy smiled, "Okay."

"Buddy, maybe it would be better if you didn't try to please her all the time. Just do what you want, what you think is best for you."

He hated to speak against Jeremy's mother, but what he hated more was what Jeremy always had to go through with HolliAnne. Sometimes Hamilton believed HolliAnne punished Jeremy for being born, and the two of them for creating him. Hamilton believed it wasn't fair to Jeremy. Jeremy never asked to be born.

CHAPTER 27

Early Christmas eve, Hamilton and Jeremy decorated the spruce tree that they bought from the lot near the shopping center. They brought it in and stood it in front of the big picture window as they'd done in the past. He wanted to decorate the tree with only things his children had made over the years. The other things that were store bought, such as a few bulbs, tinsel, and other things, except the lights were put away. When they had finished, Jeremy stood on a stool and put the star he had made in fifth grade on top. They put Jeremy's favorite reindeer he insisted on buying last Christmas, on a table. Jeremy wanted it because he said it looked just like Rudolph. They placed the bells and angels Eric and Anna had made, along with three store-bought crèches that Eric said he'd enhanced, throughout the living and family rooms. Hamilton smiled to himself when he saw the house was still filled with his children.

Later, Hamilton's parents, George and Mary, arrived carrying several big, brown shopping bags in each hand. A box wrapped in gold paper with a red ribbon protruded from the top of Mary's shopping bag.

After they got settled, Hamilton and his father ended up in the living room.

"Looks like you and me are in the same boat," George said.

"What boat is that?" Hamilton asked.

"Tell you what. I have a case of wine in the car. If you go get it," he handed Hamilton his keys, "we could get a taste see."

Hamilton brought the case in and put it in a corner in the kitchen. He took out one bottle, opened it, and poured three glasses of wine. He took one to his mother in the family room, where he overheard Jeremy tell his grandmother why he wanted to be a priest.

"No." Hamilton said to Jeremy when he saw Jeremy look up. Jeremy laughed.

Hamilton took a glass to his father, and they clinked their glasses before they each took a sip.

"Pop, where are you getting all this wine?"

"I guess I forgot to tell you. The guy who bought the vineyard didn't sell all the wine before the developers took over. He split it up and gave half of what he had left to us."

"He seemed like a nice guy the day I met him."

"Except your mother and I aren't big drinkers."

"So how are we in the same boat?"

"We are both lost souls," his father continued. "You lost something and so have I."

"You have mom, Pop. You haven't lost anything."

"This wine you're drinking is all that is left from the winery. They tore down the buildings, dug up everything that was planted, and excavated the foundation for the townhouses."

"Pop, you shouldn't be watching that."

"I know, but I can't help thinking about how I started everything. How I built up that winery from just dried out bushes to what you are sipping right now. I can't understand why anyone would want to get rid of something good just to put up townhouses."

His father's comment made him uncomfortable.

"But I can't stay lost, and you shouldn't either."

"What do you mean?"

"You know what I'm talking about, son. You've been lost for a long time. Your divorce, well, you were lost long before that. Your divorce was a happy ending."

"Pop, I'm not sure what you mean or why you think that." He couldn't help but feel a tinge of resentment he tried to hide. He didn't want to have the feeling his father's words were too late, and he should have helped him years before now. He tried to push those feelings away.

"You love those kids and you're a good father to them. I mean an exemplary father. Makes me think how I should have done better with you and Taylor."

"Pop, did mom put you up to this? Did she talk about me to you, or something?"

"Son, your mother doesn't have to say a thing to me about you. I can see for myself. I've seen for a long time how unhappy you've been. You've stored up a lot of hate and anger. You don't show it, but you have. You need to let all that go. Let it go so you can be happy."

"Pop—"

"Men, we hurt on the inside. We can't show it. We're not supposed to show it. A real man doesn't break down and cry, like you see on TV nowadays. Who would look to him for strength and courage if he's crying? A real man stands tall, finds solutions, and takes care of his family. Son, you're hurting on the inside, and you have been for a very long time. You and HolliAnne, well, that divorce, that's the best thing. But you can't continue to hurt. Find who you are and what you want so you can stop hurting."

"I'm taking care of my children."

"For me, when this wine," he pointed to the bottle of wine, "is finished, my winery will be no more. All behind me will be gone. But I can start a new project and I have. Mary and I are working together in our vegetable garden. Remember? We told you about that when we started the garden. I've gotten over my sadness with the help of your mother, and I want you to do the same."

Hamilton didn't know what or how to feel about his father. His father surely had good intentions, but was that enough? When Hamilton was a boy and a teen, he needed more from his father than just good intentions. He needed his father. In retrospect, his father's good intentions brought his family a good life. Can he still hold anything against his father? Is it right to do that?

"You're right, we're in the same place, aren't we? My family, as I knew it, has changed, but I still have my job. Your job has changed, but you still have your family."

"Find yourself a wife, son. Find yourself a wife," George paused. "You don't have to say anything. I just want to see you happy." He took a gulp of his wine and set the empty glass on the table. "Let's go see your brother, now."

Hamilton didn't think of himself as lost. He always thought he was a powerful man, as his father described. But not lost. But he was lost. He knew he needed to step out and risk his heart. The risk that Anita meant and the "When" that Franny meant. He had made progress, but he was still a little hesitant. He needed to let go all the way.

At church, Hamilton didn't expect to see how grown Jeremy had become and how much he loved being in church. He stood his ground. It cost him frustration and discomfort with his mother, but Jeremy did what he thought right. His belief in God ws strong, and he fought or took a strong stand against anyone who kept him from serving his Lord. Jeremy was much like Hamilton in that respect. Except Hamilton didn't believe in God.

When Fr. Maddox took his place at the pulpit to give his sermon, Hamilton gave him a sly wink and an eye wipe with his finger. Taylor gave him a sly wink and an eye wipe back. It was a private code between two brothers, a way they communicated with each other that said, "I believe in you. I support you." They used it with each other when the other one asked, and when one gave the other a quick glance. They had started when Hamilton was ten and Taylor was twelve. Whenever one of them had to do something like the time a boy challenged Hamilton to sled down a steep, icy hill.

They used it again when Taylor tried to climb the flagpole in high school. According to Taylor, he was so in love with his girlfriend, Gwen. She challenged him to prove it. "If you love me, then climb up that flagpole and put this sign on the top." She handed him the sign, the size of a banner. He turned to Hamilton who gave him a wink and eye wipe. Taylor tied the banner around his waist and started climbing, using his arms to pull himself up. Several times he almost slipped down; the pole was metal and hard to grip. He continued pulling himself up until he got up to the flag. He had to attach a sign saying, "Taylor and Gwen Forever." Somehow, he managed to get the sign from around his waist and tied it on the pole.

Not only did he have trouble getting down, but he also had to slide most of the way, which rubbed his hands almost raw. When the principal saw the sign, he summoned Taylor and Gwen Forever to his office. Taylor had to serve a week in detention. Gwen, who got off with a reprimand, dumped him a week later. Now, Taylor gave a sermon about the relationship between the baby Jesus and the star that shined so bright. Hamilton thought Taylor's sermon was about Jeremy.

The next day, Christmas Day, they opened their Christmas gifts before they left for church. Hamilton bought Jeremy new clothes from the "cool clothes store," Jeremy pointed out to him in the mall, and an iPad so he could do his home assignments anywhere in the house. He missed Eric and Anna but understood Eric's need to visit Paige's parents this year and Anna's need to help with the children's Christmas party at her church. Jeremy bought Hamilton a desk pen set and two dress shirts, the kind he always wore to the university, he said. Hamilton gave a quick smile to Jeremy, realizing the message Jeremy sent him. Hamilton gave his parents each a cell phone. Hamilton said they needed to have regular contact with each other. George gave Hamilton a daily journal with three pictures.

Hamilton read the note attached to the first page.

> *I want you to have these pictures. They are what I used for myself when I needed encouragement. The first picture was just after I bought the winery. The second picture was taken almost seven years later, with your mother, Taylor, and you. The third picture was during the time I received my highest awards.*
>
> *I always looked at these pictures to see my progress and made sure I was staying on track. Your mother always said I was following what God wanted me to do for us and the pictures told me I was. Your mother didn't know it, but I think she always knew I prayed everyday thanking God for her, my number one thing, my two boys, and the winery.*
>
> *Maybe these pictures will help you as you move on.*
> *I love you, son. Never doubt or forget that.*
> *Your Dad*

Hamilton tried hard to hold back his tears, while and after reading the journal.

After church, George and Mary went with Taylor and his wife, Alice, for Christmas dinner. Hamilton dropped Jeremy off at HolliAnne's and then raced home to get his Christmas dinner started.

Hamilton had asked Marilyn to Christmas dinner at his house, since she had no place to go. He promised her he would make everything and absolutely nothing would be made in a store. She accepted, teasing him, saying since he promised it, he had to, and she would search through his entire house and all the trash cans if she had to, just to see he had made everything. "Well, then I'd better be true to my word. Can't have you rummaging through trash cans," Hamilton said.

He had just taken the turkey out of the oven when he heard the doorbell ring. Marilyn stood in the doorway, agape. He looked down at himself when he saw her face. He had answered the door wrapped in his over-size Christmas apron he'd forgotten to take off. The apron had a picture of Santa winking and with the words "Santa is cooking up something special for you," written in green. "Okay, go ahead and laugh. I know you want to." He stepped aside and let her in.

"You look so cute in your new dress," she said, setting her large, brown paper bag on the hall table and taking off her coat. "I love the message."

"Make fun all you want." He took her coat to hang up in the closet next to the hall table. "Anna, my daughter, gave me this last year. She said all talented cooks should have an apron." He laughed. "Now. See? What about that?"

"We shall test out the words 'talented cook' this evening." She picked up her bag and followed him to the kitchen.

"What's in the bag?"

"I made an apple pie," she said. "I hope you don't mind. I just couldn't come empty-handed."

He stopped to gaze at her for a minute, thinking how it was like her to bring something. "How about some wine? Can I get you a glass of wine?"

"Great."

"How is your son," Hamilton asked. He gestured for her to sit at the counter.

"He's settled now, but something will happen again, and I'll be called away."

"What's the problem, if I'm not overstepping my bounds?"

"I never have understood it, but he suffered a head injury and at times he loses control of himself and hits people with his fists, or picks up things and throws it at them, or hits them with it."

"How old is he?" Hamilton said, putting the asparagus in a flat pan.

"He's twenty-three. He was in an automobile accident when he was seventeen. His mother, my husband's girlfriend," she whispered, "had just picked up Lucas from school. They were headed to David's company to pick him up. David and I were still married, but we didn't live together then." She paused. "I don't know where they were all going."

"Marilyn, you already mentioned some of this, so you don't have to—"

"No. I want to." She took a sip of the wine Hamilton placed in front of her. "Lucas was in the backseat. David said later he and his girlfriend got into a terrible fight. I would like to think the fight was about him telling her he was ending their relationship and he wanted to be with me, but that would be very naïve of me. Anyway, she wasn't watching where she was going and ran off the road. He said she tried to get control of the car and steer it back on the road, but she smashed into a boulder. She tried harder to get the car back on the road, but the car went off into the ravine below. Lucas didn't have his seatbelt on and hit his head in several places. My husband and his girlfriend had deep slashes and lacerations over their bodies. David tried to pull them both out of the car when he saw they were upside down. He helped his girlfriend out, and he got Lucas out, just before the car burst into flames. Several people stopped to help; someone called the police. A man took all three in his truck to the hospital, ten minutes away. Lucas's head wound looked severe, and there was blood everywhere, so the man said, and he didn't think they should wait on an ambulance. David gave the man permission to take them to the hospital." She paused for a moment. "Why does a man find another woman and keep his wife?"

Hamilton stopped making the dressing at her question. He didn't have to stay with HolliAnne, but he did. She could have left him, but she didn't. "I don't know. You wanted him to be the one to leave, initiate the divorce?"

"Yes."

"Why?"

"I don't know. I wasn't aware that he had another woman until Lucas reached high school. David always told me what kept him away was his work. We were together on holidays, anniversaries, birthdays, the times that mattered."

"He told you about…?"

"I answered the phone when Lucas called one day. He said he thought he was calling his father's work and when I said it was, he left a message."

"What was David like?"

"He was a good man, at first, but then at times he could be abusive. He wanted us to get married early in our relationship. I didn't want to get married right away. I wanted to wait, but I gave in. Soon after we married, he wanted us to start a family. I wasn't so sure. But we tried and when I didn't get pregnant, he blamed me for it. One day, he told me I had a problem. I didn't know he wanted a family so badly. I thought we were having a wonderful relationship, but he had found another woman."

"Why would you stay? You had different desires."

"I thought he loved me, and except for explosive bouts now and then, he treated me well. I wasn't so sure about marrying because I was afraid a marriage would mess up what we had."

"How?"

"The vows. When you marry, you make each other a promise in God's presence. That's serious—till death do us part? When you just live together, you don't make a promise to each other. You don't have an obligation to each other that you will honor each other and work things out. When times get hard, you have no obligation to stay, so you don't."

"Marilyn? Who were you afraid of? You? Or David?"

Hamilton was reminded of how he selected the right peach for his family. His father would say selecting the right grape. But, for him, it was selecting the right peach. Anna and Eric liked peaches, and when Hamilton shopped for fruit at the fruit stands, he and Anna would have to select the right peach. Selecting a mate was like picking a peach. The outside of a peach may have a nice soft fuzz with the feel of air when his hand gently touched it, a glorious yellow and a vibrant pink in color. The peach would be slightly tender to the touch, soft but strong. His mouth would water as he thought about slicing it open to taste this wonder, and with building excitement and anticipation, he would slice it open to taste and savor the sweet, juicy pulp. He would be disappointed when he cut it open to a brown decay inside.

Marilyn must have been disappointed when her husband began seeing someone else, just as he was disappointed in HolliAnne when he found out she was seeing other men. Hamilton stayed with HolliAnne because he wanted his three children to have a family structure where there was a father and mother from the time they were born until they left home. He wanted to be a father to his children. Marilyn didn't have any children, so why would she stay? In staying with HolliAnne, he didn't ask her for anything. He didn't change and at that point, he wasn't sure he even loved her. He just wanted to be a father. Why would Marilyn stay?

After dinner, Marilyn brought out her apple pie. Hamilton had vanilla ice cream they piled on top. He teased her by saying, "The pie tastes just like the one I bought at Whole Foods the other day." She broke down and admitted she bought it but reminded him he was the one who promised to make everything from scratch; she didn't make a promise.

He liked Marilyn. She was fun and sometimes easy and kind and gentle and had a smile that ended with lines on either side of her mouth, like bookmarks. This evening, she didn't flirt with him, and she helped him relax. The only thing she expected was an enjoyable dinner. She helped him clean up and put things away. While he was finishing, she took her glass of wine and sat in the living room. He brought her a shopping bag filled with several tubs of leftover food and sat in his favorite chair with a glass of wine, as they continued talking.

Marilyn decided it was time to go and as he helped her with her coat, Franny showed up for dinner.

"I hate I had to invite myself and I hope I'm not too late," Franny said, ignoring Hamilton's surprised stare, and that Marilyn was in her coat leaving. She held up a bottle of white wine. Hamilton had no idea she even knew where he lived, but he remembered he gave her his information when she hired him.

"I'm sorry, Franny. I thought you told me you were having dinner with a cousin," Hamilton said.

Franny cut her eyes down. "My mother was all I had. It was too lonely, in the apartment."

Hamilton motioned to Marilyn to come back to the kitchen. Franny ate, and they talked about the dance competition and who they thought had some chance at winning.

During the week after Christmas, before New Year's Eve, Marilyn called to say she had to go back to Lucas's hospital. Lucas threw a chair at the aide and severely injured the aide.

Eric, his girlfriend Paige, and Anna surprised Hamilton and came home. When they arrived, Hamilton convinced his parents to stay at least one more day for sightseeing. Paige was ready to see the city, and they braved the snow and cold and went sightseeing.

The first day, they went to the Lincoln Memorial and drove by the Washington Monument. Mary wanted to go in, but Hamilton remembered the elevator wasn't working and they didn't have tickets.

"You have to have tickets to go into the Monument?" George asked.

"Yes, you do," Hamilton said.

"Well, that doesn't seem right," Mary said.

"After all the taxes we pay, we should be able to just go on in," George continued.

"This world is changing now, Grandpop. You have to pay for everything, whether you've already paid for it through your taxes or not," Eric said.

"That just doesn't seem right. They're making so many changes, we won't even recognize our own country anymore," George said.

"I agree with you on that," Mary began, "everything now is the computer. Everything is all about computers."

"It's computers, and townhouses and cell phones." George said.

"Welcome to the new world," Hamilton said.

"Welcome to my world," Eric said.

Hamilton heard how his father felt displaced by the changes in his environment affecting his life, the same way he felt displaced by the changes in his life.

Hamilton gave up his room to his parents and got a blanket and pillow to sleep in the family room. Jeremy saw him and he grabbed a blanket and pillow from his bed. When Eric came down for a glass of water and saw, he got his blanket and pillow and knocked on Anna's door. Eric, Anna, and Paige came down to the family room with blankets and pillows.

Hamilton made popcorn and got a bottle of Ginger Ale. They talked about the time Eric and Anna were ten and eleven, and Anna followed Eric everywhere he went. They talked about the time in high school when they stayed out later than their curfew and how Eric tried to climb in through the window to get in. Anna stood below him outside, quietly cheering him on as only Anna would. Eric had left the window unlocked before they left. Hamilton knew it and locked the window, but the front door was open. When they came in, Hamilton was waiting for them in the living room, sitting by the window.

Hamilton was in heaven for these few minutes while he listened, laughed, and ate popcorn with his children and, most likely, his future daughter-in-law. He wanted to remember every minute of the night.

The day before New Year's Eve, George and Mary said their goodbyes and drove back home. They had tickets to a New Year's Eve party at the senior community center. Eric and Paige wanted to attend a New Year's Eve party that Eric's old high school buddy was having. Paige asked Anna to go with them. Eric had promised Paige they would also visit her parents, which meant they would have to leave early on New Year's Day. Anna wanted to visit her boyfriend. His mother wanted to meet her. Jeremy's youth group was having a party, and Jeremy wanted to stay overnight. Hamilton tried hard not to be disappointed. Instead, he let go.

CHAPTER 28

Before he was ready, the holidays had ended, and he was back at the studio for the last evening of the session. Everyone seemed so nervous on the night of the competition. All the students from both Franny's classes showed up. Franny had decorated the studio with streamers, dark lighting, and for those who may need a rest in between dances, tables and chairs were set up in the back of the studio. Most of the class members contributed refreshments and brought in punch, sandwiches, and cookies. The students from the other studio also brought refreshments, some even brought wine. "The wine was an excellent idea," Ronald began, "I think I'm gonna need it."

Emma came up with a complicated step for the cha-cha she said was her very own creation. She showed the step to Hamilton and then asked him to practice it with her. They found a spot in the studio to practice, but the step, not being a cha-cha step, was difficult for Hamilton to understand. It didn't fit with the rhythm of most cha-cha music.

"Emma, I'm not so sure about this. I just can't get it right."

"It seemed okay when I made it up."

They tried again, but Hamilton couldn't get his feet to work right, and he kept forgetting a little double step, which caused Emma to be a half step behind him. They changed course and practiced what they'd learned in the class.

Emma turned to him, "We have to get this right. I'm depending on you."

Before Hamilton had a chance to say anything, Emma added, "I mean, the others in the class are depending on us."

He put his right arm around Emma's waist, arm up and elbow out, back straight, and for a few minutes, the two of them rehearsed all the steps for the cha-cha. When they thought they could do all they could, Emma went to the dressing room to get ready.

Marilyn found Hamilton in the back of the studio, standing in front of the dressing room. She handed him something wrapped in tan paper, with a tan and purple bow.

"Open it," she said with a big smile. Marilyn waved others on the dance floor to gather around.

"Marilyn, I—"

"Just open it," Carey said.

Hamilton took the gift and unwrapped it. He pulled out a long black sash with fringed edging.

"Oh, how nice," Dacie said.

"I promised you a sash, remember?"

"Look, it has his name stitched on the front with little red balls around it," Carol said.

The others from both classes and the competitors, including Kurt, the instructor, formed a horseshoe around Hamilton. Emma, coming out of the dressing room, joined the group.

"Marilyn, what a nice thing to do," Franny said, who also joined the group.

"I don't know what to say." Hamilton looked around at everyone. "This is just very nice, and my name. I'm overwhelmed." He leaned over and kissed Marilyn on the cheek. The classes clapped.

The other team members and the instructor introduced themselves to each other. The instructor made announcements about who would compete with whom, presented the rules, and asked each side to agree on them. Everyone from both groups agreed, while clapping and singing, "Let's Dance, Let's Dance." Hamilton announced he couldn't compete since technically he was an employee. Franny suggested they hold the names of the winning couples until the end of the competition.

The music was ready, and the competition began. The first style dance was the fox-trot, and the competing teams were called.

The first couple to dance was a husband and wife team from Kurt's group. They danced the fox-trot, but they were too mechanical in their delivery. When they finished, Aileen and Albert were next. They were both smooth and not only knew the steps, but they seemed to enjoy dancing the fox-trot. Even older adults are perfervid and enjoy an amorous dalliance from time to time.

After everyone had competed, and just before Kurt announced the winners, he asked Hamilton and Marilyn to dance the tango. They performed the dance with enthusiasm and ended on a round of applause.

Hamilton looked over at Emma, who had a look of disappointment shading her face. She cast her eyes downward toward the floor. Hamilton nodded to Franny, and she turned on the music. He walked to where Emma stood and extended his hand. With a smile, she took his hand, and they circled the room, smiling at everyone watching them. After they had gone around once, Hamilton gave Emma a gentle tug and she turned, stepped to face him as he took an easy step forward and the two of them began the cha-cha.

Hamilton no longer heard the music, but felt the music radiate from her body, filling his body with the rhythm of the music. His arm was her arm and his body, her body, as he felt her an extension of him. His feet seemed to have their own mind as they automatically stepped and turned. He stared into her big, brown, round, gems that showed her happiness and seemed to say, "I'll follow you to wherever you take me." Their steps and body movements came so natural to the two of them, as they turned and circled, and she followed his lead. He took her hand, held her around her waist, as they danced side by side, stepped apart, stepped in facing each other, turned in circles. He could no longer decipher the classmates. They fell into a background of blurred masses of colors—yellows, whites, grays, blues—as he and Emma twirled and turned. The world became a magical one to him now, as he took her hands, caught her after a turn, turned her in different directions, and took her in his arms, all the while his beautiful sash swinging slightly with every move. At the end of the cha-cha, he began the waltz, and she fell right into the waltz without hesitation, making it seem like one dance.

They finished the waltz the way they began, circling around the room, and then he brought her into his arms. She pulled away, and they faced the group, took a bow. But no one clapped. Instead, they stood agape, openmouthed, astonished at the two people. Hamilton and Emma turned to each other, and Hamilton gave her a smile when he saw her terrified look.

Ronald was the first one to break out of the trance, and began clapping, encouraging others to join him. Hamilton was thankful someone at least recognized their embarrassment. As they stood together hand in hand, Hamilton tugged at Emma's hand and the two of them bowed together. The clapping continued, and they bowed again. They walked out of the center and stood with their classmates, still holding hands. The clapping continued, and everyone faced them.

The clapping went on and on, and Emma turned to smile at Hamilton. His heart had to be on his face. Her heart was on her face. He tried to raise his arms to the crowd and felt how tightly she held on to his hand. He edged closer to her and squeezed her hand as if to say, "It's okay. I'm here. I got you." The thing that makes a man feel like a man is when a woman needs him. Emma made him feel like a man. He turned to her. He wanted to be with her, hold her hand, kiss her, show her his love, and touch her soft, silky body. He wanted to kiss her entire body and hear her purr with quiet pleasure. He wanted to kiss her lips, her neck and breast, feel her tremble under him, hear her rapid breathing, and see her body beg for more. He wanted her to know how a man can love a woman, the arousal, the thrill, the beauty. But for now, he would have to keep his distance and wait for her to let him know when she was ready.

Hamilton came back to the center and held up both hands. "Everyone, let's do the waltz."

He nodded at Franny, and she started the music. Hamilton gave her an encouraging gesture toward Kurt. Franny shook her head. At that moment Kurt, with an asking smile, took Franny's hand and led her to the dance floor. After they stepped out onto the dance floor, the others followed.

During their planning, Hamilton and Franny made certificates and awards for several categories, such as best dressed, best overall, best execution of turns, and anything else they could think of so that everyone could take something home. After the dancing, Franny and Kurt handed out certificates and awards for their groups.

"Before you leave, I want to let my classes know Hamilton is leaving."

"This can't be true," Ronald said.

"No, you can't leave us," Carol said.

Hamilton looked at Franny for her to continue. "I know this is very hard. It is extremely hard for me. Hamilton has done so much for me. You just don't know." She looked at him and smiled, tears forming in her eyes. "He took some time off and now he has to get back to work. For those who can, I will have a going away party for him tomorrow evening."

Hamilton hadn't expected an announcement or party. He just wanted to slip out unnoticed.

The next evening, most of the students from all the classes, except for Franny's two ballet classes, showed up to say their goodbyes to Hamilton and to wish him well.

"Thank you everyone. So much for leaving unnoticed. I want to thank Franny for teaching me how to dance. She did a marvelous job with me, and she's done the same with you. She gave me the courage and desire to try harder and showed me I could succeed at something. I hope everyone will sign up again for Franny's next session and invite your friends and relatives to sign up. I highly recommend her."

After everyone left, Hamilton helped Franny clean up.

"Franny, I just want to thank you for hiring me. This has been an amazing experience for me."

"I wish you would stay. I'm not ready for you to leave yet."

"That's not true. You're more ready than you think. In fact, you've been ready for a while. You just needed someone to show you the way."

"I have always lived in my mother's shadow. I didn't know I had anything to offer until you came along. You made me take off that boot," she laughed.

He took her by the hands. "You never needed that boot or anything. Think about what you taught me."

"I know what I want to do. I know it's not ballet, but I want to teach dance. I had so much fun teaching the tango, the waltz, the rumba." She reached up and kissed him on the cheek. "Thank you so much, for the website, arranging the classes, my apartment, and helping me break away from my mother. I owe you so much."

"You don't owe me a thing. You owe yourself. Be the best teacher and treat your students with care and dignity. Do right by them. And don't forget to raise the price because you really weren't charging them enough."

Franny laughed. "I will."

Hamilton started out of the studio.

"Hey," Franny began. Hamilton turned around. "If the university doesn't work out or you just decide you don't want to do that, come back. You are always welcome here."

He nodded and turned to leave. He turned back to get a look at the studio, the place that made him see what controlling a person can do to the person; the place where he took hold of himself and began changing himself. He saw Franny walk back into the office. Then he left.

CHAPTER 29

Hamilton didn't believe his office would be the same when he returned, but it was. It pays to have a dutiful assistant, he said aloud after he entered and closed the door. Without thought, he took up his routine, and again, was the first one in the office. He was happy to see the brain didn't wipe out everything so quickly. The experience with Franny and all the people in the dance classes changed him, and he was thankful for the opportunity. He would miss Franny.

He was not as nervous about returning and facing everyone. He was a little more ready to talk about why he took the time off and what he did during that time. However, he wasn't ready to go too deeply into his marriage, or HolliAnne, especially since she no longer had her position of department chair at the university. He knew nothing about her plans, and he wanted to leave it like that.

As per usual, he took a few minutes to gaze out of his window at the iced over lake and the snow-covered littoral, hoping the perennials would be unharmed. He had missed looking out on his trail every day and watching the ducks take their last dip before leaving for a better climate, he supposed.

He turned to his desk. Josie had left him several notes along with packages, letters and email she had printed out for him. He picked up his box with his things he had taken with him when he left and put the things back in their places.

He turned on his computer and found he could use his password, thanks to Josie. He knew she had taken the time to call IT and gotten that already for him. He typed an email to all the department chairs under his supervision and set up a meeting to catch up. It's time to get back to work.

After his promise to Anita and months of working in the dance studio learning how to be a friend, confidant, and dancer, he was ready to make the big change, the risk that involved his heart. He was ready to release his fears and accept the challenge – the next step. He couldn't take back what he did to HolliAnne, but he would hold himself responsible in the future. His father told him he was unhappy. Hamilton wanted his happiness.

The phone on his desk rang, interrupting his thoughts.

"Dr. Maddox," he said, using his formal voice.

"Well, you're at work early, aren't you?"

"Habit, I guess. Why are you up so early? Working on a sermon for Sunday?

"I need a favor."

"So early. This is my first day back."

"I know. It has nothing to do with the university."

"I'm listening..."

"The Welcome New Members committee is having a gathering this evening at my house. We have five new members so far, and every few months we do a welcome reception for new members. We orient them to the church, informing them about all the programs and committees we have."

"I don't see how I can help."

"The chairman of the committee organizes the groups, does the speaking, and whatever else happens. I just provide the house. Larry won't be able to attend tonight. He left me with things to do and talk about, but I still need someone else. I called the other three people on the committee, and they can't come either. I'd rather not cancel this. So, here's where you come in. Can you just come? You can talk about what you do here at church and the programs and classes we have."

"Taylor, I don't know. I'm not good at that."

"You attend and have been in many classes. Jeremy is an acolyte, you're familiar with those classes and you've been to several vestry meetings. I'm asking because I know of your involvement."

Hamilton paused for a moment. He still had not told Taylor or anyone he did not believe in God.

"Plus, there will be great food," Taylor added, a laugh in his voice.

"I have to bring Jeremy. He's my support and knows more than you or I."

Alice answered the door and let in Hamilton and Jeremy. She led them to the living room where Taylor in an armchair, a man and woman seated on the couch, another man and woman in the love seat, and two other people seated in hard back chairs, were engaged in hearty laughter. As he stood, Taylor waved Hamilton and Jeremy into the living room.

"Grace, Ted, Monica, Steve, Ellen and Walter, I want you to meet my brother, Hamilton Maddox. Ham, these gracious people just joined."

"Good to meet you all," shaking hands. "I know you will love it here at St. John's. My son, Jeremy, loves this church." Jeremy extended his hand.

"Let's have something to eat. Alice made a little something for us." Taylor said.

Hamilton had not had many opportunities to see his brother as nervous as he was this evening. Taylor wasn't very good at talking about himself or trying to convince people to do things, though his sermons were often extraordinary, very encouraging, and relevant to everyday life. He imagined Taylor, beginning on Thursday in his office at the church or here in his home, walking back and forth, memorizing his points in his sermon and what he wanted to impart, the same way he used to practice his speeches when they were both in high school.

Jeremy handed Hamilton a plate of sliced chicken and rice, green salad, and green beans.

"Jeremy, I am so happy you came, tonight," Taylor said.

"Dad said there would be food, so we rushed right over."

"Are you saying you're unhappy with my cooking? I thought everything was okay," Hamilton said, a smile on his face.

"It is, Dad. It is." Jeremy laughed and left to go back to the table for his plate.

"How did the first day back go?" Taylor asked.

"Almost like I'd never left. Funny how some things just fall into place," Hamilton said, sorrow in his voice.

"You're not thinking about quitting, are you?"

"Ham, did you and Jeremy get a ticket when you came in?" Alice asked, interrupting them.

"A ticket? No."

"Well, here you go." Alice separated two tickets and handed one to Hamilton.

"What's this for?" Hamilton asked. He held it up, then stuck it in his pocket.

"We're going to put you in groups as soon as everyone gets here. You'll need your ticket for that."

"Dad? You got your ticket?" Jeremy asked, as he held up his ticket and a big smile on his face. He sat his plate on the table behind him.

"You got a ticket, too?"

"Aunt Alice thinks I'm smart enough to join the adults. What's your number?"

Hamilton showed Jeremy his ticket.

"Switch with me," Jeremy said.

"We can't switch, can we, Taylor?"

"Dad, you have my favorite number. Let's switch."

They switched tickets.

Alice entered the living room, with two ladies trailing behind her. "Taylor, Honey, am I the only one answering the door?"

Taylor moved toward the door, but Alice put her hand out, "I've already answered the door." To get their attention, she turned to look at everyone. When the room was quiet, "I would like to introduce Emma Stevens, and Veronica Howard," she stepped aside, "our two newest new members." Alice giggled at her alliteration, a habit that occasionally bothered Hamilton.

Emma gave a curt bow to the group after Mary introduced her, and Veronica gave a short wave to everyone. Hamilton's face showed both surprise and happiness when he saw Emma. "Here're your tickets."

Alice handed Emma and Veronica tickets. "Taylor, I think everyone is here now."

"I think we are all here, now. Thank you, Alice, sweetheart, for answering the door. So, let's everyone get something to eat, and then take a seat in the living room. We can get started."

In a few minutes, everyone was seated in the living room and ready for the opening prayer.

After the prayer, Taylor said, "You all have a ticket in your hand. But you only have one. Find the person with the ticket with a matching number. That is who your partner will be for the evening, and hopefully, you will have made a good friend, as well. Everyone, please find your partner now, so we can begin."

No one got up. Hamilton was a little reluctant to call out his number. Jeremy got up first. "My number is number 100. Does anyone have 100?" Grace raised her hand, and she and Jeremy sat down next to each other. Hamilton announced his number, 63. Emma raised her hand and said her number was 63. They sat together. When everyone had finished finding their partners, Taylor talked about the programs and groups at St. John's and then asked Hamilton to talk about his involvement in the church. When Hamilton finished, he asked Jeremy to talk about his programs.

Jeremy stood up and amazed both Hamilton and Taylor. He began by asking if anyone had children. Everyone raised their hand, except Emma and Veronica. Then relayed his experience in the Sunday school classes and went on to his current participation in the youth group. He related the things the youth group had done, so far, and the future events. He told them who to contact and how to get enrolled in both the Sunday school classes and the youth group. He talked about the acolyte program and the benefits of being an acolyte. When he sat down, no one spoke.

After a few minutes, Fr. Maddox said, "Wow, Jeremy. Thank you. I feel like signing up after that." The newcomers let out a chorus of "Me too," and nodded.

"I did mention that Jeremy is my nephew, right?" Taylor joked. The group laughed.

"Okay everyone. You all have heard about our programs here that you may want to join. We have leaflets, flyers, and brochures," he turned the brochure over in his hand, "many things to choose. We want you to be a part of our community here, but don't feel you must. What you choose to do or not do, how much you do or how little, of course, is your choice. Questions?" Taylor looked around the room and no one seemed to have a question. "Okay then, Larry, our newcomers leader, has asked me to lead you in the next thing. Please keep in mind, as I fumble through this, that he is usually the one doing it." Taylor cleared his throat. "Okay, then, now that you have your partner, you are to do three things. Ready?" He didn't look to see the response.

"First, find out as many things about each other as possible within the fifteen-minute time limit tonight. Focus on one thing if you can, like maybe this is the first church. Why? Or you can do something general. Second, exchange phone numbers; and third, for the next two months, call each other weekly to encourage your partner to visit a few groups and programs we have. How 'bout that? Isn't that a wonderful idea?" He queried their faces. "Okay, you will have fifteen minutes to find out as many things about your partner as possible. I will call time. Then we'll ask you to share some things you found out about each other. Okay? Okay, then, let's" he held up his hand while looking at his stopwatch on his cell phone, "begin now."

Hamilton turned to Emma, "This is a surprise. How did you find out about St. John's?"

"I was just looking for someplace close to me. I went by one day and Fr. Maddox talked to me about the church and how he could use me in the church. I came a few times and now I'm thinking about joining."

"As you can see from Jeremy's talk, it's a great place to worship."

"I'm surprised to see you here."

"Taylor is my brother. I have an obligation," he smiled.

"Just an obligation?"

He felt the same way about her as he did during their dance together. She had an alluring quality that enticed him. He tried so hard to look past it. "Why don't we tell each other something about ourselves before we run out of time. You go first."

"Okay." She paused, watched his face. "I was a nun."

"Did you say nun, like in a convent?"

"Yes, a nun, like in a convent."

He gave her an asking gaze and observed her dress. She was not dressed like someone who had just come out of the convent, though he didn't quite know what that was. She was dressed modestly.

"Five years ago, I left the convent. Now, I'm a research journalist with a research company."

Hamilton didn't know what to say to her about her past. Any question would be probing. Instead, he asked her what she did as a research journalist and what she was working on. She told him she had just completed an assignment and was waiting for the next. She didn't seem to want to talk much about herself; he offered his background. He told her a few things about his marriage, and that it was over. He wanted her to know that. He also talked about his three children and where they were now.

At the end of the fifteen minutes, Taylor called time. Each group introduced themselves to everyone in the room.

"Okay, now, we got off to a fantastic start. You guys listened to each other. Now, here's the other part of this program. Each week for the next two months, call each other and see how your partner is doing. Did they go to anything during the week? What was it like for them? Why not for those who did not? Should you attend something with them? The purpose is to stay with your partner for a while. My leader recommends two months, at least, and help each other get acclimated. Then we ask you to join us for another group coming in." He paused and looked around the room. "Are there questions?"

Several people raised their hands.

Hamilton leaned in close to say something to Emma when her hair fell across her face. She pulled it back away from her eyes and turned toward Taylor. Hamilton melted inside and sat back in his seat. The speed of his heart greatly rose, and he guessed that she could hear the beating of his heart. He gave a sideways glance to her and thought about his promise to Anita. One day he would marry this woman sitting beside him.

CHAPTER 30

The president of the college, vice presidents, associates, provosts, deans, department chairs and faculty members gave Hamilton a "Welcome Back" reception late one Friday afternoon. He suspected this was all because of his secretary, Josie, who was always up on everything. He helped himself to the food and drinks and later when Josie cut the cake, he took a small slice. People asked what he did on his leave, the paper he wrote or book he was writing, and he told them he helped a friend in a dance studio. His next paper will be about life. He thought his comment was vague enough to keep them from asking more questions.

Also, during his second week at the university, Hamilton busied himself by setting up and, or attending meetings with his department chairs, other deans, and a fund-raising committee.

Since the newcomers meeting at the church the week before, all he could do was think about Emma. He imagined what it must have been like for her as a novice working her way up to becoming a nun. He was curious about her being a nun. He wanted to know more and should have asked her more questions, but he didn't think it best.

By the end of the week, Hamilton was a little anxious. Taylor suggested everyone keep in contact with their partner for at least the next two months and should contact each other weekly. He hadn't had a chance to call Emma during the week, and he wanted to ask about any groups she may have visited.

Hamilton wasn't afraid of Emma. She was not a woman who would abuse his love. He could tell that from her honesty, her smile, and her intense gaze. He had promised Anita he wouldn't "sit on the couch and watch TV" for the rest of his life. He would "get back in the race," "climb back on the horse." He was careful about not controlling anything with Emma. He didn't want to shape things, guide her into doing things his way. He wanted to go where and how his heart led him. His heart told him Emma was the woman who could love him with all her heart and soul. She was the woman who could support him and encourage him. He called her.

At the sound of her "hello" he was delighted to hear her voice. The hello was welcoming and filled him with happiness. When he introduced himself, her voice changed to reveal her excitement, much like the excitement of children at a carnival, with the laughing, running, and surprises.

Emma said she had a sinus headache she couldn't get rid of for most of the week. He wanted to ask if he could massage her head but thought better of it. She said the melting snow, rain and dampness leaving mold and mildew didn't help much. She attended the Visiting Ministry. She explained to him the visiting ministry focused on those who could not attend church because they were in a nursing home, hospital, or were home sick.

As he listened, he heard the joy of a man and woman standing before a priest announcing them husband and wife; he heard and felt the tears mixed with laughter from a man and woman who had just given birth; he heard the laughter of children playing on a beach; he heard the happiness in her voice of a family during Christmas; and he felt the awakening of the rush of waterfalls.

Pulling him back, she joked with him, saying maybe she should have asked to be put on the list because of her sinus headache. Emma asked what he did. Hamilton told her about the reception and his meetings.

"Have you had dinner?" He asked.

"No, I haven't," she said.

There it was, now. He had officially entered the risk-taking arena.

At home, Hamilton started the dinner and asked Jeremy to help him make the house neater.

"Dad, who is this woman?" Jeremy folded the newspaper he had out earlier and stuck it under his arm.

"You know her. She's the lady from the newcomer's meeting. You met her." He tried to keep his voice even as he dusted the tops of the tables.

"Why is she coming for dinner?"

"She didn't have a pleasant week, so I thought it would be a nice thing to do."

While Jeremy went to put the newspaper in the recycle bin, Hamilton stood in the kitchen staring at the seats around the counter. He turned to the dining room and stood for a minute. Then he went to the cabinet to get out dishes and placed them on the dining room table.

"I think this woman is important to you." Jeremy stood, eyes protruding as he watched his father set the table for the three of them. He opened one of the cabinet drawers to the hutch and pulled out a white linen tablecloth. "Here. Let's put this on first."

Hamilton, a half-smile on his face, nodded and helped Jeremy remove the dishes and put down the tablecloth. Afterward, they both stood back and looked. "That's good," Hamilton said, watching Jeremy. "That's good," Jeremy confirmed.

He went about making the sauce and preparing the spaghetti. Jeremy took out the unsliced loaf of bread and spread garlic and butter on top, the way his father did. Hamilton prepared a green salad. He then poured the sauce from the jar into the pot and added sliced mushrooms and diced green peppers.

Emma arrived on time and Hamilton asked Buddy Boy to lead her into the family room where he had turned on the gas fireplace. He and Jeremy hadn't used it much this winter and Hamilton thought it would improve the atmosphere.

"What a pleasant room," Emma said. She sat on the couch.

"Jeremy, tell me more about what you do at St. John's," Emma asked.

Hamilton handed her a glass of red wine.

Jeremy and Emma took to each other, and Hamilton relaxed. He didn't have to carry the conversation.

"I enjoyed carrying the cross and the candles. That was the only thing I could do until I was confirmed."

"What made you want to serve as an acolyte?"

"It made me feel special. Being an acolyte made me feel like God asked me to serve him and carry the candles, the light, and the cross."

"Did you get confirmed?"

"I was confirmed when I was twelve." He looked at Hamilton. "I would like to become a priest someday."

Hamilton half-smiled, half-startled. He remembered Jeremy telling that to everyone during the Thanksgiving dinner.

"Wow! That's magnificent," Emma said. She turned toward Hamilton.

"I'll say. I didn't know that until recently."

"Would it be okay with you?"

"Sure. Why wouldn't it? What you want to be is your choice, not mine." There was a time not too long ago when he would have tried to change what his children and wife wanted. He paused for a moment, "Even though I am surprised, I'm not." Hamilton attempted to rustle Buddy Boy's hair, but he, expecting it, ducked.

After dinner, Hamilton and Emma had coffee in the family room. Jeremy went to his room to do his homework.

"Emma, you never told me much about the fact that you were a nun. Why did you want to be a nun?"

"I don't talk much about my background to people. My upbringing differed greatly from many people."

"I'd like to hear it, if you don't mind talking about it."

"I don't think I ever wanted to be a nun. It felt more like an obligation to me. I remember you said that one time about church."

"I may have."

"My parents were older when I was born. My mother was well into her 40s and my father was into his 50s. I never knew exactly how old they were. I was an only child. My mother had a hard time giving birth to me which left her with an illness. I was too young to understand the illness, and I never remembered the name. When I was about nine, it seemed to me my father blamed me for her illness, and I tried hard to stay away from him. When I was ten, my mother passed away. By that time, my father was almost seventy. He took me to a convent he found, one of the few still in existence, and left me there. He never said he'd be back for me. He just left me there. Seven nuns raised me. I had a group of mothers all telling me what to do. A few months after my father put me in the convent, one nun told me he died. She said he was very sick and couldn't take care of me, so he took me to a place where he knew I'd get excellent care. He couldn't leave me on my own. He had no other alternative."

"What was it like there? Did they treat you right?"

Emma laughed. "They treated me fine. I missed out on many things ten-year-old girls and older go through. Even though I had seven mothers, I never felt loved. One nun was in her nineties and very sick when I arrived. She passed away about a year later."

"You had no other relatives?"

"I think I must have. My father spoke of his brother and my mother had two sisters, but no one lived anywhere near us, as far as I knew."

Hamilton reached for her hand. "I am so sorry you had such a hard time. You seem to accept it, so complacent about your past."

"Thank you. I found there is nothing I could do to change it, so I had to accept it or go around hurt all the time. And I had lost enough time already. I wanted to spend the rest of my life savoring every moment."

Emma tried to stand; it was getting late. She pushed herself up, holding onto the arm of the couch, but lost her balance. Hamilton jumped up from his seat to steady her.

"I'm a little woozy. I guess that sinus headache is still with me somehow."

"Maybe you should wait a few minutes. Can I get you water or something?"

"I think I'll be okay." She walked around a little, allowing the dizziness to dissipate.

Hamilton walked her to her car and saw her in. "If you find you can't make it home, please pull over and call me. I'll come and get you."

She looked at him as if she wanted to say something. He leaned over and kissed her lightly. He looked at her face again and then kissed her again and again. "You'd better get home," he whispered with embarrassment.

CHAPTER 31

One of Hamilton's department chairs asked him to talk to a student who plagiarized, lied, and refused to listen. The chair said there was something else bothering the student. He refused to talk to her, and she wanted the college to do more for him than just drop him. For the next several days, Hamilton dealt with the student. He had plagiarized two essays and then cheated on his final exam. When he had received a final grade of "F," he filed an official complaint. In his written complaint, he stated he thought he should have passed the class, since he was present every day, took part in the class discussions, and did well on his quizzes. His professor responded to his complaint with the fact that not only did he fail the final exam, but he also turned in two papers he had plagiarized. The second one, the paper that counted the most, he downloaded from the internet and turned in as his work.

The guidelines for the university state that students must be heard when they make a complaint. Normally, when students protested their grade, Hamilton would look over the documents and render a decision. This time, he thought about Anna and the decision he made for her. It was the time when Anna refused to take part in the gifted and honors program at her high school because Hamilton didn't consult her.

It was because of Anna that Hamilton wanted this student to participate in the decision affecting his life. Hamilton retrieved the student's transcript and asked for written reports from each professor he had while at the university. The student, department chair, two professors from other disciplines, along with one of the student's previous professors, met together for two days, an hour each day.

On the second day, the student contested a report from a previous professor. All but two of his previous professors stated in their reports the student was not doing well in their classes.

On the third day, Hamilton met with the student alone. Just as he began to give the student the results of the previous meetings, the student broke down and cried. Through his loud crying ringing out disappointment and disgust in himself, he told Hamilton his parents wanted him to attend college. He never wanted to be a college student. He had wanted to attend broadcast school because he wanted to be a DJ. Hamilton handed him a tissue and waited for him to stop crying.

Jeremy, wanting to be a priest, came to his mind. He had to admit he didn't see that coming. Jeremy liked being an acolyte and wanted to be confirmed in the Episcopal Church, but he didn't think Jeremy would want to become a priest. His son was very social and was good with his friends. He stood up for them and when he had a chance to tell on one of them to save himself, he didn't do that. Hamilton was proud of his son. One thing Hamilton knew not to do was to tell Jeremy not to become a priest. He was brought back when he heard the student ask for another tissue.

Hamilton handed him the box to select a tissue. "Tell me about broadcast school."

"I've always wanted to be a disc jockey. Ever since I can remember I wanted to be a DJ. I applied but my parents wouldn't help me and at the time I wasn't working and wasn't able to afford the tuition. They offered scholarships, and I wanted to try for that. But even with a scholarship, that wouldn't cover everything. I couldn't do the rest on my own."

"What makes you think you're good at being a DJ?"

The student identified the qualities of a good DJ and compared them to his qualities.

"Do you have the information you need? The brochure, scholarship information, application and whatever else?"

"Yes, sir. I do."

"Why don't you get it all together and we meet back here next week and look at that for you. Maybe we can help you do that."

"What? You will help? I mean, you can do that? I — I—I don't know what to say, Sir."

"Just get everything you need, and we'll meet here in a week. And don't forget to tell your parents about what happened."

The student stood, stretched out his hand. Hamilton shook his hand and the student left. At his desk he sat back in his new chair. He had to admit his new non-control personality left him free and relaxed.

Then, February ended, and March began, slowly at first, but then as usual, the days picked up speed. He and Emma saw each other more often. They met after church on Sundays for lunch. If the weather was nice, they went for a walk. Emma asked him to go with her to a few church activities. When they could, they had dinner together before the activity.

Jeremy had his own interests, He told Hamilton he wanted to serve at the Ash Wednesday evening service and before he knew it, Easter was upon them, and Jeremy wanted to serve during the Easter service.

The weather during Easter week was miserable with its chilly temperature and constant drizzle. Eric called and he and his girlfriend, Paige, had found a nice little church where they had been attending for almost a year. During the Sunday service, the priest announced a retreat during Holy Week. When Eric and his girlfriend signed up to go, he called Anna and asked her to ride with them. Anna wanted to attend and bring her boyfriend.

Though he was disappointed, Hamilton did not let on, and even stated how happy he was he and Anna were going. Maybe he came off a little too joyous, but he wanted them to attend the retreat. Hamilton and Emma and Jeremy took the train to New York and saw, "Hello, Dolly," off Broadway. Hamilton thought Buddy Boy would complain, but he seemed to enjoy the musical.

Before Hamilton had time to miss Eric and Anna. Easter had ended and many of the church activities were ending for the year. May appeared with its colorful array of flower beds in the neighborhoods and on the islands dividing the streets. The days were longer; the rain had stopped, and the sun warmed the earth. The spring semester had also ended. How can time speed by so fast? This time last year, he was preparing himself for a court appearance. In retrospect, his life seemed so bleak then. He thought there was nothing for him to look forward to, but loneliness and the sadness that came with a tragedy — a divorce.

He wasn't aware at the time, but it was Jeremy who kept him alive, made him not give up, and showed him there was a life for him. Jeremy showed him how much he needed his father. He owed his saneness to his son who followed him around making sure he was okay. He marveled at the fact people come and go in the lives of others without realizing the effect they may have on those whom they encounter.

On the afternoon of the last day of school, Jeremy's middle school had a "Moving On" Ceremony for those students who had completed eighth grade and ready for high school. Jeremy was an honor student and recognized during the ceremony. Happiness filled his son's face and entire body. Hamilton was relieved his son didn't carry hatred or hostility in his heart. Instead, he made himself a person filled with love and someone with strong values, someone who did the right thing.

Jeremy asked to have a few of his friends over after the ceremony. Hamilton hired a caterer and rented a band. He contacted one of his old journalism students who joined a band several years ago. Jeremy invited his school and church friends.

The girl whom he liked so much attended, even though her family was moving to Chicago in a month. Her father accepted a job as a news anchor on one of the major stations. Jeremy was a little distraught about her leaving, but in thinking about it, he said he was okay with it. Hamilton suggested he would find someone in high school, someone just for him.

HolliAnne came to the party to tell Jeremy and Hamilton her parents were both very ill and she was moving to Ohio to take care of them. Her father had dementia and her mother had serious mental and physical health problems. HolliAnne said she tried too hard to take care of her husband. She was already in the hospital and HolliAnne said she needed to take her mother home. She and Tom separated.

"Sorry to hear that," Jeremy said, standing in the living room with his mother.

She held a look of surprise.

"I prayed for everything to work out for you." Jeremy kissed his mother on the cheek and gave her a hug. "Mom, take care, okay. After you get there, maybe I can visit." He gave her a wide smile.

HolliAnne leaned over and gave Jeremy a kiss on the cheek. "Go be with your friends."

Jeremy went back to his friends in the family room.

"When are you leaving?" Hamilton asked.

"Two days. My parents shouldn't be left alone and there's no one else to take care of them. They're still in their home," she said.

"Isn't this sudden?"

"Their neighbor called and said both my parents were a lot worse. She couldn't help them anymore. She had things she needed to do for her family. My mother is in the hospital which means my father is left alone in the house. I told her I'd be there before the end of the week."

"Let us know when you get there, won't you?"

"Yes, if you would like."

"Good. Jeremy will send you a card or something now and then."

"Ham, I wish it could have worked out with us."

"HolliAnne, some things are just the way they are."

"I wish I'd tried harder with you. You deserved it."

"I wish we'd both done better by each other. We deserved it. He gave her a hug and stepped back. HolliAnne left.

As per usual, Hamilton arrived at the university early the next day. To while away the time, his thoughts went to HolliAnne and the fact that she was leaving to take care of her parents. As she explained to him, during her growing-up years, HolliAnne didn't feel cared for by her parents. Now, she's going home to care for them. He hoped that HolliAnne and her parents would form a better relationship.

Just when he picked up his office phone to call Emma, she called him.

"Hello," she said.

"How've you been?" he said, a smile in his voice. "Did you see a doctor about your sinus headaches?"

"He said I had a sinus infection, again. He changed the medication and I'm feeling better."

"That's good that you got that settled."

"It was tricky at first, but everything is fine now." She paused. "I need a favor from you."

"Okay, if I can."

"This morning my boss gave me an assignment. Remember, I am now a research journalist." She sang the words and laughed. "You said you taught journalism."

"That's right. Madam research journalist! What's the assignment?"

"My boss wants me to find out how or why there are more non-native-born men and women teaching English in high schools, colleges, and universities in America than native-born men and women teaching English in America. I thought you could help me get started with the research."

"That's an interesting question. I'm thinking about my department and how that question applies to the English Department. Do you want to meet here, research the question, and put an outline together, or do you want to get started yourself and let me know what you have so far?"

"I would like to meet with you first and do a little research, if we can find anything."

"Okay then. I would also want to know how long that's been happening."

"Now, that's a good question, too."

"How about we talk about it over dinner? We can meet at a restaurant for dinner."

"That sounds great. Let me see about one thing, first. Can I text you the restaurant?"

"Sure, whatever you want." He liked hearing himself say that to her.

CHAPTER 32

Hamilton went to Emma's for dinner. She wanted to make the dinner herself rather than eat out. Even though they had been seeing each other, this was the first time he had been inside her apartment. He wasn't sure what this meant. He loved her, but something worried him and kept him from saying it. She hadn't said it to him, either.

If he had to describe her apartment, he would use the word "cozy." The living room walls were a pale-yellow color. A beautiful gold and tan rug covered most of the floor. A soft-looking fabric of light gold and yellow covered the overstuffed couch and matching armchairs. The room was dimly lit with tall crystal lamps, so Hamilton thought, and placed on each of the end tables. Hamilton sat down on the couch and ran his hand across the soft butter-like fabric. He couldn't make out the material, but it felt good to him. Emma brought two glasses of the white wine Hamilton brought and placed them on the coffee table. Hamilton took his glass, raised it.

"To your research project. May it bring you positive results."

Emma tapped her glass to his, and they each sipped their wine.

"The lasagna is ready when you are," she said.

He heard the uneasiness in her voice. He sat down at a table he thought to be an antique. He couldn't help but notice each of the four chairs were different in style, and time period, but all seemed to be of the same type of wood.

"I see you're interested in my chairs," she said. She placed a healthy platter of lasagna between them on the table. She then brought out the Italian bread sprinkled with garlic and parsley. Hamilton loved parsley and wondered how she knew.

"They are all different." The room with its different chairs gave him a sense of reverence, a respect that filled him; the same warm feeling he sometimes had during church services. But he didn't know what it meant.

"I like to think of my table as the table of The Last Supper."

"You mean where Jesus ate before they crucified him?" He placed his hands on the table and again the reverence, or holiness, filled him. This time stronger.

"Exactly. We are asked to remember Jesus, and I remember Him here. The time period of the table differs from the time period of each of the chairs. For me, this represents the length of time we have already remembered. The wood is the same and represents the basic part, The One. I find that very fascinating."

"It appears you are carrying on the teachings from the nuns in the convent." He was uncomfortable with talking about religion.

"Very much so. But let's eat. I'll bet you're starved." After she said grace, she handed him the lasagna.

"Marilyn said she signed up for the Ballroom dance class with Franny. She says she enjoys the class, and she's becoming a better dancer. She's thinking about becoming a professional and dancing in those tournaments like we saw in those videos."

"That's a bold move, isn't it?" Hamilton asked.

"It may be, but she can do it. Franny is a capable teacher."

"That's for sure and Marilyn has excellent skills. She should do well. How is Franny?"

"Marilyn says she's doing fine."

"No more boot?"

"No more boot." She gave off a slight laugh.

"What happened to you?"

"Why didn't I sign up?"

"Yes. Why didn't you?"

He loved her soft laugh that seemed to bring peace over her, over the room, over him. The sparkle in her eyes expressing curiosity, happiness and asking more from him, all captivated him. He loved the way her skin felt whenever her hand touched his. She was caring and loving, and he let himself give into her minute by minute. His mind went back to that day she came out of the dressing room. She had stopped his heart that day when he saw how the light flickered on her. He remembered he had tried with all his might and power to turn away from her, but his heart wouldn't allow him. And now, here she was, sweet, delicate, but strong and confident and he loved her. But he wanted to be cautious.

She turned away from him, then took a sip of wine. "I didn't think I should."

"Why not?" He pressed.

"Marilyn loves to dance, and dance loves her. I love to dance, but I am not sure how much dance loves me," she said looking down at the lasagna on her plate.

"The more you work at it, the more you'll see that dance loves you. You need a suitable dance partner to encourage you and show you."

"What if I can't learn the steps?"

"Your dance partner can show you the steps." He took a sip of wine.

"And help me grow?"

"Yes, and help you grow."

"Will my dance partner help me really love dance?"

"Your dance partner, who already loves dance, can help you really love dance, even more."

"Will my dance partner catch me when I fall?"

"Your dance partner will be patient, kind and have a good grip on you."

"Will my dance partner forgive all my mistakes and show me the right way?"

"I know your dance partner will cherish your mistakes, forgive you and show you."

"That sounds like a dance partner I can rely on."

"You can always rely on a suitable dance partner who understands you, who is in sync with you."

"I want a dance partner like that."

"You have a lot of potential." He paused, looked away, then cast his eyes on her, "You remember how we danced together?" He said, softly.

"Yes, I do. Yes, I do," she whispered. She turned away.

Hamilton thought it best to leave it alone. They ate in silence.

He cleared his throat, "Are we ready to get started? Or I can help you clear the table."

In silence, they cleared away the dinner items. Then Emma put the dishes in the dishwasher while Hamilton took a thick folder from his case. Emma got her laptop and opened it.

For the entire evening they worked together on the project. Hamilton was a little tensed, but he loved her easy style and even nature. They reviewed the research they both had and by the end of the evening, had a working outline of what to include in the document. She made the process uncomplicated, the reason her boss asked her to take on the assignment, he concluded.

For the next several weeks, Hamilton and Emma worked tirelessly on the essay. This was a new topic and Hamilton was excited for Emma. The paper could open the door to many opportunities for her and help her reach out in the journalism community. Since it had not been a topic of much interest, there was little research information. Hamilton explained the project to the non-American born English teachers in his department and asked them if they would give their background information and tell how they became interested in teaching English. They asked if the teachers would take an English grammar questionnaire he and Emma had devised specifically for their research. The four teachers agreed, and Hamilton and Emma began collecting data.

They contacted other universities, colleges, and high schools across the country, gathered facts and any information they needed. They visited universities, colleges, and high schools in the immediate and not so immediate area to interview English teachers.

They found many high schools taught literature beginning with American literature, in the English classes. As a result of the number of non-English born students now in high schools, many high schools have included grammar in the curriculum. This caused them to make a few changes in their questionnaire.

Weeks later, they had collected enough data and done sufficient research to begin organizing their data, and the first draft of the paper. By the end of June, Hamilton and Emma had come to an ending of one phase and were ready for the second phase. They celebrated their progress. Hamilton purchased two tickets for the dinner theater at his university.

"I love this university, but I have to say this baked lasagna isn't anywhere near as good as what you made," Hamilton said.

Emma looked up at him with an enormous smile across her entire face. He studied her face radiating a warm glow that said, "I love you." He reached over and placed his hand on hers and watched her smile grow wider and deeper. His heart sped up, and he knew she felt it from his hand on hers, but he didn't care. He loved this woman, and he wanted to make love to her.

"Emma, I—"

"Ladies and Gentlemen, welcome to the university's Summer Theater." The announcer, mic in hand, began as the lights dimmed. "We ask you to turn off your cell phones, sit back and enjoy this performance. And please, no talking during the show."

Disappointment shaded her face, and she expressed it in her eyes. He, too, was disappointed, but, for now, this was best. He slowly pulled his hand back and tried to continue eating his dinner, but he was no longer hungry. She placed her fork on her plate. He moved his chair closer to her and gave her a smile. She smiled back and with his arm around her shoulders, they settled down to watch the play.

He remembered Anita and thought about how he wanted to let her know it was becoming easier for him to let go. Even though he wasn't completely free, he didn't feel himself holding back like he had done in the past. Happiness filled his heart, and he thanked Anita for making him promise to let go.

CHAPTER 33

Hamilton was asked to apply for the position of vice president after the vice president for student affairs retired in May. He wasn't sure he wanted to, but the next day, when he brought it up in a meeting, his department chairs encouraged him to apply. He hadn't expected them to be so happy for him, patting him on the back, congratulating him before the process had even begun. He looked around the conference room, down the long table of the department chairs, the sun streaming from the long window on the opposite wall and asked, "Are you trying to get rid of me?" The department chairs laughed. Even though he joked, there were those two who gave him a challenge. One took Hamilton's advice and left. But the other one whom he thought deserved a better chance stayed and at Hamilton's question, gave Hamilton a surprise look, as if to say, "Why would you think that? You deserve the position."

Later, Hamilton called Eric to tell him about the possibility of a new position.

"Go for it, Dad. I'm with you. Do it," Eric said, happiness in his voice.

"I love your enthusiasm," Hamilton said. He wanted to ask if his plans included coming home for the summer, but he knew his oldest boy needed to make his own way.

"You've earned it. What are your plans for July and August?" Eric asked him.

Hamilton told Eric he enrolled Jeremy in two morning classes at his university so they could drive in together and have lunch together. Eric said, Anna and her boyfriend, were spending the summer working at the church Eric and Paige were now attending. The church needed volunteers to help repair the homes of the elderly people in the community. Eric also found out the church needed volunteers to go on a mission trip to Africa, for two weeks in August, and he asked Anna to go with them. The problem was he and Anna needed money. Eric promised to send Hamilton pictures of their experiences in Africa. Anna wanted to take a one-week seminar held at her university just before classes began. Hamilton told Eric about the project he and Emma were finishing and told him he would put money in their accounts.

"Dad, for the first time in a long time, you sound happy."

"I am happy. But I haven't jumped into the deep end of the pool yet."

"Dad, jump in. Jump in. Don't think about it. Just jump in. Make yourself happy."

"You don't have a problem? I mean your mom—"

"Dad, worry about you. Please. I like hearing that you're happy."

Hamilton loved the fact that Eric and Anna wanted to help people and he wanted to encourage them, but he missed them both and he thought it best to let them know. Eric's attitude made him joyful. His attitude also left him unburdened.

Hamilton needed to hear from his biggest supporter. One evening, they did their best to make a dinner out of the leftovers in the refrigerator. Hamilton pulled out several things wrapped in foil and in bowls.

"What do you think Buddy Boy?" Hamilton picked up a plastic carry out container and pulled the foil back to see what was left. He couldn't make out what it was and tossed it in the trash.

"Dad, vice president? You ask what I think?" Jeremy poured water in two glasses.

"It's not about the university. It's about us," Hamilton said, pausing. He then found a bowl of potatoes to him looked edible. He took a minute to think and remembered the potatoes were made the day before.

"I know. I don't have anything to worry about."

"You're a high school student now."

"You will always be my dad, no matter what. We will always do things together and I know you will not let your job stop us from doing things. You never have."

"You will want to be more with your friends, won't you?"

"High school is different. But you've always taught me family comes first."

"High school is different, and that's why I need to be available for you in case you need me."

"I won't go against the values you've taught me, if that's what you're worried about."

"Why don't we both remember that, okay?"

"Dad, are you saying you will miss me?" Jeremy said, as he gave his father a wide smile that turned to a laugh.

If a person could feel happiness and sunshine from inside and it could spread out all over and through their body, then Hamilton would swear he felt it at this moment.

The remainder of June sped by just as quickly as April and May. In mid-July, before the interviews for the vice president position, Hamilton took Jeremy to see his mother and father in Stevensville for a week. Hamilton wanted to see how his father was coping with the new condos and townhouses replacing his vineyard. He also wanted to tell them both he applied for the vice president position at the university.

The warm sunny July cast a heat over the area giving a feel of a warm comforting blanket to Hamilton. A blanket like the one his mother covered him with when she let him, and Taylor stay up late on the weekends and watch TV with popcorn and cocoa.

"Look at what they've done to this place," George began.

George, Hamilton, and Jeremy stood at the entrance to the townhouse community. A huge, stone sign with the words "Stevensville Estates" loomed over the entranceway where they stood. Hamilton hardly recognized the area. "But," George continued, "you have to keep up with the changes or fall behind. If you fall behind, you lose your place in this world."

"Pop, can we walk around a bit?"

"I don't see why not. There's no sign that says we can't."

They walked around looking for anything familiar, or mostly just looking. Several people drove up in cars and parked in assigned spaces, according to the sign. Many of the townhouses, had planters on the stoops. A child's bicycle was left on the grass under the window of one townhouse. Hamilton concluded that the owners had to have something to identify their home because the square, boxy-looking homes all looked alike to him. Walking farther, lights were on in another townhouse. They could hear voices coming from the rear of another townhouse. They continued through the development now covering the ground where George's life started, the ground that grew the grapes that made the best wine on the east coast. Hamilton walked all the way over to the end of the last row where they were still building. He went to where the property ended and paused there.

"I thought they were building back here, but I guess not," Hamilton said. He gazed around trying to remember if he'd ever gone this far back where weeds were growing.

"Somebody's gonna have to take care of the weeds. Pop, look. What's that? This isn't poison ivy, is it?" He pointed to something growing out of the ground. He stooped down to get a better look. "It's only a weed."

George stooped down, "Son, you might have to help me up," a smile on his face. He looked at the dark green growth coming up out of the ground, "No, Ham. It's not poison ivy." He looked at Hamilton and smiled. "It's part of a grape plant. Well, would you just look at that?"

"Shall I pull it up?"

"No. Leave it."

Hamilton helped his father stand.

"Son, you know what? You can never completely wipe out the past." He gave his son a wide smile.

Hamilton was relieved. He smiled back at his father. Instead of fighting it, his father accepted his stage of retirement, and made it productive with his vegetable garden. He could see from the look on his father's face that his father also felt a connection with this land, no matter how much it would change. The tiny plant helped George understand he would always be connected to this land in spirit. The work he'd done and all the good he put in could never be obliterated. His father gave him and Jeremy the biggest smile. Hamilton would not have to worry about his father. His father would be just fine.

Jeremy wasn't ready to return home. He wanted to spend the next two weeks at the beach. They drove to Delaware to Rehoboth and checked into a hotel. Jeremy had always loved the beach. Hamilton used to watch him walk in the sand and chase the birds or spend the entire afternoon making a sandcastle. For Hamilton, the beach was freedom. He would look up in the sky and see birds just soaring through the air, flying from one place to another without a care in the world. The beach with its mighty ocean where faraway boats came and went and the sun that sent sparkles of light through the water reflecting itself made Hamilton want to take off and travel, see the other world he was missing; the world off in the distance.

As soon as he returned home, he and Emma met on the path at his university to talk about the essay. It pleased him to see that several people were biking, running, and walking on the trail. As they strolled, he told her about the path and lake and how he fought to get it. They stopped to watch the ducks, and he checked the growth of the pond plants. He led her around, pointing out the trees, with their stately appearance and historical value, that the workers did not take down.

They talked about the next step they needed to begin the essay. They sat down on a bench and Emma talked about a theme, purpose, and introduction of the essay. Emma smiled and said she felt movement and was excited about the project and more importantly, Hamilton's help.

"Isn't it amazing how things change? One day things are one way, and the next, it's not the same," Emma said in a sad voice, according to Hamilton. He took her hand in his.

"We want things to change, don't we? Things can't remain the same." His father came to his mind.

"Some changes aren't for the good," she said.

"Things have changed for the better for you. You've been given this great assignment. Isn't that a great change?"

Hamilton was worried and called Emma the next afternoon between meetings.

"I'm afraid I haven't done much. My sinus headache is back."

"Did you go back to the doctor?"

"No. Should I? He already told me it was a sinus headache. I just took some of those left-over pills he gave me before. The last time I took them, they brought some relief, even though the headache returned."

"What can I do?"

"The essay needs finishing. I started it yesterday after our walk and did something this morning."

When Hamilton arrived at Emma's home, he found Emma had made little progress with her headache. A half-folded blanket with a pillow on top, rested on the end of the couch.

"It went away and now it's back."

"Where is it?"

"It feels like it's all over my head. Earlier it seemed only my forehead hurt, but now I can't pinpoint the pain."

"Are these migraine headaches? They're not sinus headaches, are they?"

"They could be. A migraine would be felt all over the head. This project is giving me a migraine." She tried to laugh but stopped and wrinkled her face. "I never thought I'd say that."

"I'll do something with the essay. You go call your doctor." He hated to get involved, but he had to say or do something.

Hamilton, because he was uncertain about her headaches, and the fact she seemed nervous, did much of the writing. He suggested eyestrain could be one of the causes of her headaches.

The next day, Emma told Hamilton that the doctor advised her to take more of the over-the-counter headache medicine she had been using. Emma said her headaches eased up after her trip to the doctor, but then she said she had a slight tremor in her right hand.

CHAPTER 34

In late August, Hamilton had the essay finished and wanted Emma to proofread it. He sat on her gold overstuffed couch as she read it and made notes along the side. He pretended to watch a sports game on her TV while trying to see how much she was writing. Hamilton didn't like to be corrected. When she had finished, he read over her comments.

During the following week, HR notified Hamilton that his one-week appointments for his interview for the position of vice president would begin the following week. The HR person gave him the schedule. He was to meet with several departments and respond to their concerns as part of the interview process.

By the end of September, the interviews had concluded, and the committee selected Dr. Hamilton Maddox as their next vice president for student affairs. His only disappointment was he had to move out of his office into another building and another office. The good thing was his new office was even larger, and, more importantly, he could see his lake and bike path. Jeremy and Emma attended his announcement where he gave a brief speech and later, the university had a reception for him. In the car on the way home, Buddy Boy told him how proud he was of his father.

The next day, Buddy Boy took his father and Emma to an expensive restaurant for a private celebration. Hamilton said he would open his present Eric and Anna sent him later that evening.

"How in the world did you pull this off?" Hamilton asked after they were seated at a small table at The Palm Restaurant in downtown Washington, D.C.

"I did it online. They don't ask for much online."

"This is nice Jeremy. Have you two been here before? Is this how you knew to come here?" Emma asked.

"Some friends at church said their parents have been here a lot, so I thought it would be nice for the celebration."

Hamilton looked forward to his new job and all the things he could do to establish direction and enhance strategies for his division and the university, but he was also a little melancholy in that he had to leave his old friends. He had helped all his department chairs earn their positions, groomed, and prepared them for the responsibilities early on. Over the years, he grew attached to them, and sometimes went out of his way to get them what he thought they needed. He also felt different. He was happy and for some reason life seemed light to him, like a huge weight removed itself from him. For the first time, he was happy and in love.

Hamilton hadn't had a chance to call Emma for several weeks while he focused on his interviews. To atone for that, one Sunday afternoon, in October, Hamilton took Emma to the History Museum while Jeremy helped with meals for the homeless.

The following week he took Emma to the opening of a play. She asked to leave because her headache returned after the first act when a trumpet player blasted his music so loud that it caused several people in the audience to jump and brought on Emma's headache.

"There must be something you can do. Why not go see a specialist?" Hamilton asked on the drive home.

Emma agreed, and the next day, found a specialist recommended by her doctor.

Emma told Hamilton that the specialist, Dr. Weaver, a neurologist, listened to her talk about her headaches and how off and on they were and how bad the pain was. He talked to her about typical headaches and their causes. Dr. Weaver also told her that in order to be more certain about her headaches, and the cause, he wanted to set up a time for the test that will yield the most information, an MRI.

The day after she had taken the tests, Emma called Hamilton and told him that since the day before, she was vomiting more when the headaches came on. They were more violent, lasted longer, and she was afraid.

Two days later, the nurse called Emma and told her the results were in and Emma, right then, made an appointment to talk to Dr. Weaver. She wanted Hamilton to go with her.

Hamilton and Emma entered the neurologist's office and Dr. Weaver directed them to the couch across from his desk. Dr. Weaver sat in a stiff, hardwood chair opposite them. A strong, sweet scent of apricots filled the air and Hamilton relaxed.

"I understand you've been throwing up this week," Dr. Weaver said. He looked at the information that the nurse took from Emma while they were in the waiting room.

"Yes. I can't keep any food down. What's happening to me?"

"I have your report here. I thought we would have to do more tests, but the results are clear."

Hamilton's heart pounded in his chest, and he tried to take deep breaths to relax. He couldn't fail Emma. She needed him now.

"What's wrong?" Emma asked.

Dr. Weaver put the MRI report from the radiologist on the coffee table in front of them. He then directed them to the MRI results on the screen. He turned on the light and pointed to something on the MRI. Do you see this, right here?" His finger pointed to what looked like a misshaped darkish mass. "This is a tumor in your brain."

"A tumor? A—How—A, how can it be a tumor?" She looked from the doctor to Hamilton and back.

"The tumor is pretty large. It's been growing there a while."

"How do we get it out? Do I need an operation or something?"

"Unfortunately, it's too large. That's the reason you are experiencing pain. The tumor is pressing on parts of the brain. I'd like to refer you to an oncologist."

They made an appointment to see an oncologist.

A week later, in the oncologist's office, the oncologist reviewed the test Dr. Weaver had ordered, and determined that the tumor was cancerous, likely a glioblastoma. The oncologist also said that the tumor was large and pressing on the brain.

"Do I need an operation?" Emma asked the same question of the oncologist.

"I would like to see if we can't reduce the tumor before we think about surgery."

"What? What are you saying, doctor? Things are so bad, and you can't operate? Is that what you're saying?" Emma was in tears. She took a tissue from the box on the small table next to her.

The oncologist turned toward Hamilton, like a person does when asking for help.

Hamilton said nothing. He stared in space, a frightened look on his face.

"As you can see," the oncologist began, "the tumor is of considerable size," he repeated.

"What happens now?" Hamilton asked, bringing himself back to reality. "Does she get radiation or something like that? We need to reduce the size of the tumor. That would help with the pain, wouldn't it?" Hamilton asked. His voice sounded helpless.

"Let's start with chemotherapy. These medications should reduce the tumor. Let's see what happens with this first. If we decide surgery is the best course of action, then you'll need to see a neurosurgeon."

"If the tumor is reduced, she could have an operation, couldn't she?"

"That's possible but let's take it one step at a time. I'll leave my recommendations to Dr. Weaver for chemotherapy and how to arrange chemo for you at the front desk," the oncologist said, sounding relieved.

"You two can stay here a few minutes as you need. I'll leave everything at the front desk."

Hamilton stood and extended his hand. The doctor looked at him as if he wanted to say how sorry he was. Hamilton nodded at the doctor and the doctor nodded back. Then the doctor left the room.

Hamilton had suspected something serious, but not this serious. When she was ready, they gathered themselves and he drove her home.

Once inside, they were both quiet. He had no idea what to say to her. After a few minutes, he helped her to bed. He stood over the bed watching her as she closed her eyes. She was an alive, energetic woman full of vitality and laughter. Now, she was sick, headaches driving the life out of her, changing her into someone else. He leaned down and kissed her, pulled the sheet up to her neck, then kissed her again. She opened her eyes and tried to smile at him. "Get some rest," he whispered, "You start chemotherapy tomorrow." He looked down at this beautiful woman he wanted to marry.

He had worried all along that her problem would be something he couldn't handle, or unexpected. He loved her. He had always wanted a woman who loved him as much as he loved her. He wanted a woman he could travel with, go to the theatre with, to museums and concerts and have someone to entertain with him. He was the vice president of a university; he would have to entertain people in his home. He would have to travel, respond to invitations from senators, his representative, the mayor, governor, and other people in the community. Since his divorce, he wanted someone to marry and together live a loving, long, healthy and committed life. This couldn't be his future.

CHAPTER 35

As soon as he had everything moved to his larger office in the administration building, Hamilton set up a meeting schedule. He wanted to talk with the deans and department chairs to get an idea of what they expected and to let them know what he expected. He set up appointments for his meetings and reserved a meeting room in several places throughout the university. One thing on his list was to hire a new assistant. When the previous vice president retired, the assistant also decamped, leaving a vacancy for him to fill. Josie didn't qualify and couldn't go with him, and he wasn't sure he wanted her. Confidentiality was crucial for the position, and he wasn't sure Josie could put that first.

As he was acclimating to his new position as vice president of his university, he called to see how Emma was doing. It had been a while since they had spoken last.

"Ham, I didn't think I would hear from you again. Joyce from the church has come by to help me. And the tumor is reducing. I haven't had those headaches like I had been having."

"I'm glad you're feeling better." He paused for a moment. "Emma, I'm sorry, but I've been so busy with the new job...." he allowed himself to drift off.

"I understand. I have the essay, and I've made the editor's suggested changes. Would you look it over? I need to get it to the publisher."

He hesitated a few moments. He wasn't sure he wanted to do more. It may be better to stop now.

"I don't know who else to ask and since you started it, I just thought, as a friend, but it's okay if you don't want to."

"Sure."

"Should I bring it to you?"

"No. I can come by this evening, if it's okay with you, and get it."

At Emma's, she sat on her couch, and he sat in a hardback chair next to the couch. She told him about the changes she made in the essay and the different angle she wanted to take with it. She held it out to him. He looked at her, then down at the essay as if the essay was a debilitating disease he could get, and for which there was no cure.

"Ham, as I said on the phone, I just want to know what a friend thinks."

He looked at her. There was no smile in her eyes or on her face. He took the essay from her, "Sure."

"Could I get it back by tomorrow?"

"Emma—"

"A simple yes or now will do."

"Yes."

"Hamilton, I'm not expecting anything from you. I just want a friend."

"Emma, I'm—well I—I just. I'll get this back to you tomorrow."

"Thank you. I didn't expect you to stay for dinner. Marilyn will be here in a few minutes."

Hamilton took the essay and left. He pulled into his driveway, cut the motor, and sat back in the car. He wasn't relieved or satisfied like he thought he would feel.

That night, in his study, he stayed up late going over the essay. He found a few vague comments, a few undocumented comments, and aside from that, the essay was okay. He took his time making the corrections. The essay had to excel. He had to make the effort for her. Late into the night, the essay was ready for her review.

He called her the next day from his office and told her he had emailed it to her.

"Would it be too much trouble if you came for dinner at my house? Jeremy asked if he could talk to you. He's doing a paper on women in the church and has some questions for you." He sat back in his new therapeutic chair and didn't say more. He didn't want to carry on anything that would give her the wrong impression.

Hamilton worked in the kitchen preparing the meal. Jeremy asked Emma about the role of nuns and women in the church. They sat in the family room, Emma on the couch and Jeremy in his father's chair. Jeremy had prepared a list of questions he showed Hamilton before Emma arrived. Neither one wanted to ask her anything offensive. Hamilton left a plate of stuffed mushrooms on the table for them, then went back to the kitchen to get the dinner ready.

During dinner, Jeremy asked to be excused to get started on his paper. Hamilton and Emma ate in silence until Hamilton couldn't stand it any longer.

"I want to apologize to you," Hamilton began. "I'm sorry, I—"

"I know, you're afraid. So am I."

"I'm sure what you're going through must be scary and you must be anxious—"

"But you don't want to be a caretaker," she said.

"That's not fair." He paused for a moment. "Emma, I'm not sure I'm the one for this."

"It's okay. Let's just have an enjoyable dinner," she said.

He nodded.

"What happened to those things we had earlier? Can we have that for dinner, too?"

"You mean the stuffed mushrooms?"

"Yeah, those round things. Can't we have more of those?"

"We sure can." He got up to get the stuffed mushrooms, placed them on the table near her.

Emma gazed at her plate of food and the fork in her hand. She put her fork down and picked up the sliced chicken with her fingers.

Hamilton got up to get her another fork.

"Oh, I have one of these," she held up her fork.

Hamilton took the second fork away. She seemed confused.

She took a forkful of chicken.

"I'm sorry, Emma. I shouldn't have asked you to come. Maybe we should have taken dinner to you."

"Nonsense." She took a forkful of mashed potatoes.

Her behavior was unusual, and Hamilton worried about her. "I need to drive you home."

"Ham, I can't enjoy this wonderful food if you keep worrying me about leaving."

"I don't mean for you to leave. Please, enjoy your dinner."

"Besides, I can drive myself. I don't live that far."

After dinner, Hamilton helped Emma into her coat and walked her to her car parked in front of his house.

"You know, it's no trouble. I can drive you home." He said as they walked down the driveway.

"I can drive myself and that's that." Emma got into her car, slammed the door, started the motor, and pulled out of the space onto the street, tires screeching as she sped down the street.

One evening later in the week, Jeremy found Hamilton in his study on his computer.

"Dad, I thought you liked her."

He didn't respond right away. He didn't know what to say. Then, "Some things are not always what they seem."

"What does that mean? She's a very nice lady, and she laughed at my jokes."

"She's sick, Buddy."

"How is she sick?" He sat in the chair next to his father.

"She's just sick. She's under her doctor's care."

"She told me. While you were in the kitchen, she told me."

"What did she tell you?"

"She said she had a brain tumor."

Hamilton closed his computer and turned to Jeremy. "She told you that?"

"Yes. And she said it was rough for her."

"She needs to focus on her health. What else did she say to you?"

"It was about when she stopped being a nun. She said at first, she thought it was because she just wasn't called. She wasn't very good at being a nun. She couldn't keep the vow of silence, and she questioned too many of their rituals. She thinks God led her away from the convent because He wanted her to serve him in other ways."

"Buddy, I'm not sure if I like her telling you that."

"About the brain tumor, you mean? I'm in high school, now. A boy in my class comes to school late every day because his mother has cancer, and he has to get her up and ready for the caregiver before he leaves for school."

Hamilton was silent.

"Dad, I understand she needs to get well. But I think she needs you."

"What did she say about that?"

"She just said she was blessed to have a wonderful friend, and you two were friends."

"Yes, we are friends."

"I want to see you happy. I thought you liked her. I like her and she likes me."

"I like her, and I care about her as a friend would. We worked on her project together and now it's ready for her to send to her publisher."

"Okay." Jeremy stood, started out of the room, but turned around. "Can you call her for me and thank her for the information for my paper? I got an 'A+' on it. It would be nice for her to know that."

"Sure, Bud. I'll do that."

Jeremy's comments got to him. The next morning, Hamilton called Emma to find out how her publisher accepted the essay and to deliver Jeremy's message.

"I haven't sent it to him yet."

"Why not?" He heard a strain in her voice, like she had trouble breathing.

"No reason." She told him she would have to call him back and hung up.

CHAPTER 36

For the next several days, the comments Jeremy made to him echoed throughout his brain. He wanted to explain things to Jeremy to get him to understand, but it was best for him not to. Jeremy will understand when he grows up.

During this time, his workload increased, and he had several interviews with students who wanted to see some changes made in the counselling center. Hamilton hadn't expected so many staff members to sign up to talk with him. Every time slot was filled with students with problems or staff members who had valuable suggestions for him. At the end of each day, he was exhausted and arrived home late. He and Jeremy had to communicate through notes and text messages.

One evening, after he'd talked to the last student, he received a text from Jeremy asking him to come immediately to Emma's place. When he arrived, Jeremy opened the door for him.

"Buddy—" he began.

"Dad, she's in here."

They walked to her study, where Emma sat in an armchair, her hand on her chest.

"What happened?" Hamilton asked, moving closer to her.

"Nothing, Ham. I asked Jeremy not to bother you, but he insisted. I just got out of breath, that's all."

"I'll call an ambulance," he took out his cell phone.

"No, Ham, please don't. I moved too quickly, getting up and down, got a little dizzy, and out of breath."

"How often has this happened?"

"This is the first time. I promise."

"You seem okay, now." Hamilton turned to Jeremy. "Bud, can we talk a minute?"

"Ham, I know what you're gonna say to him."

"I want to know why my son was here. What were you two doing?"

"Praying. Jeremy tries to drop by when he can to pray for me."

Hamilton looked at Jeremy in surprise.

"Dad, ever since I found out about her tumor, I come here to pray for her."

"Why didn't I know about this?"

Jeremy said nothing.

"I believe, Ham, he thought since we weren't seeing each other, you would object to him coming to pray with me."

Buddy Boy and Hamilton looked at each other. Neither spoke.

"Well, guys, I'm glad we got that settled. Ham, Jeremy was leaving, but when I got out of breath, he called you. So, I'll say goodbye to you both."

Hamilton turned to Emma. She was so beautiful, even the sickness couldn't take that away. The treatment was having a positive effect. Or was it Jeremy's prayers? He had heard how people lose their appetite, can't hold food while receiving chemotherapy. "You must be tired," he began, "Let me help you to bed."

She stood. Hamilton put his arm around her waist and guided her into the bedroom. She laid down across the bed. He put a pillow under her head, tiptoed out, and closed the door.

At home, Buddy Boy, in his bedroom with the door opened, was on his iPad, the one he got for Christmas. Hamilton knocked on the door. Jeremy put the iPad down on the desk and turned his chair toward Hamilton.

"Dad, I'm sorry. I know what you're going to say, and I'm sorry. I know I disrespected you, but I didn't mean to."

"You don't have to be sorry. You went to help her. I understand. But Buddy, why don't you tell me these things? Why do you keep these things from me?"

"I don't know. I don't intend to. Things just seem to end up that way. I just don't want to worry you."

"I understand, but do you see the problem here? When you do these things without telling me, you cause me to not trust you. Because I don't trust you, I have to put restrictions on you."

"Sometimes, I feel you would say no to the things I want to do."

"But I haven't done that, have I? Have I turned down or said no to what you want?"

"Thinking about it, maybe a few things."

"I'll tell you what I want from you. I want you to let me know what you want and want to do."

"I can do that."

Hamilton turned to leave.

"Dad."

Hamilton turned around to face Buddy Boy.

"She genuinely loves you. You know that."

He looked at Buddy, "I know. I don't know what to do about it." He said, a half-whisper.

"Yes, you do. She's really nice." He straightened himself in his chair.

"What made you go pray with her?"

"I want God to heal her. I want to see her tumor go away. Since I've been praying—"

"What? How long have you been praying with her?"

"Since she helped me with my paper."

"That's right. I remember." He paused. "What's happening now? About the tumor?"

"It's gotten smaller. I want to keep praying until the tumor is gone."

Hamilton stretched out his arms to Buddy Boy. He heard his son crying as he held his son in his arms. Hamilton held back his tears.

The next day, Hamilton made a phone call from his office at the university.

"Just thought I'd call to find out where I can read your essay."

"My publisher said we should see it in the journal in two weeks."

"Great. I guess you're happy with the outcome?"

"Yes, quite happy."

There was a lengthy pause between them, and he could hear her labored breathing.

"How do you like being a vice president?"

"Lots of work."

"You're up there, now. You have to expect the work."

"How are you?"

"What happened with you and Jeremy?"

"We talked, but I'm not sure we worked things out. I can't get him to understand that he needs to let me know things before he goes off to do them."

"He loves and respects you so much, just like many other people."

"I try to keep him close to me. Back to my question, how are you?"

She hesitated and Hamilton wanted to change the subject, but she responded.

"The headaches come and go. The treatment helps, the tumor is smaller. Ham, since Jeremy has been praying for me, I feel so much better."

"I think there's something special about him. I'm not surprised you're feeling better. Those are all positive signs."

"Does that mean he can continue praying for me?"

"I don't think I can stop him. Just don't let him leave late."

"Have you ever thought Jeremy doesn't need to tell you things because he knows you would approve? You both think alike. You both do helpful things. Has he done anything you didn't approve of? When I talk to him, it feels like I'm talking to you."

"No, he hasn't. I can't think of a time when I didn't approve. And I never thought of that. Let me know when the article is published," he paused, "or should I call you?"

"It would be nice if you called me."

After he hung up, Hamilton took a deep breath, relieved of the strain and intensity of trying to carry on a conversation. He thought for a minute about Jeremy's need to heal Emma of her tumor. He, too, wanted her tumor to shrink and disappear from her brain. He, too, wanted her healed and well. Buddy Boy was right about helping her, but Hamilton had to admit he was afraid. He loved her, but he was afraid. What should he say to Anita now?

CHAPTER 37

Two weeks later, Emma called Hamilton when the essay was published in the professional journal. He left his office and rushed over to read the article.

"How is it?" Hamilton asked, sitting back on her couch. He took a sip of water from his glass.

"I'm afraid to read it. It won't sound the same. I'll want to make changes." She handed it to him.

When he had finished reading the essay, uninterrupted, he put the journal on the table.

"What do you think? It's magnificent, isn't it?"

"That it is. You did a superb job, Emma. A really outstanding job. And it looks good in this professional journal."

They sat together on the couch that evening, talking and being quiet. She talked about the tumor; her last doctor's visit showed the tumor significantly reduced. He talked about his job and how his life was filled with meetings, and how he missed the students. She talked about how she ate more and had already gained a few pounds. He talked about how happy he was all the meetings with staff members had ended. She told him her boss loved the article, and he gave her another assignment. She accepted since she felt better. He told her not to overwork herself. She told him how Jeremy's prayers had helped. Then they were quiet for a while.

"Even though you're not saying anything, I can hear you speaking to me," Emma said.

Hamilton took her hand. "If you could do three things, any three in any order, what would those three things be?"

"I've never been to a circus. I would love to find a good circus and go. Then I think I would like to go horseback riding. I've never been, but I would like to. Third, I've always wanted to go to a Christian conference. When I was in the convent, we never had the money to go to a big Christian conference. I may have the chance to go now. It's expensive with the travel and hotel, but the conferences are inexpensive."

"What would be your next three?"

"You didn't like those, huh? I guess they don't say much about me other than I have done very little in my life. Three more. First, I always wanted to take a helicopter ride anywhere. Then I would like to be in the audience of a popular talk show. Now, you. What are three things you would like to do?"

"First, I would like to take Jeremy to see the Grand Canyon. It's a spiritual place and I know he would love it. Then, I want to enroll him in the University of his choice, and third I want to take all three of my kids to France, Germany, Italy and Sweden."

"That's nice. Why those places?"

"I'm still in touch with professors who left the university and went back to their homes. They invite me and my family to visit every year."

After a while, Emma grew tired and since Hamilton wanted her to rest, he left. But as soon as he got home, she called.

"Is everything okay?" He wished he didn't have to ask her that every time they talked. He didn't like how it seemed.

"Ham, I'm okay. I couldn't sleep. About things we wanted to do. After you left, I found a place that gives helicopter rides. I called and left a message. Someone just called back and said they don't do that anymore. I had planned to surprise you, but I can't now."

"Let me work on this and call you back tomorrow."

The next day, Hamilton called Emma back and told her they would go on a helicopter ride.

"There is only one thing."

"One thing. What do you mean?"

"The helicopter ride is in Arizona."

"I will need a little more information."

"I've arranged for you, Jeremy, and me to go see the Grand Canyon over the Thanksgiving weekend. Beginning Wednesday. Can you do that? Or rather, do you want to do that?"

"Ham, are you sure?"

"I am."

"I would love to do that. I'm sure Jeremy would love it."

Hamilton told Taylor everything about Emma and their situation. He told Taylor Jeremy was praying for Emma every day and, as a result, her tumor was reduced. Hamilton was hopeful it would get so small and dissolve itself, or small enough for the doctor to operate and remove it. Taylor said he and his congregation would pray for her.

When Hamilton called his father, George said he would call Eric and Anna, and asked them to spend the weekend with Mary and him. Hamilton said he wanted Anna and Eric to meet Emma. George told Hamilton to do what was right and what made him happy.

Hamilton, Emma, and Jeremy arrived at their hotel near the Grand Canyon on Wednesday evening. On Thursday, they started their tour of the Grand Canyon. The tour guide took the time to commemorate the day, giving thanks to the American Indians who initiated the first Thanksgiving, and those who lived around the canyon. Jeremy wanted to know whether the Navajo, Hopi and Hualapai Indian reservations still existed. Then they continued the tour. The guide allowed the tourists to take their time taking pictures and giving thanks for such a beautiful natural wonder and a beautiful day, warm and sunny, for the experience.

As he sat with Emma resting on a boulder, Hamilton gazed over at Jeremy. Jeremy snapped picture after picture and seemed to talk to himself. But Hamilton knew he was praying. Hamilton saw how different Jeremy was, so reverent, so grateful, so worshipful, and more prayerful. Maybe he is called to the priesthood.

Hamilton got up to grab a handful of the dirt. He wanted to see the difference between this dirt and the dirt around his lake. The red dirt at the Grand Canyon was dry to the touch, being exposed to the sun. Hamilton looked for dirt near a boulder and saw that it was slightly moist. He watched to see exactly when it would become fully dry, but before he could feel it in his hands, it was dry. The dirt at his lake took a second or two longer to turn from moist to dry. But his dirt was dark.

Hamilton let the dirt go, brushed his hands together and saw Jeremy standing near the barrier, and remembered the time he went to the falls in Hawaii and Superman. Time had moved so quickly for him, and he understood what he had today would not last. He stood next to Jeremy, looking down into the canyon. Hamilton realized again how small he was, how massive and expansive nature was in comparison and how much nature or God, as Buddy Boy would tell him, made up the Earth.

Maybe he should think about becoming a believer, to really believe in God, to have faith in Him and to love Him the way Buddy Boy did. He turned to Jeremy, a smile on his face, "Let's go get Emma." Jeremy followed him to Emma, and they moved to other parts of the canyon. They didn't go down into the canyon with the others. Emma couldn't make it.

As they walked, Emma commented on the beautiful weather — one of those days when it's not too cold or too hot — that created the most wondrous scene. The sun was out and cast a peaceful aura over the canyon, Emma said. The guide said that the canyon was blessed. Later, at the hotel, they enjoyed a Thanksgiving meal. This year the holiday had a different meaning for them.

On Friday, Buddy Boy's birthday, they took a helicopter ride over the canyon and over the land of the Navajo, Hopi, and Hualapai Indian reservations. Jeremy wanted to sit up front next to the pilot. Hamilton and Emma sat in the back.

Hamilton loved the way she pointed to everything from the helicopter. She reminded him of a little girl who received the doll she had been asking Santa for all year long. Emma's excitement was contagious and as they flew over what looked like any other canyon, he saw the beauty, the perfect formations, the beautiful colors in the sky and in how the colors changed in the canyon as they flew over. Everything blended into one.

He put his arm around her and drew her close, allowing her to soak up the moment, the scene, and him. From her heart, she smiled and laughed, and for the first time, prayed aloud. The beauty was so overwhelming he felt like saying, "Thank you, God." She kissed him on the cheek and said, "And thank you, God, for helping Ham plan this trip. You've made me the happiest woman in the world," she said in his ear. "I don't want you to be upset. I know you don't believe in God."

"Who told you that?"

"Jeremy."

"How would he know?"

"I don't think you can fool your son about anything. But don't worry. He still loves you." She smiled and looked up at him. "I need to tell you something," she paused. "When I first saw you, I knew right away you were sent by God to minister to me."

"Me? Are you sure? I don't believe in God," he said.

"I know. But I truly believe He sent you to me. One thing I learned at the convent is that we don't control our lives. God does. You can't fight against Him by going off doing what you want. Most people do what they want, and they get into trouble. They run into disaster, things not going right, and they don't get what they want. They don't realize that God has their life all planned. Just follow Him."

"He sent you to tell me that?"

"No, he sent you because I've always wanted to know what it would be like, what it would feel like to fall in love. He sent you to me to experience that."

Hamilton drew her closer to him and kissed her on the top of her head several times.

At the hotel, after dinner, the waiter brought out a coconut cake with the words "Happy Birthday, Buddy Boy" in blue icing. Jeremy thanked his father for the best birthday present anyone could ever have.

When Hamilton went to work on Monday, he called the Circe de sole to see if they still had tickets. They had four in the rear. Hamilton paid for three for Friday evening.

From her seat in the theater, Emma whispered, "Look how the performers twist their bodies into every unimaginable way." She pointed to the different performers and said, "Look, at that," as the performers balanced themselves on each other, and took daredevil jumps and moves.

Hamilton said, "What they do is much like dancing."

Emma laughed and said, "Performing in a circus had to be much harder than learning to dance."

"For some," he said, laughing back.

On Saturday they went to a book reading. One of Hamilton's teachers published a mystery novel, and he had a book reading and signing at The Great Reads bookstore.

Later in the week, Hamilton found a place that gave horseback riding lessons. The following Saturday, they drove to Fredericksburg, Virginia, to a farm and rode horses until they were too tired to stand.

"That wasn't quite what I thought," Emma said.

"It looks easy on TV," Jeremy said.

"You look like you've been on a horse before, Jeremy."

"Dad and I took lessons before. But I watch a lot of TV."

Hamilton and Emma laughed.

On the way home, Emma looked tired, and Hamilton decided it would be best to give her more time to rest before they did anything else. He tried not to think about what he was doing or how far he would go with Emma. He remembered Anita. He had to admit he was taking an enormous risk; in fact, risking everything with Emma.

CHAPTER 38

An afternoon after Church, again, Emma looked tired, and Hamilton took her home right after the service. They sat on her couch. Hamilton poured water in two glasses and placed them on the table in front of them.

"Ham, do you ever think about the times in Franny's dance studio?"

"Lately, I've been so busy, I haven't had the time to think about the dance studio."

"I do. I was okay then."

"You're okay, now."

"I've been so tired, and the headaches returned, though they're not as bad."

"You just need to rest, that's all."

"Ham I don't—"

"You just need to rest." He took her in his arms and held her. He didn't want her to say more. He didn't want to hear it.

"Let me finish, please. Not much has changed since my last visit to the doctor. The tumor hasn't reduced anymore. I don't expect much. But there is one thing I've always wanted. I'm talking about a sort of present."

"What is it? I'll get it for you."

"Before you say that, hear me out first."

"Tell me, sweetheart, just tell me. I'll do anything for you."

"This is a little embarrassing for me, so just bear with me. Okay?" She paused and Hamilton waited.

"I've never been with a man." She turned to see his face.

"What do you mean? I don't know if you've noticed, but I'm a man and we're here together now."

"No, I mean in the intimate sense. I've never been intimate with a man. I've only been out of the convent a few years and I haven't met anyone I wanted to be intimate with until I met you."

"Go on."

"That's what I want for a Christmas gift. I want to be intimate with you."

"That means we have to get married," Hamilton said.

"Yes, it does for me." She waited before going on. "Is that something you can do?"

"Emma, do you want us to get married for love, or get married because you want to take me to bed?"

"You shouldn't make me laugh when I get these headaches," she said, trying to stifle a laugh.

"If that's what you want, I would be honored to ask you to be my wife."

"I would be honored to accept."

"I'll call my brother tomorrow and ask if he can marry us this week."

"I always thought I'd have a big wedding with lots of flowers and a long white gown. After the convent, I never thought getting married was possible for me."

"I don't know how you would think that. I only had to see you one time."

She smiled.

"Okay, I'll ask Taylor about it this week. Will that be okay with you? You will feel up to it?"

"When someone wants to marry you, you'd better feel up to it. Yes, I will feel up to."

"Okay. Then we'll go to a hotel after that. How's that?"

"Okay."

Hamilton wanted Emma to have a will. The next day, Edwin, Hamilton's lawyer friend, went to see Emma to set up a will and explained how the contents of her estate would be handled and what to do with her remains. Hamilton thought her valuables could go to the convent.

Hamilton called Taylor and asked Taylor to perform the marriage ceremony.

"Ham, don't worry about the ceremony. I'll take care of everything," Taylor said.

"Can Alice help her with a wedding dress, veil and everything else?" He paused. "She wants a white dress. That's important to her."

"Alice, I'm sure, will help and would want to be her maiden of honor," Taylor said.

"I asked Jeremy to be best man," Hamilton said.

Two days later, Hamilton and Emma, in her white suit and veil, stood before Taylor in the chapel of his church and promised to love each other until death parted them. He was remarried.

After the small ceremony, they checked in at the Hilton on Wisconsin Avenue in Washington, D.C. Jeremy made reservations, again online, for them and after they settled in the hotel, Hamilton and Emma went to dinner at the Palm Restaurant.

During the second day, they stayed in the room most of the day. Hamilton worried about Emma. She seemed to have little strength.

"Ham, do you remember when we danced together?" They sat up in bed, his head against the headboard. She tucked under his arm, her head on his chest.

"That's not something I will forget." He looked down at her.

"I knew then that I loved you and wanted to marry you and spend my life with you. I didn't know how short my life would be. I just wanted you to know that before I leave."

"From the first time I saw you, I couldn't get you out of my mind."

"The thing that kept me going when I thought I wouldn't see you anymore, was the time we danced together. I remembered the look on your face, and I knew how you felt, too."

He turned to her and kissed her hard. His heart took over his body, and he needed to show her his love. He kissed her from head to toe, giving her nothing to think about or feel but his kisses, his caresses, and his whispering in her ear, telling her over and over how much he loved her. He heard her whimper and felt her body ask for more, and he gave her more. They met each other at the top of their canyon several times and she called out in ecstasy. They passed the day making love as many times as she asked for it.

On the morning of the third day, just before they packed, Emma's headaches and nausea returned. Emma wanted to go home. Hamilton drove her to Stevensville, his hometown. He called ahead to tell his parents he and Emma were married, and she was not doing well. Hamilton called Jeremy and asked him to call Eric and Anna and Taylor and Alice to let them know he was driving Emma to Stevensville. Hamilton wanted them all to meet him there.

When Hamilton and Emma arrived in Stevensville, Hamilton introduced her to George and Mary. Mary pulled Hamilton aside and told him she looked like death. She wanted to call an ambulance. Emma overheard her and asked her not to.

"But you need a doctor," Mary insisted.

"Thank you. But there's nothing they can do. Besides, I don't want to die in a hospital."

The next afternoon, Hamilton asked Emma to go with him to his favorite place by the water, the pier where he and his children always sat. He took a blanket and helped her walk down to the pier and sit. Since it was a little windy with a chill, he wrapped a blanket around her and held her in his arms while they sat and looked out over the water. Even at this time of year, some people were out in their boats. But it was quiet around the pier. A flock of birds flew by overhead, but this time he didn't ask himself where they were headed. They flew higher, cawing as they did, and then disappeared into the sky.

"Ham, I can't think of a more beautiful time in my life, than these times with you."

"I will always cherish these times." He tried to stop himself from crying, but he couldn't help it. Tears streamed down his face and the power of his anger about losing her now urged him on.

"Ham don't cry. I'm okay with leaving. Don't cry."

"I miss you already."

"You are such a powerful man. I love the way you care for your children."

He tried to control himself but couldn't.

"Promise me you will not be sorry you married me."

"Emma, I'm not sorry." He remembered a promise he made over a year ago to Anita, the lady he met in Hawaii. He promised her he would take a risk that resulted in him meeting the greatest love from the greatest woman who loved him like he loved her, the woman he now held in his arms.

"Ham, Hamilton, I just want to thank God for the gift of you."

He felt a little shudder from her, and when he looked down at her and saw her eyelids flutter, he kissed her goodbye. Her lips moved as if trying to say goodbye to him, and he felt the life leave her body. He sat there for some time, crying, and thinking about her.

George, Mary, Alice, Taylor, Jeremy, Eric and Anna came down to the pier with two men, one carrying a gurney. The two men took Emma from his arms and put her on the gurney. Hamilton saw from their uniforms and name tags they were EMTs. They put Emma's body in an ambulance.

"Where are you taking her," Hamilton asked.

"Mid-County Hospital," an EMT said. They both climbed into the truck and drove away. His family all gathered around him and hugged him as tightly as they could until he stopped crying.

The next day, Hamilton had her body taken to the funeral home in Rockville, the one she named in her will. Then the entire family drove back to Rockville. Emma specified in her will she wanted to be cremated. She said it would be easier for anyone who was left with disposing of her body, since she had no family.

Hamilton wanted a service for her. He called Marilyn and Franny and asked Franny to contact the people in her dance class. Hamilton notified the people at her office, and Taylor put an announcement in the church bulletin. Hamilton believed no matter what, a person should be remembered after they leave. For long or short, a person should be remembered for what they did on Earth. Emma will always be remembered for the article she wrote.

Jeremy said to his father, "Dad, you sound like a good Christian."

Hamilton smiled.

After the memorial service, Hamilton and Buddy Boy took Emma's ashes and went for a helicopter ride over the convent where she grew up. It seemed deserted and closed, but they found the spot she requested in her will, the place outdoors where almost every day, she went to pray. The cross was still there on a small, stone Altar. From the helicopter, Jeremy prayed while Hamilton poured her ashes and watched them float into the atmosphere, some landing on the Altar, her spot.

When the urn was empty, they took one more look, and then asked the pilot to take them back to Maryland. After the helicopter landed, they walked back to the car to drive home.

"Dad, you will be okay, you know," Jeremy said, turning to him in the car.

"I will? How do you know that?"

"Because of what you did."

"What do you mean, Bud?"

"Sometimes I don't understand why you don't believe in God. You do so many kind, loving things."

"I still don't understand."

"She didn't have a family. She was all alone. Remember, she told us that. She was an only child, and her parents were older and died when she was eight."

"That's right."

"You loved her. You loved her and showed her you loved her."

Hamilton was silent.

"You gave her what she needed. She told me she never felt she was loved. She always thought she was someone whom somebody had to take care of, and she never got to do anything, go any place, see God's country."

"Maybe there is a God, Jeremy. Maybe God has been living with me all this time."

He glanced over at Buddy Boy and smiled. Buddy Boy smiled back, reached over, and hugged his father.

A week after the funeral, Hamilton was back at work behind his desk, staring at the Maryland University page on his computer. It was difficult for him to concentrate as he thought about all the things that had happened over the past two years, beginning with his divorce and then to Emma. His life these past two years was different for him. He learned from Emma, that he couldn't control everything. At one time, he thought he could, but, as Emma said, he never did. If he could have controlled one thing over the past year, he would have controlled Emma's brain tumor. He would have gotten rid of it. But no one's life is rightly in the hands of another.

He heard a bing from his computer and opened his email and clicked on the first message.

> *Dear, Hamilton Maddox. I know you won't remember me, but we met about two years ago in Hawaii. You offered me a seat at your table because the restaurant was full, and later, we went for a walk along the beach. I hope you remember me. I also hope you don't mind this email. I remembered your name and looked you up at your university. I got your email address from there. Congratulations on your promotion. I have never forgotten you and the promise we made to each other. After I returned home, I did nothing to keep the promise we made. I sat on my couch eating and watching movies for about eight months. All I did was cry and eat. Then one day, still feeling sorry for myself, I found myself going through the pictures I took in Hawaii and found a picture of you. It was one of the pictures from the hike we took with the group. I thought about the promise we made to each other that evening during dinner. The next day, I enrolled in a diet program,*

a gym and threw out my couch. Later, I met Patrick, one of the nicest men ever. The company he worked for and mine merged, and we met. I stopped teaching and was hired at a PR firm. Patrick and I liked each other almost instantly and found we had so much in common. We plan to get married in six months when we, mainly me, are ready. I had promised myself, I would not be afraid to get married. You will recall my fiancé passed, and I, as you suggested, continued the honeymoon trip. I always thought you knew I didn't want to finish the trip and had made plans to return home that next morning. But after talking to you, I cancelled those plans and stayed to complete the honeymoon trip. Thank you for your encouragement. Tell me about you. I'm sure you found someone given how kind and thoughtful you are. You saved my life. I'll never forget that and thank you every day. Maybe we could all go on another trip together? I hope you email me back.

Hamilton closed out his email, got his coat and went outside to his trail and lake. He sat down on the bench facing the lake, said aloud "Than you, God," put his hands over his face, and cried. Superman.

ABOUT THE AUTHOR

Judy Kelly is an award-winning author. Her second novel, *Blessings and Curses*, is a Finalist in the Readers Favorite Award for 2020, in the Top Ten Most Popular Novels at the Frankfort, Sharjah, and Guadalajara International Book Fairs, 2018. Her first novel, *That Ever Died So Young*, was a finalist in the Somerset Literary and Contemporary Fiction Award for 2014. She presents at conferences, libraries, and meetings. She teaches fiction writing at Montgomery College, and Frederick Community College. Judy is an adjunct professor at Montgomery College teaching speech, college reading and English. She enjoys walking, live theatre, and museums.

Note from the Author

Word-of-mouth is crucial for any author to succeed. If you enjoyed *The Attractiveness of Wisdom*, please leave a review online—anywhere you are able. Even if it's just a sentence or two. It would make all the difference and would be very much appreciated.

Thanks!
Judy Kelly

We hope you enjoyed reading this title from:

www.blackrosewriting.com

Subscribe to our mailing list – *The Rosevine* – and receive **FREE** books, daily deals, and stay current with news about upcoming releases and our hottest authors.
Scan the QR code below to sign up.

Already a subscriber? Please accept a sincere thank you for being a fan of Black Rose Writing authors.

View other Black Rose Writing titles at
www.blackrosewriting.com/books and use promo code
PRINT to receive a **20% discount** when purchasing.